AF425830

LAURA WEDDLE

COLLECTED STORIES

PEOPLE LIKE US
AND
BETTER THAN MY OWN LIFE

Laura Weddle: Collected Stories. Copyright © 2023 by Laura Weddle. Printed in the United States of America. All rights reserved. No part of this book may be reproduced in any manner except for brief quotations embodied in critical articles or reviews. For information, address Sacred Chickens Publications, Huntsville, AL.
julie@sacredchickens.com

For Leo

PEOPLE LIKE US

Contents

People Like Us

Lily of the Valley

A young woman sat in a rocking chair on the narrow porch of a gray, weather-beaten farmhouse. Her thin arms moved in an easy rhythm, stringing beans, and dropping them into an aluminum pan on the floor beside her. She lifted a thick black braid of hair from her neck to catch a passing breeze and wiped sweat off her forehead with the bottom of her apron. The day was hot, even for August. Fields of tobacco and corn had ripened to a mixed array of yellows and browns, signaling the approach of autumn. No wonder they call these dog days, she thought. They sure can make you feel like one.

She was trying to decide whether she had strung enough beans for supper when she saw someone walking up the gravel road below the house. It wasn't an unusual sight. Lots of people traveled the roads these days, most of them looking for work or food, or for the chance to tell their sad stories. Some of them stopped. Others kept moving, hoping for something better down the road.

John wouldn't be home from the tobacco patch for a while yet, but she needed to start supper before Belle brought Wilma back home. She picked up the pan of green beans and shuffled toward the kitchen door. Her small body sagged with the weight of the baby that wasn't due for another month.

A voice behind her made her stop and turn around.

"Excuse me, lady."

The man was holding a black felt hat in his hand, the band discolored by sweat and dust.

"I was wondering if you had a spare bite of anything to eat," he said.

He looked away from her to the ground in front of him.

"Maybe just a piece of bread or some beans."

When she didn't answer, he looked at her again.

"I wouldn't expect you to give it to me for nothing," he said quickly. "I can do any kind of chores—chop wood, anything."

Mary stared at him. His tall thin frame was slightly stooped, and his sun-burned skin had turned a painful red. He wore a dingy white shirt, a black coat, and pants which may have once been meant for Sunday best.

These were hard times for everybody. There were no jobs to be found, and very little money anywhere. She and John were lucky to have a house to live in, and a job on Ben Taylor's farm, even if it did pay only a dollar a day. They had their garden and John's bonus money from his time in the war. The ten extra dollars a month bought whatever groceries they needed from the store and took care of unexpected expenses that came up. Little as it was, there were plenty of people that had less.

Still, it was important to keep what you had, and not just hand it out to anybody who asked.

"We just barely got enough for ourselves," she said. "Maybe if you stopped at that white house up there on the hill," she pointed at the Taylor house overlooking the fields. "They own this farm. Might be they'd have something you could do to earn you a meal."

She noticed the man's feet when he started to turn around. His shoes were worn down in the back, and there was a trace of blood on the grimy sock just above the back of his left heel.

"Wait a minute, mister," she said. "If you want to sit down out there by the shed, I'll go in and see if they was any corn bread left. It won't be much, but it might hold you a little while till you can get something else."

He didn't answer but walked past the smokehouse to the woodpile in the corner of the yard. He took a log from the pile and picked up the axe.

Mary braced her heavy body and went into the kitchen. Only

another month, but it felt like she'd been carrying this baby forever. To add to her misery, the summer heat had chafed her thighs, and every time she took a step they burned like fire. She didn't know what it was, but something about this pregnancy was different from the one with Wilma. Traces of blood had been staining her clothes lately, and Dr. George had warned her to rest as much as she could. She felt tired all the time, and sometimes she cried when nobody was around.

What a time, she thought, to bring another baby into the world.

She carried a plate with two pieces of cold corn bread out to the man and set it down beside the pile of wood.

"It ain't much, but it's all we had left."

"Much obliged, lady," he said.

He finished chopping a log into pieces the size of those John had already cut before he picked up the plate and sat down to eat. "Where's your husband?" he asked.

"Why he's out in the tobacco patch. They're topping it today." She had turned to go back into the house but stopped and looked at him directly for the first time. "You know anything about raising tobacco? It'll soon be time to cut it and put it in the barn."

"No, ma'am, I can't say I know much about the tobacco business." Mary pushed her hair back and smoothed the gray apron over her bulging stomach.

"What business was you in, mister?" she asked, and quickly looked away, her face hot with embarrassment. She hardly ever saw a stranger, much less asked nosey questions about his life.

"The man finished the bread, set the plate down beside the pile of wood, and picked up the axe before he answered.

"Worked in a vet'nary office up in Grant County." The wood made a hissing crackling sound as the sharp axe split it down the middle.

"I liked that kind of work fine, but when the hard times come people didn't have money to spend on sick animals, so the vet let me go." He raised the axe high above his head again and split the last section of the log, then set it upright against the woodpile.

"Wasn't nothing left to do but go out and look for work." He picked up his hat and turned toward the road. When he was halfway to the gate he turned and said, "I thank you for the bread, lady. I'll be getting on down the road, now."

Mary watched as the man opened the latch on the gate and walked through it. Suddenly she heard a sound like soft music and realized that he was whistling. As she listened, the words of the song came to her. Something she'd heard her mother sing when Mary was a child. "He's the lily of the valley, the bright and morning star, He's the fairest of ten thousand to my soul..." How many years since she'd heard that? For a moment her mind flew back to her childhood, and to her mother singing songs and spinning tales she'd brought with her from Ireland when she herself was only a child. Some of Mammy's old hymns and sayings still came to Mary's mind, especially when times were hard. It had been nearly ten years since her mother's passing.

There was no more time to waste on memories. She had to get the beans on for supper. John would be home a few hours from now, hungry and tired, when there wasn't enough daylight left to work.

She reached for the railing and was on the second step from the top when the pain struck—a grasping, clutching monster of a pain, that held her in its claws and refused to let her move. Her breath was frozen in her throat, and her senses had all shut off, like she was by herself in a giant white bubble.

She must have screamed. Suddenly, arms were lifting and carrying her up the steps and through the kitchen door. Time and space had no meaning for her. She was caught in a place where only pain was real, captive of a relentless agony from which even the familiar softness of her bed provided no refuge. She felt herself being cleaved apart, her bones split like the breast of a chicken or the ribs of a hog. She could hear and feel and taste the pain, like there was no way to separate herself from it, and nothing to do but die.

Then she felt gentle hands moving over her body, helping the baby force its way into the world. She felt the waves of pain ebb and flow, even harder than before. But now, over and under and around the pain, there were the hands gripping hers, helping her push, somehow making her understand that release would come only if she could see the ordeal through. She felt sweat and blood mingling in a tangle of sheets, as she thrashed and pushed and cried for release from the agony. She heard her own screams, but there was another voice too, soothing, comforting, encouraging her.

Some eternity later she heard a little mewing cry, and knew that her baby had come. She felt an incredible release from the pain, leaving in its place only a calm, blessed stillness. She lay in a quiet place, somewhere between waking and sleep. It was a place she never wanted to leave.

Gradually she became aware of the voices of John and Belle coming to her from somewhere far away. She knew she should open her eyes, but she was afraid that when she did, she would lose this feeling forever.

"Mary, please, please wake up." She felt John's hands on her shoulders, shaking her. The fear in his voice made her open her eyes.

The red and gold rays of the setting sun glinted through the window of their room. Night was not far away. She tried to remember how long it had been since the pain had struck. Surely no more than three hours, by the look of the sun.

She felt a small weight on her breast and looked down at her baby.

It's so dark, she thought, remembering the glowing pink skin and blue eyes, so much like her own, that Wilma had been born with. This one's an Indian, just like John's mother. And she remembered the dark Cherokee woman she had met only once, soon after she and John were married.

Mary looked away and saw Belle standing on the other side of the bed, her dark face marked by fear and confusion. She reached out and gripped Mary's arm.

"That man come by my house. Said you done had your baby. I run as fast as I could to the 'backer patch to get Mr. John." She stopped to catch her breath before she added, "Wilma's still up at my house playing with Nathan. Duke's watching them."

"Who was it come by, Belle?"

"I don't know who he was, but he scared me." Belle took off her bonnet and folded it over a chair.

"Him talking 'bout how you already had the baby. It didn't make no sense. Why you wasn't nowhere near due!" Belle bent over Mary and pulled the blanket aside to look at the baby.

"Did he stop, or say where he was going?" Urgency made Mary's voice stronger.

"No'm, he just said it, and then went right on down the road. I ain't seen him since."

"But where did he come from, and where did he go?" Mary asked. Something in her knew that Belle couldn't answer.

Belle looked at the clean bed. "How on earth did you get cleaned up?"

"I ain't sure," Mary said, "but I think he helped me."

Mary looked at John, on his knees by the bed. She could see his worry, and she wanted to let him know that it was all right, whatever had happened. She reached out and put her hand on his arm.

"John, I think the stranger helped me with the whole thing." He didn't answer right away, but then his face relaxed.

"Well, I guess we can just thank God that man come along when he did," John said.

He pushed her hair back and rubbed his hand across her forehead. The calluses on his fingers felt good on her face, and she inhaled the harsh odor of tobacco juice, fresh from the stalks.

"I'm going after Dr. George to come and look at you and the baby," John said.

He stood up and walked to the door. "We'll be back before it gets too dark. You'll stay with her, won't you, Belle?"

"Just as long as it takes, Mr. John. Don't you worry about nothing." Belle's hand on her arm was comforting, and Mary closed her eyes.

When she opened them again it was because she heard voices around her. The last traces of daylight were gone, and Belle had lit the coal oil lamp and set it on the dresser. A pool of yellow light covered the room like a soft, old quilt.

The doctor was holding the baby, checking her from every angle. Mary and John and Belle watched anxiously. "She looks just fine," he said finally, and handed her to Belle. "Wrap her back up, and let's see about Mother."

Relief softening their faces, Belle and John stood back and made room for Dr. George to sit down beside the bed.

"You had a hard time, Mary, like we thought you might," Dr. George said.

He examined her gently, but a sharp moan escaped her when his hand touched the raw tears the baby had made as she entered the world.

"You were mighty lucky there was somebody here to help you," he said. "No telling what might have happened if you'd been here by yourself."

He took papers and a fountain pen from his satchel.

"Who'd you say it was?"

"Nobody I knowed. Just a man looking for work."

Dr. George was quiet for a minute, then he looked down at the papers in his hand.

"Well, we have to make her a birth certificate. You all decided yet what you're gonna name her?"

Mary touched the baby's face as Belle laid the child down beside her. Her fingers traced the nose and mouth and closed around the tiny chin.

"She's a lily," she said, "like a lily of the valley, a bright and morning star."

She looked at John and Belle, and they leaned closer to her.

"I reckon I come about as close to the valley today as I'm gonna get and live to tell it."

The doctor brought the fountain pen to the paper that was propped on his knee. What he wrote was, "Lilly Adkins, born to John and Mary Adkins, August 11, 1933."

He stood up and looked at them, and then once more at the baby. "Well, I'll be going. You keep an eye on her, Belle, and you know where to find me if you need me." He tapped the birth certificate on the wooden headboard.

"I'll see this gets to Frankfort, so she's registered good and proper."

He put the paper in his satchel and turned toward the door.

"Want me to drop you by your house, Belle?"

"Yes, sir. I'd be much obliged." She stood up and looked at Mary. "And don't you worry about Wilma tonight," she said. "I'll bring her home first thing in the morning, and I'll have something good for you all to eat. Don't you try to get outta that bed." She picked up her red-flowered bonnet and followed the doctor out the door.

Silence lay between John and Mary when they were finally alone. There was never much conversation, even at normal times. John was like his mother in her "quiet turn" as people called it, accepting whatever life handed her, including the endless cruelty of her hard-drinking Scotch-Irish husband. Mary knew that John would speak only when he had something to say.

Minutes passed as they watched the sleeping baby. Finally, John touched her thick straight black hair. He smiled.

He stood up and walked over to the radio that was turned on for only half an hour every night—to save the battery. The last notes of "Turkey in the Straw" filled the room as the Grand Ole Opry finished, and radio station WSM followed with the news of the day.

"Today President Franklin D. Roosevelt presented a plan to the Congress which he said will provide..."

Suddenly there was a cry from the baby that seemed too loud and strong for such a tiny body. Her eyes were open, and she appeared to take in all the details of her surroundings.

"She's hungry," Mary said, "and she don't mind letting us know about it." She unbuttoned her dress and guided a nipple into the child's mouth.

"There, Lilly," she whispered. "We've both had a hard time today, but we're gonna be all right."

She prayed that it was so and closed her eyes.

She dreamed she was carried over wide green fields, and meadows with flowering trees, where birds flew in lazy circles under soft white clouds. In the distance a tall gray-haired woman in a long blue calico dress drifted toward her, arms outstretched.

"Hello, Mammy," she whispered. "I was hoping you'd come to see my baby."

Just beyond the pool of lamplight, Mammy held Lilly, and smiled and cooed to her. She glided shadow-like toward the bed, and placed the baby on the pillow. Outside, a pink glow rose on the eastern horizon. The new day announced its coming.

People Like Us

The bow was in a box of second-hand clothing the church ladies brought Mama on Sunday afternoon when they made their charity rounds. Usually the cardboard boxes contained only grown-up things, but this one also had a breast pin with a horse's head, a red purse with a black plastic handle, and the bow. Lilly ran her fingers over its slick round curves and felt the airy lightness of it on her head. She resisted the urge to pull it off and look at it again.

Wilma, nine years old to Lilly's five, and as blonde as Lilly was dark, ran by the porch and dropped an empty chicken-feed pan by the steps.

"Race you to the barn, Lilly," she yelled.

"Okay, wait."

Lilly jumped down the steps and ran past Wilma, beating her by four steps to the gray weathered wooden door. Lilly loved the barn. It smelled like motor oil, dried tobacco, and cow manure. Inside on the left was a line of stalls for the cows. Sometimes she would come down while Daddy was milking, and then the odor changed to that of rich warm milk, getting stronger with each squeeze of the fat tits that sent a loud echoing spray into the five-gallon tin bucket.

At feeding time, late in the afternoon when the sun was dropping behind the stand of pine trees over by the lake, Daddy tossed the cows hay from the end of a long pitchfork, and sometimes he gave Lilly a forkful and lifted her up to throw it inside. The barn was always cool and dark, and there were all kinds of tools and harnesses, and wooden boxes and benches to hide under and play on.

About midway down on the right side of the barn, a rickety wooden ladder leaned against the rafters that led to the loft, and Lilly and Wilma climbed it every time they went up or came down. Piles of straw covered the splintery plank floor, and dark corners made good places to play the games they made up. Wilma was good at thinking up things to do, and lately, stealing Uncle Duke's dinner was her favorite. They had stolen it three times before, and they knew he hid it somewhere different every day.

Wilma ran to the ladder and started to climb. "He hid it over on that side yesterday," was what she said as she reached the top. "Let's look over here today. I hope he's got something good."

She was digging around in the straw, smoothing it back over, then moving on to another spot. Lilly was close behind, catching the flying straw and tossing it over her head. It danced in the light from the cracks in the roof, making a shiny golden rain.

Suddenly Wilma shrieked. She'd found it again, far back and deeply buried, hidden under an overhanging rafter.

"Here it is," she said. "Boy, he hid it good today. I bet he thought we'd never find it."

She pulled out a blue and yellow tin bucket, "Fischer's Pure Lard" painted on the side in big black letters. The lid had been pushed down hard all the way around, forming a tight seal. Wilma clamped her thin left arm around the bucket and pushed her right hand firmly down on the top. She hooked her fingers around the edge of the lid and slowly turned the bucket, forcing the lid up a little at a time, until it finally gave.

The girls peered inside. A white cloth had been placed on top of the food, maybe while it was still warm, because little circles of grease had come through. Wilma reached in and pulled the cloth aside. Both girls gasped as the fine buttery smell swirled up around their heads like a warm, delicious cloud. Inside were three big round biscuits, each one cut through the center to make two sides of a sandwich. Lilly's mouth began to water. She noticed a little hungry gnawing in her stomach.

"Oh, don't that smell good?" Wilma reached into the bucket, lifted out two of the biscuits, and handed one to Lilly. They each tasted the sage-flavored hog sausage patty at the same time.

The girls hadn't had sausage since Mama cooked the last of theirs in February or March. Hog-killing time during the first cold spell in November was when the tenant families cured hams, made sausage and lard, and preserved all parts of the hog for use through the winter. Somehow Aunt Belle had managed to stretch what she and Uncle Duke had made until now.

Lilly and Wilma said nothing, but crammed the food into their mouths, their eyes rolling in ecstasy. The third biscuit overflowed with the blackberry jam that Aunt Belle had made last July when the berries were fat and heavy on the vines. Wilma carefully tore it into halves, and they finished off Uncle Duke's dinner.

Afterward, they replaced the cloth, put the lid back on top, and hid the bucket where they had found it. Wilma lifted the straw and smoothed it out again, making the spot look as undisturbed as possible. They sat still for a little while, heavy with the taste and bulk of the food. Finally they got up and started back toward the ladder.

Suddenly Wilma stopped. "Wait a minute, Lilly. Let's hide and watch for him today." She giggled as the idea took shape, and her face glowed with excitement. "I want to see what he does when he finds out it's gone."

Lilly had her foot on the top rung of the ladder, and she started to go on down. The other times, they had just eaten and left. The thought of staying scared her a little, but she hardly ever questioned Wilma's ideas. She climbed back up and walked slowly to a corner of the loft where Wilma had found a good place to hide.

They crawled far back under the dark rafters to wait. It wouldn't be long, because the sun was shining straight down through a crack in the tin roof, and it felt like dinner time— probably just about time for Uncle Duke to stop plowing, unharness Old Buck, and come to the barn.

It seemed like a long time to Lilly before they heard sounds below. She looked at the splintery wooden beams above their heads, each one dry and dusty from years supporting the roof of the barn. She had almost forgotten Uncle Duke, her eyes on a small black spider sitting motionless in the center of a silvery web. She was about to nudge it with a piece of straw when Wilma punched her in the side with her elbow and made a "shh" sign.

Lilly tried to lie still and listen. The sound of metal clanked against metal just inside the door—probably Uncle Duke setting his hoe up against the other tools that usually stood there. Next there was the soft padding of footsteps on the dirt floor, and the sound of something being dragged all the way to the other end of the barn. The harness was usually kept in a stall there, and Lilly recognized the scrape and thud of heavy leather pieces being placed on hooks.

The straw was beginning to itch, and Lilly didn't know how much longer she could lie still. Her dress tail had gathered up in a knot, and the straw was sticking to her arms and legs where she had sweated in the noon-day heat. When she moved just the tiniest bit, Wilma nudged her and whispered, "Be quiet."

They didn't have much longer to wait. First they saw the top of the ladder wiggle a little, and then they heard feet being placed on one rung after the other, as someone headed for the top. Lilly held her breath and hoped she could stay still.

A gray head appeared, followed by the wide shoulders of a black man in denim overalls and a faded blue work shirt. He glanced around a little before he climbed up over the ledge then sat still for a moment, his legs hanging over the side. He turned in the direction where his lunch bucket was hidden and crawled toward it, too tall to stand under the slanting two-by-fours.

Lilly was itching so much now that she didn't think she could stand it a second longer. On top of that she had to pee, and she was afraid that any minute might be the last one she could endure. She clamped her legs together and squeezed her crotch. Maybe if it started to come she could force it back inside. Gritting her teeth, she held her breath and lay as still as she could.

When he got to the spot where they had carefully piled the straw back up, way over in the corner, Uncle Duke began to dig. He stretched his arm back to where he had hidden it and pulled the bucket out. Lilly could feel Wilma giggling beside her. She closed her eyes tightly for fear that he might see or hear them. She opened her eyes just in time to see his face as he looked up.

Uncle Duke shook the bucket once or twice, then dropped it back into the straw. Lilly didn't know why, but she was scared by what she saw in his face. It was like when she was picked on by someone bigger than herself, and she knew she couldn't fight back. Like when Wilma, or one of her older cousins was mean to her in some way, and she couldn't do anything to help herself. And it was like the awful mad way she always felt when these things happened, but all she could do was cry. Lilly saw all of these things she had felt on Uncle Duke's face.

For just an instant, she thought he looked her directly in the eye, but she knew that couldn't be. Her body was hidden by the shadows and the rafters, and she had burrowed deeply into the straw. Terrified that she might do something that would give them away, she caught her breath again and didn't move a muscle.

Uncle Duke just sat there for a long time before he picked up the bucket, turned around, crawled to the ladder, and started back down. They heard the sounds of harness shuttling across the barn floor, the clink, clink, clink of metal, then nothing but the creak of timbers in the old barn, and birds singing in the trees outside.

Wilma jumped up from their hiding place and began to pick straw off her dress. "I thought he never was gonna leave," she said, and ran to the ladder. She seized the top rung in both hands and started down.

"Did you see how mad he looked?" she giggled. "Come on. Let's go on back to the house."

Lilly pulled a piece of straw off her chin and followed Wilma. "What if he saw us, and tells?" She remembered the look on Uncle Duke's face and felt uneasy.

"Oh, he can't tell on us. Nobody'd believe him." She looked at Lilly and laughed. "He's just a stupid old nigger."

The path from the barn to the house was not very long. It curved snakelike around the tool shed and meandered to the left when they reached the chicken coop. The girls picked up rocks along the way and threw them at tree trunks, and at the tin roof of the smoke house. The bantam and leghorn chickens strutted around the yard, pecking hopefully at the ground for stray kernels of dried com.

Both girls squealed and ran as a big white rooster bore down on them, wings flapping, a long sharp spur extended. Wilma reached the screen door first, hung loosely on its hinges, and flies buzzed around it, looking for any opportunity to enter the kitchen. She held it open for Lilly, and they both dashed inside. They had outrun the rooster this time, but once or twice before, they hadn't been so lucky. They both had scars to remind them.

Daddy had come home for dinner and was standing over a gray enamel wash pan on the table near the door. He was scrubbing his hands. He took a towel from a peg on the wall, and dried them. As he threw the soapy water off the porch, Mama opened the oven to take out the hot brown biscuits, and they all sat down to eat.

"I saw old Duke out in the field a while ago," Daddy said.

Only the white children on the farm called the black workers "Aunt" and "Uncle." The girls glanced at each other, and then at Daddy.

Daddy was a man of few words, and when he did say something, it was cause to listen.

"Said something got into his dinner and eat it up. Musta been rats or squirrels out there in the barn. Said he thought he saw something moving a little bit up in the loft."

Daddy took a biscuit from the plate in the middle of the table and lifted a spoonful of beans to his mouth.

"It's hard to work all day with nothing to eat."

Lilly remembered the look she had seen on Uncle Duke's face in the loft.

"I don't know why Belle don't fix his dinner bucket right," Mama said. "Why'd he tell you about it, anyway? He surely didn't expect us to feed him."

Her voice was shrill when she said, "Lord, what would them niggers do without people like us to help them out?" Then her voice softened a little, and she added, "If they's any left, you can fix him a plate and take it out to him if you want to." She paused and took a bite of biscuit. "He can set out there on the back steps and eat it."

Later, Lilly sat on the floor inside the door, bouncing the ball and grabbing the jacks while the ball was still in the air. Outside she heard the scraping of the spoon on the granite-ware plate as

Uncle Duke ate his biscuit and beans. Wilma's words came back to her. "He can't tell on us. He's just a stupid old nigger."

Out of the corner of her eye she saw Wilma and Spot going down the path to the garden, Wilma carrying a bucket and hoe to dig potatoes for supper. Lilly thought about how she liked to find the fat round potatoes under the dark soil, their tender skins peeling as she picked them up to put into the bucket. She dropped the ball and ran to the door.

"Wait, Wilma, I want to help dig the taters."

She started toward the path where Spot's short legs trotted after Wilma through the garden gate, his small black and white body almost lost among the pole beans and tomatoes. Suddenly she was aware that someone was directly in her path, and she looked up into the eyes of Uncle Duke.

"Here, Lilly," Uncle Duke said. He was holding the plate and spoon out to her, smiling as he usually did when he saw her. "Will you give these to your mama, and thank her for the beans?"

Lilly reached for the plate and noticed that he was holding something else.

"Is this yours, child?"

Lilly's hand shot up to feel for the bow that Wilma had put in her hair, but there was only a strand of straw where it had been. She looked up again, but Uncle Duke's smile was gone, replaced by the strange look she had seen earlier in the barn. It felt like a long time that she stood there, like a rabbit caught in the bright light of a lantern. When he extended the pink satin bow toward her, she grabbed it and ran. She carried the plate into the kitchen and set it, with the spoon, on the round oak table where her mother was washing the dinner dishes.

"Uncle Duke said tell you thank you for the beans," she said. She walked back into the room she shared with Wilma, forgetting about the fat potatoes in the garden, and her jacks on the floor by the door.

The bow felt strange and heavy in her hand.

The Reading Lesson

Lilly and Wilma walked along the road, each carrying a brown paper bag of groceries. Their feet, leather-like from going shoeless all summer, felt no discomfort from the small sharp rocks, and their bare arms and legs under flowered feed sack dresses were as dark as they would get this year. As they walked the half mile back toward home, Wilma answered Lilly's questions as well as she could, trying to make her understand. Lilly was six years old, and she was scared.

For weeks, now, Wilma had been preparing her for starting to school.

"Now Lilly, you have to be good. You can't turn around in your seat and talk, and you have to listen to everything the teacher says." Every time Wilma started to tell her about school, Lilly felt her stomach knot up. She was shy around strangers, and the thought of having to go to a strange place, learn rules, and be with people she didn't know, made her sick. She had never played with any other children besides Wilma and their neighbor, Nathan, and an occasional cousin, and she wasn't even sure she could.

"But why do I have to go to school, anyway? Why can't I stay home?" Lilly wanted to know.

"I already told you," Wilma said. "They make you go. If you don't, they send somebody to get you."

The girls had rounded a curve in the road, coming in sight of the small tenant house where they lived. If the house had ever been painted, there was no sign of it now. Its wooden sides and porch were weathered by years of rain, snow, and wind.

Mama was hanging clothes on a line behind the house. The wind caught in the white sheets and whipped her blue cotton dress around her legs. She bent to pick up clothes pins out of a basket on the ground, and she looked up as the girls came into the yard.

"Hurry up with them groceries so I can get the beans on for dinner," Mama said. "And go out to the garden and dig a few potatoes and peel them."

She hung up the last pair of overalls and started back toward the house.

"Alright, Mama," Wilma yelled. She ran to the shed where Daddy kept his tools and picked up a tin kettle to gather vegetables from the garden "Besides, I'll be there to ride the bus with you, but my room is upstairs from yours, and I won't see you till it's time to get back on the bus to come home. You just have to be careful and not get in trouble during the day."

"But what if the teacher thought I was talking, and I wasn't? Or if she told me to do something, and I didn't hear her. What would she do?"

"Well, she'd probably send you to Mr. Carter's office. He's really mean."

Wilma paused. Her mind was seeking just the right words to do justice to her imagination. She was watching Lilly's face.

"Minnie Smith said she heard he's got this whipping machine he makes you sit down in if you get sent to him, and it's got paddles on it that go round and round, and they smack your butt every time they go by."

Lilly's gasp was lost in the sound of the cackling hens.

"And Minnie says he can even see behind him without turning around, "Wilma continued. "I'm not sure about that part, but I wouldn't take any chances. Just be careful, and you won't get sent to his office."

Wilma shifted the bag of groceries to the other arm and slapped at a sweat bee buzzing around her head.

"And another thing, Lilly. If you have to go, raise your hand, and when she looks at you, say, 'May I be excused?' and then she'll let you go outside to the toilet."

"May I be excused?" The unfamiliar phrase echoed in Lilly's head, and she repeated it over and over to herself, wondering how she would ever remember.

Her dread increased as the days went by. The worst time was at night when she lay in bed beside Wilma, her body stiff and eyes wide open in the quiet dark room. Scary thoughts chased each other around in her head.

What if she didn't understand how to do what the teacher told her? What if she had to go to the toilet, and couldn't get out in time, and wet her pants? What if she got put in that whipping machine? She would scoot over close to Wilma and finally go to sleep, but she would dream of dark, shadowy things she could barely remember in the morning. A man with long arms and black staring eyes. Paddles chasing her down a dark empty hall.

On the Saturday before school was to start on Monday, the family got into their old Essex and went to Lancaster to get school clothes and supplies. Lilly loved the ten-mile ride to town.

Wilma read all the road signs to her. They always laughed at the Burma Shave sign, actually a bunch of wooden signs on posts a few feet apart that made a funny saying when you put them all together. This one said: Henry the eighth Prince of Friskers Lost Five Wives But kept his whiskers.

When they got to Lancaster their father pulled over to the curb and parked the car, and they all got out. A few people strolled up and down the sidewalk, going in or coming out of the stores along Main Street. Most of them were strangers to Lilly and Wilma, but once in a while their mother and father would see someone they knew from home.

"Come on, Lilly, let's go to the Ten-Cent Store first."

"Wait a minute," Mama stopped them.

"Your daddy and me's going to the hardware store to get some canning jars." She reached into the handbag she'd made from a pink flowered feed sack. "Here's the money for your paper and pencils, and a dime each for a candy bar and an ice cream cone. You all come on back to the car when you get through and wait for us if we're not back. Then we'll go look for some school clothes."

The mention of school brought back the queasy feeling in Lilly's stomach. She didn't know how yet, but some way she had to get out of going. She just wouldn't get on the bus when it stopped out on the road. And if anybody came to get her, she'd go hide in the barn until they were gone. Her mind made up; she ran to catch up with Wilma.

In Woolworth's Ten-Cent Store, they walked up and down the aisles, almost hypnotized by the variety of things to see. Rows of hardback books with colorful dust jackets lured Wilma. She loved to read, and she always managed to save up twenty-nine cents to buy one of the books. Today, she examined all of them, and then picked out The Secret of the Old Clock. She had already read three other books about the girl detective, Nancy Drew, and she wished she could be just like her.

"I can't wait to read this, Lilly, and I'll read it to you, too. But it won't be long till you can read for yourself."

Lilly wanted to be able to read. For as long as she could remember, Wilma had been reading to her. They read the funnies every day, and "The Katzenjammer Kids" was her favorite, along with "Alley Oop" and "Buck Rogers." They had a book of fairy tales, and Wilma had read them to her so many times, she had most of them memorized. To be able to read them for herself was something she dreamed about. But to learn how, she'd have to go to school.

Wilma paid for her book and wandered on down the aisle. Lilly followed, looking right and left. Wilma had stopped at one of the racks where dark blue bottles were lined up in neat rows by size, and she picked one up and read "Yardley" on the label. She held it out for Lilly to see.

"Oh, I hope whoever gets my name this year gives me one of these for Christmas. Everybody at school draws somebody else's name, and then they have to give them a present. You'll get to do it, too, and get a present under the tree."

Across the aisle were rows of glowing orange glass powder boxes with different animals on top. Lilly saw dogs and elephants and deer. Each one had a pink and blue box of dusting powder inside, with flowers around the top and sides. Wilma picked up a box with a poodle, lifted the top and sniffed.

"Or this would be nice. I bet that powder smells good."

She replaced the top, tracing the outline of the poodle's head with her finger as she set it back down.

They walked on down the long aisle, stopping to look at a row of tiny white statues of a lady with long hair and no clothes. She sat next to a jewelry display of brown plastic pins of two people in a carriage with a horse in front. Lilly picked up the statue and examined it, while Wilma held one of the pins up to her dress to see how it would look.

"Wonder why she ain't got no clothes on?" Lilly asked.

"I don't know. Maybe there's clothes to put on her, like we do our paper dolls. I don't see any, though."

The smell of oil rose from the planks of the wooden floor, and overhead fans whirred rhythmically, as Lilly and Wilma walked on. It was dark and cool inside, and Lilly thought of a cave she and Wilma had played in one day when Daddy took them fishing at the river. She could almost feel the smooth rocks on her feet, and hear the trickling water running down the dark, mossy walls inside the cave.

Suddenly Wilma stopped.

"Wait, Lilly. Here's what we need."

She was looking at a stack of writing tablets with pictures of Indians in feathered head dresses, and bins of yellow pencils with red erasers. Beside them were brown wooden pencil boxes with compartments that slid out to reveal more pencils, a hand-held eraser, a compass and a protractor. Tin boxes with watercolors and brushes were lined up in the bin next to the pencil boxes, and next to them, glue and crayons.

"This is everything we need right here," Wilma said.

She started to pick up things and hand them to Lilly. "You'll need a tablet. Here's one with a pretty Indian girl." Lilly thought of Daddy saying his Mama was Cherokee, and she wondered if her grandmother looked like the lady on the cover of the tablet.

"And a couple of these pencils." Wilma said. "They've got a pencil sharpener up on the wall, but be careful, or they won't last long."

Wilma was looking at the display of school things on the lower shelf. "And we better get some of this paste and some crayons. You have to paste and color a lot in the first grade.

I think I'll get me one of these pencil boxes," Wilma continued.

"It's got a ruler in it, and I'll probably need one for arithmetic." She also picked up a tablet and a couple of the yellow pencils, and headed toward the front of the store, where a woman sat on a tall seat behind a cash register.

Lilly had turned to follow Wilma back to the front of the store, when she noticed a display of bottles in yellow boxes covered with black lines and shapes that she recognized as writing. She had no particular interest in them, but she noticed a woman looking at the bottles. She had picked one up and was looking at it from several different angles, like she was trying to puzzle something out.

The woman looked up and said something, just as Lilly came even with her. It took a second for Lilly to realize she was speaking to her.

"Little girl, would you look at this and tell me what it says? Is this Black Draught, or something else? The doctor told me to get some Black Draught for my husband, but I can't make out what it says."

A clerk who had been listening in the next aisle over, came up behind them.

"Did you need some help?"

The clerk was looking at the woman in a way that made Lilly uneasy, like she was trying to make her feel bad. Like the time Aunt Stella and Alice came to visit when Lilly was little, and Alice laughed at her because she didn't know her numbers, or how to tell time. Lilly had hidden under the bed until Mama made her come out to say goodbye to them.

She didn't understand why, but Lilly knew the woman felt bad, too. If there had been a bed to hide under, she would have done it. Her face was red, and she kept her head down as she handed the bottle to the clerk.

"I need a bottle of Black Draught."

"Well this sure ain't it. This is Syrup of Pepsin. The Black Draught is over here."

She walked to the other side of the aisle where another stack of bottles filled a bin.

"This is the Black Draught. See, it says so, right here on the bottle."

She held the bottle close to the woman's face and pointed to the black markings.

"Thank you."

Lilly could barely hear the woman's words, and the clerk didn't answer, as she walked toward the front of the store.

Lilly was aware of the woman walking behind her, and she saw that the clerk had reached the cashier. She was whispering, but her voice was still loud enough to be heard, and she was laughing, enjoying the story she had to tell.

"And she couldn't even read good enough to tell the Black Draught from the Syrup of Pepsin. I'd sure hate to let on to people if I couldn't read."

The woman carried the bottle of medicine up to the counter and paid for it, and nothing more was said. But Lilly had a feeling that something bad had happened, and she wasn't sure what it was, or why.

"Come on, Lilly." Wilma grabbed her arm and pointed up the street. "Let's go up to the drug store and get our ice cream cone and candy bar. Then we can meet Mama and go look for our school clothes."

They had almost finished the chocolate cones before they got back to where the car was parked. Their mother was putting a cardboard box of Ball canning jars in the back seat, next to sacks of flour and beans.

"Did you all get what you needed to start in school?" she asked. "Did you have enough money?"

"We got everything. Mama," Wilma said, "and we had this quarter left over."

Her mother took the money and put it in her sweater pocket.

"Well, let's go over here to the Ben Franklin Store and see if we can find you all some school clothes." Mama looked both ways and walked across the street.

Like Woolworths, Ben Franklin was a roomy, high-ceilinged old building, with racks of clothes as far as the girls could see. It was divided into sections of men's, women's, and children's things, and on one side they could see racks of shoes, hats and purses. There were show cases with small items like billfolds and key chains in a row at the back of the store near the cash register.

The girls followed their mother up and down the aisles of dresses in their sizes. She stopped every now and then to pull out a dress and look at its price tag, figuring how much she had to spend, and what she could afford to pay. Wilma and Lilly thought some of the dresses were prettier than others, but they knew better than to complain when she put one back.

"That's a pretty little dress. Do you want to try it on?"

One by one Mama made her choices, price and durability getting the upper hand on beauty and style.

Wilma and Lilly carried the dresses into the little dressing room and took turns trying them on, stepping outside for their mother's inspection.

"No, Wilma, that one's too short," Mama said. "You wouldn't have room enough to grow a'tall. Take that one off and try this one."

"But Mama, that was the prettiest one."

Wilma knew she would never win this argument, but she couldn't help trying.

Lilly loved the smell and feel of the new dresses, but when she remembered what they were for, her stomach started to hurt. A lump came up in her throat, and she thought about the big yellow school bus that would stop out by the mailbox Monday morning, and open its folding doors, like giant wings ready to swallow her up.

"What's wrong, Lilly? Don't you love these clothes?" Wilma asked.

"Yes, but I can't go to school, Wilma. I'm afraid, and I'm not gonna go."

"Well, you have to, Lilly, so make up your mind to it. Besides, I've already told you everything to do so you won't get in trouble. The main thing is, don't talk."

When they left the store, they each had three new dresses, three changes of underwear, a pair of shoes, and five pairs of socks. By washing their clothes on Mondays and Wednesdays, their mother could keep them in clean clothes the whole week.

Their father was already waiting in the car. He was peeling and eating an apple, his sharp pocketknife cutting through the slices. He passed the sack around, and Mama and Wilma each took one, but Lilly was still full from the chocolate ice cream cone and the Pay Day candy bar. Besides, she didn't feel too well. She leaned back on the seat when they started toward home.

"Stop, Daddy, I'm sick."

Lilly often got sick riding in the back seat, and her father knew to stop the car quickly. She ran a little way from the car, the candy and ice cream coming up in a rush. When there was nothing more to come up, she turned around to look at her mother and father and Wilma. They waited by the car. Her stomach ached, her dress was dirty, and she wanted to cry.

In the car she lay back, weak from vomiting, and miserable in her soiled dress. The sour smell of chocolate and peanuts filled the car briefly before it was carried out on the wind from the open windows.

"Don't worry, Lilly." Wilma said, trying to make her feel better. "We'll soon be home, and you can take that dress off. Then we can color some with our new crayons."

Lilly could hear her mother and father talking in the front seat.

"I saw Vera Allen coming out of the Ten Cent Store today. I spoke to her, and she said she had to come to town to get some Black Draught for Pete. Said he keeps an awful hurting in his stomach," Mama said.

"Reckon it's got anything to do with him getting that cleaning fluid that time, when he thought it was tonic medicine?" Daddy said. "I remember he was sick a long time after that. Come in a hair of dying."

"I didn't ask her, but I bet it does. Wonder how on earth he could have got them two things mixed up, anyway?" Mama said. "It tells you right on the bottle that cleaning fluid is poison."

Lilly sat up, anxious to get out when the car stopped in front of the house. Mama was gathering up packages.

"Let's get these things put away so I can start supper. Wilma, you find a clean dress for Lilly, and then you all peel some potatoes." Daddy was already on his way to the barn to start the feeding and milking.

Lilly felt better since she'd napped a little on the way home, and she was getting her messy dress changed. Wilma had located one of last year's school dresses, the pink one with blue and white flowers that Lilly had grown into.

In the kitchen they got a blue granite pan from a nail on the wall, peeled potatoes from the patch in the garden, and put them on the stove to boil. Mama stood by the kitchen table rolling out dough on a board. She used a glass to cut out the biscuits, and then placed them side by side in a long pan. When she opened the oven door the girls heard sticks of burning stove wood crackle and pop, sending out waves of heat into the kitchen.

"Hurry up, girls, and get them potatoes mashed by the time these biscuits get done. We'll heat up the soup beans we had left yesterday, and then we can eat."

The table was set and the food ready when Daddy came in from the barn.

"Did you girls get everything you needed today?" Daddy passed around the potatoes and beans and took a biscuit from the plate in the middle of the table.

"We sure did," Wilma answered, "and I got a new book that we're gonna start reading right after supper."

"Are you gonna read it to Lilly?"

He poured milk from a heavy blue pitcher and handed the glass to Lilly.

"Well, it won't be long till you'll be reading your own books, will it, Lilly?' He said. "Time you get to second grade, you'll be reading everything in sight."

Lilly didn't answer.

"Come on, Lilly," Wilma said, as they washed and dried the last supper dish. "Let's go find out how the book starts." Wilma hung the cloth up on a nail beside the dish pan and headed for their bedroom.

By nine o'clock the family was in bed.

With everyone else asleep, Lilly could hear all the familiar sounds of night. The snores of her parents. The swish of a limb against the window. The whistling of the wind around the corner of the house. She put her head on Wilma's feather pillow and felt herself drifting toward sleep.

She thought of the woman holding the Syrup of Pepsin bottle, and the clerks laughing, at the cash register. And she saw a bottle of poison cleaning fluid that looked like tonic medicine.

She saw once again the long dark hallway where the tall man hovered, eyes black and staring, like a giant crow about to swoop. And all around him, the whirling, flying paddles, coming closer and closer.

Then, like shadows, or wisps of smoke, the man and the paddles faded, and she saw herself holding two bottles, reading the words, and making a choice.

"I'd sure like to learn to read," she whispered, as a big yellow school bus came toward her.

Wilma was shaking her. "Come on, Lilly, get up. It's time to get ready for school. The bus won't wait for us if we're not there when it comes."

Lilly got out of bed and walked over to the chair where her new clothes were laid out. Wilma stopped brushing her hair.

"Put 'em on, Lilly. We got to go catch the bus."

The ride to school was a blur. Lilly noticed things like the scratchy feel of her new dress where the collar buttoned around her neck. The bigger boys and girls sitting together, whispering about things she could not even guess at. Now there was only the bus, and the road, and the big, red brick building looming up ahead.

"Now remember everything I told you," Wilma said. They were walking up the concrete steps that led to the front door. Wilma found the first-grade room and stopped by the door.

"I've got to go upstairs to my room, but I'll see you right here when it's time to go home." Still turned toward Lilly, Wilma was walking away.

"Wait for me in your room, and I'll come and get you when it's time to catch the bus."

Lilly had never seen a room like this one before. It was big, with four rows of seats, most of them occupied by children about her size. From time to time one of them would turn to whisper to the one behind, creating a little hum in the room. A girl with long plaits, tied on the ends with ribbons, sat in front of Lilly, but she did not turn around.

A lady sat behind a big desk at the front of the room. She was writing in a little brown book. Every few minutes she would look up, her eyes moving around the room to focus on one child or another. Lilly sat there in fear, dreading the time when she would look at her.

"Good morning, children. I'm Miss Margaret, your teacher."

The lady stood up and moved around to the front of her desk.

"We'll be getting our new reading and spelling books tomorrow, but I see that all of you have brought your tablets and pencils with you today."

She moved up and down the rows, stopping and looking down to make sure each child had what he needed.

"The pencil sharpener is right here, and we'll line up and sharpen our pencils first," Miss Margaret said. She sharpened her own pencil, to show how it was done.

"Now that all our pencils are ready, we are going to have our first lesson in writing. Look at the row of letters above the black board behind my desk."

Miss Margaret pointed to a row of marks that stretched all the way across that side of the room.

"Those are the ABC's," she said. "We are going to begin learning to make them. First, we will learn how to hold our pencil and place our sheet of paper in front of us to begin writing."

She took a pencil in her right hand and held a sheet of paper up against the blackboard to show how the lines lay straight across in front of her.

"Put your paper down on your desk so it looks like this. Then we will practice making the first letter, which is the 'A.'"

She picked up a piece of chalk from the tray in front of the blackboard.

"Watch how I make this letter, and then see how well you can do it."

Lilly had been listening and watching, remembering Wilma's words: "You've got to do everything the teacher says, Lilly. Just do what she says, and you won't get in trouble."

This was the first test, the first thing the teacher had told her to do.

Lilly took her pencil in her right hand and placed the sheet of paper in front of her with the lines straight across, just as the teacher had said. She had watched closely as Miss Margaret formed the letter on the blackboard, and it looked so easy. She could do this.

She put her pencil down on the paper and tried to make the letter.

She couldn't do it. Her hand was cramped, and she could not make the movements that looked so easy when the teacher did it. On either side of her she could see the other children making the letter, at first slowly, and then skimming across the page faster and faster as they got the hang of it. She turned back to the sheet of paper and tried again.

She couldn't do it.

A familiar fear came up in Lilly's throat and stomach. She might have to throw up, and she might even wet her pants. What was it she was supposed to do when she had to go pee? She was choking, and tears blotted out her pencil and paper.

As though sensing her fear, the girl on her left turned to look at her.

"Haven't you made any of them yet? She's gonna get you."

Lilly felt a hand on her shoulder, and she cringed and tried to pull away. She looked around the room for some way to escape. There was none. All her worst fears were crowding in on her. She would faint or die within the next minute.

"Your name is Lilly, isn't it?" Miss Margaret was looking down at the empty sheet of paper. "What's wrong? Are you having trouble making the letter? Let me see you try."

Lilly grasped the pencil and made another awkward attempt, no more successful than before.

She remembered: it was, "May I be excused?" But before she could say it. Miss Margaret said. "Lilly, which hand do you hold your fork in?"

Without thinking, Lilly grabbed the pencil in her left hand and held it up.

"Well, let's try that. And let's turn your paper this way." She turned the sheet of paper toward Lilly until the lines were sideways facing her.

"All right, now let's see you try to make the "A."

Lilly put the pencil down on the paper, and the "A" flowed out like a crow gliding down on a morsel of corn, like a man choosing medicine over poison.

Changeling

Me and Wilma hid in the walnut tree up behind Mr. Ben's house to watch the gypsy wagon come down the road. It had a blue wooden cover painted with white stripes and red flowers, with green vines curling around the top and sides. I thought it was beautiful, but Wilma said gypsies only painted their wagons that way to hide how mean they was, and to throw people off their tracks. She said Mama knowed somebody they had robbed and beat up and left for dead.

That's why we was hiding in the tree.

As the wagon got closer, I could hear bells jingling on the horses' harness. A dark man with a red bandana around his neck held the reins, and the woman beside him dangled her feet over the front of the wagon. Her black hair hung in waves, and gold loops on her ears and arms looked like drops of dancing sunlight.

She was the prettiest lady I had ever seen.

Two girls, maybe six and ten, about mine and Wilma's ages, was sitting in the back. The younger light-haired one laughed and shoved the darker one, pretending to push her out. Just as it looked like she might fall, the first one grabbed her, and they fell back together into the wagon.

An old woman was sitting behind them. Thin strands of gray hair hung out from under a long black scarf, and she held a string of beads in her hands. It looked like she was whispering something to herself and pulling the beads through her fingers. When the wagon got under the tree, right below us, she stared straight up into my eyes and kept them there until she was too far away to see me any longer.

I shivered like it had all of a sudden turned winter.

Me and Wilma tried not to breathe. We didn't say a word until they was nearly out of sight.

"Wonder what they're doing around here?" I said and scooted over a little to get away from the rough bark that was scraping the bottom of my legs. Wilma grabbed a limb and started to climb down.

"Nobody knows where they come from, or where they go when they leave," Wilma said.

She picked up a handful of gravel and threw it at a post where a big black crow stood flapping its wings, fixing to take off. We watched it climb high, then swoop down over the corn field on the other side of the fence.

"Mr. Ben told Daddy they stopped at the store yesterday, and when they left, a twenty-five-pound sack of flour and a gallon of lard was gone. Said they stole it slick as a whistle with Fred Kestal standing right there." Wilma rolled her eyes at me like she was shocked and whispered the rest.

"Daddy said Fred was so scared they'd get the money in the cash register, he forgot to watch his groceries."

"Where you reckon they're going now?" I was still whispering too, even though we couldn't see no sign of the wagon, when I asked, "It'll soon be dark so I guess they'll find a place to stay tonight and move on in the morning?"

Wilma pulled a limb down from the persimmon tree we was passing under, and it made a swishing sound when she turned it loose.

"They just camp out wherever it suits them," she said.

We speeded up a little, thinking about that wagon stopping somewhere on Mr. Ben's farm, maybe not far from our house. As we ran, I thought I could almost hear it, still jingling along through the dark shady woods by the lake.

We rounded a curve in the road and saw Mama standing outside, throwing corn to the white leghorn hens and roosters flocking around her legs. When she saw us coming, she lifted the bucket above her head and scattered what was left of the feed in a big wide circle around her.

"You girls're later than I expected. Where've you been?"

Wilma walked over to stand next to Mama. Her hair was blonde where Mama's was dark, but both of them had blue eyes and light skin that took on the bright colors of the sun, just starting to go down. Sometimes I wished my skin was bright and shining like theirs, but Daddy said I took after my Cherokee grandma, and that she was beautiful.

Mama always worries about me and Wilma. Sometimes she meets us with a switch if we stay gone too long, and we're careful what we tell her about some of the things we do. So I didn't think we ought to tell her about the gypsies. But this time Wilma was too excited to hold it in.

"Them gypsies passed right under us, Mama. We hid in the walnut tree so they couldn't see us, but we saw them clear as anything. They was two kids and an old woman in the back, and a man and woman up front. You should've just seen how their wagon was painted up." Mama's face went pale. Wilma stopped talking.

"You was that close to them gypsies? Didn't I tell you to run if you ever seen them coming?"

For a minute I thought Mama was going for a switch, but Wilma jumped in and started talking faster.

"Oh, they're gone now, Mama. They went down the road toward the woods by the lake." Wilma ran over and picked up the feed bucket and started toward the house, with me close behind her. I turned back toward Mama as we got to the door.

"You reckon they'll camp down there tonight?" I asked.

"I hope to God they don't, but if they do, maybe they'll be gone by tomorrow morning."

She brushed away corn hulls that had stuck to the front of her apron, and used the bottom of it to wipe sweat off her forehead.

"Anyhow, I don't want you girls off this place until at least day after tomorrow. Give them gypsies plenty of time to get gone."

She opened the screen door on the back porch and called back over her shoulder.

"You all go on down and gather up the eggs, then come and help me fix supper."

The chicken house was a little gray shed next to the barn, with rows of nests Daddy had made out of boards and lined with straw. There was a good smell inside, like feathers and shelled corn and wood shavings. We had to scratch around to find the eggs, and the straw felt warm where the hens had sat. When we had found ten, Wilma said that was probably all of them.

"Why do you reckon Mama's so scared of the gypsies?" I asked, as I put in the last of the eggs I'd found into the brown basket.

"Cause they steal things. Even babies, sometimes. Mama says they take pretty little light-colored blue-eyed babies, and leave one of their own dark ugly ones in place of it."

My mind flashed back to the gypsy wagon, and I remembered something. One of the girls was lighter than the other one. Almost as light as Wilma.

It wasn't quite dark when Mr. Mackey, from the Anderson farm next to Mr. Ben's, come running up the road and pounded on our door. When Daddy got up from the table to see who it was, he was standing there panting, and his eyes had the same look I'd seen in Mama's sometimes when one of her scared spells come on her. Before Daddy could say anything, Mr. Mackey started talking loud, almost hollering.

"John, one of the boys has wandered off, and we can't find him nowhere. George and Tom was playing out by the barn last night, and when we called them for supper, George come in and said Tom had run behind the barn after old Shep and didn't come back around, and now him and the dog're both gone." Mr. Mackey stepped inside the house and dropped into a chair beside the kitchen table.

"That was about six o'clock last night," Mr. Mackey said, "and we've been looking for him all night long and all day today."

Mama poured a cup of coffee and set it down in front of Mr. Mackey. His eyes was darting all around the kitchen, but not really lighting on anything, and he didn't seem to see the coffee.

"We've covered every inch of ground over on our place, and now we're gonna scour this one." His voice sounded different from when he first come in, and I could tell he was crying.

"He's just three years old, John. How in the name of God could he've got away that quick?"

Mr. Mackey's hair was tangled and wet, with little bits of leaves and twigs in it. Sweat and dust had left brown streaks down his face, and there was a scratch with a thin red scab halfway across his forehead.

"We're getting all the men on this farm to help us look. Mr. Ben and Duke Clay and Jake Grimes are going through the fields where the corn and tobacco's so tall, and Sam Murphy and Fred Kestal have gone over to the river. I thought maybe you'd go with me through them woods down by the lake, below Mr. Ben's house." What Mr. Mackey said next was hard for me to hear.

"John, me and Stella's scared to death."

Daddy grabbed his hat off the nail by the door.

"Mary, you and the girls go on up and stay with Stella, and I'll go with Henry," he said.

They was out the door and down the path before I looked at Mama.

I had never seen her look like that before. Her face was white, and she was holding the coffee pot handle so tight her knuckles showed through. Her eyes looked darker, and she was staring out the window like she didn't know we was there.

"What's wrong, Mama?" Wilma sounded scared, like I felt.

"They're never gonna find that child," Mama said, not like she was talking to us, but to somebody far off. "Them gypsies have done got him and gone."

"What will they do with him, Mama?" I whispered.

"Nobody knows for sure. Sometimes they leave one of their own for a trade, and sometimes they just take off and you never see hide nor hair of the child or the gypsies again." Her voice had a funny sing-songy sound.

Wilma grabbed Mama's hand and started pulling her toward the door.

"Come on, Mama. Stella needs us to stay with her while they're looking for Tom."

"They always come back again, though." Mama still spoke in that strange voice.

"Always a different bunch, but gypsies always come back."

Then me and Wilma and Mama was running to get to Stella's, so we could be with her while the men looked for Tom. The sun hung big and red above the trees, and gray blue shadows covered the Mackey's house and barn up the road in front of us.

Fanny Kestal and Aunt Belle was already there. Fanny had George in the kitchen feeding him a biscuit with blackberry jam, and Aunt Belle was holding Stella's hand and talking to her in a low voice. Stella's hair hung in strings around her face, and her eyes was red and swollen. She was gripping Aunt Belle's hand like a drowning person.

"Now you just come over here and lay down and sleep for a little while." Aunt Belle was trying to ease Stella over to the day bed by the door.

"You need to be rested when they bring your boy in." But Stella held back, like she was afraid if she laid down she'd somehow miss Tom, and never see him again.

Me and Wilma walked out behind Stella's house and climbed up on the fence. Wilma pulled a splinter off the rail beside her and looked off down the road in the direction of the lake. I thought of the bright gypsy wagon I'd seen going behind those trees.

"Wilma, why is Mama so scared of them gypsies?" I asked the same question as I had at the chicken house, only now it was because of the awful way Mama had acted when she heard about Tom.

At first I didn't think Wilma was going to answer, then she leaned over close to me and whispered. "If I tell you, you got to promise not to tell."

I looked at her and nodded, almost too scared to hear what she was going to say.

"Mama had another baby once, Lilly. It was a little blonde haired girl, that died. I was too little to remember, but Aunt Pearl told me about it."

Wilma leaned closer. "Aunt Pearl said she never completely got over it. She said there was gypsies then, too. Said they come by our house the day it was born, and Aunt Pearl said Mama thought they marked the baby."

I could feel goose bumps rise up on my arms. "How?" I whispered.

"It was born dead, and Mama was so sick she never got to see it. Aunt Pearl said Mama wouldn't hardly eat or talk or nothing for a long time."

Wilma turned around and gazed back toward the house to be sure nobody was listening.

"Said, even though they tried to tell her different, Mama always thought the gypsies got her baby, was the reason she never saw it. Anyway, it wasn't hardly a year till you was born, and she got better after that, but she's been scared to death of gypsies ever since."

The light was almost gone when we saw Daddy and Mr. Mackey coming up the hill. Mr. Mackey was carrying Tom. and old Shep was running along behind them.

Me and Wilma jumped off the fence and run down to meet them. "Where was he, Daddy?" Wilma yelled, before we got halfway down the hill.

"Down by the lake with Shep and a bunch of gypsies. Looks like he must of chased Shep down the hill and fell and hit his head. He's got a little knot on it, but nothing to worry about."

Mr. Mackey hadn't said a word, just kept holding on to Tom like he'd never turn him loose again.

Me and Wilma looked at each other, knowing the question we was both thinking. Wilma spoke up first. It was like she was holding her breath, and the words was low and squeaky.

"Did you say he was with the gypsies. Daddy?"

"Yeah. He was playing with their little girls and eating some kind of sweet bread they'd give him. Feller said they was going to bring him home, but Tom couldn't tell them where he lived."

It was a sight to see when Daddy and Mr. Mackey brought Tom home, but finally all the talking and hugging and crying was done and me and Wilma and Mama and Daddy started home. The moon was big and yellow, lighting up the path almost like day. We passed the place in the road where we'd last seen the gypsy wagon, but we didn't mention it to Mama and Daddy.

The bed felt good when we got in it, and I was so sleepy I never remembered pulling the covers up. The moon out our window seemed to be playing hide and seek when the wind blew strands of gray clouds over it and stirred the branches in the oak tree out by the gate.

Sometime in the night a dream come, and I seen myself in a bright gypsy wagon in the woods. But I was a baby, not six, going on seven, like now. An old woman with black shiny eyes bent over me and lifted me out of my warm, soft bed. She carried me through the woods to a house, through a door, and into a room where a pretty blonde baby was sleeping. I felt her put me in the bed, making it shake as she dropped me, then she picked up the other baby, and slipped out the door and run off into the night.

"Wake up, Lilly. Mama's calling us for breakfast." I lay still as a ghost. My eyes felt heavy, like they didn't want to open, but Wilma was shaking me, so I sat up.

I looked out the window where the bright morning sun covered the lilac bush, and I wondered where the gypsy wagon was now, right this minute. I could almost see a campfire in the deep green woods and smell the sweet bread the lady was baking in a black iron skillet. Pretty music come from a fiddle the man was playing, and them little girls was chasing each other round and round the wagon. A little ways off from them, sitting on a purple blanket, the old woman was talking to her beads.

"Do you think they really would've brought him back?" I asked.

Wilma waited a minute, and I knew she had been wondering the same thing as me.

"I don't know, Lilly," she said. "Let's go see what Daddy thinks."

Cloudburst

Lilly and Wilma walked slowly up the narrow gravel road toward the grocery store. It was a dreary day, warm, but with a dark low sky that threatened to encircle and trap them like June bugs in an airless paper bag. Persimmon and mulberry trees on either side of the road draped heavy branches that sometimes quivered with the movement of squirrels or blue jays. Today, though, even the trees were still, with no hint of life.

Days like this made Lilly feel bad, like she wanted to cry without knowing why. Only today she did know. Her stomach gnawed where she hadn't had breakfast, and her left big toe ached and throbbed from the sharp rock she'd stubbed it on when they first started out.

"I hate this old weather, Wilma. Why can't the sun just go ahead and shine all the time?"

She knew there was no right answer, and she didn't expect any, but Wilma surprised her.

"You know as well as I do, Lilly. They's got to be water so things can grow. But I don't like it any better'n you do."

She didn't look at Lilly, and her voice sounded different, like she wanted to say something else, but couldn't.

The girls were quiet for a while after that, and the only sounds were the soft coos of mourning doves from somewhere far off. Lilly skimmed over the gravel with her already tough bare feet, even though, on this early June day, summer was not quite here yet. Their mother always made them wear their shoes until the tenth day of May, and not a day sooner could they take them off.

"Mama always says them rain-crows is a sign it's gonna rain. How you reckon they know?"

Lilly reached out to push away a shimmering spider web, its intricate threads gorged with the morning dew.

"I guess they can feel it same as we can. They're gonna get it right for sure today."

She looked at the clouds, lower and blacker now, providing a canvas for the jagged streaks of lightning that danced across the morning sky.

"Come on, Lilly. Let's hurry up and get there before it starts."

The girls usually chattered away, talking more to each other than to anyone else. The four years' difference in their ages gave the advantage to Wilma, and Lilly listened more than she talked.

Today was different, though, and while they talked some, there was something still unsaid. Fear hung between them like a curtain, and neither knew how to broach it.

Their father had roused them early, sending them out of the house without breakfast.

"You girls get up and go to the store."

Confused, they hurried into the kitchen, their eyes still heavy with sleep. He stood in front of the kitchen cupboard, holding the door open, taking stock of the groceries inside.

"Bring us back a sack of sugar and a can of lard. If you can carry it, get a five-pound bag of pinto beans, too."

His eyes darted back into his and Mama's bedroom, and the girls wondered why she wasn't already up, cooking their breakfast and planning the day.

"Run on quick, and when you get to Duke's and Belle's house, stop in there and tell Belle to come on down here. Tell her your mama's not feeling good."

His voice was louder than usual, and he clenched his teeth, like he was trying to hold something inside.

The girls stared at him. He talked little, and this was as much as he sometimes said in a whole day.

Still, there was more.

"After you get the groceries, stop on the way back at Belle's. If she's not back yet, wait there till she comes back, or I come up there after you."

Suddenly a sound came from the bedroom, a low moan rising to a shriek, and their father jumped, and bolted toward the door. Over his shoulder he yelled, "Go get Belle," and disappeared into the bedroom.

The girls' feet flew like whirling leaves over the gravel, seeming not to touch the ground until they reached Duke's and Belle's house, half a mile up the road. Out of breath, they ran up to the door and pounded on it.

The door opened immediately, as if Belle had been standing behind it, waiting. Her black face glistened in the early morning light.

She wasted no time on greetings.

"Is it your mama, girls? Did your daddy send you after me?"

She was reaching for a covered basket on the kitchen table and grabbing a shawl off a peg behind the door.

"Yes, Aunt Belle. Daddy sent us to tell you to get down there, fast as you could."

Wilma delivered this message in one breath and stepped back out of Aunt Belle's way.

Uncle Duke appeared behind Belle. His skin was equally black, but his hair had taken on a silvery look that reminded Lilly of the crown on King Arthur's head in one of Wilma's school books. "Why don't you girls come on in and wait while Belle goes back down there? I bet you all ain't even had breakfast yet."

He stepped back and held the door open for them.

"Come on in and I'll fry some hog jowl and potatoes. Maybe even make some biscuits."

He took a heavy black skillet off a nail on the wall and set a big blue and white bowl on the table.

"Nathan'll be getting up here in a minute, and he'll be starved to death."

The thought crossed Lilly's mind that she had heard Mama say lots of times that colored folks couldn't come into her house and eat. She wondered why it was alright for her and Wilma to eat with them. She didn't want to wonder about it too much, because a rumble moved through her stomach as the pork started to sizzle in the skillet.

The girls watched Aunt Belle run down the path to the gravel road, her wide green skirt whipping around her legs like snakes nipping at her heels. When she got to the fence that Duke had put up around the little gray house, she turned and looked back at them.

"Now you girls just wait here 'til I get back. You all play with Nathan, and I'll come back as soon as I can."

She ran through the gate and disappeared around a bend in the road. Wilma turned to Uncle Duke, now bending over the bowl, a dusting of white flour coating his hands.

"We can't stay right now, Uncle Duke." She was already on her way out the door.

"Daddy sent us to the store to get some things, but he told us to stop here on the way back and stay until Aunt Belle comes back."

"Alright, child." He turned to look at them, raising a wooden rolling pin over the mound of dough on the dark brown board.

"You all go on up there and get what he told you to, and when you get back, I'll have you something good fixed to eat."

Lilly and Wilma walked slowly toward the store. They were still quiet, neither of them willing to bring their fear out into the open.

When Lilly couldn't stand it any longer, she stopped in the road and faced Wilma. Her voice, when she spoke, was so low she could barely hear it herself.

"Wilma, what was wrong with Daddy this morning? Why'd he act so funny, and what made Mama yell out like that?"

She hadn't known she was going to cry, but suddenly she was.

"And why did Aunt Belle run out so fast, and why can't we go back home right now?"

"It's the baby, Lilly. It's time for Mama to have the baby. Remember what I told you about where we get 'em from?"

Lilly looked at her without answering.

"Well, Mama's is ready to come."

Lilly did remember, but wished she didn't. Wilma had made her swear not to tell, and when she heard it, she swore to herself she'd never breathe it to anybody. In fact, she wasn't even sure she believed it herself. If anybody but Wilma had told her. she wouldn't have. Anyway, she liked what Mama had told her better, how the doctor dug up babies and brought them in his black bag.

Her heart beat a little faster, like it had ever since Wilma told her about it, just thinking about the baby. Times when she was by herself she thought about how she would hold it, and play with it, and teach it things. Not even Wilma knew how hard she wished for it. Sometimes it was even there like a shadow in her dreams, and she would wake up trying to remember its face. Every so often, astonished, she would hear herself whisper, "We're getting a baby!"

Thinking about the baby had stopped her crying, but now she remembered the scream from the dark bedroom.

"But why did Mama yell out like that? She didn't even sound like herself."

Wilma walked over to the side of the road where the gravel stopped, and the grass and leaves made a soft cushion. She took her time picking out the best spot to sit, like she was putting off the answer. Finally, she looked up at a spot on the top of a fence post where a mud dauber had made its nest, and then she looked at Lilly.

"Because it hurts so much, Lilly."

She picked up a handful of gravel and threw it at the post before she said the rest.

"Mama says it hurts like the devil."

Lilly wanted to ask more, like how could a baby even get out through such a little space, but she didn't know how, and she didn't think Wilma would know, anyway.

Wilma was getting up from the cushion of leaves and brushing the back of her dress. She didn't say any more about the pain, but Lilly saw a different look in her eyes, and knew she was remembering the scream too.

For a second Lilly thought Wilma might cry, and she felt the fear crawling back up into her throat. Instead, Wilma reached out and took her by the arm. Her voice was hurried, like she wanted to get on with whatever came next.

"Come on, Lilly. Let's go get them groceries and go on back down to Uncle Duke's. Ain't you starving to death?"

The sun was still hidden behind the clouds as they lugged the sacks of groceries down the road, and a little wind had started blowing, making it chilly for June. They could see the trail of smoke spiraling up out of the chimney, and they walked a little faster, remembering the smells in the warm kitchen.

The door opened as soon as their feet touched the narrow wooden porch, and Uncle Duke stood in the doorway, his face shiny with the heat from the stove.

"Come on in here, girls. I know you're starved by now."

He held the black iron skillet, a dish towel wrapped around its handle, still smoking from the fried potatoes he'd emptied into the blue bowl on the table. Next to it sat a plate of crisp brown hog jowl, and a bowl of steaming white gravy. The biscuits were keeping hot in a pan on the back of the stove.

Lilly thought she had never smelled anything so good in her life—and probably never would again. She walked over to the table and started to pull out a chair. The taste of the food was already on her tongue.

"Get over there and wash your hands before you set down. I just brought up some water and the wash pan's there on the table. Nathan's gone out to feed the chickens, but he'll be back in a minute."

Wilma was dipping some water into the pan when Nathan came in the back door. He was two years older than Lilly, and two years younger than Wilma, putting him, at nine, right in the middle between them. He was somewhat short for his age, but sturdy, his short black hair almost the same color as his skin. Lilly and Wilma loved to play with him because he knew stuff to do like swing on grape vines and catch crawdads in the creek that ran through Mr. Ben's farm.

He ducked his head when he saw them, suddenly shy at having them inside his house, instead of in the familiar outdoors. He set the feeding pan on the floor behind the stove, and walked over to the table where Lilly and Wilma were washing their hands. He grinned at them, and started to put his hands into the pan, when Uncle Duke saw what he was about to do.

His reaction was quick and automatic, like he had touched a

red-hot cap on the cook stove. For a second Lilly thought he was going to lunge at Nathan and push him out of the way. Instead, he gripped the bread pan in both hands, his voice low and tense.

"Nathan! Don't you know no better than that? You wait till Lilly and Wilma get through washing their hands and then you can wash yours. Don't you never go sticking your hands in the same pan they's washing in."

Nathan dropped his head and backed away.

Lilly and Wilma hurried to finish and dried their hands on the white feed sack dish towel Aunt Belle had hung by the wash pan. They sat down at the table and waited for Nathan. Nobody said anything for a few minutes as they dipped food from the bowls Uncle Duke passed around.

Nathan poured gravy over a biscuit on his plate and looked inquiringly at his father.

"Mama ain't come back home yet?"

"No, she ain't, and I don't reckon she will for a while."

Uncle Duke passed the fried potatoes around for everybody to have a second helping, putting the last spoonful on his own plate.

"Why don't you all go on outside and find something to do while I get these dishes washed?" He stood up and started to rake the few leftovers into a slop bucket for the hogs.

"It sure wouldn't do for Belle to come home and find her kitchen dirty." He held the door open to let them out.

"Don't stay out there if it starts raining, though."

They wandered down to the creek behind the house, and sat on the bank, tossing pebbles into the clear water. It was a shallow creek, and minnows and crawdads darted here and there over mossy rocks. Willow trees lined the banks on either side, their branches meeting to form a protective shield.

Most days they would have been skipping flat rocks across the water or wading out to look for frogs or turtles. But today was different. The sky was almost completely black now, and there was a strange stillness in the air, as if all of nature was holding its breath.

Nathan aimed a pebble at a minnow and looked over at Wilma.

"My mama told my daddy your mama's gonna die having that baby."

"What?" Wilma bolted up from where she had been leaning back on her elbows and stared at Nathan as though she'd never seen him before.

"That's what she said. Said it's too low, and your mama too little to have a big baby like that. Said her bones too old. Ain't gonna stretch that far. Said she gonna die for sure."

"You take that back, Nathan Clay, you lying little nigger." Wilma was on him, her fists pounding into his face, neck, back, anywhere she could land a blow. "You take that back," she screamed, "or I'm gonna kill you right here."

Wilma was crying so hard that Lilly could barely make out what she said. She was so surprised by the sudden violence that her mind couldn't grasp the horror of Nathan's words or Wilma's reaction, and she looked at the two of them like she did at pictures in her story books, fascinated, but not really a part of the scene.

"You know she never said no such a thing, you lying little son of a bitch," Wilma said.

She was panting. Tears and spittle trickled down her chin. Her teeth were bared in a white snarl, her cheeks flushed scarlet.

Wilma kept up the pounding until Nathan managed to roll away from her, jump up, and run back up the hill toward his house. His muddy shirt, fresh and white this morning from Belle's vigorous scrubbing, was streaked red where blood dripped from a gash below his left eye, and one sleeve, torn from the shoulder, dangled at his side as he ran.

Watching him, Lilly was jolted back into reality, but she still felt strange, as though she might touch her own arm and not feel it. She thought about the words that had set Wilma off against Nathan, and the chill of fear, forgotten for a little while, crept through her again.

Wilma was lying on her side in a rolled-up ball, sobbing, her hair matted to her forehead, with tiny pieces of dead leaves and grass clinging to her face.

Lilly got up and started toward her, just as the downpour came.

Like a giant bucket upended, it released itself all at once, creating a roar of wind and water, and turning the light outside the canopy of leaves into a dark gray curtain. She stared at it for a moment, unable to move, caught like the motionless characters in a story book. Then the memory came back, and she looked at Wilma.

"We got to go back to the house," she yelled over the roar of the storm. "Uncle Duke said not to stay out if it started to rain."

She wasn't sure Wilma had heard her until she sat up and brushed pine needles off her face.

"He's lying, Lilly," Wilma's voice rasped from the sobs and from the energy spent on Nathan's beating. "Mama's not gonna die."

She stood up and ran her hand over her face and hair again, and shook the dried leaves and grass from her skirt. A streak of mud ran across her forehead and down her left cheek, and Lilly reached over to wipe it off, then turned back to the downpour outside the sheltering limbs. Calmer now, Wilma laid a hand on her arm.

"We'll wait a few minutes till it slacks up, then we'll go up to the house. Aunt Belle'll probably be there pretty soon, and we can go on back home."

Neither Lilly nor Wilma mentioned what had happened by the creek as they climbed the hill. Lilly thought about Nathan's torn, dirty shirt and bleeding face.

"I bet Aunt Belle gives Nathan a whipping when she sees how he looks."

"I hope she does," said Wilma. "It'll serve him right."

The rain had finally slowed to a drizzle, and for the first time that day, patches of white clouds showed on the horizon.

Wilma and Lilly were quiet as they neared the house. The back door was open, and they heard Aunt Belle inside. Her voice sounded tired, like it was an effort to make words, like she was moaning, more than talking.

"No, they wasn't no chance. Her water broke too soon. She was dry. Took too long to come, and it was turned the wrong way. No chance a'tall. There was nothing else I could do, and Miz Kestal was there to help out, so I come on home."

The girls heard Belle's words and turned and ran.

They were silent until they came in sight of their house, gray and still in the sunless afternoon. Their father was sitting on the porch in the rocker, his head resting in the crook of his arm. He looked up when he heard them.

"It was a boy," he said.

The kitchen door was open, and a kerosene lamp had been lit in their parents' bedroom. Following the light, they walked through the kitchen to the door of the bedroom and looked inside.

In the half-dark two small mounds were visible, one not much bigger than the other. Fanny Kestal stood over the smaller one, which was lying under a dark cloth on a table near the door. She unfolded a tiny white dress and laid it aside, then turned back the cover.

From where she stood, Lilly could see that it was a baby, its skin a deep dark Cherokee brown like her own. It made no movement, and when Fanny had finished dressing it, she laid it back on the table and covered it, head and all, with a small white blanket.

The other mound was on their parents' bed, and when Lilly looked closer, she could see the pale outline of her mama's face.

"Come on out, girls, your mama's got to rest." Fanny was leading them away from their mother's bed when they heard a whisper.

"No, let them stay a minute, Fanny."

They sat down by the bed and looked at her. Again, they heard the low whisper.

"Don't you worry, girls. I'm gonna be just fine."

Lilly touched her mother's arm and looked across the room to where the baby lay under the white blanket. "I saw the baby, Mama," she said, and was about to say more, when she felt a sharp pinch on the inside of her arm.

"Hush up, Lilly," Wilma whispered, and nudged her to get up. "Mama's got to rest." As they stood looking down at their mother, Fanny put her hands on their shoulders, and guided them to the kitchen door.

"I'll stay to cook some supper, girls." Fanny's eyes darted around the kitchen, wondering what there was to fix. She saw the remains of last night's pinto beans in the brown bowl on the table and was already looking for the meal and milk to make cornbread. "I'll have it ready in just a few minutes. You all go on out there and talk to your daddy."

Outside, the clouds had cleared, and the late afternoon sun was a tangle of red, yellow, and orange streaks, low in the western sky. Lilly and Wilma stood quietly on the porch, waiting for their father to speak. They knew his words would come only when he was ready.

"You girls'll have to help your mama for a while, till she gets to feeling better." He didn't look at them as he said this but turned his head instead toward the yellow-green rows of tobacco, pink-tinged now by the setting sun, in the field outside the fence.

They ate in silence, and afterwards the girls washed the dishes and put them away. They heard the low roar of a car pulling into the yard, and saw their daddy open the door to a tall man in a black suit. He took off his hat as he came in, and Lilly saw that he was young, his hair thick and wavy, and that he smiled when he shook her daddy's hand.

The man walked into the bedroom where her mother was sleeping, and when he went out the door a few minutes later, he was carrying the tiny white bundle. Their father followed him to the long black car and watched while he placed it in a special place in the back.

Alone in their room, the girls finally talked about the baby. The tears that Lilly had held back all day came now in great gasping sobs that took her breath away and clawed at her chest.

"But Wilma, I wanted that baby so bad." The crying started again, stopping her from asking the question that was crushing her. Finally, she willed herself to ask it.

"Why, Wilma? Why did it have to die?"

"I don't know, Lilly. Maybe sometimes a bad thing has to happen, just so something worse won't."

Sometime that night, late, Lilly stirred at the sound of thunder in the distance, like the rumbling of giants telling secrets. Awake, she retraced the strange events of the day. Last of all she thought of the tiny unmoving mound on the lamp table in the bedroom.

She remembered the times, sitting in the crooked branches of the cherry tree, when she had longed and waited and dreamed about the baby, and how she knew in her secret heart it would be hers alone.

Now there was a new feeling, a tearing one that hurt her to put into words, but she forced herself to whisper them into the warm dark silence.

"I'm glad it was you, you ugly little old thing, you. I'm glad it was you and not my mama.

White Trash

The long hot summer was nearing an end. Leaves, shriveled and listless, had gone from green to a dry crackling brown, and the ground had baked into zigzag lines under the blistering sun. Farm hands moved slowly in the corn and tobacco fields, stopping often to take long drinks of spring water from gray stoneware jugs. Lilly and Wilma played with Spot in the one cool place on the farm, a shaded meadow down below the barn. Under the walnut and maple trees they picked up sticks and threw them in front of the dog, who carried them back to be thrown again. Grass was waist-high in the field, and the girls ran barefoot through it, glancing down now and then to check for nettles or briars.

Lilly saw a big gnarly stick that looked perfect for throwing, and was running straight for it, when she felt a sharp jolt pass through her foot and up into her leg, like a bolt of lightning had shot down from the sky and pierced right through her, anchoring her to the ground. The shock made her look down. All she could see was a deep red stain spreading from beneath her foot, painting the grass and weeds around her.

Lilly felt like she was floating above ground, as though she had no legs at all. Slowly she lifted her foot. Blood washed over the broken half of a blue Ball canning jar, its tooth like shards buried in the soft white arch of her foot. She felt weightless, an onlooker with no connection to anything around her.

She remembered nothing more until she woke up in her bed. Mama and Daddy were standing on either side of the bed and Dr. George was sitting beside her, wrapping a white cloth around her foot. His rimless glasses clung to the tip end of his nose. A frown reflected his deep concentration. He raised his left arm and wiped a white shirt sleeve across his forehead.

"She's got an awful bad cut there, John," he said, "and she's lost a lot of blood." He touched the bandage here and there, checking his own handiwork.

"Damn lucky the ligaments didn't get severed," Dr. George said. He placed her foot carefully on the faded blue and white patchwork quilt. "A broken jar like that could have done a dang sight more damage than it did."

He reached for his black leather bag and stood up. "She'll probably sleep a while longer. I gave her a little laudanum."

He reached over and touched Mama's arm. "Come on back to the kitchen and let me tell you how to take care of it."

Lilly didn't wake up again until the morning sun was coming through the bedroom window. At first, she didn't remember the accident. She lay still, waking up slowly, looking at a picture on the 1940 wall calendar of cows under shade trees by a rocky creek. Rays of sunlight danced off Wilma's bottle of Evening in Paris perfume like tiny bolts of cobalt lightning.

Lilly pushed the sheet and quilt down to her waist. As she pulled her knees up, a pain like a scalding hot knife shot through her foot and leg. Now she remembered what had happened yesterday. She cried out and fell back on the bed, afraid to move until the pain quieted.

When it eased some, she yelled for Wilma. The kitchen door opened, and her mother came inside, wiping sweat from her face with the bottom of her green-checkered apron.

"Wilma went up to help the Taylors get the house ready for company," she said. Mr. Ben's sister and her daughter's coming."

She walked into the bedroom and sat down beside Lilly. "How's your foot feel? Dr. George said not to move it around too much."

" Ain't no danger of that," Lilly answered. "I couldn't even raise it up when I tried to get out of the bed."

"Well, you just lay there a while." Her mother pulled the covers back. A white bandage covered Lilly's whole foot and ankle.

"What am I gonna do, Mama? I can't just lay here all summer." She looked down at her foot again. "What about when school starts?" She felt a throb like a heartbeat start up in her foot. It was a pain like she'd never before imagined.

"Oh, Mama," she moaned.

Her mother got up and walked back toward the kitchen. "Now don't cry, Lilly. Just lay still. Ain't nothing we can do but let it heal up."

Mama turned at the bedroom door.

"I'm gonna get the stuff Dr. George left for me to dress it with. He did say you could get up and set in a chair pretty soon. Just not to put your weight down on it for a while."

She came back from the kitchen with a pan of hot water, cloth from a torn-up sheet, and a jar of smelly brown salve. Lilly closed her eyes while her mother carefully changed the bandage.

Afterward, she lay in her bed and looked out the window. The sky was deep soft blue, clear except for big white pillow-shaped clouds. A black crow flew in wide lazy circles, landing finally on a fence post out by the barn. She heard the occasional clang of a cowbell sounding from down in the pasture.

Late in the afternoon Wilma came home and ran into their bedroom. Lilly was dosing, drowsy from the laudanum. Wilma kneeled down beside the bed. "How's your foot, Lilly?" she asked. "Does it still hurt?"

"Not right now," Lilly yawned. She raised up a little way off the pillow and looked at Wilma. "It hurts awful if I move it, though." She shifted her foot a little, being careful not to jar the wound. "What'd you do today?"

"I helped Miz Sarah dust all the furniture and change the beds. We just did get it all done before her company got there. Boy was that something to see."

"Why?" Lilly yawned. "What was they like?"

"Well, they come in this big silver colored car Miz Sarah called a "Pierce Arrow." It was so big, you never seen nothing like it." She closed her eyes, picturing it all over again. "Then, when they got out... oh, Lilly. You should of seen 'em. They was all dressed up in these pretty flowerdy dresses, and they run in and hugged and kissed Miz Sarah and Nora."

At the mention of Nora, both girls became silent. Nora was Sarah and Ben Taylor's granddaughter. She was fifteen and she never missed an opportunity to taunt the girls. Being tenants on her grandfather's farm, they were fair game for Nora's bullying. If they didn't mind her, she told them, she'd get her Grampy to throw their whole family out of the house they lived in. And she'd do it for sure if they ever told on her. So, they stole candy bars for her from Mr. Wilson's store and packages of cigarettes when they caught him not looking.

"They never did even look at me," Wilma said.

"How many of'em was they?" Lilly asked.

"Just this one lady and her daughter about Nora's age. Miz Sarah said they was gonna stay two or three weeks."

Each day that she had to stay in bed seemed like ten to Lilly. Mama changed the bandage every day and talked about how much better her foot looked.

"It ain't got no red streaks running from it," she said. "That's what Dr. George said was a sign of infection."

It was almost two weeks later when Dr. George came by to look at Lilly's foot. He gently probed and prodded, and finally said, "Well, young lady, looks like you're gonna live."

He turned to her mother. "I think she can get some sun today, Mary. Just to sit on the porch, though. Can't risk getting dirt in that cut."

Daddy picked Lilly up and carried her to the porch, where he had fixed a chair with pillows for her to rest her leg.

"Now just sit still right there, little sugar," he said. He tucked the quilt around her, leaving her foot uncovered. "Some of this cool air might get in under the bandage and help it heal," he said.

"Oh Daddy," she whined. "Sometimes I wonder if it's ever gonna heal."

"Everything heals in time," Daddy said. "Right now, you just sit there and enjoy yourself." He squeezed her shoulder and went back inside the house.

On the third day that Lilly was allowed to sit outside, Wilma had to start school. Lilly's foot was still so sore that she could only crawl to get around. Even crawling hurt, but she was so sick of being stuck in bed or on a chair that she did it anyway. Sometimes she pretended to be Spot, and that was fun.

She watched Wilma walk down the path to catch the school bus. She almost cried. It was hard to be left out of the excitement of the first day of school after being home all summer.

"Don't worry, Lilly," Wilma said. "I'll tell everybody why you're not there."

A few minutes later Mama and Daddy headed up the hill to a field near Mr. Ben's house to shuck corn.

"Don't set out here too long, Lilly," her mother said. "Go back in and lay down after while and eat some of them beans and cornbread if you get hungry."

She hadn't been out long when Nathan came around the side of the house. He was carrying a brown paper sack with grease spots on it.

"Hi, Lilly," he said.

"Why ain't you in school today? Lilly asked.

"Ours don't start till next week," he answered. "They got to fix the roof where the storm hit it. Took off a bunch of shingles." Nathan held up the bag.

"Want a piece of Mammy's chocolate pie?"

Lilly's mouth started to water. Of all the good things in the world to eat, Aunt Belle's chocolate pie was probably her favorite. She reached for the bag in Nathan's hand.

"I brung my wagon," Nathan said, when they had finished the pie. "Get in, and I'll pull you over to the creek. We can skip rocks across."

Lilly knew she shouldn't go. For one thing. Mama didn't much like for her and Wilma to play with Nathan, on account of him being colored.

"No telling what people might say," Mama told them.

And for another, Dr. George would be mad if she left the porch and got her foot infected. She thought it over for about a minute.

"Well, all right, but just for a little while. I hafta be back before anybody comes home."

She lowered herself out of the chair and onto the floor of the porch. "Help me down the steps," she told him. Lilly leaned her weight on Nathan and held her bandaged foot in the air. At the bottom of the steps, he helped her into the red and black wooden wagon his grandpa had made him.

They sat by the creek skipping rocks and watching minnows and crawdads skitter in and out of sight in the shallow water. Birds sang in the overhead branches, and the leaves whispered secrets to the wind. Lilly loved the warmth on her skin. It seemed like forever since she'd been out the sun.

I wish I could just always stay home and sit out here, she thought. Never go back to school, or nowhere else. But then another thought came along behind it and scared her. What if I get so far behind at school I can't catch up? What if everybody else knows more'n me? With an effort she pushed the fear away, and, forgetting her injured foot, tried to reach a prime flat skipping rock lying on the bank a few feet away. As she reached for the rock, her foot banged against a piece of driftwood that had washed up on the creek bank just below where she and Nathan were sitting. Her scream shattered the morning stillness.

Nathan dropped the stone he had been about to sail across the creek. "What's the matter," he yelled. "Is it a snake?"

They had been warned of poisonous water moccasins or copperheads that slithered through the high weeds and sunned themselves on the warm flat rocks by the creek, and they knew firsthand that the snakes were there. Sometimes, if they placed their cheeks down flush with the bank, they could see them hiding between the layers of rocks.

"No, I hit my foot," Lilly tried to say, but the pain was so bad that she could only point to her foot and cry. She lay back in the mud and rocks and moaned, feeling throbs from the wound creep up over her foot and into her leg in pounding angry pulses.

Nathan stood beside her, helpless and terrified.

"Oh, God, Lilly, are you okay?"

"Oh, It hurts, it hurts," she moaned. "I think it's bleeding again."

Nathan sat down on the rocky ground and lifted her foot carefully into his lap. He moved the gauze aside to examine the wound.

"No, it ain't bleeding," he said.

"It hurts," Lilly sobbed. "It hurts so bad."

"Shhh, now," Nathan said. "We'll just set here a while. It'll quit hurting directly."

"Mama'll be so mad," Lilly cried. "I've gotta get home before she does. I'm gonna get a whipping."

"Now hush, Lilly. Ain't nobody gonna get a whipping. You just lay still a minute. We'll get you home." Nathan's voice was frightened, but somehow soothing at the same time.

"Damn this foot," she hissed. "Damn, damn this cut."

Nathan's mouth dropped open.

"Your mama'll whip you for sure if she hears that," he whispered. "You know better'n to cuss."

"It hurts, though," Lilly said.

They sat there quiet for half a minute, then voices came from the path a few feet above them. Giggles and low tones sounded like those of girls sharing secrets.

Lilly looked up. Nora and another girl came into view. They were dressed in thin voile dresses more suited to Sunday school than to the dusty path by the creek. Nora carried a dainty white picnic basket, and the other girl held a pale blue blanket. They look so pretty, Lilly thought. The girls stopped and stared at Nathan and Lilly.

"Will you look at that?" the stranger said.

"Oh, that's nobody," Nora answered. "Just some kids that belong to Grampy's tenants."

The girls stood for a minute or two, looking at Lilly and Nathan without speaking to them.

"Looks like somebody's got a boyfriend," the stranger giggled, and pointed to Lilly's foot in Nathan's lap.

"What'd you expect from niggers and white trash?" Nora asked. The girls stared at them a little longer before continuing on their way. They turned and looked back twice before passing out of sight.

Nathan and Lilly sat still. Neither spoke. After a moment, Nathan placed Lilly's foot on the ground. He left to get the wagon.

He pulled the red and black wagon along the rocky bank to where Lilly lay. He helped her get in.

They were quiet on the way back, and Lilly thought about what the girls had said. She was not surprised they called Nathan a "nigger." After all, that's what he was. But she hadn't heard herself called "white trash" before. By the way Nora said it, Lilly knew it was something bad. She looked down at her mud-streaked arm. She moistened the bottom of her dress with saliva and scrubbed her arm until it was a deep red from wrist to elbow.

Nathan didn't speak until they were almost in sight of Lilly's house.

"Who you 'spose that girl with Miss Nora was?" he finally asked.

"Oh, I know who she is," Lilly answered, moving her leg to a more comfortable position. "Her mama's Mr. Ben's sister. They come to visit for a while."

Nathan was quiet for a moment longer.

"What'd you think they meant about what we was doing back there?"

Lilly turned. She stared at Nathan. He was two years older, eleven, and a little taller than she. Now, however, he looked younger, and scared.

"You reckon Nora gonna say something to Miz Sarah?"

Lilly didn't know how to answer.

"Like what?" she said.

Nathan didn't say a thing but kept on pulling the wagon until they were in sight of Lilly's front porch. He stopped to rest on a little rise above the house.

"Mammy says I always got to be careful," he said. "Says white folks awful strange about what they like and don't like."

Lilly looked out toward the meadow where she and Wilma had played with Spot the day of the accident. A shiver passed through her.

"Take me on down and help me up on the porch," she said.

Nathan pulled the wagon to the steps and helped Lilly back into the chair. He hesitated like he might want to say something else. Instead, he jumped down the three steps to his wagon. He waved as he left the yard and got back on the road, then took off in a run toward his own house.

Lilly was sitting in the chair when Mama and Daddy came in from the field. She had dreaded to see them coming, and had closed her eyes, pretending to be sleepy. Mama went straight to the kitchen to get supper, leaving Lilly and her father alone on the porch.

"You didn't set out here all day, did you, Lilly?" he asked.

"No," she said.

She wasn't used to lying to her daddy, but right now she wished she could. *If only Nora and that girl hadn't come by and seen us,* she thought.

"Nathan brought his wagon and pulled me over to the creek for a little while," she said.

She looked for signs of anger on Daddy's face.

"We skipped rocks and I banged my foot against a piece of driftwood. It hurt something awful, but Nathan made sure it wasn't bleeding, and we sat still till it quit hurting."

"You ort not to left the porch," he said. "No telling what might happen if that foot got infected."

He was quiet for a moment. Lilly's stomach lurched. She knew more was coming.

"Mr. Ben called me out of the field while ago and said something about your foot being in Nathan's lap. Said Nora and her cousin saw you all, over by the creek."

Daddy swatted at a fly buzzing around the bandage.

"I see now how it was, but you got to be careful, Lilly. They's a lot of mean people in the world that like to cause trouble."

He stood up.

"Your mama didn't hear it. It'd just worry her, so we won't say nothing else about it."

He turned and started toward the door.

"Wait, Daddy," Lilly said.

He stopped and looked back at her.

"What's white trash?" she whispered.

Her father's face tightened. He came back and sat down.

"It's what some calls other people they look down on. Sometimes it's cause they're poor. Sometimes just cause people don't act to suit em."

He spoke slowly, as if searching for just the right words.

"It ain't a good thing to call nobody, though. You can't never tell about other people's troubles."

Daddy took Lilly's hand and looked into her eyes. The pressure of his calloused fingers sent a message more powerful than words.

"Here's the most important thing, Lilly." His voice was so low she had to strain to hear.

"You're as good as anybody. Always just do the best you can, and try to treat people right. It'll be enough."

Hours later the moon was a luminous thumbnail in a sky full of stars. Lilly looked out the bedroom window and listened to Wilma's quiet breathing. Somewhere back in the hills a dog was howling at a treed possum or coon, his voice blending with the softly moaning wind. A cloud uncovered the moon and washed the room in silver.

A chill on Lilly's shoulders made her pull the quilt up closer around her. She thought of Nora and the cousin in their pretty flowered dresses on the path by the creek, and what they had said about her and Nathan.

They're just mean, she thought, mean and ugly. If they's any white trash around here, it's them.

For My Family

Soggy flakes of snow drifted lazily out of a low flat sky. They danced and twisted, gray at first in the thin winter light, then white, as they neared the hard dark earth. The man on the road looked up as the first flakes fell, shroud-like, on his thin wool jacket. He pulled the jacket closer around his shoulders and tightened the ear flaps of his cap. He raised a hand to rub snow from his dark face, lined like stone from years in the sun. He clenched his fingers, making fists to stimulate warmth. For the tenth time since he'd left the tobacco warehouse in Lancaster, he reached his hand around to his back pocket to feel the reassuring bulge of his billfold. Beside it he also felt the hard curved outline of his leather-holstered skinning knife, the only thing his father had left him when he died. He always carried it and kept it sharp to skin and clean the squirrels and rabbits he hunted on Sundays.

The tobacco hadn't brought as much as he'd hoped, but there would be enough to pay off last year's grocery bill and leave some to lay in a supply of flour, lard, and sugar. With luck there'd also be a little left over for each of his two boys to have a toy, a length of cotton for Annie to have a dress, and maybe even enough for the family to have a bag of hard Christmas candy. It had taken the better part of the day to get this far, and his feet in the heavy work shoes felt cold and tired. If I hurry, he thought, I can make it to Wilson's store before dark.

He looked up again into the sky which now seemed darker, and saw that the flakes were smaller than before, but falling faster. A thick white curtain of snow covered the sun. He quickened his pace and looked around for a stick to steady him over the slick loose gravel. He spotted a stout straight branch that had fallen from a hickory tree beside the road.

The man picked up the stick and slogged on through the falling snow. The thick silence was broken only by the rhythm of his footsteps and the tapping of the stick. Small puffs of gray in the icy air marked the cadence of his breathing. His hands were numb in the cotton gloves, and he jammed them down into the shallow pockets of his jacket. He thought of the black pot-bellied stove at Wilson's store where he would rest and warm up before walking the two miles on home. Annie and the boys would be waiting, and his supper of thick warm soup beans and cornbread would be sitting on the back of the stove.

These thoughts of his home and family warmed him, and he was unaware of any sound until the crunch of tires startled him back to reality. A car pulled up and stopped beside him. It appeared to be a fairly new one, a black Ford coupe, with shiny steel trim around the windshield and headlights. It was hard to make out much more than that through the snow. The driver rolled down his window and peered out. He was young, and a stranger to the man. Still, there was something familiar about him. Maybe one of the onlookers at the morning's tobacco sales.

"Hey, Mister," the driver said. "Looks like you could use a ride." The man stood silently, blinking his eyes, and leaning on the broken limb. His cap and coat had taken on the heavy gray sogginess of the snow, and his face was the color of fresh-killed hog liver. His words came out in a hoarse whisper.

"I'd be much obliged to you."

He leaned in closer and looked at the driver.

"But I wouldn't want to ride for nothing. I'd pay you to take me as far as Wilson's store."

The young man laughed. "Oh, I wouldn't charge you nothing, being's we're both headed the same way. But you'll have to show me where it is. I'm just passing through."

He leaned over and opened the door on the passenger side.

"Why don't you shake some of that snow off, and get on in?"

The man stamped his feet on the gravel. He ran his hand over his cap and coat, dislodging most of the thick, soft layer of snow, and climbed into the car. The driver eased the car back into the narrow lane, and they rode silently for a few minutes. Warmth encircled the man like a blanket, and he felt a wave of drowsiness pass through him. Steam rising from his jacket and cap filled the car with the sticky sweet odor of sweat and tobacco gum. He was roused out of a groggy half-sleep by the sound of the driver's voice.

"Where you been today, Mister? Pretty bad weather to be out walking in, ain't it?"

The man was slow to answer. Finally, he said, "Had to go to Lancaster to sell my half of the tobacco crop I raised for Ben Taylor. Drove it up there in one of his wagons, then left it off at his place on my way back. Had to walk on home, 'bout eight miles."

He rubbed the steam off the window and looked out. The snow was still heavy, but a subtle fading of gray light signaled the coming of dusk.

"Didn't start to snow till I'd walked maybe four miles."

After that they were both silent for a time. The man put his head back against the seat, lulled by the rhythmic slush, slush, slush of the windshield wipers and the low hum of the car's motor.

Suddenly he felt the car veer to the side of the road and stop. Surprised, he turned toward the driver, and saw the glint of a pistol in his hand. The smile had been replaced by a steely squint that narrowed the young man's face and squeezed his eyes to tiny brown points.

"I seen you back there at the warehouse this morning," he said, "selling your tobacco."

His voice carried a new urgency, an added undertone of fear and excitement.

"So, where's your money at?"

The driver leaned closer to the man and pushed the barrel of the gun into the hollow of his narrow chest. Metal clinked on metal as the gun bit into the tin button of his jacket.

The man sat very still. He felt the trembling of the gun in the driver's hand, and felt it jab deeper into his chest.

"My back pocket," he whispered. "Let me reach around and get it." The driver was very close now, and the man could smell the odor of peanuts and whiskey on his breath. Small pits and scars dotted his face, and a curve in his nose suggested that it had been broken sometime in the past. His eyes had almost disappeared into the creases of his eyelids, and his lips drew back in a thin straight line over uneven yellow teeth.

In the split second it took the man to notice these things, he reached around as if to take his billfold from his back pocket. Instead, he snatched the skinning knife from its leather holster and brought it around in front of him. One hand buried the knife in the driver's chest. In almost the same motion, his other arm came up under the gun and knocked it toward the ceiling. The car was filled with a deafening roar as a single bullet ripped the black fabric lining in the ceiling. The driver fell back against the steering wheel. His eyes were now wide open, startled and questioning.

The man pulled the knife from the driver's body and wiped the blood on the blue cotton shirt, just below a spreading red stain. It was darker outside now, and the knife was like a heavy shadow in his hand. He looked at it, and then at the driver, then slowly reached around to replace the knife in its sheath. He opened the door and stepped out into the deep snow drift.

"I'd a paid you, Mister," he said. "But I couldn't give you my tobacco money. That's for my family."

It was almost completely dark when the man got to Wilson's store, a gray weatherboard building with tin advertising signs covering nearly every visible surface. He put his hand on the Honey Krust Bread door handle and walked into the crowded dim interior. The only light came from a small bulb dangling from the ceiling. Cans and boxes lined tall shelves along the narrow aisle on the left, and a counter topped with colorful candy jars, chewing gum boxes and a brass cash register ran the length of the right side. At the far end sat the stove with three or four straight-backed chairs around it.

A man sat beside the stove, eating a bologna sandwich and listening to a small black radio sitting on the counter near the cash register. "The Wabash Cannonball" gave way to "Wildwood Flower," as Otis Wilson looked up and nodded. "Come on in and get warmed up, Luther."

He motioned toward an empty chair.

"Cold day to be out walking. Where you been?"

The man walked to the stove and stretched out his hands. He felt the pain of the heat on his numb fingers, and drew them back a little. He pulled the plaid cap from his head and laid it on the chair. The smell of his jacket mixed with other odors in the store to form a curious mixture of sweat and fruit and motor oil.

"Went to Lancaster to sell my tobacco."

He reached into his back pocket and pulled out his billfold.

"Want to settle up with you."

"Well, that's fine, Luther. If you'll wait just a minute, I'll see how much it is."

Wilson pulled his heavy body out of the straight backed wooden chair and went behind the counter. He reached up on a shelf behind him, wheezing with the effort, and pulled down a ledger with names of farmers who'd bought their groceries "on account" all year, against the time when they would sell their tobacco crop in the late fall.

"Heard on the news while ago they was some trouble in Lancaster today."

He was searching through the ledger for Luther's name. "Said some young feller broke away from the sheriff while he was arresting him for trying to pick some farmer's pocket. Hit the sheriff in the head and stole his car and left him for dead."

He stopped and put his finger on a name in the ledger.

"Yeah. Here we are, right here."

He picked up the stub of a pencil and put it in his mouth, then started to add a column of figures.

"Lucky for the sheriff he was just knocked out. Guy's probably a long way off by now, though."

Luther walked over to a display of toys and picked up two cap pistols. He added a bag of peppermint candy canes from a stack on the floor and laid the three items on the counter. From a basket of oranges and apples he picked out a five-pound bag of each, and pointed to a bolt of blue-flowered calico.

"When you get that figured," he said, "add these other things, and three yards of that there material."

Wilson finished figuring the year's grocery bill and added the items the man had chosen.

"Looks like your total for the year with what you just bought is gonna be four hundred and sixty-eight dollars, and fifty-two cents."

He walked to the bolt of cloth and started to measure off the three yards.

"Doing a little Christmas shopping, are you, Luther?"

The man returned to the chair and picked up his red plaid cap. He buttoned his collar tighter around his neck and pulled the gloves out of his pocket. Before he put them on, he took the money out of a battered black bill fold and handed five one-hundred-dollar bills to Wilson.

The cash register rang loudly in the quiet store, drowning out the banjo music coming from the radio, as Wilson made change and handed it to him. The man put on his cap and gloves, gathered the items into his arms, and walked down the aisle toward the door. Suddenly he remembered that Wilson had asked him a question. He removed his hand from the knob and looked back toward the counter, shadowy now, in the gathering gloom.

"Yes," he answered. "I'm buying Christmas presents. For my family."

There's An Eye Watching You

Mama tries to keep us from going to the mailbox today because
of the thunder and lightning. She's always been afraid of storms,
but ever since Billy Gilpin got struck out in the hay field last
summer she's been a lot worse. Billy had lifted up a pitchfork full
of hay to throw up on the wagon, and the bolt just came right out
of the sky and hit the tip of it. Killed him in his tracks right there in
front of his daddy and his brother Jim.

Anyway, Mama says, "You all can't go out in this. It's gonna
pour down rain here in a minute. Just look at that black cloud over
there." The air in the kitchen is real heavy and warm, and I smell
the lye soap she's using to wash mine and Wilma's school clothes
and Daddy's overalls. She's up to her elbows in the tub, scrubbing
my pink and white dress on the washboard.

She wrings the dress out and lays the white square of soap on
the ledge across the top of the washboard. Raising up, she pushes
her hair back out of her eyes, then she walks over to the screen
door. Touching the wooden handle instead of the metal screen that
can draw lightning, she looks out across the yard.

"Wait a little while till it passes over," Mama says, "then you
can go."

We know better than to argue with her when she's tired, but we
walk through the water that has splashed out of the tub onto the
floor and scoot up real close to her.

Wilma kind of leans her head over on Mama's shoulder and
says, "Please Mama, let us go up there. It won't take but a minute."

Wilma looks over at me for help, then starts in again.

"We'll run all the way and be back before it starts to rain."

Wilma points outside. Her voice is all whiny like she might
start crying.

"See, there's no lightning at all now. We'll be back before you
even know we went.'"

Mama don't touch Wilma back. She hardly ever does, unless

it's to grab a switch and hit us across the legs with it if we get to worrying her too much. So, we know not to beg too hard, especially on wash day.

She stands there a minute more, taking a little break, and waiting to see if there's going to be any more thunderclaps. Me and Wilma are right behind her, holding our breath.

Finally, she says, "Well, all right, you all go on up there, but be sure to be back here in five minutes. Don't make me come after you."

Me and Wilma don't give her a chance to change her mind. We dash out the door and start running up the road. The gravels crunch every time our feet hit them, but we don't feel anything. We've gone barefooted all summer, and the bottoms of our feet are as thick as leather. We're nearly out of sight of the house when a loud clap of thunder comes, and we see a jagged streak of lightning shoot across the sky.

I hear Mama yell, "You all come back here," but I don't turn around, even though I half expect her to come running up behind us. Wilma turns and looks at me, but we don't even slow down. We have to get to that mailbox.

See, this is the day we wait for all month long. Right now we're running as fast as we can, but it's not because Mama told us to, or because we're afraid of the storm.

We're running like this because today's the day that Wilma's book comes from the Doubleday Dollar Book Club. Mama knows why we're so anxious to get to the mailbox, and we figure that's why she takes a chance on us not getting struck by lightning.

Every month is the same. The book comes in the mail, and it takes the two of us about four days to read it, give or take a little, depending on how long a book it is. Wilma gets to go first, since she's the oldest, and it comes in her name, then it's my turn. Soon as we're finished reading that book, we start in again waiting for the next one. Once in a while they send us what they call a "bonus selection," and we get two books in the same package. We love that, because then we each have one to read at the same time.

We always know the book we're getting, because they send a

piece of paper with a picture of it, and a little bit about the story. This month it's *The Foxes of Harrow*, by Frank Yerby. The picture of it shows two real pretty ladies wearing long dresses, standing by a river with a handsome man. He's got on a tall hat, and he's holding a fancy looking cane. There's a boat behind them, and a couple of negroes are carrying off a bale of cotton.

From the picture, and what we read about it last month, this is going to be a really good book about people who live on a plantation in Louisiana, and about the Civil War. Me and Wilma love books like that. The Doubleday Dollar Book Club calls them "sweeping historical novels."

Once I almost got into trouble with one of our books. See, when Wilma gets finished and it's my turn, if school is going on, I take it to school with me to read if I get finished with my homework, or we're not having a lesson. Sometimes I even sneak and read when Miss Rachel is teaching.

Anyway, one day last year, when I was in the fourth grade, and Wilma was in the eighth, I'm sitting at my desk reading *The Grapes of Wrath*. It's this really good book about this one family named Joad, and a bunch of others, having to leave their homes in Oklahoma and go to California because of a terrible dry spell, and they couldn't raise anything in Oklahoma. So, they packed up everything and went out to California, and I couldn't begin to tell you what an awful time they had there.

I'm nearly to the end of the book. This girl named Rose of Sharon's baby has died, mostly from starvation, but she still has some milk in her breasts to feed it with. And there's this man who's really sick, and he's about to die too. So, I can't believe it, but Rose of Sharon takes his head in her arms and lets him suck that milk right out of her breast.

Well, if somebody had said something to me right then, I guess I would have jumped out of my skin, because I'm right there with Rose of Sharon and that man. It's like I crawl right into the pages and I'm there with them, doing what they do and feeling what they feel.

All of a sudden, I feel somebody's hand on my shoulder, and it scares me to death. I look up and Miss Rachel is talking to me and looking at that book.

It takes me a minute to catch on to what she's saying.

"Didn't you hear me, Lilly? I've asked you twice. Does your mother know you're reading this book? It looks awfully mature to me." She reaches out like she's going to take it out of my hand, but I pretend not to notice that she wants to look at it, and I pull it back just a little bit.

Nobody's ever asked me a question before about what I'm reading, and I'm not sure what the right answer is. Something in Miss Rachel's voice scares me, like maybe she's going to tell me I can't finish reading it. I turn the page down quick and close the book, and that gives me time to think. I decide the best thing to do is just tell her the truth.

"Oh yes, ma'am, she knows. It's just a book from Wilma's book club. We get one every month. This one's about a lady who does good works and helps to save people from starving."

Something tells me to put a Christian slant on it, because Miss Rachel is one of the main workers in the Friendship Baptist Church where me and Wilma go to Sunday School, and she's always telling us how important it is to do good works.

I'm looking close to see what she thinks about what I said about the book, and she still looks a little funny, but she finally says, "Well, all right, Lilly, but just always be sure to show your books to your mother, so she'll know what you're reading."

I don't say anything else to Miss Rachel about it, but the truth is that Mama don't really know or care about what me and Wilma read. She can't read too well herself. Her daddy died when she was three, so she only got to go to the third grade in school, and then she had to quit and get a job to help her mother out.

So, she just lets us get our books and read them and never asks what they're about. She always says, "You girls go to school every day and get you a good education." I think she's glad we like to read.

I can't even remember when me and Wilma didn't read. She read to me when I was little, and then when I started to school and learned to read for myself, we just started to read the same things, like the books from the Doubleday Dollar Book Club. Wilma clipped the coupon to join it out of a *True Story* magazine about a year ago, and except for one time when they quit sending them, we've been getting the books in the mail ever since. We don't have much way to get books except once in a while at the Ten Cent Store when we go to Lancaster. When Daddy's car broke down, we never did get another one, and that's been a long time ago.

Our biggest problem is getting the dollar together to send every month, but we gather up scrap iron and sell it for a penny a pound down at the junk yard. They sell it to companies that make guns and things to fight the Germans with. If we don't have the whole dollar when it's time to send it in. Mama lets us sell a dozen eggs, or even a hen if we need to. She hates to part with the hens, though. She saves up her egg money all summer to buy us our school things in the fall.

Our feet are still flying over the gravel, and we are nearly to the mailbox. The air is still and dark, and I don't even hear any birds in the trees up over our heads. There have been two or three big claps of thunder and flashes of lightning since we left the house, but we're not scared. We just want to get our book.

When we get to it, we grab for the door handle and pull it down together. Sure enough, like always, the brown package is in there. Wilma reaches in and gets it, and we both stand in front of the mailbox looking at it. We have to remember to save the envelope that comes with it so we can send back the dollar. Otherwise, we won't get any more books.

We found that out once, way back when Wilma first joined the club. We'd been saving up our dollar for the whole month and we had it in nickels and dimes and pennies. So we put it all in the envelope and mail it back to them the day after we get the book.

Next time when the book is supposed to come to the mailbox, all we get in there is a letter, and we nearly faint when we tear it open. In big black letters it says they never got the money for the last book, and to send it in, or they won't send any more books. But the scariest thing is a big line across the top that says,

THERE'S AN EYE WATCHING YOU!

Scared to death, me and Wilma run all the way to the tobacco patch where Daddy is, to show it to him. I'm afraid to look up at the sky because I think I might see that eye.

When Daddy reads it, he says they must not have got the money. Says maybe the envelope tore, or somebody found it and kept it for themselves. He says the thing to do is take the dollar to the store and get a money order for it.

Anyway, we get another dollar saved up and send it to them that way, and we never hear from them anymore and they always send the book, but I still get scared sometimes wondering about that eye.

If it was watching us when they didn't get their money, why can't it watch us any time it wants to? Wilma says there's no need to worry as long as we send the money in on time.

So, we take the package and run over to the persimmon tree across the road. We sit down and start to open up our book. Wilma tears off the envelope and hands it to me to hold, then she pulls off the rest of the paper, and there it is.

It is so beautiful.

The picture they sent us of it last month is the same, but it is nothing like as pretty as the real book. The cover is so shiny we can almost see ourselves in it. And the people! You never saw such pretty clothes. And the river behind them, and that big boat. And the niggers carrying that big white bale of cotton!

Me and Wilma just sit there and run our hands over it for a while. Finally, she opens it up to look at the first page.

We haven't noticed how dark and still it is, until all of a sudden there's a huge clap of thunder and a flash of lightning that come together at almost the same time. The crack that comes right after the lightning hurts our ears.

Me and Wilma look at each other, both of us thinking about Mama and what she'll do if she has to come after us.

We both jump up at the same time and start running back toward the house. I'm holding the brown paper off the package and the envelope, and Wilma is holding the book up tight against her with both arms.

We round the curve in the road right close to the house and stop in our tracks. Out of nowhere comes the loudest clap I've ever heard, and the sky lights up all the way across. In the light we see Mama running toward us with a big switch in her hand. I see her face for only a second, but something about it scares me. Like she knows something awful is going to happen, and she can't do anything to stop it.

The water has started to pour down on us like a bucket, and we can't see anything except for when the big streaks of lightning chase each other across the sky. We are running toward Mama, even though we know what she's going to do with that switch.

Just then I hear another loud cracking noise right above my head, and I look up. Me and Wilma are right under the big tree that we gather walnuts from to make chocolate fudge, and I see a limb that's coming straight down at us. I don't see her, but I feel Mama grab us and pull us out of the way, just as that big limb hits the ground behind us.

We're all three on our knees beside that tree, and Mama is holding on to us and crying. It's a strange feeling, the way she's holding us, but it feels good, even with all the noise, and the water pouring over us.

The switch is on the ground where she threw it when she grabbed us. I don't notice it then, but our book is there, too.

"Come on, girls," Mama yells, and pulls us up and shoves us toward the house. Running as fast as we can, we get to the screen door, and Mama grabs it and pulls it open.

We stand inside the kitchen and watch the limbs bending and whipping, and the rain coming down in sheets. A big piece of metal flies through the yard and hits the fence, wrapping itself around the gate post.

The tub of soapy water is still sitting there in the kitchen, but the washboard and soap are floating in a puddle of water across the room, like they've been throwed there in a hurry.

"You girls get them wet clothes off," Mama finally says, that mad look on her face that me and Wilma know to watch out for.

"It's a good thing I didn't catch you all up at that mailbox. I'd a wore you out with that switch. I had to leave my washing to come after you."

We've heard her say things like that lots of times before, but this time her voice is different some way. It's quieter, like she's not really mad, but she's got to act like it anyway.

She puts the soap and washboard back in the tub, then lifts out a pair of Daddy's overalls. I'm standing close to her, and I see her turn over her hand and look at her fingers. They are wrinkly and shriveled from the water, and there's red cracks in some of them. The water on the floor almost covers my feet.

"Wilma, you and Lilly get the mop and dry this floor," Mama says, and sounds more like herself now. We hurry to get the mop and a bucket off the back porch.

When we get most of the water up, we go to the door to look outside. The storm is about over and it's starting to get lighter, so we run back down to where the limb fell, and where Wilma dropped the book when Mama pulled us out of the way. The book is still there, only now there is mud on the pretty clothes, and the pages are warped and swollen from the rain. We walk back to the house and sit down in front of the stove, wiping the mud off the cover, and drying the pages to keep them from sticking together.

Mama has started cooking supper, and Daddy is out at the barn feeding and milking the cow. There is a crackle from the wood burning in the stove, and the wind, still whistling around the corners of the house, reminds us of the storm.

"Why do you think she came out after us in that storm, as scared as she is of lightning," I ask Wilma as I finish opening up all the pages so they can dry.

Wilma has the dust jacket laid out flat on the floor, and she has wiped it nearly as clean as it was when we first opened the package.

"I don't know for sure. Maybe sometimes you find out there's something even worse to be scared of, and you just forget about the other."

The pages are dry now, and none have stuck together. The book is about twice as thick as it was, but the writing is plain and easy to read.

Wilma picks up the dust jacket and puts it back on, and we run our hands over it and look at the pretty ladies and the handsome man.

After supper we sit at the table and talk about the storm. Daddy says it took some of the roof off the barn, and he's going to have to put it back tomorrow. Says Mr. Ben wants it fixed before it's time to put up the tobacco.

"Did you girls get your book today? Let's see what it looks like." Daddy knows what day it's supposed to come, too.

Wilma brings it in and hands it to him. He looks at the picture for a minute, then turns through it looking at the pages. "Well, it sure is fat from all that water, but the writing looks clear enough."

Wilma takes the book back and opens it up to the first page. "You all want to hear a little bit about how it starts out?"

"Yes," Mama says, and we all settle back in our chairs. Wilma gets that excited look on her face and starts reading.

About fifteen miles above New Orleans the river goes very slowly. It has broadened out there until it is almost a sea and the water is yellow with the mud of half a continent. When the sun strikes it, it is golden.

At night the water talks with dark voices. It goes whispering down past the Natchez Trace, past Ormond until it reaches the old D'Estrehan place, and flows by that singing. But when it passes Harrow, it is silent....

After a few pages Daddy yawns, and we all move back from the table. Mama gets the blue jar of Vicks salve off the shelf by the stove, and sits back down and rubs it on her hands. Me and Wilma wash the supper dishes, then go to our room and change into our gowns. We blow out the lamp and go to bed.

Outside, the wind has stopped, and there's a little light from the moon coming in the window. I see the dark outline of our book on the dresser. I close my eyes and pull the blanket up around my shoulders.

Hester and Pippa

Leaning slightly forward, Carrie Stevens caught herself nodding off. She sat up straight in the hard wooden chair and glanced at her class of sixth graders, who were still engrossed in Silas Marner. The late September sun made her yawn, and she pushed up her sleeve and pinched the soft inside of her arm. She tried to focus on the classroom, but her mind wandered to the new copy of Modern Screen hidden in her satchel, with a wonderful picture of Van Johnson on the cover. True, she'd bought the magazine mostly because of Van's picture, but she could hardly wait to peek inside at Hedda Hopper's gossip column. That woman, she thought, must know everybody in Hollywood. A delicious thrill of envy sent a shiver down her spine.

Carrie was tiny, not much more than five feet. At twenty-two she still had the wispy look of a teenager. Her hair was pulled back in a bun from which a fringe of curly sprigs had escaped, framing her face like a ruffle. She wore no makeup, and her figure was hidden in a baggy sweater and a long full skirt. When she moved, she gave off a faint scent of Prince Machibelli perfume. It was the one personal grooming touch she'd refused to give up when all of the "unpleasantness," her mother's word, had occurred. There couldn't be a rule against smelling good. She hated how she looked, but the school board had given her no choice.

"Don't call attention to yourself," old lady Cruikshank in Pupil Personnel had said. "Those are good, God-fearing people down there." And I'm not, Carrie thought grimly, but held her tongue.

She blew a strand of hair off her forehead and opened her textbook. It was thick, made up of many excerpts from American and English literary classics. Skimming the pages, Carrie looked for questions to ask when the students had finished reading. Gradually, however, her mind wandered again.

What on earth am I doing here? she wondered for the thousandth time since her transfer from the school in Lancaster to this dreary place ten miles out in the county. She loved teaching, but it had been very hard to adjust. She was lucky to have a job at all. If Clayton's dad hadn't been the county school superintendent, she wouldn't have. Thinking back, she was embarrassed and humiliated all over again, and she closed her eyes and shook her head to clear it of the embarrassing memories.

One by one the students finished reading. When their books had all been put aside, Carrie stood up and walked around to the front of her desk. Force of habit made her smile, and she cleared her throat and looked around the room.

"Well, class," she said. "Did you like the story?"

Most of her students nodded. She still didn't know their names, even though school had been in session for almost two weeks. This was inexcusable, she knew, but she just hadn't been able to muster up the energy.

She searched their faces and tried to remember just one name. All eyes were on her, waiting. A trickle of perspiration ran down between her shoulder blades, and not a single name would come. Finally, she resorted to opening her roll book.

"Marie?" She waited for one of the girls to respond, but they were all quiet and still.

After a few tense seconds she said, "Where are you?"

Her face burned, but she hung on to the smile. Finally a hand went up in the middle of the first row.

"They's two of us named Marie," the girl said. She was tall and thin with reddish brown hair parted in the middle and braided into long pig tails. Her dress looked too big and baggy, as though one or more older sister might have worn it first.

"I'm Marie Grimes, and she's Marie Broaddus." She pointed to another girl in the row next to the door, who was whispering to the girl in front of her. The second Marie, a rather chubby girl, was dressed in a pretty flowered voile dress with patent leather shoes, and socks that matched her green dress. Carrie suddenly realized that this girl had not worn the same dress twice during the past two weeks.

She kicked herself mentally for not noticing the two identical first names. "Oh, I see," she said, and looked hard at the Marie who had not answered. "Well, all right. Why did we like this story? Most of you nodded that you did." She consulted her roll book again. "Lewis Mitchell, where are you?"

A sunburned boy with tobacco stains on his hands nodded at her from the back row. A faded plaid shirt hung on his narrow shoulders, and his brogans were caked with mud from last night's rain. He stared at the floor as though hoping that by some miracle he wouldn't have to speak.

"Lewis," Carrie said, "In the beginning of the story, what do you think Silas Marner cared about most in the world?"
The boy's face turned the color of a ripe beet, and he was silent. Finally, he said, "I don't know."

Whispers rustled through the class, but nobody offered to answer the question.

"You don't know," she said, staring at him. "You did read the story, didn't you?"

The boy didn't answer. He was biting his knuckles and looking at the floor. The other students watched, their faces closed and distant.

My God, she thought, how did I get myself into this? She glanced at the list of names and decided to try again.

"Well," she said. "He sure did like his money, didn't he? Does anybody know what we call someone that hoards money like he did?" Carrie's eye fell on the first name on the list. "Lilly Adkins," she said. "Where are you?"

A small girl with straight brown hair and dark eyes looked up from her desk in the middle of the second row. She raised her hand then looked back down at her textbook. The teacher's voice rose, as though she thought the girl might not have heard the question.

"So, Lilly," she repeated. Do you know what we call a stingy person like Silas Marner?"

After a long moment the girl answered. "A miser?" she asked, her face hidden behind the tall boy in front of her.

"Why, that's exactly right," Carrie said.

Thank the Lord, she thought, and hurriedly asked another

question, to keep the girl talking.

"You've got a good vocabulary, Lilly. Do you know what a vocabulary is?"

"How many words we know?"

Carrie had to strain to hear.

"Right again."

The girl had now managed to hide herself almost completely. Carrie was tempted to ask another question but decided not to press her luck.

She tried to think of a way to get the students more involved. Did they ever make a movie of this story? she wondered. Shirley Temple would've been a perfect Eppie, and maybe Claude Raines for Silas. It didn't matter anyway. She doubted that any of them had ever seen a movie.

"I know what let's do," she beamed. "Let's do parts."

Her Lancaster class had loved doing parts. These students looked blank.

"Marie Grimes, you be Eppie, and Lewis, you can be Silas."

She found a place where there was dialogue between the two characters.

"Just start right there, and read what they say to each other."

She started to suggest they come to the front of the room, but the look on Lewis' face told her that he was unlikely to budge.

Marie Grimes took a deep breath and read Eppie's line. "O the pipe! Won't you have it lit again, father?"

Lewis clenched his fists and stared at his book. Bad idea, Carrie thought, getting ready to prompt him, but then he sat up straight and read Silas' words, stumbling only once.

"Nay, child. I've done enough for today. I think, mayhap, a little of it does me more good than so much at once." Carrie wasn't sure who was more relieved, she or Lewis.

"Good job," Carrie said. "Eppie really helped Silas, didn't she? We'll do parts again when we have more time."

She glanced out the window. "I see the buses are outside, so we'll have to stop for now." She began to put papers and books into her satchel, and the students gathered up their things and hurried out the door.

When all of the buses had gone, Carrie picked up her satchel and walked out to her old blue '39 Ford, a high school graduation gift from her parents. After almost six years it still ran well. A good thing, too, she thought. No way to get a new one with this war on, even if she could afford one. She patted the dashboard affectionately, and slid her key into the ignition.

Breathing a relieved sigh that the school day was over, she turned onto the narrow road leading to the place where she was staying. "People soon forget," Clayton's dad had assured her. "Do a good job, and after a year you can come back and teach in Lancaster." That's forever, Carrie thought, but she tried to look grateful. "Ben and Sarah Taylor, she's my sister, own a farm down there," Mr. Sparks continued. "It's a big house, and they'll rent you a room. You'll probably have some of their tenants' kids in your class."

On the three-mile drive, her mind replayed the events that had brought her here. How could we've let ourselves get caught like that? she wondered. If she'd had any other kind of job, it wouldn't have mattered so much. But for a teacher the rules about conduct were ironclad. It also didn't help that Pete Sams, the deputy that caught them, had a daughter in her class.

He'd shined a flashlight in their eyes, then turned it off while they got their clothes rearranged. She knew it looked bad, but after all, she and Clayton were engaged, and he was going off to war. He needed something special to remember and look forward to while he was over there defending his country. She thought of Van and Jimmy and Clark, and all the other movie stars that were doing their part, just like Clayton, and she thought of the catchy song. "I Want Some V-Mail From My Female," from the movie they'd seen the very night they got caught. She didn't feel like humming it right now.

"You two ort to be ashamed," Pete said." I'm going straight to your father, Clayton." Then he turned on her. "And I damn sure don't want you teaching my kid no more."

Lucky for her, school was almost out. She'd been allowed to

finish the last two weeks of the year, but the students had heard the rumors, and they giggled and whispered when she tried to keep order.

"...right in the back seat," Drucie Sams whispered to Polly Collins, and clapped her hand over her mouth.

Catty little bitch, Carrie fumed, and blushed for thinking such a word. How had she ever survived those two weeks?

One of the worst things had been her parents' stricken faces. Daddy hadn't said much, but along with his disappointment, she could almost see the dollar signs spinning in his head at the thought of his wasted investment in her college education.

Mama, on the other hand, had been hysterical. She'd just been elected president of the Lancaster Womans' Club, and she sobbed at the thought of the horrible disgrace that would follow when the other members found out. There had been a time when her mother would have defended Carrie like a tiger against anybody, but they had drifted apart when Carrie left for college and Mama became a socialite. I guess she didn't know what else to do when her cub left the lair, Carrie thought.

"How could you do this to us?" Mama moaned. Then she'd had another, even more terrible thought. Turning pale and clutching her heart, she whispered, "You didn't, you're not..."

"No, mama, I'm not." But I almost wish I were, she thought. It would give me something real to hold onto. She imagined Clayton on a troop ship headed God knew where to fight the Germans.

"Be ready to get married just as soon as I get back," he'd whispered when he kissed her goodbye. Now the fear came back, making it hard for her to breathe. Please, please, please, bring him home soon, she chanted to herself as the fence posts flew by, and birds circled over rustling corn husks.

Sarah Taylor was gathering chrysanthemums when Carrie pulled into the drive. Her soft gray hair, perched in a loose top-knot high on the back of her head, almost glowed against her sun tanned skin. She's sure not a bit like Mama, Carrie thought, risking her complexion outside without a hat.

Sara waved from a flower bed that ran the full length of the big white clapboard house, and Carrie got out of the car and joined her.

"I love fall flowers," Sarah said. "The colors are so deep and bright."

"Me too." Carrie looked up as a shower of leaves drifted down from a towering red maple. "Looks like fall's coming early this year." "Yep. Soon be time to get the rake out." Sarah picked up a handful of leaves, then let the wind carry them away. "What kind of day did you have, dear?"

"Oh, I guess all right. I don't know the students very well yet."

She snapped off a blue and white pansy blossom and sniffed it. "Most of them live around here, I think. Mr. Sparks said some might live on your farm."

"I know they do," Sarah answered. "Maybe if you name some of them, I can tell you about 'em."

"Well," Carrie said. "We finished reading Silas Marner today and then discussed it. There was this one boy, Lewis Mitchell, looked like he'd read it, but then he couldn't answer any questions."

"Oh, the Mitchells," Sarah said slowly. "They just moved here last spring. Man moved his family in a wagon if you can believe that. Got a bunch of kids that work like Trojans. Can't say the same for him, though."

Sarah got quiet and looked off into the distance.

"His wife come by here one day to make some excuse for him not showing up to pull tobacco plants," she continued, "and I saw bruises on her arms and neck. Don't know how she got 'em."

She paused.

"That boy Lewis, though. Seems like he wants to go to school. Worked extra hard cutting tobacco this fall to get new shoes and a pencil box."

She looked at Carrie and shrugged.

"Maybe if you just encourage him a little."

Carrie mentioned the dark girl, Lilly Adkins, who seemed to know the meanings of lots of words but was shy when it came to speaking up in class.

"Oh, yes," Sarah answered. "John Adkins' daughter. They're

good people. Got two nice girls, but there's something special about Lilly. Seems real smart to me. She's always got a book in her hand."

Sarah laid the chrysanthemums in a willow basket, and the two women climbed the steps to the porch.

"You must be tired. Why don't you go lie down a while?" Sarah said. "I'll call you when supper's ready."

"Thank you," Carrie said, and walked down the hallway to her room.

It was an attractive room, warm and cheerful, with ruffled white curtains on the window, and a white and pink flowered chenille spread on the antique pine spool bed. Sarah and Ben had even found her a little walnut desk.

"I hope you like it," Sarah had said. "It was our granddaughter Nora's before she went away to college."

Carrie closed the door, put her satchel on the floor and flopped across the bed. Images of the afternoon reading class flitted like a bad movie through her mind. I'll never be able to do this, she thought. She remembered her room in Lancaster with its modern desks, the scrubbed children of doctors, lawyers, businessmen, even the mayor's daughter, and wanted to cry.

She reached over to her satchel and pulled out her new magazine. Movies were a secret passion for her, one that she usually kept hidden. Most people would consider them too frivolous an interest for a teacher. Turning the pages slowly, she saw Betty Grable and Lana Turner in furs and jewels, on the arms of Gregory Peck and the Aga Khan. And beautiful wedding pictures of Elizabeth Taylor and that cute Nicky Hilton, pledging to be together till death did them part.

Oh, if only I could go out there, Carrie thought, I know I could get a screen test and be discovered. It happens all the time. She could see herself sitting around a table at the Copa with Vivian Leigh and Clark Gable and a bunch of other stars, while a photographer kept snapping pictures of her.

She loosened her hair, letting a lock fall down over one eye like Veronica Lake, and raised up to look in the mirror. Not bad, she thought. Just a little peroxide and some false eyelashes and I'd look just like her. She pulled her sweater down so that just a bit of cleavage showed, and struck a sexy pose. Some day, she promised herself. Some day. Then the soft scent pink roses drifted in through the window, and she lay back and closed her eyes.

As the days passed, Carrie gradually learned the names of her students. She had to admit that as a group they were almost as smart as those in Lancaster. Not as outgoing and lively, of course, but that was probably because people out here didn't have the same social advantages as those in town.

Lewis Mitchell was especially good in arithmetic, and the two Maries competed for A's in history and geography. The Adkins girl was quiet most of the time. She seldom raised her hand, but Carrie called on her about the meanings of words or subtle points in stories that the other students missed.

The day they read a portion of the Browning poem, "Pippa Passes," Lilly seemed to forget her shyness, and pointed out how Pippa, the poor little factory girl, had helped others through her cheerful outlook on life. When Carrie read Pippa's song, "Morning's at seven, the hillside's dew-pearled, God's in his heaven, all's right with the world," she thought of Clayton and hugged the book to her. Dear God, yes, she prayed. Please let it be so.

There was an excerpt in the textbook from *The Scarlet Letter.* None of the racy stuff, of course, but only the part where Hester began to accept the letter A on her chest as a mandate to help needy people around her and began to be loved and accepted by them.

"Why was Hester able to help people like this?" Carrie asked the class. Lilly's was the only hand raised.

"Because she didn't have anything to hide," Lilly said.

In November the time came to select an entry for the annual county-wide speech contest, a highlight of the year. Carrie was thrilled. This might not be the movies, but it was, after a fashion, theater. These poor children, one of them anyway, would get a chance to feel what it was like to have all eyes on them, all ears attending their words. It would be magical, a star turn, if just for five minutes. A representative from each school competed for the county title, with the winner going to the state contest at the University of Kentucky in Lexington. Carrie knew town kids always won top honors, but the rural schools sent contestants anyway. Maybe my kids can do better, she thought, turning the words around in her head. My kids.

Mr. Pruitt, the principal, brought Carrie a list of the students in her class that she was to choose as contestants. She noticed that the six on the list were the wealthier kids, whose fathers were farm or store owners in the community.

"These students have a better chance to compete with the town kids," Mr. Pruitt said. "Besides, their parents get a kick out of seeing them perform."

Carrie felt a surprising resentment at the slight to the tenant children. Their parents get a kick, do they? she thought, and silently accepted the list.

Wondering about the best way to choose a winner, Carrie finally decided on a run-off, with the winning student selected by an independent vote. She made poetry assignments to the six students on Mr. Pruitt's list and gave them a week to prepare before inviting three people from the county school board to come out and act as judges.

There was only one student from the principal's list that Carrie thought might have a chance. Marie Broaddus' father owned a large tenant farm next to Ben and Sarah. Marie had a cute, bouncy personality that came from being the only child in a family that could give her whatever she wanted.

Knowing she was on thin ice, maybe even bordering on insubordination, Carrie made one addition to the list that Mr. Pruitt had given her. She had watched Lilly Adkins all year, marveling at her brightness.

"She's just way ahead of sixth-grade level," Carrie had told Sarah.

One afternoon when school was out, Carrie approached Lilly.

"Would you like to get a poem ready and enter the county speech contest? The way you love to read, I think you could do well with it."

Lilly hesitated. Her shyness made it hard for her to talk to the teacher, let alone refuse a direct request.

"I guess I could try if you want me to," she said.

Carrie helped her select a poem about a little beggar girl in Victorian London who had frozen to death one cold Christmas night. She listened as Lilly read it through once. Her heart fell. Lilly wasn't very good. She just didn't enunciate. Or project! Why the child had to project or nobody would hear her. Lilly tripped over the words here and there, letting the sing-song rhythm of iambic pentameter dictate her flow.

Still, Carrie knew this girl had something. Something better than Marie Broaddus, anyway. She smiled at Lilly and put her hand on her shoulder.

"'Think about what it means, Lilly," she said. "Just relax and tell the story."

Lilly recited the poem again and Carrie thought it was a little better, but not a lot. The girl was just too shy, that's all. When they finished practicing, Carrie was sure Marie Broaddus would go to Lancaster.

On the afternoon of the school competition, the three judges arrived from Lancaster and waited in the back of the room. When the last class period came, the first six students stood, according to the number they had drawn, and presented their poems.

Marie Broaddus had chosen "Maud Muller." When her turn came she practically danced up to the makeshift podium behind Carrie's desk. She paused and smiled brightly at the judges.

In a loud voice she recited the lines, paying little attention to the meaning of the poem, and surrendering to its monotonous metric regularity. Carrie was sad for the girl, but not really surprised. Marie was no better or worse than the other five, and Carrie knew there was no way any one of them could win in Lancaster, even with heavy coaching. Why do they even have to compete with the town kids, she wondered. It's cruel. Carrie felt awful for getting poor Lilly mixed up in all of this. She wasn't even going to get past this set of judges, let alone go to the state tournament.

Lilly was last with number seven. At the podium she took a deep breath and began to recite "The Little Match Girl." She said the lines as if she were telling a very sad story about someone she knew. She paid no attention to the rhythm or rhyme scheme of the poem, beginning and ending the phrases only where the meaning dictated. Her voice was clear and distinct, and she looked at everyone in the room individually, as if speaking directly to them.

This is incredible, Carrie thought. How is she able to do that? She looked at the three judges, who were staring at Lilly, fascinated. When she finished, the judges spent a few minutes huddling out of earshot about the outcome, but no one was surprised when they announced that Lilly was the winner.

Only Marie Broaddus objected.

"Mine was louder," she sobbed. "Besides, Mama already bought me a new dress to wear to Lancaster."

"Lilly," Carrie said when the others had left. "How on earth did you learn to recite like that?"

"I didn't know I could," Lilly answered. "I practiced a lot at home. Me and Wilma went over it every night. And I just tried to tell the story, like you said."

"Wilma's your older sister, isn't she?" Carrie asked, remembering Sarah's mentioning another daughter.

"Yes, ma'am. We both like to read."

"You're lucky to have a sister like that," Carrie said. "I think you'll do very well in the contest."

"I'll try my best," Lilly said.

Carrie looked at Lilly's faded dress and scuffed shoes. Some way, she thought, we'll have to get you more presentable looking.

On the drive home, as she thought about Lilly's astonishing performance, Carrie's mind wandered back to her own childhood. Mama had arranged tap dancing lessons for her, dressed her in frilly dresses, and made her sleep in tight hair rollers to produce fat bouncy curls. She could feel the pain to this day.

"You could be a movie star," her mother had said, "if we could just get you out to Hollywood." Too bad you didn't, Mama, she thought, I would have been a few years ahead of Shirley Temple.

A cloud moved over the sun, and wind picked up fallen leaves, tossing them in a whirling dance. Carrie shivered and hoped that snow was not on the way. Her parents, just getting over the shame of her firing, were planning the usual Thanksgiving dinner, still two weeks away. She pressed the gas pedal a little harder and looked out at the darkening sky. Sure be awful to get caught out here and not be able to go home for Thanksgiving.

She wondered if there would be a letter from Clayton today. The last one had come almost six weeks ago. She knew from the radio that the fighting in Europe was heavy. Clayton couldn't tell her much. His letters were censored, and sometimes there would be a black line blotting something out. She didn't even know what country he was in. But he always told her how much he loved her.

"Knowing you're there waiting for me keeps me going."

I hate this damn war. Carrie gripped the wheel and bit down hard on her lip. Damn, damn, damn this stupid war. Tears spilled out, and she had to wipe her eyes to see the road.

She knew something was wrong when she got to the Taylors' house. Sarah stood on the porch waiting for her. When she was close enough, Carrie could see that she was crying. She ran down the steps as Carrie got out of the car and threw her arms around her. "Oh Carrie," she whispered. "I'm so sorry. Clayton's dad called." She stopped and put her hand over her mouth.

"Is he...?" Carrie felt as though she might fall, but Sarah held her and led her up the steps to the house.

"No, no, Carrie," Sarah said. "The telegram said missing in action.'"

No, Carrie thought. If he was alive, I'd know it. I'd feel him there thinking about me and loving me, just like I love him. She tried to feel the closeness that had been there before, even though he was all those miles away. But it was gone, and a cold black void filled the space where her heart had been.

She went into her room and closed the door. She didn't remember getting into bed, and only realized later that Sarah had come and helped her change into her gown. The night was a passing parade of dead and dying soldiers, all with Clayton's face, and she couldn't separate nightmare from reality. When morning came, she felt as though she hadn't slept at all. In fact, she hadn't.

"Carrie, Carrie," she heard Sarah's voice from what seemed a long way off.

But when she opened her eyes, the woman was standing right over her bed, holding a steaming cup of coffee and a small plate wrapped in a napkin.

"Before you say anything, just take this coffee, and try to eat a piece of toast. You may not think so now, but it'll make you feel better."

Sarah set the things down on the bedside table and helped Carrie to sit up.

"Here," she said. "Just take a sip."

Carrie grasped the cup in both hands. The warmth and smell of the coffee began to clear her head and she remembered Clayton. She wanted to go back to sleep and never wake up. She set the cup aside and sobbed.

In the late afternoon she was roused again. "Can you wake up now, honey?" Sarah whispered. Carrie opened her eyes. Sarah was sitting in the rocking chair beside her bed.

"Me and Ben drove up to the school and told Mr. Pruitt about our bad news, and that you wouldn't be back for a few days. He said to take as much time as you need, and he'll get somebody to substitute till you get back."

"Maybe I won't even go back, Sarah," she whispered. "Just let the substitute finish out the year. These students don't need me. They need somebody more like them. Somebody that can understand them better, that's got more in common with them."

Carrie's grief let her say what she'd been feeling since the school year began. Sarah stared at her, and she hurried on. "They're just so different from the students I'm used to."

"But I thought you liked 'em. That you liked the school."

"Oh, I do. At least better than I did. But I've never felt really comfortable with the students. And I don't think they like me very much."

The days dragged by with no further word about Clayton. His parents and the Taylors clung to the hope that "missing in action" only meant that they would see him come walking back in some day, unchanged from the way they remembered him the day he went away. Carrie grieved more quietly now, but with the same terrible ache.

On the day before Thanksgiving, she packed her suitcase and walked out to her car to drive the ten miles to Lancaster. She hugged Ben and Sarah, who had walked out to the driveway with her.

"I'll be back on Sunday," she said.

Neither of them asked about her plans for returning to the classroom, and she didn't mention it. "We'll miss you," Sarah said, and waved.

"Have a good visit with your mom and dad," Ben called out as she drove away.

Although the traditional Thanksgiving dinner was outwardly the same, a dark pall fell over the day. Carrie and her parents ate the turkey and trimmings and tried to make cheerful small talk. In his prayer before the meal, her father had included a plea that Clayton be found safe and returned to his loved ones. Carrie listened and tried to offer her own prayer.

After dinner, when the three were in the kitchen washing dishes and putting things away, her mother asked about school. "Do you think you'll stay down there next year, or come back to Lancaster?"

"I don't know if I'll even finish out this year," Carrie answered.

As she spoke, she remembered the look on Lilly Adkins' face the day she'd recited "The Little Match Girl." It was hope she'd seen there. That's all she's got, Carrie thought, is hope. And it's all I have, too. She took a deep breath and dried the Thanksgiving platter with the strutting turkey decorating the middle of it.

I feel just like Hester Prynne, she thought, and traced a capital letter A on the turkey's breast. And Lilly's like Pippa. She laughed for what felt like the first time in weeks, as she said the names out loud: "Hester and Pippa."

"Who, dear?" her mother asked.

"Nobody, mama. Just two fictitious ladies who went around helping other people out." She placed the platter on the rack in the cherry hutch.

"I guess I will go back, though," she said. "I've got a student to help get ready for the county speech contest."

Ben and Sarah were watching for her on Sunday when she returned to the farm, and they met her on the front porch. A cold wind was blowing in from the west, bringing a threat of snow.

"Come on in and get warmed up," Sarah said, "I've got some hot chocolate made, and Ben's got a fire going in the fireplace."

"This feels so good," Carrie said, when she was settled in the big wing chair in the living room. "I can't sit too long, though. Have to get ready for school tomorrow."

A smile passed between Ben and Sarah.

Ben had carried her suitcase to her room and placed it on her bed. When she was alone, she started to unpack. About halfway down she came to the dress she had been thinking about ever since the day Lilly had won the chance to compete in the contest. It would be a little big on her now, but it could be cut down and hemmed, and it ought to be perfect for her. It was the dress Carrie had worn to give the valedictorian speech at her high school graduation. Mama had made it for her. and Carrie had never seen her look prouder.

A week before the contest Carrie got in her car after school and drove down to Lilly's home, a small weather-beaten tenant house not far from the Taylors. She was nervous. What will they think of me offering this? she wondered. Before she could change her mind, she picked up the bag with the dress and got out of the car. She walked through the small yard and climbed the porch steps.

A pale, blue-eyed woman with wavy black hair opened the door. How different she looks from Lilly, Carrie thought. "Are you Mrs. Adkins?" she asked.

The woman nodded.

"Well, I'm Carrie Stevens, Lilly's teacher," Carrie said.

The woman smiled. "Yes ma'am," she said. Carrie was

flustered by the deference in her voice. "Lilly's talked a lot about you." She opened the screen door. "I'm her mother. Come in."

The room was small and dark and very warm. One window looked out on a path leading to a barnyard where chickens cackled and pecked for elusive grains of corn. The strong smell of soup beans and fried pork seemed to have soaked into the walls of the house. Carrie saw a coal oil lamp and a stack of schoolbooks on a round oak table in the middle of the room. Against the wall, which was decorated with family pictures and a grocery store calendar, was a day bed covered by a red and white patchwork quilt. Two wooden rocking chairs sat near a black iron heating stove.

"Here," Mary Adkins pulled out the chair closer to Carrie. "Sit down by the stove, and I'll light the lamp."

She struck a match from a box on the table and lifted the clear glass chimney, touching the flame to the wick.

"Lilly and Wilma's down at the shed gathering the eggs."

She replaced the chimney and sat down in the other rocker. The lamp cast a soft glow over the room.

Carrie collected her thoughts. She hadn't expected this to be so hard.

"Mrs. Adkins," she said finally. "I'm sure you know about the speech contest Lilly's going to be in." The woman nodded. "Well, I thought maybe, if you didn't care," she could feel her face turn red as she tried to think how to begin.

"Well, see. I've got this dress. I always thought of it as my lucky dress, and I just wondered if you'd let Lilly wear it in the speech contest." She opened the sack and pulled out the navy blue voile dress with tiny white polka dots, a white lace collar and sleeves. "My mother made it for me to wear for a special speech, and it would mean a lot to me if you'd let Lilly wear it." She held it up. "I know it's a little big like it is, but it could be altered..."

"Thank you," Lilly's mother said. "She'd look pretty in that." She took the dress and held it up, mentally measuring it. "It might be a little long, but I can hem it for her."

Relief made Carrie smile when she left the Adkins house. She hadn't deceived Lilly's mother about her reason for offering the dress. She just hadn't understood it herself until now. Maybe it could be Lilly's lucky dress, too. Thank you, thank you, she said, to no one in particular, and got into her car to go home.

Carrie saw Sarah Taylor waiting on the porch when she neared the house. Strange, she thought, as chilly as it is. When she pulled off the road into the driveway, Sarah ran down the steps and up to Carrie, who had stepped out of her car. In her hand was a yellow sheet of paper that could only be a telegram. Carrie felt a jolt, like someone punching her hard in the chest. She was suddenly and completely terrified.

"He's alive, Carrie, he's alive," Sarah yelled. She waved the telegram in the air, then pushed it into Carrie's hand. "He's been in a hospital in Italy, and now he's coming..." It was all Carrie heard before the ground came up to meet her.

Clayton's letter arrived three days later and filled in the details. His unit had been trapped by enemy fire and he had suffered severe shrapnel wounds. He'd lain unconscious for two months, unable to send word to Carrie and his family. Recuperation would take a few months longer, but everything pointed to a full recovery. "I'll soon be home, Carrie," his letter said. "And the first thing we'll do is get married. It's the only thought that's kept me alive."

"Oh yes, Clayton," Carrie wrote back. "Just get well and come back home to me."

My heart lied to me, she thought. Thank God, it lied. It's the only secret I'll ever keep from you, Clayton. That I knew in my heart you were dead.

To fill the time, Carrie threw herself into getting Lilly ready for the contest.

When the day finally came, Carrie stopped by Lilly's house to pick her up. She caught her breath when the girl came out. The dress had been altered to fit Lilly as though it had been made for her, and the shade of blue was perfect for her dark skin and eyes. Someone, her sister, Carrie guessed, had curled Lily's hair.

"It's perfect, Lilly," she said. "You look beautiful."

Lilly blushed and smiled.

Two hours later Carrie sat in the front row of the auditorium and watched Lilly walk up to the stage. There was a look in her eyes, confidence, and she walked tall and straight. Win or lose, Carrie thought, she'll never look back.

The dress reminded Carrie of her mother's dreams for her, of the times when the two of them were close. And of her own fantasies of going to Hollywood to be discovered. But now I'm going to be an old married lady, she thought, almost giddy with happiness. Carrie Sparks. Mrs. Clayton Sparks. Mr. and Mrs. Clayton Sparks. The words played like a love song in her mind. Then Lilly stepped forward and looked directly at Carrie, and beyond her to the waiting audience.

Oh child, Carrie thought. Oh Lilly. Be a star. Be a star.

The Summer of Billy

Wilma would always remember the summer of her sixteenth birthday. The summer the tornado came and carried old Mrs. Bailey's house away while she was still shelling beans in her rocking chair on the front porch. The summer polio struck the Corley family and left two of their kids in iron lungs, and Wilma's mama took sick with the walking pneumonia in the middle of July and had to stay in bed until the last of August. It was the worst of summers, and the best of summers, it was the summer Wilma fell in love.

A stranger in the tobacco field was unusual. The workers, for the most part, were tenants on Mr. Ben's farm or on neighboring ones, and Wilma had known them all her life. She paid little attention to them, except to say hello or comment on the weather, and they, in turn, moved past her, doing the various tasks necessary for growing tobacco, like the interchangeable parts of a quiet machine.

Today, though, there was a newcomer.

He was young, not much older than Wilma, by the looks of him, and handsomer than any boy she had ever seen. His eyes were dark, his skin smooth and unmarked by long hot days in the fields. His new straw hat, so clean that sweat had not yet stained the headband, sat squarely on the back of his head. Every now and then he would lift it to wipe the sweat beads off his face, and Wilma could see where the straw had made a bright red halo around his temple.

Wilma had to help chop out the tobacco while her daddy went with Mr. Ben to deliver some heifers to the Anderson farm down the road. She dreaded it. The sun was unusually hot for so early in the summer, and she could see heat waves rising from the steel hood of the tractor that had been left in the field after the last plowing. It was bound to get bad before quitting time at sunset.

She wore the thin yellow feed-sack dress Mama had just

finished making her. The sleeves left her arms bare, and any breeze that stirred could find its way under the full skirt that hung loosely around her legs. She had pulled back her short blonde hair and tied it with a ribbon, but a few wisps had already escaped to form a damp fringe across her forehead.

The Murphy brothers had also come to help with the chopping, but they had gone ahead, leaving Wilma and the newcomer nearly side by side in two adjoining rows. They had not yet spoken. He stopped and leaned on his hoe. Without knowing why, exactly, Wilma stopped too. But she didn't look at him directly. Instead, she watched a buzzard tracing lazy circles above the field, its keen eyes peeled for an unsuspecting field mouse. She turned at the sound of the boy's voice coming across the ten or twelve feet that separated them.

"I'm Billy Compton. What's your name?" he asked.

"Wilma Adkins. My dad raises tobacco for Mr. Ben."

"So, you all live on this farm?"

"Yeah, me and my mother and dad and my sister Lilly. She's twelve."

Surprised by her own shyness, Wilma couldn't think of anything else to say.

"Well, I guess you know I'm new here," Billy answered quickly. "We just moved in up the road. That white house near the Methodist Church."

He reached up to swat a sweat bee buzzing in ever narrowing circles around his head.

"My dad's the preacher. Is that where you all go to church?"

"No, we go to Friendship Baptist, on down the road a little piece."

Wilma was beginning to feel more comfortable with each new conversational exchange.

"You don't look like no work hand. How come you're out here hoeing tobacco?"

"You're sure right about that. I'm not used to this kind of work. Heat's awful."

Billy mopped at his face and neck again. "I'm working this

summer to make some extra money for clothes and books when I start in at Methodist College this fall."

Wilma had never known anybody who had gone to college, and she was once more at a loss for words. She chopped at a clump of red clover and pulled it away from the young green tobacco stalks. With one hand she caught the bottom of her skirt and fanned her legs, enjoying the brief movement of cool air. After a few minutes she broke the silence.

"Are you gonna be a preacher like your daddy?"

"Lord, I hope not."

Billy pulled off the straw hat and rubbed his arm across his forehead. Wilma noticed that his hair was as black as the feathers of the buzzard that had stopped circling and settled itself on a nearby fence post.

"No, I've seen too much of that kind of life."

He picked up a rock and threw it at the post.

"My daddy wants me to study preaching," he said. "It's the only way he'll let me go to college."

Billy paused and looked out over the long row of tobacco, his voice taking on a low, almost dream-like tone. "What I really want to do is travel," he said. "I don't know how or when, but I'm gonna see the world."

They didn't speak for a while after that, subdued by the late-morning heat. The Murphy boys came up even with them and said they were going to stop and go to the house for dinner.

"Me too," said Wilma. "I'll have to help Mama and Lilly get it ready before Daddy gets there."

She looked over at Billy, who was propping his hoe against the wooden gate that stood between the tobacco field and the road.

"Are you gonna come back after dinner?" she asked.

"I wouldn't miss it for nothing," he said.

Wilma didn't know why she ran, but there was an energy inside her that seemed to lift and carry her feet above the ground, all the way back to the house. While she and her family ate dinner she kept reliving the morning in the tobacco field, and had to be asked twice to pass Lilly the fried potatoes.

After washing the dishes, Wilma and Lilly sat on the porch resting before going back to the afternoon chores. "He told me about how he's going away to college this fall," Wilma said, "and how his daddy don't even know he don't want to be a preacher."

"But what about when his daddy finds out?" Lilly asked.

"I guess he'll find a way to tell him when the time comes. Besides, he says his daddy don't have to know for a while." Wilma smiled, thinking about Billy's plan to fool his father. "By the time he finds out, it'll be too late to do anything about it."

Lilly stood up to take the glasses to the kitchen. "Well, I never saw you get this excited over nobody before," she said. "He sure must be something."

All the way back to the tobacco field Wilma prayed that Billy would be there. As soon as she rounded the bend in the road where she could see the patch, there he was, leaning against the slats of the gate, hoe in hand. Frank and Jimmy Murphy were already out in the middle of the field, and Wilma saw that Billy had waited for her before he started back to work.

"What kept you? Time's a-wasting," he said.

"I hurried to get back as fast as I could."

Wilma's face felt hot. She grabbed the hoe and hurried toward the tobacco patch, searching her mind for something to say.

"Where'd you all live before you moved here?"

"Dad had a church up in Ohio, but they moved him down here," Billy said. "I didn't want to move at first, but now that I'm here, this place is looking a whole lot better."

His look seemed to cut a hole right through Wilma, and she shivered in spite of the heat.

They worked on into the afternoon, stopping now and then to drink from the jug of spring water Wilma had brought from the house, and to talk in an easy flow of give and take. Wilma told him about her life from her earliest memories up until now. Billy listened and asked questions, and Wilma couldn't believe that somebody so wonderful could be interested in her.

When the sun was almost touching the horizon, blanketing the fields with pink and gold, Wilma and Billy stood under the big oak tree beside the road.

"Well, I guess we made short work of those weeds," he said. "Won't be any excuse to come back here tomorrow."

Wilma looked over at the clean rows of tobacco and tried desperately to think of a reason why they should come back. As though reading her thoughts, Billy broke in quickly.

"Have you got anything to do tomorrow afternoon?"

Before she could answer, he rushed on.

"I've got a key to the church house, and there's nobody there then. I'd like to take you up there and show you around."

Wilma's answer was in her face.

That was early May.

By July, Wilma and Billy had spent many afternoons in the Methodist church house, in a small room where the choir robes were stored for use on Sundays. They were careful to approach the church by a path that led from a grove of pine and maple trees, right up close to the back door. Billy always went ahead and unlocked the door, and Wilma waited to be sure no one was around to see her follow him in.

She'd never "gone all the way" with a boy before, never had a totally clear understanding of what they meant when her girlfriends snickered about girls who did. Now that she did understand, she knew those whispers could never apply to her. What she and Billy had was special. He loved her in a way that left her breathless when she thought about it, which was most all the time.

She thought about when she would be Mrs. Billy Compton, and she covered the pages of her diary with the name. She dreamed day and night of what their future would be like. Billy would take her someplace far away and beautiful where it would always be just them, and nobody else would matter.

"What in the world is wrong with you, Wilma?"

Lilly's voice startled her, and she rolled over on her bed, loosening the grip on her diary. "You mope around here all the time, like all you ever do is think about that Billy Compton. What are you gonna do when he goes off to college?"

Billy's college plans had faded from Wilma's mind. As a matter of fact, now that she thought about it, he hadn't even mentioned college since that first day in the tobacco field.

"Why Lilly," she answered patiently, dreamily. "He's not going to college. Don't you know me and him's gonna get married just as soon as he can get a job?"

Wilma closed her eyes and turned away again, burrowing into her pillow and the privacy of her thoughts.

She vaguely heard the door close when Lilly left the room.

Had he mentioned getting a job? Of course, he had; she just couldn't remember exactly when. They had talked about so many things in the heat of that dark little room, on the red and white choir robes.

Only one tiny thing skittered around the edges of her mind like a mouse in a cellar. A wonderful thing, really. She had missed her "monthly," as Mama called it. Billy would be so happy when she told him. All it meant was that they'd have to move up their plans a little.

She raised up and looked at the alarm clock on the small round table by her bed. Four o'clock. Still another hour before she was to meet him.

She was restless. Why not go on up to the woods behind the church and wait for him? It was cool and quiet there, and no one would see her. Besides, the time would go quicker that way.

She walked to her favorite spot, a smooth mossy green boulder, and settled back to wait. Through a break in the branches that hung over her head she could see puffs of white clouds against a clear blue sky. She tried to make out shapes, and saw women in pretty, white bride dresses, carrying bouquets of flowers with long ribbons trailing behind them.

A murmur of voices came to her from the back door of the church. Her heart jumped. Nobody was supposed to be here at this time of day. She crept forward to peer through a thick curtain of bushes.

Preacher Compton's wife and Cora Mitchell stood on the church's tiny back porch. Cora shook a mop vigorously over the railing, as if attempting to roust out demons with the dust, while

Billy's mother beat a small rug against the railing.

"I'm glad we got the sanctuary cleaned today, Cora, "she said. "They'll be a lot of new people coming in for the revival tomorrow night."

She opened the door behind her and tossed the rug back inside.

"Well, you and me both know cleanliness is next to godliness." Cora said, hanging the mop on a nail beside the door, and she looked at a patch of scraggly petunias whose petals drooped in the late evening sun.

"I'll declare, I don't know where this summer's gone. First thing we know, winter'll be here."

She lifted the bottom of her pink-flowered apron and wiped her face.

"I guess Billy's excited about going away to college. Getting started on his work for the Lord."

"Oh, he is, Cora. We're so proud of him," Mrs. Compton answered, almost reverently.

Then her voice sparkled with even greater excitement.

"But what we're really praising God for is him and Celeste. She's that lovely girl he met at Bible camp two summers ago. Well, they've decided to study to be missionaries in Africa and get married and go there when they graduate."

Cora clapped her hands over her mouth, gasping as if she were in a fit of religious ecstasy.

"Oh, Sister Compton. Just imagine! A son and his bride who are gonna take the word of the Lord to them heathens in Africa, and who knows where-all else? Why you and Brother Compton must be just about drownded in the overflowing blessings of Jesus."

Suddenly the two women looked out at the woods behind the church, startled by what sounded like a small animal's cry. They listened for a minute longer but heard nothing more. Then they went inside and closed the door.

Wilma didn't know how much longer she sat there. The sun was getting lower in the sky, dribbling down in golden patterns on the decaying leaves around her. There were no sounds except for the crackle of a dead limb now and then, or the caw of a crow over in Mr. Ben's cornfield. She sat still, trapped in a place inside herself where no feeling or thought could penetrate.

When she heard Billy's footsteps on the path behind her, Wilma stood up and moved toward him. He stopped when he saw her face.

"I heard your mother and Miz Mitchell," she said. "You're gonna marry some girl and go to Africa to be a missionary."

His face went pale, and she wondered if he would speak. When he did, he sounded far away, his voice like cold ashes.

"Wilma, you knew I was going away to school. And I told you I was gonna travel. Marrying Celeste and becoming a missionary's my best chance."

"There's gonna be a baby, Billy," Wilma said.

He stared at her blankly, as though she was suddenly speaking in tongues. The silence between them became a stone wall. It was a stranger's voice she finally heard.

"Not for me, there ain't, Wilma," he said. "My parents would die." His eyes shot icicles through her.

"Nobody knows about us coming here. If you say we did, I'll deny it." An angry laugh sharpened his voice. "My daddy's the preacher. Who d'you think they're gonna believe?"

Wilma stood very still, struggling to control the hurt and panic that was raging inside.

She moved close to this stranger who would always be some small part of her and spoke quietly. Her voice sounded strange. She felt like an onlooker to the scene under the cool green canopy.

"You go carry the message of the Lord, Billy."

He backed away from her.

"You go on and see the world. You tell them heathens about the Lord, Billy, before it comes your turn to rot in Hell, quicker'n any one of them ever does."

Knight at Arms

God had warned the Reverend Billy Compton if he wanted to save his immortal soul, he'd have to stop lusting after Labella Damsan. Billy had heard Him plain as day when he got down on his knees last night to ask for help in staving off this latest attack of the devil.

"You've got to be strong," God said, "and shut that Jezebel, that unholy whore of Babylon, out of your mind."

Lack of sleep had left dark smudges around Billy's eyes and his nerves teetered on the thin edge of a razor. He moved his head a little to the left to escape a piercing ray of sunshine that had found its way into the parsonage study. At least morning had finally come. He rubbed his eyes with the heels of both hands and leaned his head back on the hard rung of his oak swivel chair.

I've got nothing but contempt for that woman, he assured God, as he raked his fingers through his thick unruly black hair. Why she can't even hold a candle to Celeste.

But he felt perspiration pop out on his forehead as he pictured Labella cutting her big round blue eyes at him from behind the Broadman Hymnal and felt her body "accidentally" brush against him on her way to the choir loft. Last Sunday she'd even winked at him and whispered something he hadn't heard but had got the gist of anyway.

A witch is what she is, he thought, nothing but a beautiful sinful temptress witch. Labella's slim body seemed to float into the room and arrange itself in soft curving folds on top of the big black King James Bible on Billy's desk.

God help me, he shuddered, as chills, like hungry rats, ran up and down his spine. Shaking his head to clear it, Billy stumbled out of the hot little room.

Celeste was in the kitchen breaking large brown eggs into a yellow mixing bowl for Billy's breakfast. When she heard him come in, she wiped her hands on her daisy print apron and turned toward him. The hot buttered biscuit with blackberry jam she was sampling from the batch just out of the oven had left a faint purple smudge in the corner of her mouth. She smiled as though she hadn't seen Billy for a week, although after two years of marriage they had seldom been more than a mile away from each other.

"Morning, Billy," she said. "Finished with your devotional?"

"Finished," he answered, looking over her head into the dark accusing eyes of Jesus in a print above the kitchen table.

At that moment Labella's bright blue eyes flashed before him, and the spot on his arm her smooth skin had brushed felt scorched. Billy's head swam, and he waited for the dizziness to pass. Turning to the gray enamel wash pan on the table behind him, he dipped his hands into the warm soapy water Celeste had prepared for him.

"Right after breakfast," Billy said, "I'm going down to the post office and see if the new Sunday School tracts have come."

He scrubbed his hands and dried them on a feed-sack towel hanging on the wall beside the table. "It's been over a week since we ordered 'em."

"Want me to go to the post office with you?" Celeste asked when they had finished breakfast. She had washed and dried the last dish and returned it to the cabinet by the stove. Her eyes were fixed on a fence post in the garden where a robin preened its orange and brown feathers in the morning sun.

"I'll go if you want me to." She turned from the window and smiled up at him. "Otherwise, I'll stay here and get everything ready for Sunday."

Little Eden Holy Name Chapel observed the rite of communion only once a month, and Celeste always prepared purple grape juice for the church members to drink. Not sinful wine like the Catholics used. Billy understood how Celeste looked up to him as minister of the church, and how much she liked feeling useful. Doing such chores as preparing the juice made her feel almost like she was his equal. God knew Billy would never deprive her of such a pleasure.

"No, you just stay right here and do that," Billy answered quickly. "I won't be gone long."

His voice was husky, as though he had suddenly gone hoarse or swallowed something the wrong way. He cleared his throat and wiped sweat off his forehead with a crisply ironed white handkerchief. Celeste looked him over carefully and brushed a speck of lint off his lapel.

"You look awful nice," she said.

He had put on his black Sunday suit. The red and black striped necktie was a gift from Wilma Adkins, a girl he'd once dated. Billy barely remembered what Wilma looked like, but he liked the tie.

Celeste lifted her face to be kissed, and Billy brushed his lips across her cheek.

"I won't be gone long," he repeated, and dashed for the door.

"Just a minute, before you go." Celeste picked up a small brown bag from the pie safe and handed it to him. "Here's a little treat I made for Sister Damsan. Give it to her when you get to the post office."

Billy's heart tightened up as though a giant hand had grabbed it. He couldn't answer. He put the small brown sack under his arm, and tried not to meet Celeste's eyes as he walked out the door.

The old black Buick was parked in the backyard under a tall maple tree which usually vibrated with the songs of finches and warblers and wrens. Sometimes great flocks would fly away all at once and disappear into the morning sun. Today, though, their voices were silent. The hedge that outlined the backyard was dry from lack of rain. Some of the leaves were beginning to wither. Billy made a mental note to add rain to the list of things he needed to ask God for.

The car was seldom moved. Bird droppings covered its black body like the white and green speckles of some dread disease. Billy said a silent prayer each time he needed to go somewhere. He feared it was only a matter of time until the car simply stopped and never ran again.

Just once more, God, he'd say, and turn on the ignition.

Today the car started right off, as though anxious to get on the road. Excitement tinged with dread made breathing difficult for Billy as he backed out onto the narrow road to the post office.

What'll I say to her if it's just the two of us in there by

ourselves? he wondered. Maybe it won't even be her in there today. Maybe she had business in Lancaster and left somebody else in charge.

No, he thought, she's gonna be there.

Billy felt both shame and anger toward God and Celeste for letting him get into this fix. God knew how hard he tried to be faithful and devout, even though all of his boyhood dreams of travel and adventure had been denied when he gave in to his dad's wishes and became a preacher. Still, God gave him no help with his struggle. It seemed that the harder Billy tried, the more God demanded that he keep on proving himself.

And as for Celeste, if she was a really top-notch wife, Labella wouldn't even be able to catch his eye, much less get this kind of a hold on him. He couldn't quite put his finger on where Celeste was failing him. True enough, she was a good hand to cook and take care of the house and help him with church matters. And she was good at her wifely duties. But any fool could see that she was falling down somewhere.

The road to the post office was lined with persimmon and walnut trees on either side, and their overhanging branches made a rhythmic swish-swish every few feet on the car's windshield. Although Billy expected these small assaults, he still cringed. They reminded him vaguely of his mother, her willow switch always handy, always ready to put whelps on his bare legs for real or imagined sins. He shivered and saw that his knuckles were white from gripping the steering wheel. Somebody ought to cut these blasted limbs, he thought, before they cause a wreck.

The post office was a weather-beaten gray structure, hovering like an anxious mother bird at the edge of the gravel road. A faded wooden sign above the front door read, "Little Eden, Kentucky." No other cars were parked anywhere near the building. Billy's stomach gave a sudden lurch, and he was struck with the horrible fear that he might throw up.

Inside, he knew, Labella Damsan, the post mistress, would be sitting behind the counter, selling an occasional book of stamps and handing out letters and Sears and Roebuck catalogs to the people of Little Eden.

He sat very still, giving his insides a chance to settle, trying to muster up his courage. His heart pounded at the prospect of seeing Labella again without the protective armor of the church. It would be just him and her, and the heat that passed between them each time they met. A vivid image of what might happen in the little office at the back of the post office made him gasp, and he felt a tightening in his groin. Minutes passed before he mustered the courage to go in.

Celeste's brown paper bag sat like a silent passenger on the seat beside him. He grabbed it and opened the car door, giving himself no time to think of turning back. He took a second to give his jacket a quick brush and finger the knot of his tie.

The entrance to the post office was about fifteen feet away. Billy covered the distance in four long strides. He flung open the door and entered the dimly lit room. Momentarily blinded, he stood for a few seconds waiting for his eyes to adjust.

Labella glanced up and her eyes widened. Her face broke into a smile, and she stood up and came around the counter. There was a scent in the room like the deep purple fragrance of lilacs after a rain. A light seemed to envelop Labella, like a halo around the moon on a foggy night. Billy's hand clutched at his throat, and he knew what it must feel like to drown. Before she could say anything Billy raised the bag and thrust it toward her.

"I came to get the Sunday School tracts," he gasped, "and here's something Celeste sent you."

A snug white sweater emphasized Labella's full breasts. In the dimness they looked to Billy like the high beams of a coal truck bearing down upon him. Wide hips filled out a red flowered broomstick skirt, which swirled around her tan muscular legs. Her smile seemed to grow until her whole face was covered, and Billy had the sensation that he was about to be devoured like a morsel of chocolate pie. Fear and anticipation weakened him, and he reached for the counter to steady himself.

Labella stopped a foot from him and took the bag. Her eyes caressed his face as she slowly pushed her hand inside the bag and pulled out its contents. A large slice of pound cake wrapped in wax paper lay in her hand, covered by another piece of paper that appeared to be a note.

"What's this, Reverend?" she grinned, placing heavy emphasis on Billy's church title, as though by saying it that way, she let him know that she considered him anything but saintly. Billy searched for words that wouldn't come. He tried to smile, but his face felt frozen. He wanted to reach out for her, but he was pinned like a captured butterfly. Habit almost made him ask God for help.

Labella finally looked away and unfolded the piece of lined tablet paper. She read through it once and then again, as though she hadn't understood it the first time. Her expression changed, sliding from anticipation to anger to fear, and the rosy glow of her cheeks faded to a sallow gray. He watched her smile crumble like one of Celeste's oatmeal cookies in a cup of warm milk. She looked at Billy as though expecting some kind of help. When none came, she turned her back on him and snatched something from the counter.

"Here's your package," she said, and pushed it against his chest, as if trying to propel him backwards toward the door. Her eyes, which had shone so blue in the stained-glass reflection of the church choir loft, now bore into him like the cold gray chill of winter sleet. The room seemed to darken in the midday silence.

Billy stood still for a few seconds, a mixture of confusion, disappointment and relief anchoring him to the floor. Then, like a man granted a last-minute reprieve, he turned and ran. He opened the car door, dropped the Sunday School tracts onto the seat, rammed the key into the ignition, and started the motor.

When Billy arrived back at the parsonage, Celeste was in the kitchen where he had left her, stirring a pan of purple grapes. She had changed from pajamas into a thin cotton house dress printed with roses and dabbed a little pink on her lips and cheeks. A light fragrance of Ivory soap and talcum powder filled the space around her.

"The juice is almost done," she said. "Did you get the tracts?"

Billy laid the package on the table. His hands trembled. Several seconds passed before he could find his voice.

"What did you say to Sister Damsan in the note you sent with the cake?" he finally asked, struggling to keep any emotion out of his voice.

"Oh, I just told her to render unto God what was God's, and unto Caesar what was Caesar's, and that you belong to God and me, and the money she's stealing out of the stamp fund is Caesar's."

Celeste stopped stirring the pot of grape juice and gazed up into Billy's eyes. "I told her I wouldn't tell about the stamp money," she said, "if she gave God and me back our property."

Billy's mouth dropped open. He stared at Celeste as if she were a stranger. A chill passed through him, and he fought off the crazy notion that some otherworldly being had invaded her body and set up residence where his dependable, trusting wife used to be.

"But how could you know such a thing?" he whispered.

"Well, she was either stealing or she wasn't," Celeste answered. "I took a chance she was."

She cupped his face in her hands. "Looks like I was right."

She patted his cheek and turned back to the stove. Billy had the eerie feeling that she could still see his expression.

"Anyway," she laughed, "maybe God tells me things sometimes, too."

By Sunday morning Billy felt like a knight at arms in the service of the Lord. Three nights of uninterrupted, dreamless slumber had left him rested and refreshed. He approached the pulpit and stood still, as though searching for just the right words.

"I tell you brothers and sisters," he began quietly, "you've got to take on the whole armor of God." His volume rose gradually with each new phrase. "You've got to fight against evil everywhere you find it, and if you don't find it, it'll find you." He began to rock back and forth as his cadences slid into a sing-song chant.

"Ah, brothers, ah you got to fight... ah, sisters... ah you got to fight... ah, children and babes in arms... ah you got to fight, or it'll get you in its thrall..."

The chant went into overdrive and Billy looked out over his congregation. Some stared at him in rapt attention, their expressions registering a range of emotions from fear to morbid fascination.

The Wilhoits were sitting in their usual pew about midways back on the left-hand side of the church. Alma sat up straight, her eyes and face nearly hidden behind dark glasses and a black scarf tied around her forehead. Her husband had not looked up during the whole sermon. Alma called the law on Olin last Tuesday for beating her up, Billy thought. Looks like she's decided to take him back.

"...ah, sisters, you got to fight..."

Chester Turpin, on the other side of the church, looked as though he'd like nothing better than to stretch out on the pew and go to sleep. Looks like he tied another one on last night, Billy thought, noticing Chester's bloodshot eyes and hangdog expression. His shirt looked wrinkled and dingy, as though he'd come straight from his bed to church.

"you got to stay on guard, ah..."

Billy noticed that Chester's cute little wife Angie sat as far away from her husband as possible without drawing undue attention to herself. The baby in her lap had squirmed and fretted until Angie's dress had knotted up, exposing thighs that looked milky white in the morning sun.

"against the lures of Satan, ah..."

Bet Angie'll be coming in for counseling one of these days, he thought, and felt a familiar reminder of his own potency.

"Yes," he shouted, and pounded the pulpit for emphasis.

After twenty minutes Billy's words resumed the normal patterns of everyday speech, and he concluded his sermon.

"And I say unto you, brethren," he whispered, "be not deceived. God is not mocked. Be sure your sins will find you out."

The choir loft seemed strangely vacant. Everyone who usually sang in it was there except the post mistress. The hearty gusto of her voice, which had added an almost militant authority to "Onward Christian Soldiers," left a silent reminder of her. The gray-robed choir members filed out quietly after the service. Some of them glanced briefly at the spot where Labella had always sat.

"Wonder where Sister Damsan is this morning," Hattie Buffin said, as she walked up to Billy to congratulate him on his message.

Before he could answer, Ester Taylor, in line behind Hattie, spoke up.

"Me and Amos heard she'd decided to join the Baptists, them hard-shells. Can't imagine why, less it's closer to where she lives."

She reached out her hand to shake Billy's.

"That was a real good message, Brother Compton," she said. "Sounded like it come right straight from God's own lips."

"Praise God, Sister Taylor," Billy said. He looked at the pulpit where Celeste was tidying up, gathering up his notes and the Bible he had used today. As if she felt his eyes on her, she looked over her shoulder and smiled.

That green striped dress don't do much for her, Billy thought. Makes her behind look too big. He'd suggest she wear the yellow polka dot next Sunday.

Out the window behind the pulpit the hills rolled back in hazy lines to a distant horizon. Billy's mind wandered to his lifelong dream. Must be a little like England looks, or Greece. To get to go where King Arthur and his knights lived, or where Ulysses sailed the seas, running into all those beautiful Sirens—boy, would I love to see that. Maybe sometime I'll just take off and go, he thought, just get up in the night and go.

Suddenly a realization, almost too good to be believed, washed over him like the waters of a total baptismal immersion.

Praise God! he thought. Is that what you're telling me to do? Just go? He glanced in Celeste's direction, but she was busy stacking hymnals. Celeste would never go. All she could talk about was building up the church and having a baby soon.

He thought of another possibility. You want me to go by myself, to seek Your will for my life in some faraway land?

He suddenly realized that Ester was still looking at him, and he drew himself up, trying to hide his excitement. Messages sometimes take strange detour from God's lips to ours.

"Sister Taylor," he said in his most holy tone. "God's always watching us, always making His plans known to us, if we do but heed His signs."

He looked at the beckoning hills beyond the window. Labella's luminous blue eyes floated up over the horizon of his consciousness, and he pushed them down again with a gentle mental nudge. His words trailed off, leaving the last sentence unspoken except in the privacy of his own mind.

Just always be on the lookout, ready to obey His messages when they come.

Cold

She checked the coal bucket to see if she ought to refill it before it got any later. It was still half full, but she knew she would need more before dark, and if she brought in another bucket and used it sparingly, there might even be enough to last through the night. The decision made, she took her black wool overcoat from the hook beside the door.

She stepped outside, and a blast of cold air forced her backward, stinging and burning her nose and cheeks. It was the kind of January day that casts a vague uneasy pall, like the sky might suddenly discharge a great avalanche of snow and smother the whole world. Between routine household chores, Callie had made several trips to the window to look outside, but the cold gray air never seemed to move or change color, and only the moving hands on her clock told her that the day was moving on into mid-afternoon. Moving carefully, she walked to the wooden steps that led off her porch to the frozen ground below. A thin coating of ice made her wary, and she grasped the railing, taking the steps very slowly, one after the other.

When she got to the bottom, she pulled the coat closer around her and walked the few steps to the shed where the ton of coal that Eldon had ordered lay in a scattered black pile.

"Now where is that shovel?" she wondered aloud and saw it on the other side of the pile where she had dropped it early that morning. It hurt her back to bend over, but she put one hand on her hip to brace herself and bent over to shovel the pieces into the bucket, filling it almost to the top.

She stood and rested for a moment before starting the slow climb back up the steps. She didn't see the small patch of coal about halfway up, probably dropped on her first trip to the coal pile. Her foot slipped, scattering the coal, and tearing her hand from the railing. She felt herself falling, and fought to catch herself, but felt only empty cold air closing around her.

Fear grabbed her throat, choking a scream, and then she heard the familiar voice behind her.

"Callie! What on earth do you think you're doing? Why didn't you wait till I got home to carry that coal in?"

She felt George's arms lifting her, bringing her up the steps and into the house. He carried her to the bed in the small room beside the kitchen and laid her on top of the patchwork quilt. Working swiftly, he pulled another quilt from the oak chifforobe and wrapped it around her.

He went back into the kitchen, and she heard the sound of water being poured into the coffeepot.

"You just lay there and rest while I make some hot coffee." Insistent, delicious waves of sleep engulfed her, and she wanted to relax and surrender to them. Instead, she was aroused by George, speaking to her, as he came back into the room, carrying the steaming coffee.

"Here, Callie, drink this. Don't go to sleep right now. How do you feel? You don't reckon you hurt the baby when you fell, do you?"

She wanted to answer him, and tried to, but her eyes kept closing, and only the hot liquid entering her mouth as he held the cup and cradled her head against his shoulder, kept her from drifting off.

She placed her hand over his, and together they felt the familiar movement of a tiny hand or foot moving across the width of her stomach. Smiling, she thought of how much George wanted a boy, and how happy she was that their long wait was almost over.

They sat there for a long time, Callie's head resting on his shoulder, and George stroking her hair, and arranging the quilt around her feet to keep them warm. Through the window on the other side of the room she could see the snow falling like a great gray cape, shrouding the bare branches of the oak and maple trees down by the creek. There was a wild beauty about it that almost made her want to go outside and stand with her arms outstretched, letting the wind blow her long black hair and blanket it with whiteness.

"You stay still, now, Callie. I'm going back out to the field. I'll be back pretty soon and put the tractor in the barn. You'll be warm there on the bed. You just lay there and don't move till I come back."

His voice had a soft, faraway tone that made her want to get up and follow him. To tell him not to go out ever again, to stay here with her where she could see him and touch him. But when she tried to speak, no words would come, and her legs refused to allow her to stand up and run after him.

"No, George, please don't go. Please, please don't go." The words turned into screams in her head, repeating over and over like a phonograph needle stuck in an endless groove.

She heard voices in the kitchen and lay still, listening to the words that came clearly to her through the open door.

"I really appreciate you coming all the way out here, Doctor Franklin. I was scared to death she was dead when I saw her there on the steps." His voice quivered. "She was covered up in snow like she'd been there for hours."

"That's the strange part." The doctor's voice sounded mystified. "In most every case I've ever seen, especially ones in her age range, the patient has suffered severe hypothermia, very often causing death. But I can't see any evidence of that in her case, almost like something kept her from getting too cold. Of course, she'll need watching for the next few days, but I really think she'll recover fully."

"This time"— Callie heard a resolve in Eldon's voice that she had never heard before — "I'm going to insist that she come to Lancaster to live with Gwen and me, or at least let me get her an apartment where we can look in on her every day. Being the only child, I feel completely responsible for her, but there's just no reasoning with her. She and my father moved into this house when they first married, and she's always flat refused to move away from it."

"I never knew your father, Eldon. He was gone before I started my practice in Lancaster, and that's been nearly thirty-five years now."

“I never knew him either, Doctor. He died in a tractor accident three weeks before I was born.”

Abner and Eva

Friendship Baptist Church sat on a small grassy hill beside a winding, tree-lined country road. White in the morning light of summer, its clapboard sides faded to a pasty gray in the evening, and in the short cold days of winter. Weekdays it was still and silent, nestled squat like a brooding leghorn hen. But on Sundays the church roused itself to claim its rightful role in the community. Since Stanley Kirby served as chairman of the deacons, he and Thelma always arrived first, to open the door and prepare the sanctuary for the weekly service. Today they walked inside and paused, breathing the familiar odors of old varnish and musty hymnals, their voices silenced by the echoes of their own footsteps.

Thelma moved around the church, straightening the Bible and vase of dried flowers that decorated the table in front of the pulpit. Satisfied, she walked to the front of the church where a stack of cardboard boxes with clothing donations had been left by the door.

"Get them boxes out of sight before Brother Carney gets here," she sniffed. "They look tacky setting there."

She picked up a pink sweater and held it between two fingers before dropping it back into the box.

"Me and Loretta are gonna go around and hand things out to some of the poor and less fortunate next week."

She noticed a fan with a picture of Jesus talking to some little children and smiled. "It just makes you feel good all over to do good works for the Lord," she said, glancing back at the boxes before she started back up the aisle. "Maybe some different clothes'll fire up a little ambition in them people."

Stanley didn't answer her. He was trying to decide on the best arrangement of chairs for a meeting of the deacons after the sermon.

"Ben Taylor'll want to set next to Doc George so they can talk the sermon over," he mumbled. "Them two always agrees with each other, then tries to push their opinions off on the rest of us."

Stanley looked at the chairs again, then scooted them a foot or two farther apart.

Thelma watched Stanley pick up the boxes and carry them to a closet at the back of the church. He had removed his coat and laid it over the back of the last pew. A roll of fat rode along the top of his black leather belt, jiggling a little when he walked. Dark sweat stained a line down the center of his back. Thelma saw him pull his white handkerchief out of his back pocket and dab it to his neck and brow, and at the round bare crown at the back of his head. A memory passed through her mind, of when they were young, and his hair had felt like strands of silk through her fingers. Other secret, almost hidden memories of their courtship sometimes came to her late at night when she couldn't sleep, as Stanley lay snoring on his side of the bed. She pushed them aside and tried to doze off by reciting, "The Lord is my Shepherd, I shall not want..." Then she reached up and swatted at a fly that must have come in when they opened the door and continued stacking hymnals.

Her thoughts went to the young preacher who would visit the church again today. He had sat near the piano stool a month ago, so close she could have reached out and touched him. His fingers were long and delicate where he held his Bible, almost caressing it, waiting to be introduced to the congregation. Fine black hair fell over a wide forehead and high cheekbones, suggesting the proud features of a Cherokee brave. She had tried to catch his eyes, to probe their depths, to sense his dedication to the work of the Lord. If he had noticed, he made no sign. She felt an unfamiliar lightness in her head. Her hand fluttered upward to straighten her collar, and on up to pat her hair and adjust her glasses. A little shiver went up her back. Thelma almost felt sixteen again, and pretty.

"He's coming," said Stanley, who had spotted a car from the window.

Thelma heard a crunch of gravel and moved over to stand beside her husband. Her heart was beating a little faster, and she glanced over at Stanley, who was concentrating on the approaching car. She saw a small, black Ford coupe pull into the churchyard. Dents here and there made it look old and well-used. The window on the passenger side had been broken and patched with a strip of brown tape. Scratches in the matte black paint had been touched up with a shiny black, giving the car an uneven glow in the morning sunlight.

As Thelma and Stanley watched from inside the church, the driver's door opened, and Abner Carney stepped out. A new black suit, serious and reverent in color and style, hung loosely on his tall frame, and a worn Bible was tucked securely under his arm. He stepped around the back of the car and opened the door on the passenger side. A young woman climbed out, grasping his hand. The air in the church turned white, and Thelma wasn't sure for a moment if she remembered how to breathe.

"Wonder who she is," Thelma whispered.

She turned and looked at Stanley.

"We didn't bargain for no woman," she said.

Stanley was looking at the woman's reddish brown hair, her lightly freckled skin, and the thin ankles just visible under a long gray coat.

"He didn't mention no wife, did he?" Thelma snapped.

"No, he didn't say nothing about none when we talked to him in April," Stanley replied. "Course that was a month ago. I guess he coulda got married since then."

"Looks like he'da mentioned something that important," Thelma mused. "Less he got married in a awful hurry."

The young woman looked up at the preacher and slid her hand through the crook of his arm. Together they walked toward the church.

Stanley moved to the door, a broad smile fixed on his face as he swung it open. He extended his hand to the young man and nodded to the woman.

"Good to see you again, Reverend," his voice boomed in the quiet church. "We met last month. I'm Deacon Stanley Kirby. We're awful pleased you're here today to deliver us a message from the Lord."

Stanley led the way to the front of the church.

"You remember Sister Kirby, from when you was here last

month."

He pointed toward Thelma.

"She leads the music."

"Why yes, I do remember Sister Kirby," Abner smiled and nodded in Thelma's direction, then took the elbow of the young woman and pulled her forward. "And I want you all to meet my fiancée, Eva Simpson."

The girl stepped up beside Reverend Carney and smiled.

"I'm pleased to meet you," she said, in a voice that could not have been heard more than a foot away. A fragrance surrounded her, like a cross between Johnson's baby powder and Evening in Paris perfume.

"Me and Eva's planning to be married next week," the preacher said. "We're both anxious to start our lives together in the work of the Lord."

Thelma felt like all the light in the church had vanished. Her chest hurt, and all at once a sharp twinge of arthritis jolted her left knee. Eva was pretty and young, probably flighty too. Much too flighty to ever fit in at Friendship. Then Thelma got a better look. Something about the girl reminded her of a deer she had once seen caught in the headlights of a car. She took in the frightened eyes, the lips that seemed to tremble with some nameless apprehension. Wonder what she's got to be so scared of, Thelma mused, and she felt a little better.

One by one the church members started to arrive, and Stanley introduced them to Reverend Carney as they entered the church. Most of the men carried newly dusted black felt hats, and the women were vaguely formal in flowered print dresses that they seldom wore except on Sundays. Calloused brown hands reached out to grasp the preacher's, and then were pulled quickly away.

Eva had taken a seat on the first row, just in front of the pulpit. She sat very still, her hands folded in her lap, an unwavering smile on her face. The members looked at her curiously and took their places in their usual pews. Some carried babies, whom they shushed and rocked to still their fussing, and they made a special effort to curb the whispers and giggles of restless teenagers.

Stanley moved to the front of the church, followed closely by the Reverend Carney, and led the congregation in a lengthy prayer. He then turned to the preacher, who had seated himself in the high-backed wooden chair at the right of the pulpit.

"Brothers and sisters," Stanley began. "Today the Lord has sent us Brother Abner Carney from the Baptist Seminary. He's been studying to be a preacher for the last three years, and today he's come with his future wife Eva to pay us a visit." Stanley lifted his open right hand toward Eva, who had not changed her position or her smile. "Brother Carney is gonna bring us a message from the Lord today, and after the service there'll be a brief meeting of the deacons there at the back of the church." Stanley pointed to the carefully arranged chairs.

"First, Sister Kirby'll lead us in all four stanzas of 'Blessed Assurance, Jesus is Mine.'"

The singing was loud and enthusiastic, but two voices could be heard above the rest, as Sister Corley and Sister Huffman tried to drown out everybody else. They peaked on the chorus and the song ended with Thelma's closing notes on the aging piano. Them two would have to make a spectacle of theirselves today of all days, Thelma thought. Out of the corner of her eye, she could see Irene looking at her outfit. Too bad she's too fat to wear anything stylish like this, she said to herself, and gave a little pat to her hair. She smiled inwardly, making herself comfortable on the narrow bench. Thelma never moved, once the service started, preferring instead to listen to the message from where she could see the whole congregation, and be ready to launch into the "Invitational" at the end.

When the last echoes of the music had faded, Abner Carney walked to the pulpit. He placed the Bible in front of him and looked out at the congregation. Thelma felt a little catch in her throat, and she gripped the sharp edge of the bench. The preacher's handsome face had the same intensity that had been there a month ago. There was the same fire in his eyes, the same passionate way he grasped the Bible. Thelma saw his long look at the picture of Jesus mounted on the wall above his head. And she saw the way he looked at Eva.

The preacher's first words were quiet and tentative, as though the task before him were too difficult, too awesome a responsibility for him to undertake.

"Brothers and sisters in the blood of the Lamb…" he paused, and the congregation seemed to hold its breath, watching him curiously, seeming to wonder if he would continue. He stood unmoving and quiet for a moment or two more, then raised his Bible in both hands above his head and repeated his opening words. There was the difference of daylight and dark in the timber of his voice. The raised Bible became a shield against the wiles of Satan, a sword of vengeance in the army of the Lord. His face seemed to be subtly transformed—to both absorb and reflect the rays of the sun coming through the clear shadeless windows. Almost as one person the congregation sighed and settled into their pews, like outnumbered soldiers sighting unexpected reinforcements.

The minister's voice rose and fell in cadences that ceased to carry everyday meanings, but moved instead directly into the wordless centers of the heart.

"Do you feel His hands upon you, brethren?" he sang. "Is His warm breath filling you with the blessed Spirit?"

His eyes looked heavenward, and his hands extended toward the congregation, seeming to invite them to a place that only he could see. "Do you feel it, brothers and sisters, do you feel His holy touch?" He began to march back and forth, first behind and then in front of the pulpit, his feet moving in rhythm with his voice. Thelma and the congregation lost track of time and space, transported by the music of his words. Babies were quiet, and the older children sat motionless, their eyes wide and fixed on the minister.

"Oh, I say to you today, brothers and sisters, let His boundless love wash over you, let it lead you to Glory."

Oh yes, yes, I will, muttered Thelma. Praise God, yes, I do, I feel his touch upon me. She wrapped her thin arms across her chest, shivering and swaying a little on the wooden bench. A murmur flowed through the congregation like the sighing of wind through new spring leaves.

"Praise the Lord," Sister Corley sobbed, and "aaamen and amen" rose like a hallelujah chorus over the church.

Silence filled the sanctuary when the minister hushed, gathered up his Bible, and returned to his seat behind the pulpit. Stanley came to the front of the church and stood quiet and pale, as though empty of words.

Finally, he whispered, "The Lord has sure blessed us with that fine message, Brother Carney." He raised his arms to the congregation in a beckoning, silent altar call, motioned toward Thelma at the piano and walked slowly back toward his seat.

Thelma's fingers felt like they were moving by themselves over the keys, as she pounded out an inspiring rendition of "Almost Persuaded." Members from all over the church rose and came forward to rededicate their lives. Even God knew this was just about Thelma's favorite part of the service, when sinners got convicted of their sins and came forth to profess it. She smiled and cast her eyes on the likeness of Jesus as each one came forward. Today, however, impatience made her hands tremble. She longed to get up and walk around, to hear what was being said about Brother Carney and the woman he'd brought with him. Why don't you just sit down and be quiet, she wanted to yell, as one after another came up to give testimony and ask forgiveness for a variety of sins.

When the service finally ended those who had come forward thanked Brother Carney for helping them get back on track with God. Thelma looked at Eva who sat quietly watching the minister, not moving from her seat on the front row.

Mealy-mouthed little thing, Thelma said to herself. Why she wouldn't be no kind of a wife for him. He needs somebody to stand up beside him and help him fight off the Devil ever day of his life. Not no weak-kneed little slip of a girl. Thelma closed the cover of the piano and returned her attention to the preacher.

Abner, standing smiling in the aisle, gave Thelma a quizzical look as if he thought she had spoken to him, then he quickly looked away and extended his hand to each of the repentant church members. His eyes followed the movement of the four deacons making their way to the back of the church. Thelma felt herself flush. For no good reason she could think of, she remembered the time she and Willard Strunk had stayed behind after school, and he talked her into a kiss in the dark cloakroom.

The women shuffled from their pews to the basement to get the food they had stashed for today's dinner on the grounds. Warm smells of pork jowl seasoning wafted up from bowls of green beans and mingled with those of yeast and vinegar as each lady carried her dish outside and uncovered it. When the long wooden table under a whitewashed shelter at the side of the church was ready, they would call the men and children to come and fill their plates. Each lady would watch to see who would try her dish, and who would pass it up. Each would remember, and unspoken scores would be tallied by how much food remained in each bowl at the end of the meal. Thelma carried out her own famous potato salad, and the women moved aside to leave a place of honor for her bowl.

Eva made her way to the head of the food line, where the ladies insisted she take her place. She hesitated at first, as if embarrassed or afraid to dip into the bowls. Finally, after coaxing, Eva began to fill her plate. Thelma saw the scoops of green beans and cole slaw, potato salad and corn, the two pieces of fried chicken she took from the platter Loretta had brought, and the helping of bread and butter pickles Irene Corley always insisted on bringing, even though they were hardly ever touched.

Thelma smiled to herself. Well, Irene, she thought, you finally found somebody brave enough to try your pickles. Eva sat down in one of the folding wooden chairs and placed her napkin neatly on her lap. Finally, she began to eat, daintily, but with obvious enjoyment. She sure eats enough, Thelma thought, to be as little as she is. Go ahead, honey, eat, Thelma muttered silently. Get yourself fat as a hog. She watched as Eva took one small bite of the pickles, then another, seeming to enjoy them more than any of the other food on her plate.

A light of understanding dawned on Thelma's face. She

elbowed her way around the group of women and children, trying to get a closer look at Eva's eyes. A thought so incredible had come to her that her cheeks reddened, and her glasses slid down a notch on her nose. Thelma didn't know whether to laugh or cry. She heard a small hallelujah and wasn't sure whether it was in her head, on her lips, or maybe even somewhere else. Maybe the voice of God Himself. Eva had still not removed the coat, but Thelma's attention dropped to her middle, just below the one luminous mother-of pearl button. Thelma's eyes widened and her heart beat faster as the thought took shape. Why, it's just now starting to grow and grow until its shame can't be covered up no longer. That's it, she thought. That's the reason she's so scared.

The deacons had stopped their visiting and small talk with other members of the church and were hurrying to their chairs, anxious to finish their meeting before all the food was gone. Thelma knew she had to catch Stanley before he started the meeting. She saw him finally, standing in a group of men near the front of the church.

Stanley jumped at the unexpected feel of a hand grasping at the back of his shirt.

"Come over here," Thelma said, pushing Stanley toward an empty spot at the end of a pew.

Confusion and irritation turned Stanley's heavy round face a deep red.

"What on earth's wrong with you?" he hissed. "Don't you know the deacons is waiting on me to lead this meeting?"

A few of the church members standing nearby stared in their direction.

"What'd you stop me for, anyway?"

"I had to catch you 'fore you got started."

Thelma was still clutching at his shirt, and Stanley made a futile effort to pull away.

She leaned closer to him and whispered in his ear.

"You all can't vote to bring her in here. That woman's in the fam'ly way, and I bet she's already more'n a month along."

His mouth dropped open and Stanley stared at Thelma as if

she'd lost her mind. Finally, he was able to gasp out a question.

"Whadaya mean she's...?" he choked. "Why she's thin as a rail, and she never even taken her coat off."

"No wonder," Thelma smiled, and her eyes narrowed. "I knowed there was something funny about her when I first seen her," she said. "They's a kinda yella color about a body's eyes when they're that way."

She glanced around the church to be sure nobody was close enough to hear, and she looked intently into Stanley's face. Then she put her hand to his ear again and whispered, "Sides that, you ought to seen her eating Irene's bread and butter pickles."

Stanley looked uncertain and fearful. He glanced back at the deacons who were fidgeting in their chairs. He had already sensed their unqualified approval of Reverend Carney and his betrothed. The deacons would quickly vote to call him to be pastor of the church so they could go eat their dinner.

"Maybe I better go tell the preacher we'll let him know later," he said.

"Stanley," Thelma said, clutching at the lapel of his coat. Her chest ached, and her words spilled out in low quick gasps. She had to make Stanley understand, so he wouldn't let this tragedy happen.

"We've got to have him," she cried, "get the deacons to invite Brother Carney, but tell'em she can't come."

Stanley's face was red, almost purple. He pulled loose from her and stomped away.

The sound of her voice had carried to the deacons, and she saw Ben Taylor and Dr. George eyeing her curiously. Thelma stared back at them. If only you knowed how close we come to making a big mistake, she thought, you'd be thanking me right now. Light-headed, she grabbed one of the Jesus fans and waved it in front of her face. She felt one of the hot flashes coming on and snatched a handkerchief out of her pocket. As daintily as she could, she mopped up the perspiration pouring off her forehead. God, why did you send this on me now, she wondered. With as much dignity as she could summon, she lifted her chin and pushed her glasses higher on her nose. Without looking at the deacons again, she turned and marched toward the open front door.

Thelma watched her husband make his way to the young couple sitting beside the table outside. The preacher was just about to finish his plate which he had piled high with food, taking something from every dish on the table. The women watched with satisfaction as he seemed to relish each bite. He smiled at them, and although Thelma could not hear the words, she could tell that he had bragged on their cooking.

Thelma gazed at the preacher. His face glowed with pleasure as he talked to Stanley and shook hands with the people standing near him. He smiled at Eva and reached down to take her elbow and lead her away from the table. In spite of the sun's warmth, Thelma shivered as Abner's hand caressed Eva's arm and back.

He must not know, she thought. Why I bet it ain't even his. Her mouth dropped open at the horrible implications of this thought. She was unable to move for an instant, then a slight shudder moved through her body. She stepped quickly back inside as the couple headed toward the front door of the church.

"Well, Sister Kirby," Abner Carney said as he entered, "that was a most inspiring musical message you brought us today."

He reached out and caught her hand in a quick firm handshake.

"Eva'n I'll be getting on back."

His eyes went to the pulpit where its rich brown wood glowed in the noonday sun.

"Brother Kirby says he'll let us know of the church's decision later this week."

He nodded and smiled at the four waiting deacons who sat whispering among themselves, looking restless and uncomfortable in their stiff Sunday clothes.

Eva took a small step forward and held out her hand. Her fingers had a soft moist feel like the hot underbelly of a puppy. "Thank you for the wonderful welcome you gave us, Sister Kirby," she whispered.

Thelma snatched her hand back as if she'd been burned.

"You'll be in my prayers till we meet again," Eva said.

The couple took a last look around the sanctuary and stepped out onto the gray, stone steps. Thelma watched them walk back toward their car. Church members gathered around them, trying to get close enough to shake the preacher's hand and congratulate him one last time on his sermon. When they reached the car, she saw Abner bend down to whisper something into Eva's ear, and heard her laugh as he opened the door and took her hand to help her inside.

"Little hussy bitch," Thelma hissed and started back up the aisle toward her piano. She hadn't meant to say it out loud and didn't know she had until she heard a gasp from the back of the church. Ben Taylor and Dr. George stared at her, their faces red with shocked embarrassment.

"What did you say, Sister Kirby?" Spencer Grimes gasped.

Thelma's heart gave a lurch and her hand flew to her chest. She stared back at the deacons.

"Why I didn't say nothing," she said. Tears of panic and rage made tiny rivulets down her powdered cheeks. She swiped at them and rubbed her hand on her collar, leaving a long brown smear.

All at once the church was gone, the pews, the pulpit, even the picture of Jesus, and she was alone in a tiny room with only herself at one end and four scrawny old men at the other, daring to make her defend herself.

"What are you old busybodies looking at anyway?" she screamed.

Stanley ran up beside her, bewilderment replacing his anger, as he stared first at her and then at the silent deacons. They had not moved, nor had they taken their eyes off Thelma's face. She slumped against him, her body going limp.

"I didn't say nothing, Stanley," she sobbed. "Make 'em leave me alone."

Behind Stanley, through the open door, she saw the women running in from the yard. Elly Turner had her arms around her whiny little twins as if they needed protecting, and Loretta, holding what was left of her platter of greasy fried chicken, stood with her mouth open and her eyes bulging. As if from a great distance

Thelma heard screams and sobs that seemed to be coming from somebody else, somebody who was either crazy or dying. Who in the name'a God is making all that racket? she wondered.

Thelma sat motionless beside Stanley on the back row of the church. It was August, and this was her first time back since her sick spell back in the spring. Damp strands of hair escaped from a thin coil at the back of her head. Behind her glasses, her eyes, ringed with dark circles, darted here and there, and she twisted a small, flowered handkerchief through pale, thin fingers. Church members whispered behind funeral-home fans and tried to look at her without being obvious about it.

Lord help me, she prayed silently, and looked at the shadowy ceiling, but she could almost see her prayer hovering up there somewhere right under the rafters. If God's anywhere around here, I sure don't see no sign of him, she said to herself.

"Wonder if she's back at herself," Thelma heard Irene Corley say to Loretta as they sidled up the aisle, casting a quick glance in her direction. "It musta been the change a life that made her go off."

Both women turned their heads as if to look at a floral arrangement on the other side of the church, but Thelma knew they did it to avoid having to make eye contact with her.

"Looks to me like she's fell off some," Loretta answered.

Irene snickered and said something else that Thelma didn't catch, as they passed out of earshot.

Spiteful old hypocrites, Thelma thought, and made a little tapping noise with her fan on the wooden pew. Beside her, Stanley sat rigid and quiet. He kept his eyes on a church bulletin in his lap and looked at no one.

Ben Taylor, the new chairman of the deacons, walked to the front of the church.

"Brothers and Sisters," he said, "please turn in your hymn books to page fifty-one, and let's praise the Lord with all four verses of "Onward Christian Soldiers.""

He opened the hymnal and motioned toward the piano.

Eva Carney, as slender and trim as she had been back in April, smoothed her white cotton dress with tiny pink roses, smiled, and placed her hands on the keys. Her fingers moved effortlessly as the notes pealed through the church and the congregation sang with joyous enthusiasm.

Abner Carney sat watching Eva from the high-backed wooden chair at the right of the pulpit. His eyes caressed her face and body, while he fingered the worn black Bible in his lap. Thelma's hand trembled as she lifted it to her mouth and bit hard on her clenched fingers.

"Hussy." She heard the word thunder through her head like the angry voice of Jesus in the Temple. She hoped no one could hear, but she couldn't stop the word booming through her head. "Hussy, hussy, hussy."

A Path to the Lake

As Sarah Taylor stood at the sink, drying and putting away her breakfast dishes, she watched the morning mist rising over Harrison Lake. Nearly eight o'clock. She and Ben would have already been hurrying to get their fishing poles and gear together before the sun got too high. She resisted the temptation to look out the window, to see him lugging things out of the shed, knocking over her gardening tools, making her lose her temper and yell at him. Instead, she forced herself to look at the trees and the cloudless sky, and face the cold reality that she was alone.

Her house sat back off the road, shaded by the gold and yellow of giant oaks and maples. In the front yard a curving, fieldstone walk was bordered by rose bushes and peonies. A dense hedge of evergreens framed the wide front porch. To the back, and visible from her kitchen window was an open field that bordered the lake, just out of sight behind a line of willows and pines.

She thought she could almost hear the birds and crickets, and the faint splash, as a shiny black bass broke the surface and leaped out of the water. She wished she could be out there in her own private spot by the lake, but she couldn't. Not today. She had too much to do. She stood there a few seconds longer, then turned away from the window.

Sarah picked up the cane she always kept close at hand, and she started the slow walk from her kitchen to the white wooden swing on her front porch. She remembered to pick up one of two small medicine bottles from the window ledge above the sink and drop it into her apron pocket. She never ventured anywhere, even from room to room, without her bottle of "little pills." Dr. George had given her the nitroglycerin, along with a prescription for renewal, after the last bad spell she had with her heart.

"Now Sarah, be sure you carry these with you all the time," Dr. George opened the bottle and shook out a few for her to see. "And if you get any pain, just slip one of these little pills under your

"

tongue." He replaced the pills and patted her hand. "And don't you move around too much, either. You didn't have a heart attack this time, but you did have a warning, and I'll feel a lot better about you when you're with your granddaughter."

He let her leave the hospital only after she promised to stay with Nora and Jim until she was a little stronger. She had resisted making the promise as long as possible. The thought of leaving her home, even for a little while, was scary. She needed the security of the room she and Ben had shared, surrounded by all the years of accumulated memories.

"A place for everything, and everything in its place," she used to tell Ellen and Nora, and she had never wanted anybody to move her things around. Her only consolation was that she could leave Nora's and come home the minute she was back up to par. After all, Nora and Jim were family. It wasn't like she'd be at the mercy of strangers.

Using her cane for balance, she carried a plate of cookies to the front porch and set it down next to a pitcher of icy lemonade. When the sun was warm, she sometimes sat in her swing, knitting or reading, watching for people on the road. Usually children were running an errand, or one or another of her tenants passing, and they were used to her calling out to them, offering them cookies or a cold drink.

These small acts of kindness were tempered with a subtle though unconscious sense of noblesse oblige—she would have called it responsibility—toward her tenants, and she had passed it on to her granddaughter through occasional remarks designed to instill compassion for the less fortunate.

"Grammy says the poor are always with us, and you are the poor," was the way Nora put it when she lorded it over the other children on the farm. But both Sarah and her tenants understood the natural order of things, and they accepted and enjoyed the benefits of her largess.

Today was perfect for porch-sitting. She was nearly finished with the pink and blue blanket for Nora's baby. Probably she could have it done by the time Nora got here this afternoon. As she knitted, she watched the narrow road in front of her house. Eventually she saw a man walking slowly, raising a small dust swirl around his feet. He was probably on his way to the grocery store up the hill where tenants bought their groceries "on account," until they sold their tobacco in December. When he was near the front gate, she recognized him and called out.

"Mr. Adkins. Good morning. Come over here and have a cookie and rest a minute."

John Adkins stopped and looked over at the shaded porch. He had seen her sitting there, probably before she had noticed him, and was waiting for the call. Twenty years as a tenant on her farm had been long enough to get to know most of Sarah Taylor's habits, the good and the bad. She could be Hell-on-wheels if things didn't go just to suit her, but then she'd turn right around and do something kind and you'd forget the rest. Like the time he almost lost Mary after the miscarriage, and she was too sick for weeks to take care of the girls. Sarah was there with food every day until his wife was back on her feet. He'd never forget that.

Waving from the road, he turned in at the gate.

"Thank you, Mrs. Taylor. I'd be much obliged."

He fanned himself with his straw hat as he walked toward the porch.

Sarah held out the plate of cookies.

"Take two, Mr. Adkins, and sit down there on the step and rest before you go on up the hill. Was you started to the store?"

"Yes, ma'am. I just got through shucking the rest of the corn, and since I was this close, I thought I'd go by the store before I went back to the house."

"Beautiful day, Mr. Adkins."

She took a blue glass from the tray beside the plate of cookies and poured him some lemonade.

"I'm finishing Nora's baby blanket today," she said, unrolling a longer strand of the yarn that she was knitting into a pattern of alternating pink and blue squares.

"Since we don't know what it's going to be, I'm playing it safe."

Sarah was quiet for a few minutes while the knitting needles moved rhythmically in her fingers.

"I've been thinking about going to stay a while with Nora and Jim," she said. "They've been begging me to come ever since Ben died, but I couldn't bring myself to leave."

There was an unfamiliar quaver in her voice, and Mr. Adkins listened more closely.

"Now I've got my orders from the doctor, though, so I guess I'll have to go for a few days."

Adkins sat looking at the ground in front of the steps, remembering Nora when she was little, before she grew up and married. He remembered the way she bossed Lilly and Wilma around, telling them her grandfather owned the house they lived in, and she could kick them out any time she wanted, if they didn't do as she said. Really had the girls going for a while.

He hadn't thought about Nora in a very long time. Strange how time changes things.

Sarah held the plate out to him, and he took a second cookie, nodding his thanks. The condensation on the glass of icy lemonade felt cool to his hand as he took a long swallow, and let his mind drift back.

It wasn't hard to understand the way Ben and Sarah had doted on Nora. Everybody knew both of them nearly went crazy after a car wreck killed their only child, Ellen, and her husband. It was just by some miracle the baby had lived. No wonder they spoiled her. Nora was the only grandchild they'd ever have.

He hadn't seen much of Nora the last few years, since she grew up and married. People said she didn't come home very often.

"He says it's dangerous for me to stay by myself with my heart like it is." Sarah's voice brought him back to the present. "I feel all right, though, and I'm coming right back home in a few days."

Her voice dropped, and he had to strain to hear the rest.

"I don't believe I could stand it if I ever thought I had to leave for good," Sarah said.

He thanked her again, replacing the straw hat on his head as he crossed the porch to the wide stone steps. The clack of the knitting needles followed him to the gate and out into the road.

Sarah finished the blanket and remained in the swing, her eye fixed on a particular spot on the road just beyond the tobacco barn where Adkins and the other tenants put up her crop every year. Presently she saw a cloud of dust raised by an automobile, and she watched it until it slowed and pulled into her driveway.

When the small, red convertible stopped, Nora opened the door and got out. She glanced at the car, noticing a fine coating of dust on the hood, and made a mental note to wash it before she took it back home.

"Hello, Grammy," Nora smiled and waved. She brushed wind-blown and wavy blonde hair back from her face.

Sarah smiled and stood, leaning on the arm of the swing for support. Her hand trembled a little as she picked up her cane and moved toward Nora, who was now halfway up the porch steps.

"Should you be out here walking around like this, Gram? I thought the doctor told you not to move around much."

"There's nothing wrong with me that a good hug won't cure. Let me look at you."

She held her arms out to Nora as they met at the top of the steps.

"Why you're getting as round as a partridge." She laughed, and patted Nora's stomach.

Nora put her hand under her grandmother's arm and helped her back to the swing.

"Let's sit down over here a minute, Gram. There's something I want to talk to you about."

Nora had been watching her grandmother while they settled into the old wooden swing. Now her eyes dropped to her lap, and she studied her pale pink nail polish. She began to talk rapidly, as if she wanted to get through an ordeal.

"Now Grammy, I know what we talked about on the phone, but Jim says we just can't have you right now. His business is just beginning to get built up, and we need to be able to go out with clients a lot, and it just wouldn't work out. He says it's going to be hard enough with the baby..."

All of this came out in one breath, and she rushed on before Sarah could answer.

"But we've found something even better, Grammy. There's a really nice rest home over in Andersonville, real close to where we live."

Her grandmother's quiet gasp almost stopped her, but she hurried on.

"I could come and see you every little bit, and I would. Why I'd be there every day or two. And after the baby comes I could bring it to see you, too."

She finally turned to look at her grandmother, relieved that she had been able to tell her how it was going to be. For the first time, Nora noticed how pale she was, her skin almost transparent in the blue October light.

When Sarah spoke, her voice had the old fiery, spirited tone that Nora remembered so well.

"A rest home? But I only need to be somewhere for a little while, Nora, just until I get my strength back. Oh, no. I wouldn't think of going to a rest home."

Sarah attempted a small laugh.

"Why a rest home sounds so permanent," she said. Her hands had started to twist and untwist the ruffle around the bottom of her apron.

"No, I'll have to be back home in time for tobacco-cutting. Why, what would the tenants do if I left? And what about my house, and my flowers? Oh, no Nora, a rest home is completely out of the question."

Nora bit her lip and looked at her grandmother in the same scared way she had as a child when she heard that tone.

But things were different now. Nora was in charge, and what she and Jim had done was for her grandmother's own good.

"But you don't understand. Gram. You'll be there from now on. You won't ever have to worry about anything. They'll take care of you and do everything for you."

Nora was speaking brightly, but her eyes had left her grandmother's, and were fixed on a colorful clump of chrysanthemums out by the fence.

"You can take some of your pictures and things, and you'll have your own room—maybe even a roommate for company. Why it'll be just like being at home, only better."

Nora paused. Again she had to remind herself that whether her grandmother understood or not, some things just had to be done, and that she might as well just go ahead and get it all out in the open right now.

"Now Grammy, there's something else. Remember when you were so sick in the hospital, and you needed someone to sign the papers for your insurance and the hospital arrangements, and you gave Jim your Power of Attorney?"

Nora faltered at this point, and her nerve almost failed her, but she took a deep breath and rushed on. "Well, he knew you might not want to do it, but that it was by far the best thing for you. See, the doctor had already told us you shouldn't stay here alone. So Jim looked around and found a buyer for this old place. He got a really good offer, too." Nora's nervousness made her voice shrill.

"That's why you don't have to worry anymore," she said. "He's already done the paper work for you. and you don't even have to go to the courthouse to sign over the deed."

Sarah was silent, but Nora sensed something different about her. Her face had a stricken look, as though she wanted to speak, but couldn't. And her body seemed to shrink and wither in the wide, old swing.

Looking at her. Nora thought the illness had left her Grammy even weaker than she had imagined. She had to get her away from here as soon as possible.

The blanket had been lying on the arm of the swing, and Sarah's hand touched it as her fingers groped for the familiar wood. She had almost forgotten it, as her mind reeled, trying to grasp the meaning of Nora's words. Feeling it now, she lifted it and handed it to Nora.

"Oh, Grammy! How pretty. And just feel how soft that is."

Nora held the blanket to her face for a few seconds, then laid it aside and turned to look at her grandmother. She only half noticed the little medicine bottle that Sarah was replacing in her apron pocket as she placed a small pill in her mouth. For the first time, Nora felt an unfamiliar twinge of fear. She stood up quickly and touched her grandmother's hair.

She walked over to the front door and stuck her head in the living room. The place looked the same, old-fashioned, and crowded, with the same tired old family pictures and whatnots that had been there all her life. And there was that smell, like a combination of dried flowers and yesterday's baking. Sniffing slightly, she turned back to her grandmother.

"We'll have to see about closing this musty old place up until the buyer is ready to take possession. I never did like it out here, Grammy. There was never anything to do, or anybody for me to hang around with." Sarah was rocking slightly back and forth in the swing, and looking out toward the road. When she spoke her voice sounded far away.

"John Adkins was by a little while ago. Sat for a minute and had a cookie. Do you remember his little girls, Lilly, and Wilma? You used to play with them."

"Don't be silly, Gram. Those little rag-tag girls? Didn't they live down the road in one of Granddaddy's tenant houses?"

Nora frowned, trying to picture the two girls.

"I never actually played with them. I guess I teased them a little, though. I probably ought to be ashamed, but kids will be kids."

Nora was quiet, remembering some of the things she'd done and said to the Adkins girls, but she didn't share these thoughts with her grandmother. Instead, she turned and looked at her closely.

"You're not still feeding every straggler that comes by here, are you? That's another reason you shouldn't stay here any longer. You just don't need to be putting out all that extra energy."

Nora walked back over to the swing and sat down, taking both of Sarah's hands in her own.

"Just wait and see, Gram, she said. "You'll be so much better off when there's somebody to look after you all the time."

She wondered if Sarah even heard her, gazing as she was out toward the ridge of trees that bordered the lake.

She glanced down at a small square, gold, watch, its black leather band circling her wrist.

"Now, Grammy, I'm going to have to get back home," she said. "Jim's expecting me back in time for us to go out to dinner with some people tonight."

She waited a long time for an answer. When it finally came, Sarah's voice had regained some of its old asperity, and she was smiling.

"I know you have to get back, sweetheart. I'm just always so glad to see you. And I'm so glad you like the blanket."

"Oh, it's gorgeous, Gram. This baby's going to be just so proud of what its great-grammy made it."

Nora stood up and carefully folded the blanket. She pushed back a wispy strand of gray hair from Sarah's forehead and kissed her there.

"Now don't you be exerting yourself to do anything until we get those arrangements made. I'll be back to see you in a day or two, and by then, I'll have everything worked out."

Nora was off the porch and backing toward the car as she spoke.

"When I come back, I'll help you decide what you want to take with you, and I'll pack it for you, so don't you try to do any of that stuff yourself."

Something about her grandmother's look made her hesitate, and she almost ran back toward the steps. Instead, she opened the car door, got inside, and blew Sarah a kiss.

"I love you, Grammy," she yelled out the window. She waved and backed the car out of the driveway, swirling dust in the narrow road.

Sarah watched as Nora drove out of sight. Then she grasped her cane, walked toward the front door, and into her living room.

Inside, she looked around, stopping at a table near the door. She picked up a picture in a small silver frame—a young family, herself and Ben and Ellen, taken when they went to the State Fair that time when Ellen was five. She looked at it for a moment, then put it back and picked up another one—Ellen and Cecil on their wedding day. And another picture of them a year later, holding their baby girl, Nora. Sarah traced her fingers over the faces, wiping away imaginary dust.

"Close up this musty old place and go to a rest home. Sell our house. Have you ever heard of anything so ridiculous, Ben?" Sarah was holding a picture of the two of them, taken by a photographer in Lancaster on their fiftieth wedding anniversary.

"What do you reckon has come over that girl? Maybe it's the baby. You always did say I was crazy when I was that way."

Sarah laughed as she replaced the picture and moved around the room, straightening a doily here, a vase there, as though reacquainting herself with old friends.

Then she walked to the kitchen, taking care not to slip on the shiny linoleum. Standing at her kitchen window, she watched birds flying in and out among the tree branches. She and Ben had dug the saplings out in the woods and planted those trees, keeping them watered and nurtured until their roots took hold. Now they towered over the yard, forming a canopy of color. Her eye wandered past the yard to the path, and she pictured the lake beyond.

She didn't go there as often anymore, but she still loved it. She thought of the walk through the trees, along the rocky shoreline where she and Ben had taken first Ellen, then Nora for picnics. She remembered sitting by the water, watching the wind ripple the blue-green surface, and she could almost feel the warm afternoon sun. A walk to the lake. She stood there thinking for a long minute.

She reached into her apron pocket and took out the bottle of little white pills and set them on the window ledge. Then she picked up the other bottle and put it in her pocket.

Walking out under the trees along the path, she felt a lightness in her step, and a surge of energy. She eased her grip on her cane, no longer afraid of falling. Here and there she bent to pick up the fallen leaves, until she held a bouquet of glowing sunshine.

She arrived at her spot under a dark old pine tree, on a wide flat rock that overlooked the lake. She sat still for a long time, eyes closed, absorbing the silence. She felt the brush of the wind on her shoulders, and the rocks and leaves under her fingertips. The fragrance of pine and grass was mixed with the smoke of a distant campfire, and she opened her eyes and looked around. Two cardinals were perched on a lower limb of a maple tree over to her left. The bright scarlet male lifted his wings and flew, leaving his less colorful mate to follow soon after. Sarah gasped at their beauty. She focused on this detail and that, wanting to miss nothing.

Satisfied, she put her hand in her apron pocket and took out the bottle. She looked at the instructions and remembered the doctor's words.

"Now remember, Sarah. Only one of these if you absolutely cannot go to sleep. And don't use them at all if you don't have to."

"Well," she said softly, "it looks like I finally have to."

She opened the bottle and emptied the five capsules into her hand. She held them cupped there, noticing how deeply red they appeared against her palm. Then she swallowed them one by one and lay back against the rock.

John Adkins had finished the last of the feeding and milking for the day. The sun was sinking in a red and gold, pink and purple mishmash of color behind the horizon. He got his fishing pole from the barn where he kept it handy for days like this and set out along his own path to the lake. The sun was gone now, but the twilight cast a luminous glow over the landscape.

At first, he thought Sarah Taylor was sitting on the bank looking at the water. But as he came closer, he saw that she was lying down, sleeping maybe, after walking out to this spot where he'd seen her many times before.

It was only when he bent over her and touched her hand that he knew. Her skin was as cold as a slab of bacon from the smokehouse on a winter morning. His hand flew to his mouth, and he stifled an impulse to scream. Terrified in the presence of death, he stood motionless, uncertain of what to do. His eyes darted this way and that, as though expecting help from some unexpected source.

Gradually forcing himself to control his fear, he looked at her again.

It was then that he noticed it. On the ground beside her lay a small empty medicine bottle. He picked it up and read the doctor's instructions. "Take one capsule at night as needed for sleep."

He dropped the green glass bottle to the ground where he had found it, then turned and ran.

The little country Baptist chapel was crowded the day of Sarah's funeral. People from neighboring farms, and a few of her tenants filed by and hugged Nora and Jim. Some whispered to Nora about her grandmother's kindness. Some she had loaned money to take a sick child to the doctor. Some she had given food from her own garden when theirs had failed. Dozens of little things that defined Sarah Taylor's memory.

"Yes, she was kind," Nora sobbed, "Thank you for coming." "Thank God I'd just been to see her that morning. She gave me a blanket she'd just finished knitting for the baby." Nora broke down and couldn't continue.

"What do they think it was, Nora?" Eva Jenkins whispered to her, expressing her deepest sympathy.

"Oh, Eva, you know how bad her heart was. Well, she just went out there for a walk and forgot her nitroglycerin. How many times had I warned her to always carry it with her? And why she decided to walk out there, all by herself, I'll never know."

John Adkins stood waiting to pay his respects.

"I'm very sorry about your grandmother, Nora."

"Thank you, Mr. Adkins."

He saw fear in her eyes as she looked away. He had not told anyone about the little bottle beside Sarah Taylor's body. He wondered how Nora would deal with it. Now he knew.

Still looking away, she whispered. "And thank you for everything you did for the family."

She sensed his waiting, and she slowly raised her head. She wanted to look away, but his eyes held her.

"Your grandmother must've had good reason for going the way she did, Nora. And she wouldn't have wanted you to be embarrassed by it. She loved you."

A shiver ran through her as he turned and walked away, down the long aisle, and out into the bright October day. Somewhere deep inside she felt the baby move.

A Good Boy, Bradley

It was the first day of July and hotter than blazes. Nellie Grimes sat on her front porch, rocking, and peeling apples to dry for the winter. Her knotted little bird-claw hands worked with mechanical precision, almost independently of her mind and body. As she worked, her eyes darted around the yard, taking in the sagging front gate, the broken bottom porch step, and the weather-beaten mailbox leaning drunkenly to one side. She could count at least six things that needed fixing in the front yard alone, never mind the back yard and the barn.

She was trying to figure how would be the best way to get her nephew Bradley to come up and do some work for her. He was just fifteen, but big and strapping like his daddy. Not too smart, as far as she could tell. Had a faraway, meandering look about his eyes that sometimes made her wonder if there was anybody home.

She was alone and had been for so long she hardly ever noticed it. Mr. Ben had let her stay on in the tenant house after Spencer died ten years ago. Then when his granddaughter Nora inherited the farm, she never asked Nellie to move either, and all they had ever expected was for her to keep things up in reasonably good repair.

That never had been a problem until just the last couple of years. Hard work was as natural to her as walking or breathing, but the pains in her hip joint were getting to the point where it was hard to get up when she was down, much less fix a broken gate or plant a mailbox post.

So, she sat there and plotted and schemed about how to get Bradley to come and do the chores without having to pay him an arm and a leg. It was ridiculous. The boy wanted five dollars for every day's work he did around the place—and him her blood kin. She got mad every time she thought about it. He liked to hang around her place, even when he wasn't working for her. She had a suspicion that he smoked in her barn and might burn it down some day. She'd confronted him about it more than once, but he always denied it.

Nellie had a good view of the road and fields around the farm, situated as she was on a little rise, and her porch another ten feet off the ground. A dark green line of trees over to the right stood like sentinels between her house and the rocky banks of Harrison Lake. The county road ran by the front of her house, and most weekends during the summer, a stream of cars pulling boats or trailers would head for the cool shelter of camping and fishing sites on the lake. Sometimes one would pass without the camping gear, and she knew that it was probably going on into Lancaster.

She had almost finished peeling the last of the apples when she saw dust a long way down the road that told her a car or truck was coming. She watched idly as the dust cloud came closer to her gate, and when it moved past, she saw that it had been raised by a big black car she'd never seen before.

Nellie squinted to try to get a better view. She set the pan of apples aside and eased up to walk over to the porch railing. "Ohhh," she breathed, and rubbed her hip. She held on to the back of the rocker and stretched out her other arm to catch the railing. Above all things she dreaded the thought of falling, alone as she was out here.

She was tiny, with shoulders that had continued to bend steadily over the years, until now she looked a little like one of those wooden bows that hunters sometimes carried past her house in deer season. She had to peer upward to see over the railing, but there was nothing wrong with her eyes. She could still see as well as she could when she was twenty, and without glasses, too.

The car had passed her gate and gone on down the road, obviously in a hurry to get somewhere. Nellie was about to turn around to get her apples and take them into the kitchen when she saw the car stop in the road. Two men got out.

She wondered what on earth they could be stopping out here for. They sure weren't fishermen—wearing black suits, it looked like—and there wasn't much to see around here, especially nothing that warranted stopping a car.

She was puzzling it over when a curious thing happened. The two men looked up toward her house, then turned to talk to each other. From where she stood, they appeared to be arguing, and although she could not hear words from that distance, she had the impression that the discussion was heated.

Nellie didn't get many visitors, and the few that did come never stayed long. Mostly it was just the occasional Jehovah's Witness, or some gushy do-gooder church lady. Sometimes, even an unsuspecting encyclopedia salesman ventured up to her door.

She could always tell which was which, and already had her heave-ho strategy planned before they got to the door. Over the years she'd acquired a widespread reputation as a cranky old witch. She knew this and was not the least bit bothered by it. In fact, she had cultivated the image, and took some pride in it.

While she stood peering up over the railing, with only her eyes and the wispy gray topknot on her head showing, she saw the two men come around the side of their car and look again in her direction. Their discussion had taken on the appearance of a full-scale argument, and, for the first time, she felt a little uneasy. These two didn't look like either preachers or traveling salesmen. They looked like strangers that had no business bothering anybody out here, her in particular. Besides, she had no ready plan for dealing with people that looked like them.

She still wasn't able to make out what they were saying, but suddenly, as though they had come to a decision, they got back into the car and backed it up to the gate that separated her field from the road. One of them got out to open the gate, and now she knew for sure they were coming to her house.

She stood by the railing for a few seconds longer, then turned and scuttled back to the screen door. Her green dotted cotton dress was covered by a red and white apron that had faded to a soft pink after countless washings, and its long ties hung down her back almost to the tops of her shoes. She smoothed the wrinkles in her apron, pushed a wisp of hair out of her eyes, and went inside.

She hooked the latch and stood waiting. She'd get rid of these two in a hurry. One thing was certain. They didn't have anything she wanted, even if they were giving it away, and she sure didn't have anything for them.

The car came to a stop in front of her house, and up close she could see its battered look, as though it had seen plenty of hard use. A window on the passenger side was broken, and a crisscross pattern of duct tape held the pieces in place. The left front fender had a deep rusty dent, and a piece of pitted chrome from the bumper dangled near the ground.

Both front doors opened, and the men got out.

At this range there were some obvious differences in the two. One appeared older, his hair just beginning to turn gray around the sides, while the other still had the long gangly look of a kid. Something about him told Nellie that he was probably older than he looked, and from this distance, he seemed to be doing most of the talking. He lifted a wide-brimmed black hat, rubbed the arm of his white shirt across his forehead and jammed the felt hat back down so far that his ears seemed to stand out at right angles to his head. He spoke to his companion, who had both hands pushed deep into his pockets like he might be hiding something inside.

"We got to get this damn car hid, or we'll be sitting ducks."

He pointed in the direction of Nellie's barn, just visible from the corner of the house.

"Soon's we see them pass we got to go the other way, and get as far away from here as possible."

The panic in his voice carried across the yard.

"Jesus! Why'd you have to shoot that guard anyway? We already had the money."

Then the other man spoke, and Nellie felt a chill go up her spine. "You're stupid, you know that, Stoner? That guy could identify both of us down to a T. How long you think it'd take them to figure out who we are? Now quit sniveling and get this car out of sight, so when they stop looking for us out here, we can slip out and get on back up to Cincinnati."

Nellie choked on a knot in her throat. These two had killed somebody, and they actually meant to hide their car in her barn and wait around until they could get away. Panic set in. She tried to think.

It was going take more to persuade them to leave than just the force of her personality, and she searched the kitchen for a possible weapon. The only other time she had ever needed such a thing was last spring when she ran up on a copperhead in her cucumber patch and had beaten it to death with her hoe.

She heard the rake and scrape of footsteps climbing the steps to her porch, and her eyes darted back to the latched screen door. Barely breathing, she shrank back out of sight against the wall, hoping that if they didn't see her, maybe they'd give up and go away.

"Is anybody home?"

A soft knock followed, and Nellie saw that it was the older, quieter man who had spoken. She abandoned the idea of hiding and faced the door. She screwed her face into a scowl and opened her mouth, intending to spit out the sharpest rebuke she could muster.

"Hello, Lady."

The words were soft and pleasant, uttered like a man about to bestow a compliment. Instead, he reached out his hand and pushed open the screen door, breaking the flimsy latch and sending it flying across the room to bounce off the wall at Nellie's feet.

He walked into her kitchen, his companion close on his heels.

"We're sorry to intrude on you this afternoon, lady, but me and my friend here just need a little while to rest and use your barn to put our car in while we're here."

His voice hadn't changed, but now he stood toe to toe with Nellie, and his eyes glittered as he took in the details of the room. When he finally fixed them on her, she was reminded of the copperhead in the garden.

Nellie's mind flew from the broken latch on her kitchen floor to the two strange men standing in front of her. Fear paralyzed her for an instant, and then she realized she couldn't just stand there and do nothing. With a supreme effort she pulled her wits together and opened her mouth, with no idea of what she was about to say.

"I'm sorry I can't let you gentlemen stay."

Her voice was shrill, almost a squeak.

"I was just getting ready to go to the store with my nephew."

She darted her head around the man and pretended to be looking at the road.

"He ort to be here just any minute."

Cunning joined the fear on her wrinkled face.

"He's the sheriff of this county, and he comes out here on his rounds every day and checks on me to be sure I'm all right."

Stoner had been standing in the open doorway, his hat still pushed solidly down on his forehead. Now he jerked it off and waved it in the air.

"Did you hear that. Mason? Let's get out of here right now."

He was already out the door and bolting down the steps when Mason's voice stopped him cold.

"You idiot, Stoner. Get back in here and shut that door."

His eyes had not left Nellie's, and now he took a half step closer to her.

"Now, now, little lady, you wouldn't lie to us, would you?"

Nellie felt her scowl crumble. The voice of the man called Mason had a soothing, almost hypnotizing effect.

"Like I said, we only wanted to impose on your hospitality for a little while, but you don't sound much in the mood to be neighborly, so we're just gonna make you comfortable while we're here. Give you a chance to take your afternoon nap."

She never saw the fist streaking toward her, and remembered nothing until she woke up on her bed in the gathering shadows of late afternoon.

Her mouth was dry, and she felt paralyzed. Gradually she realized that her hands and feet were bound with the twine she used to tie up her tomato plants to their supports in the garden, and her mouth was glued together with some kind of tape. Her hip ached from lying in a rigid prone position, and she could not move herself to relieve it.

The pungent odor of tobacco and the sound of low voices came from the kitchen. She willed herself to hear the conversation.

"That was a good one she tried to pull about the sheriff. What kind of fools did she take us for?"

Stoner was laughing, and he seemed to be speaking through a mouth full of food. Nellie remembered the blackberry cobbler she'd left on the kitchen table.

"I bet nobody hardly ever comes out to this God-forsaken place. If we just leave her tied up, they'll not find her for maybe a week, and we'll be long gone."

"Now you listen to me, Stoner."

Nellie cringed, and a jolt of pain shot through her legs. She gathered all her strength to roll over but could only manage a tiny shift to her right side. She felt moisture and wondered if she'd wet herself. Before she could decide whether it was urine or sweat, she heard Mason speak again.

"We done what we had to do back at that store, and we'll keep right on doing it till we get out of this mess. When it gets good and dark, we'll slip down to the lake and follow the bank to the highway, then stay out of sight in the woods and brush along the road till we get to Ohio. Once we get there, we're home free."

"But what about her?" Stoner asked. "What're we gonna do about the old lady?"

"Shut up and let me think. We can't just leave her and hope nobody finds her. What if she does have somebody that comes by regular?" He was silent for a moment.

"No, damn it, we got to finish her before we leave."

He paused, and his icy voice warmed with pleasure.

"What we'll do is, we'll push her and the car over one of them cliffs down at the lake," he said. "Then we can take our time getting back north, and there'll be no trace of her or the car either."

The full meaning of what Mason had said rolled through Nellie's mind like a freight train. Somehow, she had to find a way to get out of its path. Screams exploded in her head and echoed through every room in her house. But the tiny cat-like moan and the merest shift of her weight on the iron bed was the only real sound in the dark bedroom, and Mason and Stoner did not hear it.

What happened next would not be completely clear to Nellie for a long time.

The crash of breaking glass was followed by a volley of bullets through her kitchen window. Running feet clattered over her polished linoleum floor. Although she couldn't move, she imagined that she drew herself up into a tiny invisible ball.

It was almost dark when she awoke to feel hands at her face, and the sting of tape being ripped from her mouth. She didn't dare open her eyes until she heard the snip of scissors and felt the twine being cut from her wrists and ankles. Only then did she open one eye a tiny crack, and she made out the stolid form of Bradley bending over her.

"Wake up, Aunt Nellie. They're not gonna bother you no more."

She tried to jump up off the bed, but the pain in her hip threw her back, and blackness covered her again.

She was awakened by the feel of hands rubbing her wrists where the twine had made long red welts on her skin. When she opened her eyes, Bradley had turned on the table lamp beside the bed, and the familiar setting quieted the panic in her chest. This time she did not try to get up, but lay still, enjoying the soothing massage, as pin pricks of feeling gradually replaced the numbness in her arms.

When he saw that she was awake, Bradley stopped rubbing her wrists and bent close to her. Nellie noticed that his round face was flushed and sweaty, and that the collar of his red and white plaid work shirt dangled by a thread. A scratch ran down the side of his face from his eyebrow to his chin, and his breathing was raw and uneven.

"I saw that black car in your barn, Aunt Nellie, and I thought you might have company, so I walked on up here, and when I got just under the window, I heard them men talking. Sounded like they'd robbed a place and killed somebody and was trying to decide whether to kill you or not."

"I knew I couldn't do nothing, and I couldn't take time to go get help."

Bradley was getting more excited.

"And then I remembered I'd left my firecrackers in your barn to have for the fourth of July.”

At the mention of the fireworks, his face changed. He turned a darker shade of red, and his eyes darted away from her. He paused, but when she said nothing, he went on.

“So, I went back down there and got a big rock and taped a string of firecrackers around it, and put a match to it, and throwed it through your window. Then I dashed around to the door, and when them fellers run out, I hit them with your hoe.”

Bradley laughed, forgetting to be afraid of Nellie’s anger.

“They’re tied up so tight out there, there ain’t no way they can ever get loose. I’m gonna go get Daddy right now to bring the sheriff.”

As he started to get up, Nellie reached up and put her hand on Bradley’s arm. He looked down at her with those strange faraway eyes, waiting for what she had to say.

And there was so much that needed saying.

He had stored firecrackers in her barn. Sure as the world, he’d burn it down one of these days, and all her stuff in it. She felt the rebuke forming on her tongue, ready to spill out and singe his ears and curl his toes.

She hesitated. There was a long streak of drying blood where something sharp had dug a deep scratch into Bradley’s forearm. He winced when he started to lift it. Outside she heard a rustle of maple leaves against her window, and the sound of bodies struggling helplessly against the weathered boards below her porch.

She raised herself, exerting a little pressure on Bradley’s shoulder. The pain in her hip streaked through her body like a bolt of jagged lightning in a summer sky, but she hardly noticed it. Agony and fear had been replaced by a sense of relief more profound than any she had ever felt before.

The rebuke died on her lips.

What she said was, “You’re a good boy, Bradley. I’m sure glad you come by when you did.”

Hello, Mr. Buffin

Old Charlie got to his usual spot under the draping branches of the big willow by the river at about the same time as the two fellows that were bent on pulling off the robbery. Charlie was a great one for setting trot lines all up and down the river, and sometimes he'd come home carrying a thirty or forty pound catfish on his back. He knew exactly where to set the lines, and when to go back and check on them. There was no doubt he enjoyed the fishing, but he loved even more to come and sit in this spot and think his thoughts.

On this particular day—a sunny Sunday afternoon—he was sitting there resting for his long walk home, when he heard voices a little way up the bank. There was a lot of brush and undergrowth around, and he was leaning up against the willow, with the branches coming down like a shroud around him. So, he couldn't be seen, no matter how close anyone came to him.

He heard the voices, clear as could be, but he wasn't about to let on that he was there. He sat very still so as not to rustle the leaves, and he waited to find out who they were and what they were up to. Not many people came around this spot, and those that did might be into something a person had better stay away from.

Just before he heard the voices, Charlie'd been thinking his usual thoughts. Outside the everyday things—like taking care of his trot lines and keeping up with home chores—he never thought about much else.

What he was thinking about was how he could do away with his brother Patrick. He'd hated Patrick for forty years, ever since Patrick stole Lutie and then let her die. There was no use for it. Lutie had taken the kind of flu that was killing people, and Patrick knew she needed a doctor, but he didn't go get her one—he thought he could cure her himself. So, when she took bad sick, he decided he would just fix her up a poultice and put it on her chest, and the fever would break, and the stuff in her lungs would come up, and she'd be all right. But she just lay there and got worse until it was too late for a doctor or anybody else to do her any good, and she died. They'd only been married two years when it happened, and Patrick had spent the last thirty-eight years grieving over her. Five miles away Charlie'd been grieving over her, too, but he'd also been building up a case of hate against Patrick that he couldn't let go of.

It was a shame, too, because those two brothers—twins, at that— were as close as two peas, growing up. They went everywhere together, hunted squirrels and rabbits in the woods, and fished the river for turtles and catfish. They worked side by side to help farm their daddy's corn and tobacco. And if any disputes arose that required the use of fists, each one could count on the other's support.

But the beginning of the end came when that new family—the Wilsons—moved into the rent house on the Jackson farm, right next to the Buffins—Patrick and Charlie and their ma and pa.

There was a big family of the Wilsons. Lutie was the oldest, with five or six younger brothers and sisters. She was a tall girl with dark hair pulled back from her face, and warm brown eyes that always seemed to smile. Her daddy was a sharecropper who'd contracted to help put out Jim Jackson's tobacco for a part of the profit, and all of the bigger children helped with the planting.

It was early spring when Patrick and Charlie first saw Lutie. The young green tobacco plants were pushing up under the canvas in the beds, ready to be planted, and the Wilsons had gone out to start the back-breaking job. Patrick and Charlie were there to swap work, so that in a few days when their plants were ready to pull, the Wilsons would do the same for them.

Patrick and Charlie both saw Lutie at the same time. She was about fifteen, same as them. Both boys thought she was the prettiest girl they'd ever seen, and both of them fell in love, then and there.

Lutie didn't seem to pay much attention to either one, but she did notice them, even though they didn't know it. She'd watch them from under her wide straw hat. her dark brown eyes following them without anybody knowing.

Kneeling on the ground beside the tobacco bed, she pulled the plants and listened to the others talking and laughing, and she watched Patrick and Charlie trying to outdo each other to get her attention.

That same thing went on all day, and from then on, as long as Lutie came out to help with the planting. Gradually, as they got more used to being around her, and the newness wore off, some of the horseplay and monkeyshines eased up a little, but that didn't mean that either one of the boys was any less interested in Lutie. The truth was that both Patrick and Charlie loved her a little more every day. Both boys wanted to court her, but Lutie showed no special preference.

Late November the year they were seventeen, Charlie decided he was going to make his move. Unbeknownst to Patrick, he spent the better part of two weeks carving a statue of a horse out of an old piece of cherry wood he'd been saving for this very thing. As much as the boys looked alike—identical, most people thought—in some ways they were different. For one thing, Charlie had this wonderful knack for wood-carving—some called it whittling—but anything he carved out of a piece of wood looked like it ought to move or speak. Patrick couldn't do that. He was good at everyday things, like plowing a straight row, or setting up a perfect shock of corn, but when it came to making something special, he didn't have Charlie's touch.

Charlie worked on that horse until it gleamed and glimmered and pranced in the glow of the lamplight. The red cherry color gave the high-stepping horse and its flying mane a warm, rare beauty.

When Charlie got finished with the horse, he hid it away where nobody could find it. He hadn't even told Patrick about the little cubbyhole he'd made behind the wall of the shed to hide special things.

He waited until about a week before Christmas to take the little horse out of its hiding place. He had decided that this was the day he would take it over and give it to Lutie as a special Christmas present, tell her once and for all that he loved her, and ask her to marry him.

He got up early on that Saturday morning, six days before Christmas. He noticed that Patrick was already up. Patrick didn't mind doing some of the early morning chores—he was quicker at most things, like milking and feeding—and usually went on out and got started before Charlie was awake.

Since nobody was around, he decided to go ahead and get the horse out, so he'd have it ready to go right after the chores were done. The house was cold up in the rafters where the boys slept, and Charlie hurried to get into his blue denim pants, his good white shirt, and the heavy, green wool sweater his ma had knitted for him last Christmas. Might as well be dressed and ready to go. When he was ready, he climbed down the narrow stairs to the kitchen and splashed water on his face from a bucket that sat on the table by the stove. He couldn't wait to go out to the shed and get the horse. He'd just stop and have a look at it before he went on to the barn to help Patrick with the chores.

He was still a little ways back from his hiding place, when he knew something was wrong. He couldn't have said exactly what it was, but it was like he knew somebody had been there ahead of him. And they shouldn't have been, because this was a part of the shed where nobody ever came—a place where you had to get down and crawl around an old broken plow and a roll of chicken wire, and then squeeze through to the place where the board had been pried loose and put back. But in some way—maybe because things appeared to have been moved around a little—he knew somebody had been there ahead of him. He still wasn't worried— probably just somebody looking for a piece of wire to mend a hole in the fence—so he crawled on around and eased up to the board.

As soon as he saw it, he knew. Somebody had pulled the board loose and left it standing open just wide enough for Charlie to see through the crack in the hiding place. Still not understanding all of what it meant, he jerked the board loose from the wall and stuck his hand in to pull out the horse. At first, he thought it must have fallen down a little deeper into a crack behind the wall, until he felt all around, pushing his whole arm in as far as it would go. The side of his face was mashed against the rough board as his arm flailed around, searching for the horse. He felt his heart jump and his breath tighten in his throat. Panic washed over him like a cold bucket of water.

Patrick. He must have seen him whittle out the horse and then watched where he hid it. Might've already known about his hiding place. They had never kept secrets from each other before, so he'd probably not taken enough pains to conceal it.

He knew what Patrick intended to do with the horse. They both knew about how Lutie loved the horses, how she would stand beside the fence and watch them grazing in the pasture, and how she could ride at a gallop over the fields with nothing but a bridle to hold on to. She would love this beautiful little horse, and the one who gave it to her.

Charlie knew what he had to do. If he could just beat Patrick there, it still wouldn't be too late. Even if he didn't have the horse, he could tell her about it and make her understand that every little curve and glimmer of it was a sign of how much he loved her.

Without stopping for anything else, he ran out of the shed and down the path to the road that would take him to Lutie's house. He ran with the speed and energy of someone possessed. Love, fear, panic, and anger, all churned inside him, as his feet flew over the gravels on the narrow little road.

He knocked, and she opened the door. When he saw her face his heart lurched. She had never looked like this before. Her face was flushed, she was smiling, and her eyes were shining with tears ready to overflow. She didn't wait for him to speak.

"Oh, Charlie, has Patrick told you yet? Of course, he has. You probably knew before I did, knowing how you two are. Oh, Charlie, I'm so happy. I didn't think he was ever going to ask me, and when he came in so early this morning, carrying that little horse and asking me to marry him, I couldn't hardly answer him. You two've been so special to me ever since we was kids, and I've always knowed that someday me and Patrick'd get married. He did too, but some way he just couldn't get up the nerve to ask. I don't know what finally done it, but I'm just thankful for it. I love him so much, Charlie."

He could see it now. He never had wanted to admit it, but thinking back, there was always something a little different and special about the way Lutie was with Patrick. When Charlie would tell his stories about strange, faraway places he'd read about in books, Lutie'd be interested, and she'd laugh at the funny stories he made up to tell her. But she'd get still and thoughtful when Patrick would tell about the farm he was going to have someday, and about how he would grow his own tobacco and take care of his animals.

In the end he didn't tell her about the horse. He could see that it wouldn't make any difference, and there was no use to cause any more trouble than there already was. He also knew that he would never forgive Patrick.

So, Lutie and Patrick got married that spring. Patrick had spent January, February, March, and April putting them up a little house, and by May tenth, their wedding day, he had everything ready.

Everybody was happy—their folks, people that knew them in the community—this was the way things were supposed to be. Everybody, that is, but Charlie. From the minute he felt around in that hole in the shed and understood what had happened—from that minute on he hated Patrick, and passed very few days not thinking about what Patrick had done to him, and how he could get even with him.

It was bad enough the first two years after the marriage. Charlie thought about Patrick and Lutie together in that little house over on the other side of the ridge, and how it ought to be him and Lutie, and he stewed and simmered till it became a pastime for him to think up ways to get back at Patrick.

When Lutie died, Charlie's hatred got so bad that sometimes he thought about killing Patrick. To steal Lutie from him like he did, and then let her die—it was just too much to stand.

Right after the funeral was over, and all the mourners had left, Patrick came over to see Charlie. It was the first time, and the last, that he ever tried to explain.

"Charlie, you've got to understand. I loved her so much, and when I saw you making that little horse I knowed that would be what would make the difference. I could never make nothing like that, but if I could just take it with me, and tell her how I felt....

"Well, I couldn't help myself, Charlie. I've never got over feeling guilty about taking it, but I had to. I never could have told her without having that little horse in my hand.

"And Charlie, she did love me, just as much as I loved her. And when she got sick, I tried to get her to let me go after the doctor, but she wouldn't. You know how she always gathered up them herbs and roots for healing. And she told me just how to fix 'em up to put on her chest. I done it just like she said, but she just kept on choking and getting weaker to where I couldn't leave her to go nowhere."

Patrick was sobbing now, so hard it was hard for Charlie to hear his words.

"And when she died, I died some too. I don't see how I'm gonna go on. But Charlie, you've got to forgive me, and let us be brothers like we was before."

But, of course, Charlie never did. He'd spent all these years at the home place. Never got married. Took care of their parents when they got too old to do for themselves, and then stayed on and kept the place going as well as he could. Raised most of what he ate and got plenty of good catfish from his trot lines in the river. Once in a while over the years, he'd see Patrick at the feed store, or somewhere else that people were likely to run into each other, and every time, he'd sensed that Patrick wanted to reach out to him or say something to close the gap between them, but Charlie never gave him that chance.

So, when he heard those men talking on the other side of the willow tree, he first thought he'd dosed off and was dreaming. Because what they were saying was the kind of thing he had thought about or seen in his dreams at night for the last forty years.

"You mean old Patrick Buffin, over on Beaver Fork?"

"Yep."

"Are you sure he's got money hid away over there?"

"Hell yes, I'm sure. I told you how he asked me to fix up that log fence that part of it fell down out behind his house? Well, I fixed it, and when I went up to his door to tell him I was done, I seen him go to an old trunk back in his front room and get a box out of it. And I seen him take out some bills to pay me and then put the lid on it and put it back in that trunk and close it up. He didn't know I seen him 'cause he turned his back to me and I was out on the porch, but he was standing facing a dresser with a mirror in it, and I could see what he was doing just as plain as I'm seeing you right now. Oh, he's got it in there, all right. They's no telling how much he's got, neither. He sure don't spend much, as I can see, and he raises them calves and sells them, and he still puts out a tobacco crop. I bet he's still got nearly every cent he ever made, right there in that trunk."

"And you ain't told a soul about seeing it?"

"Nobody but you, Hank. I knowed you'd be interested, and I didn't want to try nothing by myself."

When he first heard them mention Patrick, Charlie got a feeling like a cold chill running right up his spine. For so many years he'd thought about Patrick by himself, in the loneliness and silence of his own thoughts, that when he heard somebody else talking about him, it was like it wasn't really happening. It took him a minute to get adjusted to it—to realize that he was hearing two strangers say these things about Patrick. He sat very still, hardly breathing.

"Well, what do you think we ought to do?"

"There ain't nobody lives close to him, and he stays there by hisself. We could either wait till it gets dark and go over there, or we could just go on now. I don't think there's any chance of anybody seeing us. We can just go along the river here, and when we get to that place close to his house, just cut over and go right up to it. Once we get there, if he won't let us in, we can just push that little old door open and go on in."

"But it's broad daylight. He knows who I am from where I fixed that fence."

"Hell, I know that. He knows me, too, from being down at the feed store when I was working there. So, we might's well make up our mind right now. We damn shore can't leave him alive. Even if we done it at night, he might get a look at us. I got my rifle in the pickup. Where's yours? Ain't you got it?"

"No, but I got my hunting knife right here in my belt. We can do it whichever way seems best at the time."

"Well, do you want to just go on over there, now, then?"

"Hell, I guess so. I always heard there ain't no time like the present. How far is it, anyway? Must be about two mile, following the river bank."

Their voices grew fainter as they walked away from the willow tree toward the river, a hundred yards away.

Charlie was confused. The words he'd heard were a lot of the same ones he'd played over in his mind for the last forty years. How to pay Patrick back for stealing his life. Stealing her and letting her die. He might've even laughed if he hadn't been so stunned. This plan was better than any he'd ever conjured up late at night when his arthritis hurt and he couldn't sleep. His mind played a game that would sometimes lull him off. The game was to make up the perfect plan to do away with Patrick. Sometimes it was digging a deep hole and baiting it with some kind of lure to get Patrick to walk over it, then let him drop into the hole, never to be heard of again. Or put just enough sleeping pills in his coffee that he would just fall over at the table and never wake up.

Now that their parents were gone, and Charlie was all alone, the plans were all he had. When he closed his eyes at night, he recited his hatred and the details of his latest plan, a litany closing out the small room and the darkness.

He had made up a hundred, maybe even a thousand different plans over the years, and he'd enjoyed every one. The more cruel and hateful details he could think up, the more he enjoyed it.

It was like he knew, though, that he would never carry one out. The plans had become like a scratchy old blanket to wrap up in and go someplace deep inside himself where the hurt and anger couldn't follow.

But this! These fellows had the perfect plan. Charlie didn't have to do a thing, and all his fantasies and dreams would come true. Finally, he would be avenged. All he had to do was sit still under the tree until they had time to get to that spot where the fence separated Patrick's back pasture from the river, climb over it, and go right on up to his house.

Probably take them about two hours to make the walk, time they had to break through the limbs and weeds and climb over all the slippery rocks alongside the river.

He sat there for another five minutes, just rolling the whole thing over and over in his head. Then he got up, started up the hill toward a shortcut through the woods, and ran to warn his brother.

His mind was racing as he came to the fence. He wasn't sure where to cross it to make the best time. The road to Patrick's house was a hundred yards on the other side, running through a stand of cedars along the top of the ridge. The house was a mile down that road. He stopped for a minute to look around and tried to decide the shortest distance to the narrow, wooded path that would lead him to Patrick's farm. As he started to climb over, he forgot the row of barbwire stretched along the top, and too late, he felt his baggy old work pants get caught on the sharp points. He knew he was losing his balance as he swung his leg over the side, but he was helpless to stop his fall.

He came down hard on his ankle, and a sickening pain made him think he'd broken it. He sat there in agony, not able to move, for what seemed like a long time. Gradually the pain eased, and he was able to move his foot. Pulling himself up by the fence post, he gasped at the pain of putting his weight down on his ankle.

"Must be sprained. If I can find a good strong tree limb, I can make me a crutch."

Almost in a panic now, he scoured the area near him. Finally, he spotted a branch not too far from where he'd fallen, that looked like it might be strong enough to carry his weight. Pulling himself up on his elbows, he half crawled, half dragged himself to where it lay. He grasped the limb in both hands and pulled himself up into a sitting position. Holding the limb in front of him, he forced himself to his knees, and then to his feet, placing the fork under his arm, and leaning on it for support.

He knew that the distance he had to cover to get to Patrick's house was a lot shorter than what the men had, going all the way around by the river, but now he didn't know if his leg would slow him down enough to let them get there first.

The terror of this thought reminded him of the worst feelings he'd ever had in his life up to now. The day Patrick stole the horse. The day Patrick and Lutie got married. The day Lutie died.

As terrible as all those feelings had been, this one was just as bad—in ways maybe even worse. He could not control any of those things. Lutie loved Patrick more than she did him, and neither the horse nor anything else could have changed that. And he guessed he'd always known that Patrick would have done anything to save her—even to dying himself if he could. But this thing that he was trying to do now—save Patrick from these murderers—was something within his power. If only he could get there in time.

The pain was worse now, and the swelling was coming up over his shoe top. He'd have to take the shoe off and leave it there. Slowly pulling the tie out of his lace to keep from jarring his ankle, he loosened the shoe and pulled it off. He laid the shoe aside and felt the cool grass against his foot. The leg was black, and swollen to twice its normal size. He sat looking at it for a moment, then he ran his fingers along the calf from ankle to knee. Pulling himself up, and placing the limb under his arm, he moved ahead, hopping, limping, dragging his leg, inches at a time.

The loose rock hidden under the tall grass rolled when the tip of the limb came down on it, upsetting his balance, and pitching him headlong into the leaves and underbrush. The pain was huge. Disoriented, unable to move, he lay crying. Panic came in waves. He didn't know how far he'd come, or how much time had passed. Summoning his remaining strength, he dragged himself forward to look over a little rise just ahead of him. Then he saw it, and his gasp was very close to a sob. Just down the hill he saw the little square lot that Patrick's house sat on—the house that Patrick had built for himself and Lutie forty years ago. He looked at it now, and it seemed strange—like it belonged to someone he'd never known.

He knew now that he had to be careful. If the men had come straight on after they left the willow tree, they must be pretty close.

Easing down close to the ground, he pulled himself over to the log fence that separated Patrick's property from the field that Charlie'd just crossed. He took a long, careful look around. The house seemed very quiet and still.

From this spot he could see the front door and both sides of the house. A few shrubs in the yard and a maple tree with long spreading limbs would block the view of anybody near the house, and make it possible for Charlie to get all the way to the front door without being seen.

What if Patrick came to the door and wouldn't let him in? How could he explain showing up like this after all these years? What if Patrick thought he was here to settle accounts? God knows he'd dreamed about doing that for years, but maybe Patrick didn't know. There was no time left to worry about it—he'd just have to find the right words when Patrick opened the door.

He found a place in the fence where one of the logs had fallen. There was still one log about eighteen inches off the ground that he would have to climb over. Leaning against the post that the log was attached to, he managed to pull the injured leg up and over. Still holding on, to save putting down all his weight, he swung the other one over.

Leaning through to the other side he got the limb, and now, crawling more than walking, he made it to the big maple tree near the front door.

Looking at the door, he felt better. No sign of trouble. Surely if they'd been here, he'd be able to tell it. There was still time to warn Patrick.

Then he heard a sound that chilled him. Voices coming from down the hill on the other side of the house—the side by the river. They were here and making no effort to be quiet. Must be planning to tell Patrick some story to get him to open the door.

He gauged the distance that the men had to come, compared to the distance to the front door. He still had an edge on them. He closed his fist around the limb, moved from his cover under the maple, and began to close the distance to the door. He felt no pain, and the limb dropped to the ground. He was running—three more steps—arm raised and extended to push Patrick back through the open door.

"Patrick! It's Charlie! Let me in! Let me in! Grab your gun, and let me in!"

"Charlie?" Patrick, still a mirror image of himself, stood there in the open door, staring.

"Patrick! Them fellers—"

The voices were louder now, and closer. Charlie made a lunge for the front door as the two men rounded the corner. He knew he wouldn't make it. Charlie's back was to the men, but Patrick still stood in the open door, unmoving.

"Hello, Mr. Buffin," came a smiling voice.

Charlie looked at his brother. "Patrick," he said. "I'm sorry, Patrick. Oh, my God, I'm sorry."

The Kiss

It's early when the sheriff gets to our house. My bedroom door is closed, but I see the light from the kitchen lamp underneath, so I know it's not even good daylight yet. The smell of Mama's coffee and biscuits usually wakes me up, but today all I want to do is to sink back under the covers of my dark safe bed and hide.

I hear a short, quick knock. It's strange because nobody ever comes to our house this early. Daddy's chair scrapes on the floor as he scoots back and steps over to the door. Another knock comes, louder than the first, like whoever's out there won't wait much longer. The iron latch rubs on the wooden boards as daddy opens it and the door creaks like somebody's pushing it from the outside.

Daddy is quiet, but there's a strange voice, and I strain to hear the words.

"Sorry to bother you this early, mister, but we're looking for somebody. Thought you might've seen him or could give us some idea where he might be. Name's Nathan Clay and we understand him and his family live on this farm."

When I hear Nathan's name, my heart leaps up in my mouth, and I jump out of bed and run to my door. I put my eye up to a little crack, and I can see two men on the porch and daddy standing in the doorway. The men are wearing blue uniforms and carrying shotguns. The tall black-headed one is doing the talking, while the shorter fat one glances up and down the road, and around the corner of our house. He cradles his gun, and his finger's near the trigger. For a second, I think he looks straight at me through the crack, and I shiver. My heart pounds so hard I'm afraid they'll hear it and know I'm listening. I hold tight to the door, so my hands won't shake and give me away.

Daddy's already dressed to go to the tobacco patch. He puts his hands in his overalls pocket and shakes his head.

"Nathan and his mama and daddy live up the road a little piece, but I ain't seen Nathan lately. I don't have no idea where he is."

"Well, if you see or hear tell of him, get in touch with me. If I ain't at my office there in Lancaster, somebody'll be there. Much obliged for your time." The sheriff touches his hand to his hat and turns around and starts off the porch. The other man puts his shotgun on his shoulder and follows him.

Mama's been setting the kitchen table for breakfast. I can tell she's listening too, because she's just standing there, holding the three plates up against her chest. Finally she calls out after them.

"Why was you looking for Nathan?"

Both men turn around at once, like they're surprised to hear another voice, especially a woman's. They look at her for a minute, then at each other, like they don't know what to say. Finally the sheriff starts back up the steps.

"Well, we're not at liberty to say too much, ma'am, but the fact is that somebody's complained that he attacked their daughter, and they want him caught. That's about all we can tell you right now." They turn around fast, the two of them nearly running down the steps toward the gate.

Mama and Daddy watch them leave, then Daddy closes the door and sits down at the table. Mama stays by the door for a minute before she goes to the stove.

"Lord, John. I never would've thought such a thing of that boy."

She speaks in a whisper, like she's afraid somebody will hear her.

"I never heard of him causing no trouble before, especially nothing like that."

She reaches into the oven and pulls out the biscuits.

"If they was to hurt him, it'd kill Belle and Duke. That boy's all they've got."

Everybody knows Nathan is Aunt Belle's and Uncle Duke's grandson. Bertha Mae ran away at fifteen and came back home a year later, just long enough to have Nathan and leave without him. As far as anybody knows, they never heard from her again. Nathan's always called them Mama and Daddy, just like he was their own son. Maybe he thinks he is.

Mama puts the biscuits in the middle of the table, brings the bowl of gravy from the back of the stove, and looks toward my door.

"If it was a white girl he attacked, they're liable to lynch him," Daddy says quietly.

Mama doesn't answer but calls out to me.

"Lilly, get up and come on to breakfast."

I'm still standing behind my door, and it's like I'm paralyzed. Like some giant has reached down and caught me under his thumb, and he's holding me down so tight I can't move my legs. A cold shiver runs through my whole body, and I pull my gown tighter around me and force myself to walk into the kitchen.

"Hurry up, Lilly, or you'll miss the school bus," Mama says and passes the biscuits to me. She pours Daddy a cup of coffee from the gray pot and sets it back on the stove.

Then she says, "Lilly, you haven't seen nothing of Nathan, have you? They was two sheriffs by here looking for him for bothering some girl. Wouldn't say who it was, was she white or colored, where she lived, or nothing."

She passes me the gravy and pours milk into my glass from the blue pitcher with the broken handle that used to be her mother's.

"You be careful when you go out to the school bus. Them men had guns, and they might shoot if they get sight of Nathan around here. It won't be safe to walk outside till they catch him."

I don't say anything but just keep my head down like I'm too sleepy to talk, which is about the truth, because I sure didn't sleep much last night. Truth is, I know exactly what's going on, only I wish to God I didn't.

Me and my sister Wilma used to play with Nathan when we were little kids. Mama made us quit when I got old enough to go to school. She said people would talk about us for playing with a colored boy. We'd still slip around with him sometimes anyway, and go down to the creek, or hunt scrap iron to sell for the war effort against the Japs and Germans.

Once when I was ten. we were out running in tall weeds and my foot came down on a broken jar. Cut it almost in half, and I couldn't walk all summer. Nathan would wait till everybody was out working in the tobacco, then he'd come to the house and bring some of Aunt Belle's cookies or chocolate pie, and make up games for us to play, so I wouldn't have to be by myself all day. We played together close as any brother and sister.

I hardly ever see him any more now, though, since I'm in high school and Wilma's gone to work as a waitress at the Mercer Grill in Lancaster. Nathan went to a colored school over at Lackey for a while, but now he mostly just helps Uncle Duke and Mr. Ben with the tobacco and farm chores.

Anyway, I've got this friend, Louise, who's been my very best friend since first grade, even though we're totally different. In about sixth grade, she starts wanting to go out with boys really bad. She flirts with the older boys and tries to get me to. but I don't know what to say to them.

Now that we're in high school she's a lot prettier than I am. I'm skinny, with straight brown hair, but hers is blonde and curly. She wears makeup and tight clothes, and boys like her. She slips around so her mama and daddy don't know it and has dates almost every weekend. I feel left out. but she always tells me about them on Monday. Sometimes she tells me some pretty scary things.

I was surprised yesterday morning when she come and sat down behind me in study hall and said she had to talk to me. We usually wait till school's out and talk on the bus going home, but I see right away there's something wrong. She looks over her shoulder like she's scared, like maybe somebody's chasing her.

"'I'm gonna ask to be excused," she whispers, "then you wait a little while and ask too. I'll meet you in the typing room. Nobody's in there this hour."

"But what if a teacher walks in and sees us, and sends us to Mr. Broaddus' office?" Just getting sent to the principal's office guarantees you'll have to stay in for a week at lunch time and not see or talk to anybody, whether you've done anything wrong or not.

By now Louise is practically crying, and her knuckles are white where she's holding on to her notebook so tight. So, I tell her

I'll do it, even though I'm scared to death.

She waits a few minutes, then raises her hand to be excused, and in a little while I do the same thing, praying Mr. Hoskins won't remember that Louise is out and not let me go.

"You may be excused, Lilly," he says, and I'm out of my seat so fast I know everybody thinks I'm about to wet my pants. When I get to the typing room, there's Louise, crouching down in a seat way in the back.

"Come here, Lilly," she whispers, and motions for me to sit next to her.

I sit down in a chair facing a big black Remington, and automatically think "asdf, jkl;." Louise whimpers, and I turn around to face her.

"Louise, what on earth is wrong with you? You look awful."

Her hand trembles. Her eyes are surrounded by dark blue circles, and a strand of hair has come loose from a barrette and fallen across her face. She pushes it back, grabs my hand, and holds on tight.

"Now listen, Lilly," she says. "You've got to promise me you won't tell nobody about this. You can't never breathe it out loud, not to a living soul."

I'm confused, because we always keep each other's secrets, knowing there's no way either one of us would ever tell anything on the other.

She's beginning to scare me more than I already was, and I look at her, trying to listen for footsteps in the hall at the same time. Suddenly she's talking in a rush, like she has to get rid of the words all at once.

"Lilly, do you remember once I told you I thought Nathan Clay was cute, and you thought I was joking, and we both knew people would die if they ever heard me say such a thing?"

"Sure, I remember," I whisper.

I lean over close to her so I can hear better. Then is when I notice she's wearing the same dress she had on yesterday, and her hair looks like it hasn't been combed. She takes a deep breath and starts talking again.

"You know how our house sits on up the road about a mile above Nathan's, and there's a barn about halfway between our house and his, where Mr. Ben keeps feed for the stock?"

Her face is so close to mine I can feel her breath. The words spill out of her mouth, and her clammy hand grips my arm so hard it hurts.

"Well, yesterday after school I went to the barn to get a milk bucket for mama, and when I went in, I saw Nathan in there, throwing down some hay for the cows."

She stops, like she doesn't want to tell me the rest. I crazy urge to put my hand over her mouth, to shut her up suddenly the words start up again, like some invisible ha dragging them out of her.

"I just kinda smiled at him, and he acted like he didn't want to talk to me at first, but finally I got him to sit down by me on the pile of hay." She catches her breath and hurries on. "I swear to God, Lilly, I don't know what come over me.

She stops and looks away from me, her eyes on the picture of Abraham Lincoln above the chalk board, like she's trying to figure out how to put the rest of it into words.

"It was like I just lost my mind, and before either one of us knew what happened, I leaned over and kissed him right on the lips."

Suddenly she slows down a little, and looks at me in a different way, almost like she's laughing at me.

"Come on, Lilly. Don't tell me you never wondered what it would be like to kiss Nathan."

I'm staring back into Louise's eyes, but my heart knots up, and I can't say a word. I feel the blood rising up my neck, and my cheeks get hot. But then she seems to forget about me, and looks off again like she's reliving what happened next.

"He looked so scared at first, and then he looked mad, and he reached out his hands to push me away."

Now her face gets all strange and twisted. I don't want to hear any more, but I know we're both caught in this story, and there can be no stopping her until it is finished.

"When he pushed me I fell back on the hay, and just then I heard somebody coming into the barn. I looked up and my daddy was standing there at the barn door with a pitchfork in his hand. His mouth was open, but nothing was coming out.

Then he screamed and lunged at Nathan with that pitchfork, and it came down in a hair of going through him."

"What did you do?" I whisper. "What did you tell your daddy?"

"What could I tell him? Nathan jumped up and run out the other door, and daddy was still standing there holding that pitchfork up over his head like he was gonna hit me with it. He looked so wild, like he didn't even know me. So, I run over to him, and I told him that when I went in the barn to get the bucket, Nathan come up behind me before I even knew he was in there, and grabbed me, and pushed me down on the straw."

"But don't you know what they'll do to Nathan for attacking a white girl?" She doesn't answer, and I whisper, "What did your daddy do then?"

"Well, he didn't wait to hear nothing else. He just run back out the door, yelling that he was going after the sheriff, and that's the last I saw of him. He didn't even come home last night. Me and Mama waited up all night for him. She's scared to death he'll kill somebody and get sent to prison."

"Did you tell her what really happened? I mean the truth about Nathan?" Her eyes drop like she can't look me in the eyes, and I already know the answer.

"I couldn't, Lilly. You know how she is. She's wild right now. anyway, and she'd die if she ever thought I'd kiss a colored boy. Besides, I couldn't change what I'd already told daddy."

She grips my arm harder. I want to jerk it away, but I don't. It's like I'm caught in a trap with her and neither one of us can escape. So, I just look at her and don't say a word.

"Lilly, you've got to swear to God you won't never tell this to nobody." Her face is the color of dirty chalk dust, and I'm afraid to look at her anymore. All I want to do is get out of there.

"I swear," I whisper, and jerk my arm away.

I tiptoe to the door and go back to study hall and in a few minutes, Louise comes back in, and somehow we get through the rest of the day.

When I get home, I tell Mama I've got the cramps and don't want any supper, and go to my room, even though it's not even dark yet. Later I hear Mama and Daddy go to bed, and my eyes feel like they're being propped open with sticks. The house creaks, and somewhere far off I hear dogs barking. A wind comes up and swishes the limbs on the maple tree outside my window, and I see black shadows dancing on the curtains.

I see Nathan running through the willows down by the creek with dogs chasing him, and somebody's behind him with a shotgun. I wake up with my heart pounding, and I know it was a nightmare.

Morning comes, and I hear the sheriff on the porch.

When I'm dressed for school, I say goodbye to Mama and Daddy and walk out the door onto the porch. The dew sparkles in the sunlight, and smoke rises from the chimney of the Buffin's house on the Jackson farm, down the lane from ours. I start toward the road to where the bus stops.

From behind me a car comes up the road, and as it passes, I see that it's the sheriff's car, going toward Nathan's house. It's moving slow, and if I run fast enough, I can catch it.

The road is like a swollen river with waves lapping around my legs, forcing me back. My books are a dead weight in my arms, and I toss them aside like another misplaced promise. I come in sight of Nathan's house, and I see Aunt Belle standing on the porch. The sheriff is walking toward her, holding out a bloody jacket.

I hear her scream as I fight against the current, and I know that whatever happens all the rest of my life will be measured against that scream.

The Ride Home

W ell, here we are Lilly," Mr. Kirby pulled the blue showroom-new '52 Buick over to the shoulder of the blacktop and left the motor running. Its wavering yellow headlights pierced only a little way into the darkness ahead.

"I guess we'll see you in church Sunday," he said.

He kept his large hands on the steering wheel, staring into the shadows beyond the windshield.

Lilly sat still in the back seat. The narrow gravel road that led to her house was marked by a row of mailboxes, dimly outlined in the moonlight. To her left, out the window, she could see the entrance to the road, and the overhanging branches of persimmon and maple trees on either side.

She reached down for the handle of her suitcase, the tan Samsonite Wilma had given her when she graduated from high school a year ago. She remembered how heavy it had been when she lifted it into the car this afternoon, full of clothes, books, and a year's accumulation of small, meaningful things. Beside Lilly, in the back seat, Janet Kirby said nothing, but Mrs. Kirby turned and spoke for the first time since they had left Lancaster.

"Tell your mother they's still some boxes of clothes and things at the church that was donated and sent down here from up north, if she wants to come and pick some out."

Lilly opened the door, pulling the suitcase after her, and leaned back into the dark car.

"Thank you. I'll tell her. And thank you for the ride. Mr. Kirby."

The car pulled away, leaving Lilly standing alone in the darkness.

She faced the shrouded entrance to the narrow road. It was two miles to her house, where her mother and father would already be in bed.

"Why I guess so. Lilly," Mrs. Kirby had responded to Lilly's request for a ride home when the semester ended. "We're picking Janet up at the University and we can come on over there and get you. Just be sure to have your things ready outside your dormitory."

She watched the red taillights disappear. The Kirbys lived five miles further down the main road, near Friendship Baptist Church, where Mr. Kirby was a deacon, and Mrs. Kirby played the piano and led the singing. Lilly and her family went there too, when they could get a ride.

It was a cool night in late May. The quiet was broken only by an occasional breeze through the new spring leaves, or a snapping of twigs in the dry undergrowth. Somewhere, she heard the sound of a whippoorwill and knew there would be many more as the night wore on.

How many times had she and Wilma walked over this road during her growing-up years? How many times had they gone to the store for Mama, to the fields to help in the tobacco and corn, and in late summer, to pick blackberries for jam and cobblers? Everything in her early life could eventually be reached by walking up or down this road.

Now, in the darkness, it looked different. Bushes and weeds grew thick on both sides, and sudden curves came after straight stretches, hiding what lay beyond. She thought of the last part of the road, more than a mile further on. and hesitated for a minute longer. Then she picked up the suitcase and started the long walk home.

She tried to think of the school year she had just completed. It had been a good year, her first away from home as a college freshman. She had missed home at first, but her adjustment had not taken long. She was in a wonderful new world that she could only have imagined before.

"Are you glad school's out for this year, Lilly?" Mrs. Kirby had asked her when she got into the car.

"Yes ma'am, but I'll miss it. I'll be ready to go back in the fall."

"I guess you done good in your grades. Kept up your scholarship all right?"

Mrs. Kirby brushed back a strand of steel gray hair that had escaped from a coil at the back of her head, and with one finger adjusted her wire-rimmed glasses.

"Yes, I had three A's and two B's this semester. Thank goodness my math's out of the way."

Mrs. Kirby was quiet after that, and she and Mr. Kirby rode in silence for the next few miles.

In the back seat, Lilly and Janet had talked about their different college experiences.

"I'm majoring in Home Ec," Janet said. "That way, even if I don't meet somebody and get married right away, I can still get a teaching certificate to fall back on."

Walking slowly in the darkness, stumbling occasionally in the loose gravel, Lilly moved the heavy suitcase from one hand to the other, trying to find a way to maintain a steady pace. She stopped often to rest, each time setting a goal to reach before putting her burden down again.

The moon went behind a blanket of silver-gray clouds, hiding the row of fenceposts beside the road. Lilly hit her foot on a rock and barely managed to keep from falling. Even though she hadn't reached her next goal, she sat down on the suitcase and squeezed her toes until they stopped aching, and bit her lip to keep from crying.

Her thoughts drifted back to the Kirbys. When they got to Lancaster, Mr. Kirby had pulled into the parking lot of the Southern States Co-op where county farmers bought feed and supplies.

"Got to go in here and see about having some feed sent out for the cows." He spoke through teeth clamped together on an unlit cigar. "Shouldn't take too long," he said, walking away.

Lilly looked out the window at the bank of orange, pink and purple clouds hanging low in the western sky. She loved this time of day. Since childhood she had felt an emotional response to the quiet of twilight, as though in those moments she merged with every other living thing.

Time passed, and one by one, the businesses along Main Street closed their doors. Lights came on in houses. Cars pulled away from the curb, leaving only the Kirbys and Lilly in the Co-op parking lot. Mr. Kirby had been gone a long time, and Lilly wondered if Janet and her mother were used to this kind of waiting. Conversation had long since dwindled to an awkward silence.

Mrs. Kirby finally turned toward the back seat.

"We was all so pleased you got that scholarship," she said.

She was looking closely at Lilly, a perpetual smile set firmly on her small face, her gray eyes almost transparent through thick round lenses. But Lilly heard a sharp edge in her voice.

"Course Janet could a had one too, us giving so much to the Baptist church, but then she really didn't have a need like you did."

She turned her head and looked toward the feed store, then down at the gold-plated Bulova on her wrist. Without commenting on the length of her husband's absence, she turned back toward Lilly.

"We prayed that God would provide you a way to go to college."

"I think it was because of the speech contests I won," Lilly answered, her face getting hot. She knew that it was also her grades that had made the Rotary Club choose her for an academic scholarship to the prestigious private Baptist college, but she couldn't say that.

"Well as far as that goes, Janet can make speeches. She's spoke in church all her life." Mrs. Kirby's face still wore a tight smile, but her voice was almost shrill.

Beside Lilly in the dark back seat, Janet seemed to shrink into the dark corner.

At last Mr. Kirby appeared. He ambled toward the car, opened the door, and climbed into the driver's seat. He started the car without commenting on his business in the feed store and pulled out of the parking lot. At the corner he turned onto the highway that led to their community, ten miles away. Lilly looked out the window. The beautiful colors had faded to gray, and night would soon cover the rolling hills.

Lilly had not told her parents that she would be coming home tonight. They didn't have a telephone, and she had not written, because she thought the Kirbys would drive her all the way home. She was glad she had not told them to wait up for her.

She had walked almost a mile now, and her hands were hot and raw from the heavy swinging of her suitcase. Now and then she saw a shadow move among the trees, and reminded herself that it was only the movement of clouds over the moon.

Somewhere off in the distance she heard a dog howling and forced herself not to let her imagination take over. She thought of one of her childhood books with the story of "The Hound of the Baskervilles," and the horrible full-page picture of the hound. She and Wilma had shuddered at the dagger-like fangs in the snarling, dripping mouth, and they never read the story at bedtime.

She rounded a curve in the road and found herself at the spot she had dreaded since her walk began. It was a hill descending through dense woods, leading down into an even narrower stretch of gravel road. At the bottom was a creek spanned by an iron bridge, where she and Wilma and Nathan had played on summer days.

She looked toward the place where the hill began, a black void that she could almost reach out and touch. A chill drifted out of the trees, moving finger-like up and down her arms. Standing very still, she heard a crashing sound that could be a tree limb falling, or feet running through dry, dead leaves.

She would never be able to enter the wood. Fatigue made her legs tremble, and she dropped the suitcase into the gravel. In panic, she pressed her hands against her mouth. She sat down on the edge of the suitcase and rocked back and forth, hugging herself in the deepening chill.

She tried to think more clearly. What other option did she have, but to follow the road and go on to her house? She stood and looked toward the spot where the road began to drop away, the trees closing in like black caped arms, shutting out the moon.

Come on, she thought, goading herself to move. You know you can't just sit here like this. Pretend it's daylight, and Wilma and me and Nathan are down here catching bullfrogs. Feel how warm the sun is, coming through the trees and hitting the water down there in the creek.

She made herself pick up the suitcase and take one step, then another, into the wood. "Stay in the middle of the road." she whispered, as she half dragged, half carried the heavy suitcase.

Remember how we used to come down here and walk straight down the hill to the creek, Wilma? And how we could almost reach out and touch the weeds and grass on both sides, it was so narrow? And how you and Nathan would race each other to see who could get down to the creek first, but I couldn't keep up because my legs were so short? As her thoughts reached out to Wilma, she could no longer hang on to the illusion of daylight.

Instead, her mind jumped back to that awful day in the barn. Bits of straw the color of her hair stuck to Wilma's arms where she had been lying curled up in the loft. Lilly had to lean down close to hear what she was saying.

"I thought Billy loved me."

Her voice was hoarse from crying. "He said he did, but now he says he can't marry me on account of his parents. And he says he don't want no baby."

Lilly thought Wilma sounded like a baby herself.

"I don't know what to do, Lilly." Wilma's voice was hollow, like the life had been drained from it.

"I'll help you, Wilma. Please don't cry," Lilly begged.

She had put her arms around her sister and held her, rocking her, soothing her, in the dark warm barn. And she had tried to help her, but she hadn't known how.

"You know you can't stay here and have that baby," Mama had shrieked. "Why we'd be run out of this county."

Wilma cried, and Mama cried, and they both screamed words that were too awful to bear.

So, Wilma had gone to stay with Aunt Sarah in Indiana until the baby came, and then to Lancaster to get a job at the Mercer Grill, where her childhood soon became a distant memory.

The blackness became more dense and frightening. She could

feel the trees on both sides, and hear leaves and branches crackling, like footsteps creeping closer and closer. She wanted to scream and run, but fear paralyzed her.

Then came the worst memory, the one she had struggled with for three years, and would have to hide from for the rest of her life.

Nathan.

Louise had told her at school, how she had lied about him to her parents, and Lilly hadn't told anyone, even though she knew that a white girl lying about a black boy could get him killed. A day and a night she had known, and hadn't told, and then it was too late.

"I was on my way to tell them, Nathan," she whispered. "I swear to God I was."

This was the place where the sheriff and his men had found Nathan hiding and shot him when his terror made him run.

Unable to take another step, Lilly sank down in the dark road and surrendered herself to the enfolding darkness.

Time passed, and after a while she raised her head. She had no idea how long she'd been sitting there, but the sharp gravel hurt her legs, and she felt stiff when she tried to stand up. The sounds around her were different from those she had heard earlier. Whippoorwills were calling out to each other from many trees, and the din in the woods had died away.

Suddenly, through the trees, she saw a dim light in the window of a house up the hill on her left. She had forgotten the house was there until now. It had been empty for a long time, and she remembered being six or eight years old, going inside and finding old magazines and jars and cans that had been left by earlier tenants.

Who, she wondered, could be living there now? She was certain the house had been empty when she left for college. Filtered as it was through tree branches and fog, the light was pale, and seemed to waver as though a hand were moving it back and forth. Her hands trembled, but she hesitated for only a moment, then picked up her suitcase and started up the hill toward the light.

The house was shabby. Even in the darkness Lilly could see

where panes of glass were cracked in some of the windows, and two steps leading up to the porch had rotted and fallen through. A clothesline was strung along the porch, and three or four diapers and a pair of men's overalls hung on it.

She knocked once, and then again more loudly, until she heard footsteps. The door opened, and a woman stood there, holding a baby against her shoulder. She was thin, and her black hair hung in a plait over one shoulder. The woman blinked and opened her mouth, but no words came out. Lilly realized how strange she must look, standing on the porch in the moonlight in her thin cotton dress. She was afraid the woman might slam the door in her face.

"Please, ma'am, please don't close the door. My name is Lilly Adkins, and my family lives right up yonder over the hill."

Her words sounded like babbling, even to her. "Is there somebody here that could take me on home? I've walked all the way from the main road, and I just can't go any further."

The woman suddenly seemed to realize who Lilly was.

"Are you Miz Adkins' daughter? I met her at the store, and she told me about you. Said you was away at college."

She shifted the baby to the other shoulder and patted its back. "Yes!" Lilly felt almost faint with relief. "That's who I am. I'm so glad you know my mother."

The woman held the door open and motioned for Lilly to come inside.

"Wait just a minute and let me call my husband. He'll take you on home, soon as he puts his shoes back on."

The woman went into the next room, and Lilly could hear whispered conversation. A tall man followed her when she came back into the room. Uncombed black hair framed his face, which was darkened by a stubble of beard, and the leathery tan of a farm hand.

"This is my husband, Raymond Lane, and I'm Peggy. I'm glad you seen our light and come on up here." She opened the front door and stood to one side.

"Come on out to the truck," the man said. "It won't take a minute to drive you up the hill." He picked up her suitcase and walked out the door.

Her house was dark when they stopped in front of it, and Lilly climbed out of the rusty old pickup.

"Mr. Lane, I sure appreciate you bringing me on home. You just about saved my life."

"It wasn't no trouble." He looked at her, and Lilly smelled the faint sweet odor of whiskey on his breath. "Besides, I always thought that's what neighbors was for."

Lilly pulled her suitcase out and walked to the front door. She turned the knob slowly, trying to be as quiet as possible. As the door opened she heard the little creak in the hinge that had been there as long as she could remember.

A voice came from the bedroom.

"Who is it?"

"It's me, Mama. I got a ride and came on home tonight."

Lilly heard a rustle of bedclothes, and the sound of her mother's feet on the floor. She appeared in the doorway in a blue cotton gown, pushing strands of gray hair back from her face.

"Lilly, we didn't know you was coming home tonight. I was just dreaming about you, and something about the dream scared me, but I can't remember now what it was."

She stood there blinking, trying to wake up.

"It's ten o'clock. What on earth are you doing out so late? Who brought you home?"

"Well, the Kirbys brought me to the turn-off, and I walked as far as the Lanes. Raymond Lane brought me on up the hill from their house." "Oh, the Lanes. They just moved into the old Grider house two or three months ago."

Her mother started toward the kitchen. "Me and your daddy don't know too much about them. They don't go to church."

She stopped at the stove and took a pan out of the oven.

"Nellie Grimes said she heard he drinks."

Her mother took a bowl down from the shelf above the old iron cook stove.

"Are you hungry? I just made this peach cobbler today."

She scooped some of the cobbler into a bowl and poured a

glass of milk out of a blue stoneware pitcher.

"But why'd you have to walk as far as the Lanes? Why didn't the Kirbys bring you on home?"

"I don't know, Mama. They just let me out, and said they'd see me in church Sunday."

Her mother was quiet for a moment. When she spoke, Lilly heard a sharp edge of anger in her voice.

"Well, it ain't always the church people that help you out when you need it the most."

"No, Mama," Lilly said. "Not always."

As Lilly ate, her eyelids began to feel heavy, and she wondered if she could make it into bed without falling asleep. Her mother helped her drag the suitcase into her room and set it at the foot of the bed. Lilly took off her shoes and peeled the sock back from her blistered heel.

"You want some Cloverine salve to put on your feet? They look almost raw."

"No, I'm just too tired tonight."

She was rummaging in her suitcase, looking for a gown. "I'll put some on tomorrow, though."

"Well, goodnight, Lilly," her mother said. "I'm sure glad you got home all right."

She wished her mother would come over and put her arms around her and tell her how glad she was to see her, but she knew that would never happen. It just wasn't Mama's way.

"Me too," she said. "You don't know how glad I am to be here."

Lilly lay in the dark and thought about college, and how much she wanted to go back in the fall. She thought of Wilma and Nathan, and of how different the paths their lives had taken from her own. And of her mother's reaction to the Kirbys leaving her to walk home in the dark alone.

One thing was sure. She would never tell her mother about the charity boxes of clothes at the church.

"Damn you anyway, Mrs. Kirby," she whispered, and closed her eyes. "Damn you and your silly little prayers.

Acknowledgments

"The Reading Lesson" was published in the September, 1997 issue of *The Journal of Kentucky Studies.* Northern Kentucky University, Highland Heights, Kentucky.

"There's An Eye Watching You" was published in the September, 1998 issue of *The Journal of Kentucky Studies.* Northern Kentucky University, Highland Heights, Kentucky.

"Hello, Mr. Buffin" was published in the Spring, 1999 issue of *Eureka Literary Magazine.* Eureka College, Eureka, Illinois.

"A Good Boy, Bradley" was published in the Summer, 1999 issue of *Appalachian Heritage.* Berea College, Berea, Kentucky.

"Cloudburst" was published in the Summer, 1999 issue of *Pangolin Papers.* Turtle Press, Marrowstone Island, Washington.

"The Ride Home" was published in the September, 2000 issue of *The Journal of Kentucky Studies.* Northern Kentucky University, Highland Heights, Kentucky.

"Cold" was published in the Winter, 2000 issue *of Appalachian Heritage.* Berea College, Berea, Kentucky.

"Lily of the Valley" was published in the Spring, 2001 issue of *Pangolin Papers.* Turtle Press, Marrowstone Island, Washington.

"Changeling" was published in the Summer, 2001 issue of *Now and Then.* East Tennessee State University, Johnson City, Tennessee.

"For My Family" was published in the Winter, 2002 issue of *Appalachian Heritage.* Berea college, Berea, Kentucky.

"People Like Us" was published in the Fall, 2002 issue of *Virginia Adversaria.* Empire Publishing Co., Poquoson, Virginia.

"A Path to the Lake" was published in the Fall, 2002 issue of *Eureka Literary Magazine.* Eureka College, Eureka, Illinois.

"Abner and Eva" was published in the Spring, 2002 issue of *Pangolin Papers.* Turtle Press, Marrowstone Island, Washington. (Nominated by Pangolin Papers for 2002 Pushcart Prize).

"Knight At Arms" was published in the Summer, 2003 issue of
    Pangolin Papers. Turtle Press, Marrowstone Island,
    Washington.
"Hester and Pippa" was published in the Fall, 2004 issue of *Eureka
    Literary Magazine.* Eureka College, Eureka, Illinois.
"The Kiss" was published in the Fall, 2004 issue of *Pangolin
    Papers.* Turtle Press, Marrowstone Island, Washington.
    (Nominated by Pangolin Papers for 2004 Pushcart Prize).

I owe a debt of gratitude to the following people who helped
make this book a reality. First, I am indebted to my family, who
encouraged me to write these stories, to my son Jeff, who told me
that I could, and must do it; to my daughter Lynn who read the
stories and praised them, but saw to it that none of them depicted
any suffering animals; to my daughter-in-law Jill, who was always
there to offer love and confidence in my ability to bring the stories
to fruition; to my grandson Gus and his soon to arrive brother or
sister, whom I love beyond measure; and of course to my husband
Leo, my staunchest supporter and soul mate.

Secondly, I am indebted to my friend Sandy Robertson, who
read the stories and talked to me about the characters as though she
knew them personally, and in so doing, made them even more real
to me; to my friend Marie Parsons, who loves the language as
much as I do, and often helped me to "get it right;" to my friends
Mary Hodges and Karen Adams who traveled miles to read my
stories as I read theirs, and gave me priceless feedback; to my
friend Dr. Sonya Jones, my best student in all of my years of
college teaching, who later became my editor, my agent, and my
most enthusiastic cheerleader.

Three teachers must also be acknowledged: Lillian McGuire,
Wyatt Shely and Rena Calhoun, each of whom saw something in
me that they chose to nourish and encourage. These teachers made
a great difference in my life, and I shall always be grateful to them.

I am indebted to the participants and staff of the Hindman
Settlement School's Appalachian Writers' Workshop, whose

unceasing encouragement motivated me to keep going. Without them this book would not exist.

I am indebted to my close friends, the Ladies of the Club, my reading group in Prestonsburg, Kentucky with whom I shared so many years in reading and discussing good books and forging friendships that have endured over the years. Thank you, Clara, Sandy, Marge, Julie. Drema. Carolyn, Leatha and Jan.

To the "Usual Suspects" of the LaGrange-Coxs' Creek connection, who always knew this book would eventually come to be, and who never stopped adding their encouraging words to the chorus, my heartfelt thanks to B.J. and Vicki, Ed and Merrie, Nolan and Marcia, Jim and Janice, and Don and Lynn.

I am indebted to the editors of all the literary magazines who saw fit to publish my stories, but most especially to Sidney Saylor Farr, then editor of *Appalachian Heritage*, who published my first one.

I am blessed to have had as my parents, John and Elizabeth Thomas, and my siblings, John Wesley, Betty Jane and Sandy, with whom I have always shared an unconditional love. A very special tribute must be given to my older sister, Wanda,who instilled in me a love of books, reading and learning from my earliest childhood. Without her the path of my life might have taken a very different turn.

To these and countless others who have influenced and nurtured me along the course of my life, I extend a heartfelt "Thank you."

BETTER THAN MY OWN LIFE

Contents

Book I

Book II

Better Than My Own Life

The Gods Don't Smile

Lilly reads the newspaper cover to cover every morning.
Not because it interests her all that much, but because the
routine helps her wake up enough to face another day with a
room full of giggling high school teenagers. She promises
herself that soon she will go back to the University to work
on a Master's degree, but so far she hasn't. If she earns one,
she can probably get a job at a small private college in
Kentucky. Maybe even become a drama coach at Bethany,
her alma mater, now that Professor Riley has finally decided
to retire. At least two people she graduated with are teaching
there now.

She often wonders why she can't do something, anything,
to get out of the mind-numbing rut she's in. She can't decide
whether she's too lazy, too comfortable, or just too afraid to make a
move.

A change is what I need, she thinks. Something new.
Something that will shake me loose, make a real difference in my
life.

She nearly drops her coffee cup when she spots a story in
the entertainment section. She slowly sets the cup down and brings

the newspaper closer, reading the headline again to make sure her eyes haven't deceived her. "Ben Stevens to Appear in a Community Theater Production of *The Glass Menagerie*."

She stares at the name on the page. Five years really have passed since she last saw Ben. She reads the date at the top of the page: March 15, 1961. Almost exactly five years, she thinks. Beware the Ides.

Suddenly, she is back at Bethany College, standing on a high ladder, hanging lights for a production of *The Book of Job*.

Lilly knew practically nothing about electricity or any other technical aspect of theater production, but this assignment was a requirement for graduation in her speech and drama major. The sounds of saws and hammers blended with those of a fierce storm coming from the sound system as Professor Riley and the tech crew prepared for dress rehearsal before opening night.

"Hey, Lilly," the stage manager called, "hurry up and finish with that, so we can do a run-through on the lighting."

"Just about done," she answered, twisting the second of two wires into an electrical plug. With a nervous shiver, she inserted the plug into an outlet. One wrong wire could shut down the whole system. She looked back at the lines of wires she had connected to the banks of lights illuminating the stage and crossed her fingers.

She climbed down the ladder and stood beside Ben, the star of the play, holding a rustic walking stick and dressed in the ragged robe of a beleaguered Job. He threw his arm around her shoulders.

"Come on," he said. "Let's go get a Coke while we've still got time."

Ben towered over Lilly's slender five-two frame by at least a foot. His blond hair and beard had grown longer for his role in the play, and his sea-surf eyes seemed even brighter against the dark brown layer of grease paint on his face. His smile was quick and easy. He drew people to him like bears to a honey tree.

Everybody knew that Ben Stevens would be a big star someday. He got all the best roles in the college plays and slid into his characters as effortlessly as putting on his well-pressed khaki slacks and shiny brown loafers. He could be cold and remote when the role called for it, not at all like the real Ben, or happy and jovial when necessary. His rendition of Tartuffe in his junior year brought new definition to the meaning of *hypocrite* and drew ecstatic raves from the drama critic and everyone else who saw the play.

"Soon as I graduate, I'm heading straight to New York to try my luck on Broadway," he'd say. "I know it's hard to break in, but. . ." He nodded toward a large bulletin board where the programs of all of the plays produced in the last four years featured his picture. His eyes would focus on some faraway point as though he could already see his name on a giant marquee.

"Even if I have to start with bit parts and work my way up, I know I can make it."

Everybody believed him, too, including Professor Riley. "Ben is the best natural talent I've ever directed," she said. Her eyes, somewhat dull from advancing age and the onset of cataracts, regained some of their old sparkle. "He just may be the one that puts Bethany College on the map."

Lilly and Ben had been a romantic item on campus for the last two years. She smiled up at him and felt the closeness that shut other people out when they were together. She reached to the back of a chair for her black cashmere sweater, Ben's Christmas gift, and put it around her shoulders, relishing, as usual, its softness on her arms.

"Let's go," she said. "I could use a Coke after all that climbing around in the rafters."

Ben led the way to the Green Room, where a snack had been set out for the cast and crew. A built-in shelf ran the entire length of the room, above which hung a wall of mirrors. Stools in front of the shelf gave actors a place to sit and apply makeup. The smell of brownies and pimiento cheese sandwiches mixed with that of grease paint and musty costumes stored on racks around the walls.

Lilly felt a pang of hunger. "I only hope I got all those wires in the right places," she said, reaching for a sandwich. "Can you just imagine what Riley would do if the whole thing blew up?"

She waited for some silly answer from Ben, but when none came, she turned around to look at him. His eyes were fixed on the open doorway where a prop girl had come in, carrying a ragged burlap bag that Job would use in the first scene of the play. She moved quickly, radiating energy through the shadowy room. As though sensing someone looking at her, she dropped the bag onto the crowded prop table and turned to look at Lilly and Ben.

She was a small girl, thin, almost waif-like. A black slouch hat was draped around her head, hiding one eye, and accenting the other, as though she were looking at them through a makeshift telescope. She wore no makeup, and a black sleeveless peasant blouse emphasized her pale skin. She made no effort to smile or say hello. A look like a beam of light crossed the twenty feet that separated Ben and the girl. Surprise, like a response to some preconscious level of recognition, registered on both their faces.

Only a few seconds had elapsed, but to Lilly it felt like much more. She looked up at Ben. When she turned her head back, the girl was gone. Ben's hand clenched her shoulder, then fell away. *What on earth was that*, she wondered. She felt dazed, like a witness to a head-on collision, a fatal accident on a busy highway. She moved away from the table. Ben followed closely behind her.

"Who is that girl?" he whispered.

"I'm pretty sure she's in my stage craft class," Lilly answered, trying to pretend that nothing unusual had happened. "Her name is Catherine something, I don't recall what, and she's just transferred here from some university in California." You sound like a babbling idiot, she thought, trying to laugh at herself, but an uneasy feeling sent a shiver through her.

Ben handed Lilly a Coke and got one for himself. "I guess I'd better go check to be sure my props are all where they're supposed to be," he said, looking at the open door. Without tasting it, he set the Coke back on the table and walked away.

Lilly watched him stride past the prop table and out into the hallway. The stage manager appeared and asked the cast and crew to take their places to begin dress rehearsal. In a few minutes, Ben came back inside, flushing visibly through his makeup. Lilly tried to catch his eye, to give him her usual good wishes for his performance, but he didn't seem to see her as he took his place on stage.

"Break a leg, Ben," she whispered. "Break a leg."

Lilly moves to the coffee maker to pour herself another cup. She still has half an hour before time to get ready for school. I need to do something about my hands, she thinks, looking at her ragged, unpainted nails. "When did this start?" she wonders, pushing a long strand of hair away from her face. Five years out of college, and I've turned into a frump.

The shrill ring of her telephone startles her. "Hello," she says, her voice still a little hoarse from sleep.

"Good morning. Why aren't you practically out the door?"

"Oh, hi," she smiles, recognizing the voice. "Just getting ready to go. What's up?"

Steve Warren calls her frequently to ask her out for dinner and a movie or to a concert at the University. They were debate partners at Bethany, and his political science major has led him to a law degree and a thriving practice. He returned home last year to open an office, so now they live only thirty minutes apart.

"Did you know that Professor Riley's finally retiring? I got an invitation to a party for her a couple of weeks from now."

"So did I," Lilly laughs. "It's about time. Wonder how old she is."

"God knows, but she probably wasn't as old as she seemed to us back then. Over thirty was way over the hill, remember?" He pauses. "So would you like to go?"

He keeps his voice light, but Lilly senses the intensity just below the surface. She glances down at the newspaper, checking the date of the play.

"Let me get back to you on that, Steve. I've got something else the night before, and I'm not sure how I'll feel."

"Sure, Lilly," he says.

She's known for a while that Steve is unhappy with things as they are. He wants more from their relationship than the casual affection she has been willing to give. Sometimes she does, too, but she always resists the temptation, just as she has with the other men who have drifted in and out of her life since graduation.

She carries her coffee back to the table, looks at the news item again and remembers how things changed for her and Ben after the night of the dress rehearsal.

It was gradual at first. They still saw each other at play rehearsals, still went to a movie once in a while, even necked occasionally under the big trees down behind Lilly's dorm. But as the weeks passed and they saw less and less of each other, a feeling of helplessness gripped her, and she knew she was losing him. Finally, there was no longer even a pretense that they were a couple.

On the small Bethany campus, it was impossible to miss seeing Catherine and Ben, holding hands in the cafeteria or having intense conversations in dark corners of the library. One day Lilly sat two tables away from them, searching the current issue of *Time* for evidence to use in debate. Although anyone in that part of the library could have heard their conversation, Lilly still felt like a spy.

"Listen, Ben," Catherine said, "Ginsberg's new poem, 'Sunflower Sutra.' Just listen to this. 'Jack Kerouac sat beside me on a busted rusty pole, companion, we thought the same thoughts of the soul.' Can't you just see the two of them sitting there together," she whispered, "talking about thoughts of the soul?"

Ben's answer was lost in rustling pages and the librarian's warning "shh."

Sometimes they appeared to argue. At other times the intensity of their feelings almost spilled over onto passersby. Faculty and students watched them without bothering to hide their interest, sensing that Ben and Catherine wouldn't notice or care.

There was a quality about Catherine that set her apart from other girls on the campus. A kind of indifference to what people might think of her. She made no effort to hide her boredom with the small college town. Sometimes she walked across the campus with a cigarette in her fingers, a wispy, fragrant trail of smoke in her wake. She wore long full skirts that rustled around her legs when she walked as though stirred by a secret breeze. People wondered where she bought the off-beat garments, but they didn't ask. Something about Catherine reminded Lilly of the mysterious gypsy women who came through the countryside in the summertime when she was a child.

That year Lilly served as Dean Adams' student assistant. One morning on her way to work, she overheard the Dean and housemother, Sally Parsons, discussing Catherine.

"Her uncle is our trustee, Mr. Samuel Cranston. And you know how generous he's been with his donations to the college," Dean Adams said. "Also, Catherine's parents think our policy of *in loco parentis* will be good for Catherine after the permissiveness of Berkeley."

"Yes, especially after her problems there," Mom Parsons said.

Lilly puts her hands around her warm coffee cup and looks out the window. Traffic is beginning to pick up as people start their morning commute. A dull gray drizzle sends a pattern of rivulets down her window, causing a patch of goose bumps to form on her bare upper arms. She debates whether to smoke a cigarette with her last few swallows of coffee but rejects the idea when she considers the extra time it would take to brush her teeth again.

When did I take up that nasty habit, anyway, she wonders, and the answer, as always, leads her back to Ben. Not while she was going with him, but later, after Catherine entered the picture. Smoking was a calming thing, an act of defiance, a pretense that she didn't care about Ben's taking up with Catherine. I need to quit, she thinks, adding one more need to the stack of needs she can't seem to address.

It was subtle at first, the transformation in Ben. Some mornings he would come to class grungy and unshaven, looking as if he hadn't changed since the day before. He seemed vaguely distracted and out of touch with what went on around him. Worst of all, he began to appear late to rehearsals and had to be cued when he flubbed his lines.

"Ben," Professor Riley began, hesitating as though afraid to continue. The other cast members watched guardedly, pretending that they were busy with some detail of stage business. "Please have your lines down by tomorrow night. Remember that opening night is only two weeks away."

"Of course, I will, Professor Riley." Ben seemed to arouse from a daydream. His smile momentarily restored the features of the Ben they all knew. There was a tangible release of tension in the Green Room.

"Did you ever know me not to have my lines down perfect?"

Professor Riley's answering smile was tentative, as though she didn't know whether to laugh or cry. As always, Ben's responsibility for the success of the play was too important to risk upsetting him.

Once Ben skipped classes all day and missed play rehearsal that night. Word got around that Catherine had left campus without signing out or telling anyone where she was going, and that Ben had gone off to look for her.

The next day Lilly saw Ben and Catherine coming into Dean Adams' office. Ben's face was pale, and Catherine's eyes were covered by dark, oversized sunglasses that further diminished her small features. Although they passed very close to Lilly, neither of them seemed to notice her.

Later that week, Dean Adams asked Lilly to send a memo to the women administrators, calling for a meeting in her office. When they arrived at the appointed time, their usual gossipy laughter was replaced with silence. As soon as they were all inside, the dean closed the door, but Lilly had noticed that the open transom above the office door allowed conversations to be heard clearly if one stood directly beneath it.

Knowing she shouldn't, Lilly gathered an armload of files and stood with her hand on the doorknob, ready to knock if anyone came into the reception room. Mouth dry, heart pounding, she listened.

"Couldn't we reconsider?" Professor Riley asked. Her voice sounded hoarse and weak as though she were very tired or had been crying for a long time.

"No, Rebecca," Dean Adams answered, her voice stern and determined "it's just too much. You know we must stand firm on this."

"Such a waste," Mom Parsons whispered, so quietly that Lilly could scarcely hear.

Lilly had been watching the big round clock on the outer office wall. She knew that she couldn't listen any longer. I can't be late for debate practice, she thought. Everyone knew about Professor Henderson's near mania for punctuality. But her mind was racing to make sense of what was going on with Ben, and the meaning of the strange conversation she had just overheard.

She dashed across the campus to get her debate files from her room and ran, almost literally, into Sarah Jane Kemper, who was standing in the doorway of Parker Hall, their rambling old Gothic style dormitory.

"Wait a minute, Lilly." Sarah Jane caught her arm in a tight grip, reminding Lilly of Coleridge's Ancient Mariner, who had to tell his story or die.

"Have you heard about Ben and Catherine?" Sarah Jane whispered.

"No," Lilly answered. "What about them?"

"Well, Friday, Catherine signed out to go home, and she never got there." Sarah Jane stared at Lilly, waiting for her reaction.

"Oh, God," Lilly whispered. "Were they killed?"

"Oh, no, no, no, nothing like that." Sarah Jane smiled and paused for effect as long as she dared. "No, they just ran off to get married."

Even though she had seen something like this coming for months, Lilly felt her heart jump into her mouth. How long had she been holding out hope, thinking that somehow, some way, Ben would tire of Catherine and come back to her. The dark walls of the old mansion closed around her, and for a moment she thought she might fall. Normal sounds like the roar of a lawn mower outside the window seemed to dull, and she felt herself caught in a silent vacuum.

She stared at Sarah Jane, with no idea of what to say. "Married," she finally managed. "But what about Ben's career? What about Broadway?"

"Guess he'll just have to take Catherine with him," Sarah Jane said. She turned and ran out the door and down the steps, leaving Lilly alone.

The maples lining the sidewalks of the campus rustled, as a breeze, cool for late May, stole through their branches, as though sending secret messages to the azaleas and rhododendrons. A passing train shook the ground.

Lilly came to herself, standing in the doorway of the hollow old mansion, knowing that events had occurred in her life, and in those of Ben and Catherine, that would change them all forever.

The regal old turn-of-the-century Opera House in Lexington flaunts its renovated finery like a dowager queen. Lilly has wasted no time in reserving her seat for opening night of *The Glass Menagerie*, asking for the one closest to the stage. She has spent half a day at the Shear Genius beauty salon and her dark straight hair has been cut and permed into a suitably sophisticated style, befitting a high school speech and English teacher. She's even let Sally talk her into a manicure and moderately long fingernails. Big mistake, Lilly thinks. The nails keep getting in her way and making her drop things. But she can't stop glancing at them, cherry red against the beige and green theater program. She has also invested in a black turtleneck merino wool sweater and a black and red plaid skirt. The fabric clings to her body in a way that emphasizes her small compact figure, which hasn't changed much since college. She shifts her weight in the narrow seat and crosses her legs, checking her gray nylons to be sure she hasn't snagged a run.

Inside her black leather clutch purse, she has tucked the press pass and memo pad she uses to interview minor celebrities for occasional contributions to the "Arts and Entertainment" section of the paper. The press credential helps her get past stage managers.

She turns in her seat to look at the audience. People are being ushered in from three large doors at the back. Three rows back from Lilly, in the center aisle, sits Professor Riley. A halo of soft white hair frames her face. Her eyes shine, and her cheeks glow with excitement. Dean Adams and another woman Lilly does not recognize sit on either side of her. The three women are quiet, gazing at the stage.

A familiar figure walks through the center door and is shown to a seat near the back of the auditorium. Steve Warren. Of course, he would be here. Ben was his friend, too. And, of course, he would remember about Ben and Lilly. She feels her face flush. She draws her arms and legs close to her body and sinks a little deeper into her seat, glad that a heavy-set man is seated directly behind her.

She opens the program and begins to read. She stares at a picture of Ben with the same old jovial smile, the shining blond hair, and the neatly trimmed beard, now slightly shorter than she remembers. A list of his acting credits cites summer stock in New England, an occasional role as a doctor in "Days of our Lives," and two minor roles in off-Broadway productions in New York. *The Glass Menagerie* is touring in a dozen southern cities, with one performance in each.

The house lights dim, and Lilly's heart lurches. Her body responds as it used to when she was near Ben, when she wanted nothing so much as to be in his arms. Steady, she tells herself.

A hush settles as the heavy stage curtain begins to part from its center in blue and gold waves, and an old-fashioned southern living room is set for the arrival of "the gentleman caller."

On cue, Ben takes his place on stage. For a long time, Lilly hears no lines, sees no other actors, is unaware of anyone else in the theater. She watches Ben, scenes floating through her mind, remembering roles in which she thought he was so good that Tennessee Williams himself might write a part for him. Momentarily, she is transformed into Stella or Maggie the Cat, with Ben opposite her, pouring out his love. Only slowly does she return to the here and now, herself a member of an audience, watching an actor she no longer knows. He's neither better nor worse now than he was then, Lilly thinks. But there is another quality about him that she can't quite name. It's more than just maturity, but that's part of it. Something more, though, she thinks. He delivers his lines like the pro that he is, but something tells her he's not there, not really there. Where are you, Ben, she whispers. Where did you go?

A sudden movement of Ben's hand, a piece of stage business that doesn't quite seem to fit, prompts Lilly to look at him more closely, and she knows that he has seen her, somehow knows that she is watching. Not that he will ever look at her directly, never break character for an instant. But Lilly knows that he knows. Even his leading lady looks at him curiously when the timber of his voice deepens, and she seems to sense a much closer connection than before with her "gentleman caller."

When the curtain closes for the final time, Lilly joins the audience in applause. Hers is a message of approval to the Ben she once knew. More enthusiastic than that of the people around her, she tries to restrain her clapping, to avoid drawing attention to herself.

Lilly waits until Steve and everyone else have left the theater, pins the pass to the front of her sweater and heads backstage. A tall man with arms folded across his chest guards the door. Lilly recognizes him as a stage manager, smiles and points to her press pass.

"I'm here to interview Mr. Stevens for the *Herald*," she says.

"Second door on your right's his dressing room," he says, making a move as if to touch the pass to verify its validity.

"Close enough," she smiles and is gone.

The door of the dressing room is open a crack, and Lilly can see Ben inside. He is sitting in front of a round lighted mirror, rubbing cold cream on his face to remove a thick layer of stage makeup. His blond hair is standing up in random peaks, and his beard glistens with cream.

Ben looks up at her through the mirror when he hears the door creak. "Lilly?"

He grabs a hand full of tissue and rubs hard at the cold cream. "I knew you were out there, Lilly." Giving the cream one more swipe, he gets up and starts toward her.

"Hello, Ben," she says quietly. "It's been a long time."

She points to the small patches of cream still clinging to his face and backs away. "Do they still use that stuff to get the paint off?" She laughs. "I guess some things never change."

"Okay, Lilly." He grins at her, and she could swear he's the old Ben, still as sincere as ever and as anxious to please. "You always did know how to ruin a perfect moment," he laughs, sitting back down in front of the mirror. "Let me get this stuff off so we can have a proper reunion."

Lilly sits on a stool near Ben as he applies more tissue to the cream and makeup. "So, tell me about yourself, Ben," she says. "By now, we all thought you'd be a Broadway star." *O, God, did I say that*, she chides herself, and opens her memo pad to hide her embarrassment.

"Hey, don't give up on me yet," Ben says. He runs a comb through his hair and beard. "Didn't you see all my credits in the program? And I've got an audition for a part in *Death of a Salesman* next week." He examines his face closely in the mirror now, absently patting an area under his chin where he's missed a streak of paint. "It's opening in a couple of months in a really good theater off Broadway."

There are dark circles under his eyes, and Lilly notices for the first time how tired he looks. "What about Catherine, Ben?" she asks. "How does she feel about being married to a budding star like yourself?" She tries to keep her voice light, but cringes at the sharpness of her tone.

"You knew she was pregnant when we left school, didn't you, Lilly?"

Ben is looking at her intently now. "Hell, you know how it was then, especially at a place like Bethany." He hesitates. "And, unfortunately, Catherine had scored a little pot from some of her friends out west, and Dean Adams caught her with it."

He laughs, but there is a touch of bitterness in his voice that Lilly has never heard before.

"So, you see we didn't have many choices about going or staying." Lilly closes her eyes, remembering and finally understanding the scene she had witnessed in Dean Adams' office. Ye gods, she thinks, drugs on the Bethany campus. She remembers the grief on Professor Riley's face and her futile attempt to save her young star; and Mom Parsons expressing the eternal bewilderment of the elderly toward the follies of the young: Such a waste indeed. She shifts her body on the backless stool, crosses her ankles and swings her foot, gazing at the toe of her black leather pump. "So, you have a four-year old child, Ben? A son, or a daughter?" The little room is stuffy, making it difficult for Lilly to breathe. She wants a cigarette but has not brought her pack of Tareytons. She pulls a tissue from the box beside Ben and touches it to her throat.

"Well, yeah, we had a little girl," he answers slowly. "But it was no kind of life for any of us. Me working and going to auditions all the time, and Catherine and the baby stuck in a dinky, little one-room apartment, which was all we could afford." His voice trails off, and he is quiet for a few seconds. "We had a little television set, and she sat all day watching shows like "*The Lone Ranger*" and "*Ozzie and Harriet.*" He laughs. "Can you imagine Catherine watching '*I Love Lucy*'?"

Lilly smiles and shakes her head. She remembers the

intense young girl who read the Beats and flaunted her rebellion for all the world to see. "What a disappointment New York must have been for her," she says.

"Anyway," Ben says, "after about a year she decided she'd had enough and took herself and Drema back home to California." His look makes Lilly wonder if he is trying to gauge her reaction. "She sent divorce papers six months later, and I signed them and sent them back." He's quiet for a minute, and Lilly wonders if there's more to tell. "I heard from her when the divorce was final, but I haven't seen her or the baby but once since they left."

Lilly clutches the note pad and pencil and stares at him. "Divorce." She whispers the word, tasting its strangeness on her tongue. She pauses, unsure of what to say next. She feels a slight shudder in the floor as if the old theater is moving, resettling itself into some secret new configuration. "And you've not even seen the baby but once in all that time?" she finally asks. "How could you stand it?"

"It was hard to let them go. And Catherine didn't really want to." Something in his answer confuses Lilly until she realizes that he has deftly sidestepped her question. He pauses, seeming to remember things he has not thought about in a long time. "She tried hard to make it work, I guess." He gives a brief little laugh. "'Course, she married somebody else last year." He stops and looks at Lilly as if convinced she'll understand what he's going to say next. "Anyway, you know I couldn't just up and leave New York with my career ready to take off."

The silence stretches to a minute, then two. Lilly closes the note pad and rises. It seems strange that there's not more to say.

"It's been good to see you, Ben —"

"Wait, Lilly." Ben stands, and Lilly is surprised that he doesn't seem as tall as he once did. A web of lines radiates from the corners of his eyes, reminding her of the laughter that used to light up his face. "You can't just walk away after all this time." He lifts his hand as if to touch her hair. "Let's go somewhere and talk."

Lilly is startled by the urgency in his voice.

"We can have a night cap and talk about old times," he smiles. He produces a room key from a pocket of his rumpled khaki pants. "My hotel is just around the corner."

"Oh, I don't think so, Ben," Lilly says. "I think we both know how our story ends." She reaches up and kisses him lightly on the lips. "Tomorrow's a busy day for me." She tucks her bag under her arm and takes her first deep breath since entering the room. "I'm going over to the University in the morning to check on a Master's degree program. And tomorrow night I'm meeting someone for a very special evening." She takes one last look into Ben's eyes. "I think I'm ready for something new in my life," she says. Somewhere down the hall, a door closes, and Lilly turns to go.

"Good luck with your audition, Ben," she says. "You'll make a good Willie Loman."

It is a quarter to seven in the evening, and Angela Adams is putting the finishing touches on her hair and makeup. She wants to look as nice as possible tonight. She picks up her black leather shoulder-strap bag and walks out of the front door of her small white bungalow, located just a block north of Parker Hall, where she will meet Sally Parsons, for the short walk to Creighton Hall, home of Bethany College's drama department.

A chilly breeze whips up an eddy of dead leaves along the sidewalk, and she pulls her beige woolen jacket more snugly around her. No telling who all will be there, she thinks. Rebecca's been here a long time. She allows her mind to drift back over the years, guiding it like she would a well-trained horse, reining it in to avoid one memory, letting it run hard at another.

A few steps further, and she stops in front of Parker Hall.

At the stone steps of the dormitory, polished and deeply grooved by ninety years of footsteps, the dean grasps the iron railing and climbs to the wide, chair-lined veranda which spans the front of the building. Even with strategically placed spotlights, the veranda has small pockets of shadow, and the low voices and laughter of the girl residents and their dates arise here and there.

Silence falls when the dean appears at the top of the steps. She does not pause on the porch, but goes to the heavy wooden door and lets herself in. The living room is bathed in light from the glass prisms of a large crystal chandelier. Couches and chairs form reading and conversation areas around the room. A piano on the left side of the room holds a bronze bust of Dr. Augustus Parker, the early benefactor for whom the building is named. A long-time professor of mathematics at Bethany, Dr. Parker left his considerable estate to the college at the time of his death.

Mom Parsons checks Dr. Parker each morning to remove a cigarette from his slightly parted lips or the occasional item of apparel that one of the girls' dates may have used to adorn him the night before. Hats and scarves are common, undergarments less so.

Angela waves to Sally from the doorway. She smiles, and deep dimples appear in her cheeks, reminding Angela, as always, of an elderly Shirley Temple.

Sally pushes herself up from a couch near the sign-out desk, where she has been waiting. A hint of Blue Grass cologne accompanies her movements.

"Hello, Angela," she says, pulling on an aqua gabardine jacket over a white silk blouse and navy-blue calf-length skirt. Short gray curls that normally frame her plump face have been pulled back and anchored with brown tortoise-shell combs. Her deeply set blue eyes, accented by rimless bifocals, shine in the blazing light.

"All set for Rebecca's bacchanal?" Sally asks.

She picks up an ebony cane with a gold-plated handle, a gift last year on her seventieth birthday from the girls in the dorm and turns toward the door. Only a slight limp remains as evidence of the hip replacement she underwent three months ago.

"All set, I guess," Angela says. She steps back and allows Sally to lead the way. "Have you seen Rebecca today?" At the top of the steps, she slides her hand under Sally's elbow, and they walk down together. "We were a little late getting home from the play last night, and I thought she'd probably be tired today."

"She wasn't in the cafeteria at lunch time," Sally answers.

She stumbles and catches herself as her cane tip hits a crack in the sidewalk. "She's probably just resting up for tonight."

Angela slows her pace for the older woman and looks across the campus to the lights of Creighton Hall. A row of shrubs in front of the building has been strung with hundreds of tiny white lights, and the walk leading up to it is lined with brown sacks that glow from within like captured fireflies. "It looks like they're all set up over there."

"So pretty," Sally says. "Rebecca will like that. By the way, how'd she like the play?"

"Well, she cried when she first saw Ben," Angela answers. "But she loved it. Said it was the best thing she'd ever seen him do." She sneezes and opens her purse to find a Kleenex. "She tried to send a note backstage to let him know she was there, but they wouldn't take it. Said it was against theater policy." She puts extra emphasis on the last two words and looks at Sally with a wry smile. "You can imagine how much she would've loved to see him."

They stop to let a car pass, then cross to the walk leading to Creighton Hall. The wind has picked up again, sending chilly gusts along the street. Angela dabs at her nose and replaces the Kleenex in her purse. She stops and looks up at the ten steps they must climb to get to the party.

"Shall we give it a try?" she asks, hooking her arm through Sally's.

Creighton Hall is one of the oldest buildings on campus. Its imposing columns inspire the same kind of awe that first-time visitors must feel for the Parthenon. The elegant, old oratorical societies had their beginnings here. Its halls have seen the plays, heard the orations and listened to the debates of generations of Bethany students. Tonight, it will witness the retirement party of Rebecca Riley, herself one of the most enduring institutions of the college.

Entering the large hall, Sally and Angela are dazzled by green and yellow streamers descending from an antique globe ceiling light and secured with white ribbons at various points along the walls. Guest tables are draped with white cloths and adorned with center pieces of yellow roses. They are invited to sign a guest book, presided over by a young member of the Harlequins Drama Club.

Rebecca is seated in a place of honor, designated for her by the Chairman of the Special Events Committee. Angela notices that they have placed Rebecca in a brand-new rocking chair that creaks with the slightest movement of her body and barely allows her feet to touch the floor.

"Hello, Rebecca," Angela says, "what are you doing in that god-awful chair?"

"Hello, girls." Rebecca's cheeks glow with small round spots of red, as though a painter has dabbed an identical circle on each.

She's nervous, Angela thinks. Or maybe she's been at the silver flask. The three women have been friends for so long they keep few secrets from each other.

Not that the little brandy flask has ever caused Rebecca a problem. The only evidence of her tippling has been slightly brighter eyes or a flushed neck, signs detectable only by Angela and Sally.

In troubled times, Rebecca has poured the three of them a thimbleful to ease their pain. In happy times, they have shared many a toast in celebration. But they all understand the unhappy consequences of disclosure of the practice, so it is never mentioned by any of them, even in their most private moments.

Angela glances at Sally, who has been standing quietly beside Rebecca's chair. "Can you move around, Rebecca, or are you stuck here for the duration?" Sally asks.

"I've got my orders to sit in this so-called place of honor," Rebecca laughs. "But I'm about ready to move." Her voice is soft and well-modulated, reflecting years of teaching students the elements of good diction and the subtle nuances of acting. Her fair skin, crisscrossed with fine blue veins, covers a delicate bone structure.

"Well, come on, then," Sally says, extending a white-gloved hand to Rebecca. With a slight heave, Rebecca escapes from the chair, landing on the floor between Angela and Sally, who tower over her. They each take an elbow and guide her toward the buffet table on the opposite side of the room.

"Let's get a cup of tea," Angela says, "and you can start mingling."

The buffet is laden with finger sandwiches, green vegetables with dip, and nuts in small colorful wax paper cups. A large, square white cake sits on a table beside the buffet. Outlined with green and yellow roses, the middle is inscribed, "Congratulations, Professor Riley." Beneath these words, more yellow frosting has been used to draw comic and tragic masks.

Beside the cake is a big cut-glass bowl filled with cranberry-orange punch. The bowl is always brought out for special events, then carefully cleaned, polished, and put away. No one knows for sure where the bowl came from, but tradition maintains that it was donated at the turn of the century by the notorious Madam Belle Breezing in honor of a professor who died while visiting her Lexington establishment.

People are coming into the room through a large door at the back. Angela notices that most of the older faculty are there and a few of the younger ones, especially some who have not yet achieved tenure. Tom Hawkins, a third-year English instructor, approaches Professor Simms, chairman of the Promotion and Tenure Committee. Although Angela can't catch all the words, she reads the body language: *Hello, Dr. Simms. I'm here. Remember that when I come up for tenure.*

She hides a smile behind her hand.

Some people spot the buffet table and go straight for it. Carrying plates of food, they look embarrassed when they see Rebecca, and search for a place to set the plate down so they can greet her. Rebecca stands as each one approaches, smiles graciously, and makes noncommittal comments to those she can't quite place. Old friends get a hug or a pat on the arm.

"Where have all the years gone?" some lament. Others assure her that she hasn't aged a bit since they last saw her twenty years ago. Her hand goes occasionally to her neck to finger a small pendant on a silver chain.

"A gift from one of my drama students several years ago," she says, in answer to a question from one of her well-wishers.

A young man and woman rush up to her. The woman grabs her hand and looks into her eyes. "Professor Riley," she begins, "I don't think you'll remember me, but I was in your Interpretation class and in some of your plays, and ..."

Professor Riley looks at the woman intently. "Why, Lilly Adkins, why on earth wouldn't I remember you?" She grabs Lilly's hand and looks at her again. "You're the young woman that wired the gymnasium wrong for the May Day festivities that time. Took a couple of our boys all night to fix it. The other students called you Miss GE for the rest of the semester." She pats Lilly's hand and laughs again. "Bet you didn't know I knew that did you?"

Rebecca turns to Angela and pulls her toward Lilly.

"Dean Adams, you remember Lilly Adkins, of course."

"Hello, Lilly," Angela says, "it would be hard to forget one of my best student assistants." She grasps Lilly's hand. "I remember the famous May Day caper, too." *It happened right after Ben and Catherine left*, Angela thinks. *You had a lot on your mind.* She smiles at Lilly. "You left a bunch of work undone in my office that week."

"How embarrassing that whole thing was," Lilly says. "I still don't like to think about it." She lifts a festive napkin off the buffet table and pretends to fan herself.

"Hello, Dean Adams, Professor Riley," Steve Warren greets the two women, and extending his hand to Rebecca, he says, "Congratulations on your retirement." Steve looks prosperous in a gray, Harris Tweed jacket and black wool trousers. "You may not remember me, Professor. I was more into debate than drama, but I certainly remember you."

"Of course, I remember." Rebecca takes his hand and squeezes it. "You and Lilly did us proud with all your forensic success."

She looks up at him through thick lens that magnify the faint blue circles under her eyes. "And I also know that you have a law office right here in town." She smiles slightly and taps him on the chest with her small black satin handbag. "Next time somebody threatens to sue me, I'll know where to come for advice."

Five years, and it still bothers her, Angela thinks. She seldom dwells on the traumatic chain of events that followed Catherine's untimely departure, but incidents like this one bring it back in full detail. The lawsuit by Catherine's family for the college's failure to protect the girl through *in loco parentis* had hit Rebecca harder than anyone.

As if anyone could have controlled Catherine. Angela's hand goes to her mouth as she realizes that she has almost spoken the words aloud.

A slight palsy shakes Rebecca's hand as she replaces her handbag on the table. The red in her cheeks has faded to a grayish pallor.

The room falls silent as someone enters the hall through the back door. As though drawn by a magnetic source, all faces turn toward the newcomer. Dressed in a navy-blue blazer, a red and blue striped tie, and sharply creased khaki trousers, Ben Stevens strides toward Professor Riley. He spots the centerpieces on the tables and grabs a yellow rose. The other guests step aside as he moves forward. A few seem to recognize him and whisper to those near them. Others merely sense a strange new presence.

Like the parting of the Red Sea, Angela thinks. She edges to a spot directly behind Rebecca. With Sally, Lilly, and Steve, the four form a motionless tableau in the midst of the whispering crowd.

Ben's hands are outstretched, and his smile glows. In the subdued light, he looks no older than he did the day five years ago when he and Catherine left the campus for good.

Rebecca looks up as he approaches. Her body sways and Angela reaches out to steady her. Beside her, Angela feels Lilly Adkins stiffen and hears her sharp intake of breath.

"Ben," Rebecca says, "I thought you'd probably gone on to

Knoxville for your next performance." Although Angela can't see her face, she hears tears in Rebecca's voice. "Why are you here?"

Ben reaches out and takes both of Rebecca's hands, holding them together against his chest. He makes an exaggerated bow and places the rose in her hand. His deep blue eyes, lacking only a little of their earlier luster, are fixed intently on Rebecca's face.

"Why, Professor Riley," he says, "did you think for one minute that I would be this close and not come to your retirement party?" He laughs. "Besides, when your role in the play is as important as mine, you have an understudy. He's filling in for me tonight."

Rebecca stands very still.

"Hey," he says, noticing the pendant at her throat. "You're wearing the little praying mantis I gave you when we finished *Tartuffe*."

"Yes," Rebecca smiles and touches the tiny pendant. "It's always been a particular favorite of mine. By the way," she says, "I saw your performance last night."

Angela hears more strength in her friend's voice as though she has received an invisible shot of adrenalin.

"Your pacing was good, but I thought your projection could have been more forceful at times." She pulls her hands free and reaches high to place one on each of Ben's shoulders. "You must always make your audience believe your character means what he says." She flicks an imaginary piece of lint off his collar. "I didn't always believe yours last night."

Angela can't take her eyes off Ben. His hearty smile has become a mask. Surprise and uncertainty shadow his face.

"You honestly thought I didn't project well?" he finally asks. His voice has lost the bravado it had held when he entered the room.

"I didn't exactly say that," Rebecca says. "You did well most of the time."

She pauses as if trying to make sure her next remark will be phrased exactly as she wants it to be. "Just think back, Ben. Remember your intensity in *Job*? And how every single soul in the audience believed you were a total hypocrite in *Tartuffe*? She smiles and squeezes his shoulders.

"That's the kind of performance you always want to give."

Ben reaches up and takes Professor Riley's hands in his own. Angela sees that he is using them to push away from her.

"Congratulations on your retirement," he says, "and thanks for your review of my performance. You always were my biggest fan and severest critic."

He pauses and takes a deep breath. Angela senses that he has somehow regained some of his old confidence. Either that she thinks, or he's putting on the best performance of his life.

"Not to mention the best coach an actor could ever want," he says, hugging her lightly.

"I'd better be going. Got to drive to Knoxville to rejoin the company. Tomorrow night we play Atlanta."

Beside her Angela hears Lilly Adkins whisper, "Break a leg, Ben."

An hour later, Angela, Sally and Rebecca leave the party in the hands of the clean-up crew and the few remaining guests still talking in groups of twos and threes.

A cool wind sweeps across the concrete steps as they start back to Parker Hall. Angela walks between the two older women, an arm hooked through each of theirs. They walk slowly, careful not to trip over a fallen limb or stray rock.

"Well, Rebecca, I thought it was a very nice party," Angela says. "Can you imagine Ben Stevens taking a night off from his play to come back to see you?"

When Rebecca doesn't answer, Sally chimes in. "And why in the world wouldn't he?" she asks. "Rebecca taught him everything he knows about acting."

They continue in silence a few minutes longer. Across the campus on the porch of Linus Hall, a group of students are broiling hamburgers on an outdoor grill. The aroma carries on the wind.

"You just never know, do you?" Rebecca says. "You try to give them all you have and hope that somehow it'll see them through." She sighs and looks back as if trying to call up an image of a faraway time and place. "Sometimes it takes, and sometimes it doesn't."

The three women have reached the steps of Parker Hall and start up toward the door.

"Shall we go inside and rest a little while until you all have to go on home?" Sally asks.

Inside, they sit on the antique needlepoint chairs in Sally Parsons' apartment. A subtle floral fragrance hangs in the air as if someone has shaken a can of talcum powder over everything. Outside the chintz-curtained windows, a cloud passes over the moon.

"I'll make us a cup of tea, Sally says, picking up three hand-painted bone china cups from a collection on her windowsill, gifts from her girls over the many years that she has been the dorm mother. When it has brewed she pours steaming tea into each cup and sits down.

Without a word Rebecca pulls a little silver brandy flask from a deep pocket in her black cashmere evening coat and pours a jigger into each cup.

"Here's to retirement," says Angela, and the three of them drink quietly.

"Another?" asks Sally, refilling their cups with the steaming tea.

Rebecca replenishes their brandy.

"Here's to Rebecca," says Sally.

"Here's to Ben," says Rebecca.

"I thought you loved Ben's performance last night," Angela says.

"Oh, yes," Rebecca answers, taking another sip. "Without a doubt, his best ever."

"Then why?"

"The gods don't smile upon hubris," she says.

Quiet laughter, like an early spring breeze fills the room as the three lift their cups in silent salute.

Topsy

Wilma sat in a rickety old wooden rocker by the window, listening to its rhythmic *skreek, skreek, skreek* as she moved back and forth. Sounds like the rocker Lilly and I used to play going to school in, she thought, when she was five and I was nine. Just the two of us, teacher and student, us against the world.

Rain trickled down the windowpane, distorting trees, houses, cars, and the few people who had ventured outside. Wilma held a cigarette in her fingers and let the ash grow until it burned them. Not because she wanted to hurt herself. She didn't. But because memories sometimes made her forget her presence in the here and now. She crushed out the stub and dropped it into an overflowing ashtray.

A child walked by on the street below her window. A black child, a little girl holding a carefully wrapped doll in her arms. A soggy gray kitten, ears and tail drooping, crossed the sidewalk. The child stopped and watched it. A young woman, a few steps ahead of the child, paused and shifted two grocery sacks on her hips. She turned and spoke to the child. Although the wind and rain muffled the sound of the woman's voice, her expression reflected an impatience born of worry and fatigue.

I know where you're coming from, lady, Wilma thought. Hang in there. Been there, done that. You got lotsa company. Some a lot younger and worse off than you. This too shall pass away. We don't know what's in store for us, and if we did know it'd probably drive us crazy.

Wilma's eyes returned to the child, who had pulled the doll even closer. Topsy, she thought. That doll's name might be Topsy. Memories flooded Wilma's mind of the Christmas morning years ago when Santa had left Lilly a black doll under the tree. Daddy had bought it at the neighborhood grocery store. He'd had to wait until Christmas Eve to shop after he'd sold his share of the tobacco crop at the warehouse in Lancaster.

Mama'd been angry when she saw it.

"Why'd he get her a doll like that?" she asked Wilma, after he'd gone to the barn to milk.

"Daddy said it was the only one they had left."

Wilma had carried a blue pottery bowl to the back of the stove. She took the top off a gray kettle, poured thick brown soup beans from it into the bowl and set it on the table.

"Besides, Lilly loves it just the same as if it was white." She set a milk pitcher beside the beans and got glasses out of the kitchen cabinet.

Mama wasn't a bigot, she thought. It was just that there was such a sharp dividing line back then. She and Aunt Belle were about as close as blood kin.

"I told Lilly about a little slave girl named Topsy in *Uncle Tom s Cabin* and that's why she named it that."

Lilly had carried Topsy everywhere.

We made clothes for it out of old scraps of feedsacks. Made us a playhouse under that big old maple tree. It's gone now. Lightning struck it right after I left home and burned it to the ground. Shame. We had a lot of fun under that old tree.

I'd always be the big sister and Lilly'd be Topsy's mother. So ironic, the way things turned out. Lilly wanting to be the mother. Billy took care of that little detail when I was sixteen. Let me show you around the church. My daddy won't care. He's the preacher. Come on over here and lay down by me on these choir robes.

Sometimes, all these years later, she thought she could still feel his warm breath on her neck. Hear his ragged breathing that she took to be a sign of his love for her, as strong as hers for him. Billy'd go on to college and be a preacher, like his daddy; she'd be a perfect wife, and they'd live happily ever after.

Idiotic me, little Hester Prynne. Everything but a big letter A.

Wilma's laugh dissolved into a coughing spell. She pulled her sweater closer around her. The sight of the rain raised chill bumps on her arms. She glanced at the clock and back to the scene outside her window. The wind was stronger now. Leaves were blowing wildly on their branches. Some hit the window, making little whipping sounds, like the sting of a switch on bare skin. Oh, lift me as a wave, a leaf a cloud. I fall upon the thorns of life. I bleed.

I dread to go out in that, she thought. Would anybody even care if I didn't show up? Probably not. Only if I didn't keep the appointment. Not because they care about me. Because of the money. Got to fill up the time. If I'm not there somebody else needs to be. Money makes the world go round. First chemo, then radiation, the doctor had said. Or was it the other way around?

Swing Low, Sweet Chariot, comin' for to carry me . . . She hummed a little snatch of the old song before her mind wandered back to Lilly and Topsy.

One night after supper Lilly'd been playing with Topsy in the kitchen. Mama and Daddy were sitting by the Warm Morning stove in the front room. Daddy was always tired after the long days in the fields, walking behind a plow, cutting tobacco, and spearing it onto sharp sticks, doing any one of a thousand other year-round tasks. So, bedtime came early. Sometimes it would still be light outside.

Wilma remembered how restless she'd been at those times. How she'd look out the window and see cows and horses, even people still moving about. She and Lilly didn't talk much then. They knew better than to keep Daddy awake. Sometimes Wilma read before it got too dark to see.

Titles of some of her favorite books floated up. *The Sword in the Mountains*, about the Civil War, snippets from *Silas Marner* and *Les Miserables* in her third-grade reader. Even that old, ragged copy of *The Complete Works of Shakespeare* that Sarah Taylor had given her once for hoeing out the garden. She read them all to Lilly, all the way through.

Stories and characters like Eppie and Cosette, Ophelia and Iago skittered through her mind like mice playing in the corners.

Lilly had come into their room that night and crawled up on

the bed beside Wilma. She usually pulled up the covers and tucked her doll in beside her, but tonight she was alone.

"Where's Topsy?" Wilma had asked.

"She was cold, so I found her a good place to sleep," Lilly answered.

I guess I was so anxious to get back to my book, I didn't think to ask her where she'd put Topsy, Wilma thought. She pulled a tissue out of a box on the table beside her and held it to her mouth, coughing into it, trying to catch her breath. I've got to cut back on this smoking, she thought. Seems pretty silly to try to stop now, though.

The clinic doctor had seemed distracted when he told her to stop smoking. Maybe it was the room full of patients waiting in line to see him. It's a free clinic.

"The damage is already done," he had said, not pulling any punches. "But it might make your breathing a little easier when we start the treatments."

The time for getting up in the morning back in their childhood was as early as bedtime the night before. When it was cold and dark outside, Wilma had hated leaving the warm covers to go into the kitchen for breakfast.

She shivered at the thought of it, even after all these years, and pulled her sweater sleeves down over her hands. The heat in her third-floor walkup was never quite warm enough in winter, and in summer she roasted. Chicago was as cold as a witch's tit, but this apartment was what she could afford on her waitress pay, and anyway, she was used to it.

Why'd I ever come to Chicago in the first place? She wondered.

Because of Allen, of course. Said he had a good job up here and we'd make it just fine. How could I resist that coal-black hair and those icy blue eyes? You'd think I would have learned after Billy. I guess I just kept looking for love in all the wrong places. Maybe I was just born under a dark star. Or maybe not. "The fault, something, something, is not in our stars, but in ourselves, something, something . . .”

You had an answer for everything, didn’t you, Mr. Will?

When Allen pulled out after a year, he’d taken a piece of her soul with him. Along with what little savings she had. Even the little gold locket with their pictures Lilly’d given her when she left home. Thieving bastard.

Mama’s screams before daylight had terrified Wilma and Lilly. “John, John, come in here!” The panic in her voice made her words hard to understand. “They’s a rat that’s crawled up in the oven and burned up, and I can’t get it out.” The rest was lost in her screams.

Wilma and Lilly were right behind Daddy as they all ran for the kitchen. There was Mama on the floor in front of the stove, waving a dish towel, trying to dispel the thick black smoke pouring out of the oven.

“Get it out before it sets the house on fire,” Mama yelled.

Grabbing the towel, Daddy dropped to the floor, opened the oven door and stuck his hand inside. He slung a black smoky thing across the room. It landed on a chair beside the back door.

The instant she saw it, Lilly recognized Topsy. She ran to the chair and tried to lift her doll, but the melting rubber and hot singed hair made it impossible. She fell down in front of the chair and tried to get her arms around it. “Topsy’s burnt up, she’s all burnt up,” Lilly sobbed, over and over, until all she could manage were gasps and hiccups.

I wonder how much of that day Lilly remembers, Wilma thought.

She pictured Lilly now, all grown up, teaching at Bethany, back home in Kentucky. Literature, of course. What else? Neither one of us could ever get enough of books. Still can’t. They help me endure life’s slings and arrows. God knows I’ve had my share. I’ve never even got to see Lilly teach. Oh, how I’d like to. I’ll go see her sometime. Maybe next spring. Maybe when the leaves come out and the wildflowers bloom. That's when I'll go.

Her finger felt the sting of a burn. She stuck it into her mouth to cool it. How did that cigarette get in my hand, she wondered. I don't remember lighting it.

She glanced at the clock. Two-thirty. Her appointment was at four. How was it that every day just seemed to slide into the next with her barely noticing? She walked to the kitchenette and found the cup she'd drunk from the night before. She rinsed it out and poured in two fingers of Southern Comfort from the half-empty bottle on the counter. Mary Kate sent her a bottle every so often. The Liquor Locker she managed in Lexington gave her good discounts. She smiled at the thought of her bright, overly serious, hard-working daughter. She must've got whatever little bit of good was in Billy and me. Good thing she dodged the bad.

I can just hear her now: Mama, you drink this up too quick. Just sip along on it slow, and I'll send you some more the next time it goes on sale.

Wilma loved her daughter, but they weren't close. Distance separated them more than a lack of love. Billy had never acknowledged her, and Wilma'd had to raise her as best she could. She had been little more than a baby herself at the time. Maybe she could have done a better job, but she didn't know how. She'd managed to get Kate through high school and two years of business at the community college. Enough to fit her for a decent job.

Poor Billy, she thought. Being a preacher might have been a worse fate for him than mine was for me. His big dream was to travel and see the world. Instead, he'd had to settle for being a small-time country preacher, his every move seen and judged by the flock, not to mention his devout wife.

Oh, Billy, Billy.

She carried the glass back to the window and sat down. She sipped the sweet liqueur and let her mind drift back to the day Topsy had burned. Seeing Lilly's grief had made her search her mind for a solution. The answer came like a flash of lightning. She ran to Lilly and put her arms around her.

"I know what let's do, Lilly," she said. "Let's bury her. Let's give her a real nice funeral."

It took me a while to convince her but after a while she gave in. Me being a right smart older, she'd usually follow my lead. 'Course, that wasn't always a good thing. I could think up some pretty mean things for us to do. Poor old Uncle Duke had to go hungry more than once when we stole his lunch out of the barn loft.

Wilma had made a dress for Topsy out of white tissue paper, and they'd fashioned a coffin out of an old shoebox from the back of their closet.

"Don't she look pretty, Lilly?" Wilma said. "Let's take her down in the field and put her under that tree where the violets come up every spring." They'd dug a hole under the bare branches of the walnut tree down in the pasture. The sun was shining, and the air had a certain warmth to it, like the promise of an early spring. Cows in the next field eyed them curiously, but soon lost interest and turned back to their grazing.

They sang a few lines of "Shall We Gather at the River," and Wilma talked about what a good doll Topsy had been before her unfortunate accident. About how much Lilly loved her and how much she'd be missed.

Finally, the time came to place Topsy in her grave. Until then Lilly had done well with the ceremony. But when she saw Wilma lowering the covered shoebox into the hole, her crying came back louder than ever.

I couldn't think what to say to her, Wilma thought, but then I remembered the violets.

"Don't cry, Lilly," she'd said. She put her arms around Lilly and held her close. "Topsy's not gone." Her voice was soft, like a lullaby. "Next spring she'll come back as beautiful purple violets, right here under this tree. When you see the flowers, you'll know it's her."

The words had an almost magical effect on Lilly. Her crying stopped.

"I'll come back to see her every year," she said.

Their contact was much less frequent now than it had been in those early years. Now they sent cards on birthdays and at Christmas, always enclosing short notes. Most of Lilly's ended with "I'm going to visit our tree again soon."

It was like a pledge between them. Wilma looked at the clock. Four fifteen. Time to go. She was weaker now, and it was harder to make the trip. She had taken to using a cane, and that steadied her. She put on her coat and a plastic rain hat and closed the door behind her.

That's when I'll go see her, she thought. Next spring when the violets bloom.

Summons to Chicago

The call had come three days ago, from an unknown doctor in a hospital in Chicago. It was neither expected, nor unexpected. All her life she'd heard people say of death, "You're never really ready for something like this. It's always hard." She'd never fully understood the meaning of those words, until now.

Lilly walked down the hall to Steve's office. Her face told him the story.

"So, she's gone," he said. He stood up and gathered Lilly into his arms. "I'm so sorry," he whispered. "Have you contacted Mary Kate?"

"No, but I'm pretty sure she won't be able to go with us." She let Steve help her into a chair usually reserved for students before he sat back down. "She gets only two weeks off for vacation, and she took them last month."

"But wouldn't they let her off for her own mother's funeral arrangements?"

"Probably, but you know how bad the job situation is now. They might use it as an excuse to let her go if their business falls off."

"Not likely," Steve said. "People seem to drink more when times are hard." He put his arm around her shoulder. "Let's go talk to the dean."

Fifteen years ago, Steve had decided to leave his law practice and join Lilly in academia. He'd never been sorry. It didn't take him long to prefer the classroom to the courtroom. As members of the faculty of the local UK Community College, they and their two children had become fixtures in the community.

Lilly wiped her eyes and replaced the Kleenex in her jacket pocket as they headed to the Administration Building.

Outside the Sword Building, where most of the faculty offices were located, spring had brought new life to the campus. Forsythia and daffodils lent bright yellow touches to bare branches and clumps of dry grass. Students moved in twos and threes on walkways between buildings or sat on scattered concrete benches where some studied their open textbooks while others chatted with fellow students. All seemed to luxuriate in the warm afternoon sun. Lilly imagined she could hear them purring like contented cats.

It was raining the morning they headed for the airport and still very dark. The two-hour ride down the Mountain Parkway had been quiet. Neither of them felt like talking. When they reached Lexington, they looked out their windows at the darkened store fronts as drops of rain cast distorted reflections on the glass. The few people stirring hurried along the sidewalks with umbrellas clutched in front of them like weapons against the piercing raindrops.

"Are you all right?" Steve asked.

"More or less," Lilly answered. "Or maybe all right wouldn't be quite the word. I'm just trying to hold myself together." She reached for his hand in the darkness. "I owe everything to her, you know."

Steve squeezed her hand and didn't intrude upon her silence again until they reached the airport.

They boarded the plane and located their seats in the economy section over the wing, near the back. In a few minutes, they lifted off in a soggy, overcast haze. The tears, never far from the surface since she'd learned of Wilma's illness a short five months ago, welled up again.

By the time the plane had reached cruising level, her eyes were tightly shut against the reality of what awaited her in Chicago. A few minutes later she became aware that Steve was speaking. "Lilly," he said, squeezing her hand, "come on, baby, open your eyes."

They were bathed in a world of sunshine, high above a blanket of billowy white clouds. At first it was hard for her to grasp the change. The transformation from chill to warmth, from dark to light, from despair to elation was too ironic to absorb.

"You look like you've just had a reprieve," Steve said.

"Wilma would have called it an epiphany," she whispered. "Reprieve would've been too lame for her."

Lilly's gloom lifted, replaced by an incredible lightness that seemed to carry her from the confines of the plane to a luxurious cloud floating in the distance, one which Wilma would doubtless have chosen to rest upon. "How she would have loved this," Lilly said. She put her head on Steve's shoulder, prepared to sleep until they reached O'Hare.

The Peaceful Rest Funeral Home was a dark old stone structure, set back on a spacious lawn from the din of traffic in the busy street. Inside, there was a quiet that seemed to defy any threat to the building's determined tranquility.

A small, slightly stooped man appeared as soon as they opened the heavy, wooden beveled glass door. He reached for Lilly's hand and grasped Steve's shoulder.

"You must be the Warrens, Ms. Adkins' sister and brother-in- law?" he asked. His somber voice echoed through the spacious hallway.

"Why, yes," Lilly said. "We want to arrange to have my sister's body sent back to our home in Kentucky."

"Of course," the man answered. He hesitated and rubbed his scrubbed dry hands together. Lilly imagined that she could hear a rustle like cornstalks.

"And how did you wish to pay for these arrangements?"

Lilly opened her mouth to answer, but nothing came out.

Steve answered for her.

"My sister-in-law had a burial policy. Lilly and I intend to claim it for her and pay any debts she may have incurred before we leave Chicago." His tone was cold. "Yours, sir, will certainly be at the top of our list."

Crab-like, the little man sidestepped as though trying to crawl into a protective shell. "Certainly, Mr. Warren," he whispered. "Everything will be taken care of."

As an apparent afterthought, he added, "We're sorry for your loss."

They got out of their cab in front of a dingy, old brownstone building where Wilma had lived for the last six years of her life. It was located in one of the many neighborhoods that made up Chicago. There were several small shops and restaurants along the street, mom and pop establishments, whose names reflected an ethnic preponderance of Italian and Greek. Looking at them, Lilly remembered the many such Lexington restaurants where Wilma had worked when she first left home.

She was so young and pretty, Lilly thought. No wonder so many of the owners wanted to take her into their own homes and shelter her, offering her room and board while she worked for them.

She remembered the times when Wilma would take her to the restaurants and give her foods that she had never tasted before. Things like thick creamy pimento cheese and lemon icebox pie made with sweetened condensed milk. Memories that still made her mouth water.

Steve had been watching her as they stood in front of the apartment building. He touched her elbow. "Why don't we go on inside and look for the manager? We still have to go through her things and decide what to do with them."

Lilly forced herself to return to the here and now. She put aside the memories that had flooded her constantly since the arrival of the call and allowed Steve to guide her up the five steps to the front door. He knocked, and after a few minutes, the door opened.

An elderly woman stood there, wiping her hands on a green linen dishtowel. Her wispy white hair had been gathered into a small bun and secured with tortoise shell pins to the top of her head. She was smiling, and the corners of her eyes and the bridge of her nose crinkled as though drawn together by a single invisible thread. She pushed the towel into the pocket of a starched apron, printed all over with vines and violets.

"Hello," she said. "What can I do for you?"

"Hello," Steve responded, extending his hand, as she

offered hers. "I'm Steve Warren, and this is my wife, Lilly. Wilma Adkins was my wife's sister. We've come to see about her things."

"I've been expecting you. Come on in. I'm Sophie Kindal. Been manager here for thirty-five years."

She led them past a staircase to a tiny sitting room beside the foyer. "Sit down a minute. Then I'll show you upstairs to where Wilma lived." She pointed to a floral chintz teapot. "I was just about to have a cup of tea. I know you're in a hurry, but won't you have a cup with me?"

Nothing had sounded so good to Lilly since she and Steve had left home that morning. "Why, that would be lovely," she said.

Steve squeezed her hand when Sophie left the room to get the cups. "This place is a lot more welcoming than the funeral home, isn't it?" he whispered.

"Isn't it, though?" she said. Lilly put her head back on the velour sofa and might have gone to sleep if not for Sophie's returning footsteps.

"You don't need to worry about Wilma, you know," she said, placing tiny bone china cups, saucers and napkins in front of them. "She was mighty sick toward the end, but she was never no trouble to anybody." Sophie poured the tea and offered them sugar and cream. "Took care of her own problems, paid her rent on time, and you never heard a sound out of her once she got in her apartment and closed the door."

The building was very quiet as they sipped their tea, and Sophie told them things about Wilma.

"She had a boyfriend a long time back, right after she got here, I think it was." She spoke in a quiet, musing, almost hypnotic voice. "Seemed crazy about him. But he went away after a while, and I never did see her take up with anybody else. Her voice trailed off, remembering. "There was something special about Wilma. Everybody loved her. She smoked too much, though. Drank a little, too. There's a bar down the street about a block away, and she used to go down there two or three times a week. She had some mighty good friends there. When she got so sick toward the end, several of them drove her to and from her radiation treatments."

Lilly listened intently, as though Sophie were sending her a lifeline.

"Death was a blessing for her, though. I don't think she suffered a minute."

"Myocardial infarction," Lilly whispered.

"Yes," Sophie said. "Lung cancer, diabetes, smoking, hard work. My God, she was a worker. Went to that restaurant every day till she just couldn't go anymore."

Sophie looked intently at Lilly. "Her heart just finally gave up. I'll tell you one thing, though. And I'm pretty sure you already know it. She loved you more than anything else in the world. You were about all she talked about. Said she was going to see you soon." Lilly stood up and felt herself sway. Steve reached out to steady her.

"Mrs. Kindal," he said, "your hospitality has been wonderful, and we appreciate it more than you know. But could we please go up to Wilma's apartment and sort through her things? Our plane back to Kentucky leaves tomorrow, and we still have a few more arrangements to take care of."

"Of course," Sophie said. "Let me give you the key. Take all the time you need."

"We'll be taking a few small things as keepsakes for Wilma's loved ones back home," Steve said. "Will you be kind enough to donate her other things to Goodwill or do whatever else you think would be appropriate?"

As Lilly and Steve climbed the stairs to Wilma's apartment, they slowed down to catch their breath. "Can you imagine that she had to walk up and down these three flights every time she went out?" Lilly said.

Her chest ached from the steep climb and from the dread of what they might find behind the brown oak door. Her hand felt cold in Steve's, and she sensed his gentle pressure, urging her on.

He took the key from his pocket and unlocked the door.

The quiet inside Wilma's apartment was absolute. Lilly had the impression that the place was wrapped in gauze, where neither light nor sound could penetrate. A faint odor of lemon and Pinesol hung over the room, reminding Lilly of the fastidious attention Wilma gave to housekeeping.

Steve found a switch just inside the door and turned on the overhead light. Not a speck of dust or clutter to be seen.

"She must have done all this just before the attack," Lilly whispered. "Do you suppose she knew?"

"Maybe," Steve said.

They walked slowly around the room looking in a drawer here, a closet there. On the dresser in Wilma's bedroom Lilly found an Omega wristwatch. "I'll take this back to Mary Kate," she said.

In the tiny kitchenette she found a figurine of two little girls, one reading to the other. "This is for me," she said.

In the top drawer of a small desk, she found a letter addressed to herself. A stamp had been pasted on the upper right-hand corner of the envelope. She carried the letter into the living room where Steve sat on the couch, thumbing through a stack of *Good Old Days* magazines.

"Can you open this and read it to me? Lilly asked. "There's no way I can do it."

Steve took the envelope, turning it over twice and looking at it before tearing it open.

"I'm coming to see you this spring," he read, "in just a few weeks from now, when the radiation is finished. Let's go visit our tree and see if the violets are up."

Lilly sank into Steve's lap and cried for a long time. "They'll be up," she whispered. "I'll see you and Topsy there."

Epiphanies

Lilly and Callie gazed through the window at the beautiful English countryside as their tour bus wound through the Cotswolds. Its rolling green hills and tiny villages reminded them of poems like Gray's "Elegy Written in a Country Churchyard," and any number of pastoral poems by Keats and Shelley. Lilly turned to Callie and whispered, "The curfew tolls the knell of parting day,"

"The lowing herd winds slowly o'er the lea," Callie added.

"The plowman homeward plods his weary way," said Lilly.

And in unison with mock solemnity, they said, "And leaves the world to darkness and to me."

"By George," said Callie. "I think we've still got it." The two women had taught English literature together for twenty years, sometimes dreaming of the day when they could retire and visit the British Isles, but never quite believing it would happen.

Lilly's husband, Steve, a retired psychology professor, sat in the seat directly behind them. He leaned forward and laughed. "Listening to you two makes me almost homesick for the classroom. Almost," he added, "but not quite." He had loved teaching, but, as he sometimes remarked, "After about a week out of the classroom, I discovered that I was a confirmed expert on the subject of retirement." The freedom from committees, class schedules and school politics was a more than satisfactory trade off.

Steve turned back to his seatmate, Samantha, a woman from Cincinnati who called herself "Sam." She was traveling with her twenty-something daughters, Maxie and Flora, who related to the tour with a mixture of boredom and exasperation at the shortage of young men their age on the trip. They took some consolation in the fact that they had a full three weeks away from their tedious stenographic jobs.

"Guess you have to take the bitter with the sweet," Maxie had said during the get-acquainted party in London. "Maybe we'll at least see what cool people wear over here and pick up some new ideas about hair and makeup." She touched her own highlighted brown locks that looked like strips of yarn in the dim light of the hotel meeting room. Her sweeping glance at the other tourists, most of whom were middle-aged or older, conveyed the doubt of such a positive outcome.

Their mother, on the other hand, found much to marvel at.

"Look over there at those quaint little houses," she said, nudging Steve's arm. "Wonder how they even find room to turn around, especially if they have kids." She looked across the aisle at her daughters, dozing in the warm afternoon sun. She lowered her voice a little, but her comments still carried throughout the bus. "I'll have to say I'm glad we're more prosperous in our country."

Steve acknowledged Sam's remark with a small nod. He would have preferred to gaze out the window and think his own thoughts. Or, better still, to open the book he had started that morning, on English cathedrals. He had enjoyed *Pillars of the Earth*, a novel about the building of a medieval cathedral, and this new book promised to be a good follow up, especially here in the British Isles, where castles and cathedrals dotted the landscape. As he was reaching for the book in his backpack, Sam spoke again. Steve gave up the idea of reading.

"You know, we're real lucky to be from the good old USA," she said. "Sometimes you have to leave it to appreciate it." She paused as if to consider this insight for a few seconds. "You take me and Melvin, for instance," she continued. "Some might wonder how me and my girls could afford to take this expensive trip, but there again you've got an example of the American dream. Now me and Melvin loved kids, and in our thirty-five years together before he passed away, the two of us took in over two hundred foster children. We'd have 'em for a while and then they'd age out or be adopted. I can't even remember most of their names anymore." She was quiet for a moment.

Steve looked hopefully at her closed eyes, which suddenly

reopened as if on a spring.

"But you know what?" she asked. "That's exactly where the American dream comes in. For every one of those young'uns we took pity on, the government gave us a check. Of course, we always saved some for a rainy day. What a wonderful country!

There were twenty-five travelers on the Pilgrims' Choice Tour from several states and countries. Lilly and Callie had laughed at the title of the company.

"Wouldn't Chaucer love this?" said Callie.

"Guess I get to be the Wyf of Bath," Lilly mused. "The only thing is, I'd hate to be gap-toothed."

"And what about all those marital misadventures she had," Callie asked. "Wouldn't you be mortified about those?"

"Au contraire," Lilly laughed. "She probably enjoyed those."

"Well, I refuse to be the nun," Callie answered. "Where's the fun in that?"

Steve, though not as well versed in The Canterbury Tales, wanted in on the banter. "Well, who do I get to be?" he asked. "Is there a part for a somewhat studious ex-professor type?"

"Of course," laughed Callie. "You can be the Knight. Just don't get too chivalrous on us," she giggled. Most of their fellow tourists were friendly and outgoing, fascinated with promised sights listed in the Pilgrims' Choice Catalog and anxious to have pictures to take home to show friends and family. They took the opportunity to be snapped in front of every famous landmark they'd ever heard of.

One couple came from Canada. They were middle aged, a well-dressed, quiet pair, whose slightly standoffish air made the other tourists shy away from them.

"John and Penny Cavanaugh," the woman had said when they were asked to introduce themselves on get-acquainted night.

"From Quebec, Canada," the man had added, as though, Lilly thought, he only wanted to have something to say.

Lilly, Steve, and Callie wondered about the chilly response of the couple to any overtures of friendliness. Furthermore, there appeared to be a distance between the two of them, as though they occupied different worlds.

"Why on earth would a couple like that join a tour?" Callie said. "If they wanted to be alone, looks like they'd have been better off to stay home, unless they wanted to hide in a crowd."

Lilly laughed. "Isn't it ironic," she said. "Sometimes the more you try to hide, the more visible you become."

"Ladies and gentlemen," came the voice of Dave, the pudgy, somewhat apoplectic tour guide. "We will be stopping soon for the evening. We will spend the night in Pembrokeshire, and tomorrow we will board the ferry to cross the Irish Sea. Remember to put your luggage out beside your bedroom door tonight so that it can be carried onto the ferry in the morning. A dark flush deepened as he spoke. "And always remember the importance of being on time. You must not make your fellow travelers wait."

The bus pulled to a stop in front of the hotel where they would have dinner and spend the night. Lilly and Callie got off and waited for Steve to join them.

"I guess you all heard what the man said," Steve grinned. "We must not keep our fellow travelers waiting."

Their trouble with Dave had started on the first day of the tour. Callie had left her camera beside one of the tall stone pillars at Stonehenge. The tour bus was parked within a few hundred yards of the ancient landmark, and Lilly volunteered to run back to see if the camera was still lying where Callie had left it. Not surprisingly, it was no longer anywhere to be seen. Lilly spent little time searching for it and hurried back. But before she had covered the short distance, she could see Dave waiting for her outside the bus. His face was the bright red color of a stove-top burner turned to "high." Lilly had the fleeting impression that if she accidentally touched it, her finger would be burned.

"Madam," Dave began. "You must remember that this bus follows a very tight schedule. Whenever, by being late, you impede the progress of the tour, you inconvenience all of your fellow travelers." He paused to catch his breath and his voice was now almost a squeak. "This must not happen again." He gave a short wave to the bus driver, who was obviously waiting for Dave's signal to reopen the door.

Lilly was too mortified to try to explain or apologize. Her entrance into the bus was met with a few claps and giggles from the other tourists. Spotting Steve and Callie, she slid into the seat behind them.

"What in the hell was that all about?" Steve asked.

"What a dictator," Callie said.

"We may be in for a very interesting tour," Lilly said, when she was able to find her voice.

When the three of them went out to the bus the next morning, the sky was gray and overcast. They had come to realize in the short time they had been in England that many of the days began this way. But none of the three was particularly bothered by the weather. They had looked forward to this trip for so long that the thrill of finally being here took precedence over everything else.

"I'm going back inside to get some hot coffee and a scone to take on the bus," Callie said.

Steve put his arm around Lilly's shoulders, and the two of them walked to a wooden stand from which to view the slate-gray waves of the Irish Sea. Lilly pulled her jacket more closely around her, as a shiver ran down her spine. She sensed that someone had come up behind them.

She and Steve turned and found John and Penny standing nearby. The strange couple seemed not to see them. Lilly noticed a large diamond ring on Penny's finger and a fine wool cape around her shoulders. A small alligator bag hung on her arm, like a kitten waiting to be stroked. The mixed metaphor tickled Lilly, and she felt her "grammar girdle" pinch. You've been an English teacher too long, she thought.

"Good morning," Steve said. "Looks like we might have a rainy crossing today."

"Yes," said John. He turned away as if discouraging further

conversation.

Penny looked toward them with a vague smile, as though just then realizing she was not alone. She was a pretty woman in a pale sort of way, her hair and makeup carefully arranged and applied. Something about her reminded Lilly of a knight in a suit of armor - a layer of protection between herself and the world. A female knight, Lilly thought, amused at her own imagination. Maybe Joan of Arc.

"Are you all enjoying the tour so far?" Lilly knew how inane the question sounded, but she couldn't think of anything better. To cover her embarrassment, she added, "This is our first trip out of the states, and we're trying to take it all in. How about you two?"

At first Penny just looked at her, puzzled. Lilly noticed that she was trembling. The purse jiggled slightly, and she dropped her arm as if to cover the movement. When she spoke, her voice was quiet, but there was a hoarseness to it, like someone with a cold or a chronic cigarette cough.

"The tour's fine," Penny said. After a pause she added, "Sometimes you just need to get away, to focus on something besides yourself." John was now making his way toward the group gathered beside the bus. Without another word, Penny followed him.

Lilly and Steve looked at each other and shrugged. "What do you make of that?" Steve asked.

"Who knows?" said Lilly. "They're a strange pair."

Callie walked up, holding a box with coffee and scones for them. "Wait'll you taste the clotted cream," she said. "Toto, I don't think we're in Kentucky anymore."

They boarded the bus, rotating their seats as instructed by Dave. "So, everybody will have a chance to sit up front near me."

"Now don't you two fight over who gets to sit closest to him," Steve grinned.

Sam and her girls, who always returned to the bus ahead of the others, seemed delighted with the rule. "It'll be great to get to sit up front," said Maxie.

"Now, don't you all distract the driver," said Sam. "He needs to keep his eyes on the road."

Up ahead in the narrow two-lane road, Flora spotted a truck approaching fast. She leaned over and grabbed Maxie's shoulder. "This driving on the wrong side of the road like they do over here scares me to death," she said, as the truck whizzed past. "I'm not gonna say a word to him."

This time Steve and Callie were in the next to last seat on the left side, and Lilly found herself directly across the aisle from Penny and John. Penny gave Lilly a vague smile. Lilly noticed that the couple looked straight ahead and made no effort to relate to each other.

"I'm excited about going to Ireland," Lilly said. "My grandmother was born there and came to America when she was very young." Penny and John said nothing, but Penny turned toward her and gave her another smile and nod. Encouraged, Lilly continued. "I don't know exactly where she came from, but I'm going to try to do a little genealogy if there's time."

Suddenly, a small click signaled that the intercom had been turned on. Dave's voice boomed.

"Good morning, ladies and gentlemen," he said. "As you know, today we will cross the Irish Sea." His tone was weary, as if he had made this speech and this trip so many times that he could hardly stand to repeat either. He reminded her of an old professor colleague of hers, long overdue for retirement.

"When we reach the ferry, we will find ourselves on a spacious craft that will carry us on our short voyage. You will find all of the necessary amenities. Food and drink will be served on board, and you may move freely about or find a quiet place to visit or read. Make yourselves comfortable until we arrive at our destination." The small click sounded again, and Dave dropped back into his padded seat.

The ferry was adequate, although lacking in decorative frills. It reminded Lilly of the inside of a huge gray semi, fitted with chairs, bathrooms, and a bar, carrying a group of travelers down a winding highway or a slightly rolling sea.

"Not much to write home about, is it?" Callie said.

"No," said Lilly, "but just think of what's waiting for us when we get there."

Steve pulled out his book. "Finally, a chance to do some uninterrupted reading," he said. He wandered off to the bar and came back holding a mug of Guinness. "Something to wash the serious historical facts down with," he laughed and headed toward an empty chair along the wall.

The water was choppy, and a light drizzle kept most of the group inside the ferry. On a bright day they might have stood outside, leaning on the rail, enjoying the breeze and the occasional spray of water. Lilly and Callie looked for a place to sit and compare notes on the places in Ireland they wanted to see if only Dave would give them time. So far, the prospects didn't look good. He seemed bent on finishing the tour as soon as possible regardless of the wishes of the group.

"He must be about ready to retire," said Callie. "The way his blood pressure climbs every time he gets frustrated, it's a wonder he hasn't stroked out already."

"It wouldn't take much to push him over the edge," Lilly answered. "He reminds me of Chaucer's Monk, remember? 'Fat was this lord ... / His bulging eyes he rolled about, and hot / they gleamed and red, like fire beneath a pot.'"

"Ooh, good one," laughed Callie. "You nailed him."

Lilly opened a colorful brochure about the town of Limerick, one of the many they had brought with them. "I just hope we get to finish this trip before he self-destructs."

"Just our luck to get a guide like him," said Callie. "What did we do to deserve it?"

"Hey, gals." Steve came up to where they were sitting, still poring over the brochures. "Looks like we're pretty close to landing." He reached for Lilly's hand and pulled her up. "I think the rain's stopped. Let's go stand by the rail until time to disembark." He said the last word with a distinct English accent, stressing the pomposity of it. The ferry came to rest beside a pier where stewards began to gather luggage. They could see the bus on the road that ran parallel to the pier.

Dave left his conversation with the bus driver and came down to address the group. "Let's board the bus as quickly as possible. Remember where you were seated, and we will keep the same arrangement. Follow me, please."

Lilly, Callie and Steve fell dutifully into line and made their way to the bus. The big green and white vehicle, with Pilgrims' Choice Tours emblazoned on the side, was almost a duplicate of the one back in England. It was not difficult to find their assigned seats and prepare for the trip to the hotel.

Lilly glanced around the bus, noticing that most of the tourists had found their seats. John and Penny, however, were nowhere to be seen.

Neither was Dave.

In the seat in front of her, Steve and Callie sat quietly, waiting for Dave to announce their departure for the hotel.

Gradually, Lilly became aware that something was amiss. Dave's carefully prepared itinerary was behind by at least twenty minutes. By now they should be pulling into their hotel parking lot, going inside, and preparing for dinner and a night's rest.

Callie and Steve turned to each other, and Lilly leaned her head in. "Where's Dave?" she asked. Around them the other tourists, now settled into their assigned seats, were asking the same question. Only two seats, aside from Dave's amply padded one in the front of the bus, remained empty.

"Where's Dave?" came Sam's loud voice from two seats in front of Steve and Callie.

"Who's missing?" asked Maxie.

"It's that couple from Canada," said Callie. "They got on the bus with us this morning."

A hush fell over the bus as the passengers sat back in their seats, waiting, and wondering. There had been a mystique about the couple from the beginning. One thing they knew for certain. Dave would wait for nobody unless it was a total necessity, and then he wouldn't wait long.

Suddenly, their silence was broken by the sight of four people approaching the bus. Dave marched stiffly in front, and behind him a tall burly man was leading two people. Each with an arm around his shoulder, their heads bobbing up and down with each step, John and Penny approached the bus.

Dave reached the bus a second or two before the others and climbed to the first step. His crimson face appeared to be lit from within.

His pause was either for effect or from an inability to speak at that moment. At last, with obvious effort, he pulled in a deep breath. "Ladies and gentlemen," he rasped. "Your fellow travelers were overserved at the bar."

Lilly was aware of the proverbial pin drop as Dave stepped aside and the burly man propelled John and Penny into the bus and dropped them into their assigned seats. They didn't open their eyes, but leaned toward each other as if for support.

Without another word, Dave took his accustomed seat beside the driver.

A cold air settled over the bus. From the beginning Dave had intimidated them all. But now they had John and Penny to blame should any one of them accidentally break one of his rules. They had found a scapegoat. Lilly turned her attention to Callie and Steve. Major eye roll from Callie. A can you believe it shrug from Steve.

From his vantage point, Dave had turned his back on the entire group. Lilly could see his face reflected in the round mirror which hung like a halo above his head, its angle slanted to include them all in its scope. The angry glow on his face reminded Lilly of her childish fears of a wrathful, all-seeing God who judged every human action. She drew her sweater closer around her shoulders. The chill was seeping into her bones.

John and Penny, oblivious to the drama surrounding them, slept through the slowly passing hours to the next destination. Lilly gazed out the window at the beautiful Ring of Kerry. The road followed the path of the sea below. Blue waves washed against white boulders lining the shore. The radiance of grass and trees on the gently rising slopes reminded Lilly of the reason why Ireland was called the Emerald Isle. Images from "A Modest Proposal" crossed her mind, and with them the contrast of beauty and brutality that too often coexist in human society. She smiled in spite of herself at the saber-like wit of Jonathan Swift, who could evoke laughter with his outrageous suggestions. Eat the tender babies indeed! Not surprisingly, her students had often missed both the satire and Swift's benign intent.

Another click signaled an announcement from Dave. In her reverie Lilly had nearly forgotten about him. From his reflection in the mirror, she saw that some of the crimson had faded from his face and that he seemed about to communicate with his charges.

"Ladies and gentlemen, we are approaching Blarney Castle, which I'm sure most of you have heard of, and of the folk stories about the fabled Blarney Stone. Because of our unfortunate experience earlier this morning," he paused and settled a baleful glare on John and Penny, "we are off our schedule and can only stop here for fifteen minutes. This will give you time to have a look at the castle and then we will be on our way. I urge you, in consideration of the rights of your fellow tourists, to be back here in fifteen minutes so that we can continue our journey."

Callie had been busying herself with a new kind of puzzle, Sudoku, which had recently become popular in the United States. Callie, who liked anything to do with numbers, had immediately taken it up. Lilly preferred crossword puzzles, and although Callie had tried to help her master Sudoku, she hadn't been able to get the hang of it. Steve was finally making headway with his book on medieval cathedrals. The rest of the passengers were rousing themselves from afternoon naps.

Callie put her Sudoku book away and yawned. "We'd better hurry and get off," she said, "or our fifteen minutes'll be up before we even get to the Blarney Stone."

They were practically running when they left the bus and followed a sign with an arrow pointing toward the castle. The walk was not far. When they reached the imposing dark gray stone walls of the famous old landmark, they stopped to gaze up at it.

"It's not as big as I always thought it would be," whispered Callie. "Me either," Lilly answered. "I guess we enlarge things in our minds when we're little. Places like this seem so far away. Almost unreal, in a way. My sister Wilma used to read to me about the Blarney Stone. She'd be so thrilled if she could see me standing here now."

Steve, who had been looking at the surrounding features of the area, came up to where Lilly and Callie stood.

"Girls," he said, "you've got exactly ten minutes to climb those steps over there, kiss the Blarney Stone, and get back to the bus before Dave blows a gasket."

Lilly saw that at least five other people were ahead of them. "What do you think?" asked Callie. "Should we chance it, or go back to the bus right now?" Her expression said she already knew Lilly's answer.

They ran to the stairway with Steve following closely. Directly in front of them stood Maxie and Flo.

"Oh my God," said Maxie when she realized what time it was. "Come on, Flo." She was already halfway down the steps. "There's no way we've got time to do this."

"Mama'll die if we're not back to the bus in time," said Flo. The clatter of their flying feet broke the silence of the afternoon.

Lilly and Callie looked at Steve. They all smiled grimly and took the girls' places on the steps. Only three ahead of them.

Twenty minutes later, the cool feel of the famous old stone still lingering on her lips, Lilly found herself a few steps behind Callie and Steve, who had already climbed into the bus. Although she had been moving as fast as possible, she could see that it had not been fast enough.

Dave, in his accustomed place beside the bus door, loomed over her like the angel of death. If it were possible, his face had assumed a red hue, even darker than before. Lilly was rooted in her tracks like a butterfly skewered by a collector's pin.

"Madam," he began, "do I have to remind you again of

your obligation to your fellow travelers?"

Lilly ignored him and, seeming to have suddenly become unentranced, if that was even a word, stepped onto the bus. She made her way to her assigned seat, but she did not sit down. From the middle of the bus, she began to speak.

"Sir," said Lilly, "we will hear no more about being back late to the bus." She was seeing Dave now through a red haze, anger possessing her like a demon. "Do you honestly believe that at least some of us, having spent thousands of dollars and traveled thousands of miles to come on this wretched tour, would get this close to Blarney Castle and not stay to kiss the Blarney Stone? Just remember that if it were not for our hard-earned dollars, you would not even have a job. You are here at our pleasure, sir, and not the other way around." Her haze was beginning to clear, and she became aware of Dave standing slack-jawed at the front of the bus, his rutabaga countenance turning slowly to the gray pallor of a shell-shocked bully.

"My friend and I, Dr. Callie Carson, here, taught English literature for many years, always hoping that one day we might get to come to this country and see the places we had so often told our students about."

"So just remember," she continued, her voice softer but just as firm, "that we all have the right to expect a reasonable consideration for ourselves as individuals, not just as a flock of sheep that you can herd together, playing us against each other, trying to make us feel guilty for wanting to see what we've paid for and been promised." With that she dropped into her seat, to the sound of scattered clapping throughout the bus.

"Wow, Lilly," said Steve, "that Blarney Stone sure lived up to its reputation." He pulled his book out of his backpack and turned to the page where he'd left off. "Maybe you need to kiss it more often."

"Speak the speech, I pray you, as I pronounced it to you, trippingly on the tongue," said Callie. "Even Hamlet couldn't have asked for a delivery more tripping than that." She reached over and patted Lilly on the arm. "I bet a lot of people on this bus wish they'd been the one to do what you just did."

"I really don't know where it came from," whispered Lilly. Her heart was pounding, and her head felt like if she stood up she might fall in a heap. "It was like something came over me and I couldn't stop myself."

Across the aisle, John and Penny were staring blankly at her. "I was speaking for all of us," she whispered to Penny. "Sometimes you just have to challenge a bully."

Penny reached over and touched Lilly's hand. "Thank you," she said. John gave her the first real smile she'd seen on his face since the start of the tour.

The last stop of the day was a spot on the shore that Lilly had often heard of and was sometimes reminded of by the words of a song running through her head. It came back to her now:

If you ever go across the sea to Ireland,
Then maybe at the closing of your day,
You can sit and watch the moon rise over Claddagh
And see the sun go down on Galway Bay.

See the sun go down on Galway Bay. The realization of a dream. By some quirk of fate, Dave had actually brought them to this place at sunset. He had signaled to the driver to stop the bus and had pointed to a wide expanse of water below. Streaks of purple, red and gold lit up the western sky, as a cloak of shadows settled over the quiet landscape.

"That is Galway Bay," he said. "Of course, you may go down for a moment and look, but please return immediately to the bus." Again, he looked at John and Penny. "As you know, we are severely curtailed in our time for sightseeing."

Something on Dave's face prompted Lilly to glance at John and Penny. No longer were they cowering in the face of Dave's wrath. Defiance had replaced the shame with something like dignity. Penny's face was so pale that a pattern of faint blue lines etching her forehead made her skin appear transparent. John's eyes, hooded and black, projected a measure of pain that — how did Wordsworth put it? — "lay too deep for tears."

Some of the other tourists were getting out of their seats, preparing to catch a running glimpse of the famed Galway Bay. Sam and her daughters debated for a few minutes, weighing the possibility of getting back late to the bus against the prospect of missing one of the sights that had been singled out as a must-see in the catalog. Finally, the lure of the famous attraction won out, and Sam laid out their strategy.

"Okay, now girls," she said. "We'll run about halfway down that hill to where we can see it, enough so we can tell people back home what it looked like. Then we'll run right back up to the bus."

With that she elbowed her way past the Flanagans, an elderly, retired couple from Pennsylvania who sometimes had trouble negotiating the more rigorous physical demands of the tour. Mr. Flanagan had had a hip replacement fifteen years before and often recounted the circumstances of his four hip dislocations over the years.

"One of them," he said, "happened in Israel on the banks of the Jordan River, near the Sea of Galilee."

Sam, who had never really listened to his stories, didn't see his cane and came close to tripping him as she rushed by. "Better run if you want to see the bay," she said, as Mrs. Flanagan grabbed her husband before he toppled over.

Callie, Lilly, and Steve slipped out of the bus and hurried down the cobblestone walkway to the shore. The shadows were deepening, and a sliver of moon hung like a golden pendant on a chain of stars. The three stood still as Galway Bay took its place in the album of their memories.

Dave was unusually quiet as the tourists boarded the bus for the ride to the hotel where they would spend the night. Lilly and Steve sat together behind Callie and Sam, who had rotated to about midway on the left side of the bus. Maxie and Flora had finally made it to the seats directly behind Gerald, the driver, a ruddy giant of a man whose Cockney accent rendered him almost unintelligible to most of the tourists. He didn't actually say very much, as if he knew who the real star was and didn't want to risk Dave's wrath. Both girls thought Gerald was cute, but Maxie had already declared dibs on him, and Flora knew not to flirt or even speak to him until her sister gave her the go-ahead.

"Remember what Mama said," Flora reminded Maxie. "Don't distract him while he's driving on the wrong side of the road." She leaned as far as possible to the left as a lorry barreled straight toward them in the right lane. "Wouldn't you hate to be killed over here in this boring place where nobody even knows who we are? I know I would."

"Don't be an idiot, Flo," Maxie said. "I'm just going to introduce myself and tell him how much we're enjoying the tour." She opened her backpack and took out her makeup bag. Smiling into her mirror, she examined her teeth for remnants of the spinach salad they'd had for lunch. She patted her nose with a powder puff and dabbed on a bit of lipstick. "I'm ready for my close up, Mr. DeMille," she drawled, summoning her best imitation of Gloria Swanson.

Flora covered her mouth and tried not to giggle.

Although not as loud as their mother, the girls' plotting could still be heard by those seated nearby, and Steve laughed and winked at Lilly. "Sounds like the Cincinnati kids are on the prowl."

"I hope they don't wake up Dave," Callie whispered. "He's sure had a day of it."

"I'd say he's earned a nap," Lilly said.

"And so have they," Steve said. He inclined his head slightly toward John and Penny, seated two rows back on the opposite side of the bus. Their heads were resting on the backs of their seats, their eyes closed. Consciously or not, Lilly noticed, their hands were lightly entwined. She wondered if they were sleeping.

Gradually, the bus became quiet as the tourists napped or reflected on the activities of the day. Outside the bus the wind had risen, and wispy, white clouds floated and swirled across the moon like young girls dancing around a maypole. Lilly closed her eyes and thought of herself as a child with Wilma, the two of them pretending that Wilma was the teacher and Lilly the student, learning a lesson on some subject that Wilma had recently studied.

"You're going to be a teacher when you grow up," Wilma had often told her, and Lilly had accepted it as a simple truth. She had never considered any other path for her life.

Lilly did not know when the memory became a dream. In it, she and Wilma were completely alone on the bus save for the driver, far away in the front, being yelled at by a person she couldn't see. A sudden lurch of the bus awakened her. Outside, small trees and shrubs flew past as the bus bumped along over sharp rocks and gravel. The terrified driver fought the wheel to get the bus back onto the highway. All eyes were looking to the front of the bus where Maxie, leaning far forward, was patting down a loose sprig of the bus driver's thinning hair. "There now," she giggled, "isn't that better?"

A look of horror on Flora's face replaced the grin that had been there before Maxie's gesture backfired. "Oh my God, Max," she whispered, as her sister, thrown off balance, fell into her lap. "Now look what you've done."

"Dammit, Gerald!" screamed Dave. All eyes were fixed on the reflection of his purple face in the overhead mirror. "Don't you know better than to fraternize with the tourists? You keep your eyes on that road and get this bloody God-forsaken bus to the hotel without a smashup." He seemed to run out of breath at that moment and fell back into his seat like a sack of turnips. "I'll deal with you when we get there," he growled, mopping his face with a handkerchief that appeared to be already sopping from overuse.

Maxie and Flora cowered in their seats as Sam rose up and grabbed the two girls by their collars. "Didn't I tell you not to do that?" she hissed. Her face was roughly the same color as Dave's, and the degree of her humiliation more than matched his wrath. She grabbed the girls by their collars and jerked them off their seats. "You just wait and see if I ever take you two any place else again." Then with a force that must have rattled their teeth, she shoved them back down.

Lilly thought of the old mother cat she and Wilma used to have that grabbed her kittens up by the scruff of the neck and carried them from one place to another. Old Nellie must've felt a sight more maternal than Sam did just then, she thought.

Callie turned around and gave the two of them a look that said, "Are we ever going to have a lot to talk about tonight." They glanced at Sam, who now sat stiffly in the seat next to Callie. Her body seemed to have hardened and compacted in the minutes since the near accident, like a turtle retreating into its shell.

The excited whispers of the tourists gradually died down as they settled back for what they hoped would be an uneventful ride the rest of the way. It had been a long day. Lights outside the bus became brighter as they neared a small town. The familiar click signaling a pronouncement from Dave aroused their attention.

"Ladies and gentlemen," he announced. "We are approaching the town of Limerick and the hotel where we will spend the night. I urge you to get a good night's rest. Tomorrow will be another full day." He paused for only a heartbeat, but in it Lilly heard a silent message: I hope and pray to God it will not be as catastrophic as today.

"Breakfast will be at seven and we will board the bus at eight. I need not remind you of the necessity to be prompt."

"I could use a drink," said Steve as the three of them entered the hotel. They had spotted a pub to the right of the lobby. Some wag had named it, "The Rhyme or Reason."

"Me too," said Callie. "I think we've all earned a pint, after an especially delightful day on our delightful tour, with our delightful leader."

"'Tis," said Lilly.

Steve and Callie laughed at the abbreviation of the Bard's famous line: "'Tis a consummation devoutly to be wished."

"Then let's devoutly consume it" paraphrased Lilly, and they walked into the pub.

They relaxed and slowly sipped their Guinness while

talking about the day's memorable events. After a brief laugh about their brush with disaster at the hands of the Cincinnati Kids, they turned to the spectacle that had been created by John and Penny.

"Who could've ever seen that coming?" asked Callie. "That uptight, standoffish couple getting plastered like that?"

"Almost makes me pity poor old Dave," Steve said. "Who knows? Maybe he's projecting some hang up of his own. Total jerk that he is, you gotta feel a little bit bad for him."

"Yeah, but it's hard to do," Callie said. "I can't help thinking about that couple, John and Penny, I mean. They must have known how much trouble they'd be in when they got off the ferry."

On that note, they left the pub, heading for the elevator that served the three floors of the hotel. Callie's room was next to Steve and Lilly's. All of the tourists' rooms were on that floor, and looking up and down the corridor, they could see some suitcases already placed outside the rooms, waiting for the morning pickup.

"Gotta get 'em out there," Steve said. "Heaven forbid that we should mess up Dave's timetable."

"See you all in the morning," Callie said, as she dug in her purse for the heavy brass room key they'd picked up at the registration desk.

"'Night," laughed Lilly. "Try not to dream of bus wrecks and vengeful guides, or things that go bump in the night."

Inside their room, Lilly began to empty her backpack. "Oh, I meant to mail these postcards today," she told Steve. "I'll run them down to the lobby right now, so I won't forget them in the morning. Be right back."

As she approached the elevator, she saw that the door was open. "Hey," she called out, as quietly as possible. "Could you please hold it for me?" Penny Cavanaugh's finger was on the "Open Door" button when Lilly reached the elevator.

"Hello, again," said Penny. Her face was pale, her blue eyes marked by angry red circles. "I was just going down to the desk to try to get something for John's headache."

"Well," Lilly answered, "when we got to our room, I remembered I needed to mail these. Our kids, grown though they are, would never forgive us if we didn't send cards. Isn't it funny how we never stop thinking about them that way, just like we did when they were little, still not wanting to disappoint them?"

Something about Penny's face changed. It was like a piece of cellophane that had been dropped on a hot stove and started to shrink and shrivel up.

"We thought this trip would be good for us," she said finally, so softly that Lilly had to lean toward her to hear. "John and I used to be so close, like you and your husband obviously are. After the accident we tried to get past it, to get on with our lives, but all we could feel was pain. We both started to drink to "self-medicate," as one doctor put it. What an irony."

The anger in her voice seemed to lower the temperature in the room.

"What a Goddamn irony."

The elevator door opened. There was no one in the lobby, and Lilly took Penny's arm and led her to a small adjacent sitting room. Penny sat at one end of the sofa. She didn't look at Lilly, almost as if she were unaware of her presence.

"That was five years ago. We thought we had whipped it, the alcoholism, I mean," she said. "We joined Alcoholics Anonymous and everything." Her voice trailed off and Lilly wondered if she would continue.

"So, we actually thought we could do it." Hurt and grief mottled her face. "But today. Who knows what unexpected things trigger the old memories and pain? Maybe we'll never be safe again." She was quiet for so long that Lilly thought she might have finished speaking - that maybe she had withdrawn beyond reach.

"Penny," Lilly whispered. "Do you want to tell me what happened?" She hesitated, unsure if she should ask the question. "Do you want to tell me about the accident?"

A grandfather clock across the room began to toll the hour of ten. Penny gazed at it until it was quiet.

"Our twins," she said, "Roland and Amy. They were nine

years old. We let them walk to school because it was very near our house." She looked at Lilly for the first time since she had begun her story. "One beautiful spring morning a drunken driver struck and killed them when they were only a few steps from the schoolhouse door."

Lilly knew that Penny had finished her story and that she herself had no comforting words. Suddenly, Lilly felt an iron-like grip on her arm and Penny's eyes boring into hers as if seeking— what? Comfort, absolution, redemption?

"But don't you see the irony, Lilly?" she said.

"The awful unbearable irony of it all?"

Lilly stood still for a moment after Penny had left her. The impact of the woman's story was overwhelming. Finally, she turned in the direction of the mail drop she'd noticed just outside the door of the Rhyme or Reason. As she neared it, she glanced inside the dimly lit barroom. It appeared deserted except for one lone customer who sat on a stool sipping from a half empty mug of dark ale. Near his elbow sat two empties. He appeared to be alternately reading something — a letter, perhaps — and gazing at a photograph in front of him. Although she could see only the back of his head, there was no mistaking who he was. Before she could look away, he turned toward her, and his eyes opened widely in recognition.

"Well, if it isn't the Literary Lady," he said, his words noticeably slurred. "And where's the Good Doctor tonight?" He raised his mug in a mock salute and took a long swallow. His face shone with its usual bright red hue, and beads of perspiration stood out on his forehead as if defying gravity. Despair covered his shoulders like a shroud.

"Callie's retired for the evening," Lilly said, acknowledging him with a lift of her envelopes. "Good night, Dave. See you in the morning."

He had already turned back to whatever the paper was that had held his attention before. She saw it shake in his hand.

She felt a curious lightness of spirit as she walked away. She did not know the nature of Dave's pain. Maybe she never would. But she knew that tomorrow would be different. For her, at least, and maybe for Steve and Callie, too, when she told them.

"To understand all is to forgive all," somebody had written, and for once she couldn't remember who it was. Maybe Callie would.

She only knew that twice tonight she had been permitted a tiny glimpse behind the curtain that hides us all, one from another.

The Token

Say you come down to Polly's Bend to sell Cloverine brand salve?

Well, I don't know how much you'll sell. Most of us along here don't do much for cuts and scratches 'cept maybe put on a little coal oil or rubbing alcohol. My daddy used to trap polecats and render out the grease after he'd skinned off the hides. That was a good salve, but people don't take the trouble to make it no more. Most druther have a fancy store remedy than one they could just as easy make theirself.

Somebody might buy a box from you, though, just to get one of them pictures you're giving away with it. I'm partial to that one there.

No, that one next to it, of the angel flying over them children. Makes it look like God's always gonna be there to protect them. Shame how often it don't work out that way.

Why don't you set down on the step there and rest a little while till Sam comes in for supper? You can eat a bite with us. Besides, he might want to buy some of your salve to use on the cow's tits. Sometimes in the winter they crack open and get so sore she won't hardly stand still for him to milk her. Bonnie Bell Anne, Sam calls her. She won a blue ribbon one year at the county fair, and he's got it framed, hanging up in there over our bed. Sometimes I wonder if he thinks more of that cow than he does of me.

No, sir, no trouble a 'tall. I've already got a big pot of soup beans and a skillet of cornbread cooked. I'll slice some tomatoes and onions to go with it and bring up some cool buttermilk from the cellar to wash it down.

To me, this is the prettiest time of the day. I like to set out here of an evening and watch the sun go down. They's a kind of warm glow that settles over everything, like a big old soft blanket. And it gets so quiet you can hear the least sound up and down the holler.

Last night old man Watkins — they live down around that bend there — was yelling at Berthy because she hadn't fried the taters brown enough to suit him, and her so stove up with the rheumatiz she can't hardly walk. Probably drinking again. Goes off ever morning and runs the road till dark sees him home. Sorriest thing that ever had a mother. You just bet I'd a told him what to do with them taters.

I ain't saying my Sam's perfect, neither. He takes a notion for a little dram once in a while, just like the next feller. Gambles a little, too, around Christmas, when he goes to town to sell his tobaccer. But he knows better'n to lay into me like Pete does to Berthy, about anything, much less my cooking.

Here, let me pour you a little tea.

See that house on up the road there? The one with the big maple tree in front. My neighbor Stelly lives up there. I try to run up and check on her about ever day. Her husband brought her here from up around Lancaster, and she don't have no kin close by. She's in the family way and about ready to have it. Her first, if it lives. Two others was born dead and only about a year apart. She liked to never stopped crying. The second one was nearly two years ago. We all watched her for a long time after that. Didn't know what she might do to herself. Sometimes still yet, I'll see her out in the yard just gazing off at nothing, far as I can tell. Don't do no good to even speak to her at them times. She don't hear you.

Truth be told, I lost a baby once, and I was relieved. Me with one still at the breast and another one in diapers. 'Course, I wasn't near as far along as she was — her carrying them two almost to the full time. I honestly didn't know how I was gonna manage. I never willed it to happen, nothing like that. But I tell you, I never grieved over it, neither. It was like God suddenly reached down and lifted a burden right offa my shoulders. Back then I never told another soul how I felt about it, knowing what a scandal some would make out of a thing like that. Still, like the old feller says, we can't always harness our wayward thoughts.

Stelly looks awful frail. Pale as she can be, with all that

black hair down her back, and her eyes like two shiny buttons of coal. She fell off a right smart after she lost them other two babies, and she couldn't stand to lose much. Ain't gained much of it back, neither, even with the few extra pounds she's carrying now.

I tell you, mister, I know her man has to travel to put grub on their table, but he ort not to be leaving her by herself this close to her time. For one thing, it don't look good for him to be gone days and nights at a time. Everbody knows how easy it is for men to get tempted by loose women, and God knows they're everwhere, just waiting to toll a weak man off. I know I don't let Sam go nowhere without me. Not that he'd ever think of doing such a thing.

Anyway, when I went up there this morning, she was standing still as a pin by the screen door, staring straight ahead like she'd been charmed by a snake and couldn't move. At the same time, she was kinda patting her stomach and crooning a little song like you might sing to a baby to calm it and make it go to sleep. She jumped like she come to herself when she heared me come in.

"I heared Ethan singing last night just before it got good and dark," was the first thing out of her mouth. "I heared him stepping on the planks crossing the bridge over the creek, and all the time he was singing, 'She'll be comin' round the mountain when she comes,' just like he used to when we was little. Only that one line was all the words he would ever sing. I guess he didn't know the rest. Sometimes he'd whistle it, too, but I could always fill in the words."

All the time she was talkin,' Stelly never did look at me, and I wondered if she even knowed I was there. I raised my hand to touch her shoulder, but then I pulled it back. Something told me she was somewhere beyond touching.

"But last night he was only singing," she said.

Her voice was so low I had to strain to hear.

"Being twins like we was, and me a girl, I was always afraid he'd go off and leave me when we got older, so I'd beg him not to, but he'd only laugh. "'Oh, you're just a silly little old girl, Stelly,'" he'd say. "'You know you can't come with me when I go.'

"But then when he'd see that I was sulling up, about to cry, he'd quit teasing."

"'Now don't you worry, Sis,'" he'd say. "No matter where I am, if ever you get scared and need me, I'll come back. And when I do, you'll know that whatever it is, it's gonna be all right.'

"Last night when I heared him coming, I started walking down the hill to the creek. I didn't go far, though. Patrick's afraid I'll slip and fall in the gravel and hurt me and the baby both. So, I just stood out there a minute or two and then come on back to the house."

She took her hand off her stomach and reached for the screen door like she might need it for support. Her eyes was still set as if on some far off thing only she could see. She put her hand back on her stomach, and she had the prettiest smile on her face I'd seen since she got that way with that first baby. And she started crooning that little song again, under her breath.

"Come on and set down now, Stelly," I said, "and rest a spell. I don't think Patrick could stand it if you all lost another one."

"No, no, Pearl, don't you see?" she said.

It was the first time since I come in her house that morning that I was sure she even knowed I was there. She sounded excited as a mama bird when somebody gets too close to its nest.

"It was what else Ethan told me back then. He said, 'When I do come back, you'll know that whatever it is, it's gonna be all right.' Pearl, he never did come back before. Neither time before when I was that way did I hear the slightest sound out of him. Not the least hint that he was nowhere near me. And now I know why." She was sobbing, but they was a joy to it, like she'd had the answer to a prayer. "This one is safe," she whispered.

When I realized what she was telling me, I felt like somebody hexed. I couldn't move a muscle. I knowed it was a token soon's I heared it. That's what Mammy always called it. One of them Irish words she brought across the waters when she come.

Ethan'd been in the war. France is where they sent him, I think, or maybe it was Italy. Been about four years now since they got the word. He's buried in the family graveyard up around Lancaster.

The Writer

Nell Amanda Parker awoke just before sunrise and lay still beneath the thick red quilt that had been her great-grandmother's, listening to the sound of her own breath. Her sister, Alma, lay sprawled beside her, snoring lightly, and together they were snug and safe. Without even looking, Nell knew that it was dark outside, and cold. It had been raining for days, and she dreaded going out into the weather. There was something missing this morning, though. Every day for a week she had awakened to the sound of rain pounding their house's old tin roof. Today, everything was still. If she imagined hard enough, it was like she could stay in her lovely cocoon forever. But the school bus would come soon, and she would have to leave the good warm covers and get ready for the long walk out the muddy road to the bus stop at Mr. Jessup's feed store. She didn't want to go to school today, and besides, she told herself, she didn't feel very good.

"All right kids, everybody roll out. Time to get ready for school. Rise and shine. The early bird gets the worm!" Her mother's voice, always the same, every morning. "I've got your oatmeal ready. Hurry up so you can eat before you go."

Nell was the middle child. Kenny was fifteen and Alma was nine. School was okay, but every once in a while Nell liked to stay home. She could read or listen to the radio, or just feel special with her mother all to herself. Today she had something different in mind. Lately, she had been writing. Her best friend, Sarah, whom she had known since first grade, had given her a diary for her birthday a month earlier, and Nell immediately began filling the pages. At first, she wrote about things that happened to her during the day, but that soon changed into stories about her family and about the places she would go when she grew up, the things she would do. It all went into the diary, and the diary always stayed with her. She wrote when she was alone, and no one knew that she was even doing it.

The story she was writing now was about Kenny. He was a good basketball player, maybe not as good as he thought he was and surely not as good as their daddy seemed to believe, but he was still good. Nell was writing a story about Kenny playing in a big game and being the hero. Maybe he would make the winning shot at the buzzer. Nell couldn't decide if that was too dumb, but she liked the idea of Kenny being good at something. He didn't do well in school and, it seemed to Nell, always looked a little sad. Writing about things the way she wanted them to be made Nell happy.

Nell heard a thump and a bang as Kenny began to stir in the next room, and beside her in their bed, Alma sat up and yawned.

"I sure am glad today's Friday." She stretched and kicked the covers aside. "If only I didn't have that stupid old arithmetic test." Alma didn't like school much. Kids teased her and called her Chubby Checkers. Her sweet tooth made her fat, but she wasn't ready to give up candy yet, not just to look good.

Nell didn't say anything, but she got up and padded into the kitchen.

"Mommy, I don't think I feel like going to school today, Nell said, sinking into a chair at the table. My stomach hurts, and I feel like I might throw up. Come, feel my head. Do I feel hot?" The weak little whine usually worked. "Can I stay home? I just don't think I can go."

She didn't try this often enough to make her mother suspicious. Going to school was at least as important as telling the truth, as far as her parents were concerned, and breaking both rules at once would be to invite trouble.

Her mother looked a little dubious, but she put a pan of hot biscuits on the table and walked over to where Nell was slumped in her best suffering posture.

"I'm just not sure, honey. You don't feel all that hot to me." Her mother held the back of her hand to Nell's forehead and frowned.

For a moment, it seemed to Nell that Mama was teetering between yes and no. That maybe there was a chance she would say today would be a good day for Nell to stay home and rest. Nell gritted her teeth and held her breath. "Please, please, please." The word skittered across her mind like a stone skipping across the creek.

Her hopes were dashed the next second. There was no chance for appeal when her mother made up her mind. "Tell you what. You go on to school. See if maybe it's only a little upset stomach. Then if you feel bad later on, you call and I'll come and get you."

"Damn it," Nell thought to herself. That was a habit she had taken up lately, cursing. She and Sarah said damn at least a dozen times a day and it felt good saying it. Still trying her best to look sick, Nell turned back toward the bedroom and saw Alma standing in the door. Alma threw a disgusted look at Nell and went to the table to eat her oatmeal. Nell did the same, but between bites she was busy figuring how long she would have to stay at school before she told her teacher she felt awful and needed to go home.

Her daddy came in from the porch with a load of wood and dropped it on the floor behind the stove. He lifted the iron lid and shoved in two sticks, then stood in front of the stove, his hands extended, palms down. "Chilly out there this morning," he said. He took off his fleece-lined jacket and hung it on a nail behind the kitchen door.

"You kids better wrap up good to wait on the bus. River's way up from all that rain. He turned his back to the stove and shivered, as if to shake off a chill that ran through his whole body. "Better be careful not to get your feet wet when you go down the path. They's lots of puddles out there."

Right then, Kenny, looking sleepy, came into the kitchen. He yawned and sat down at the table, moving his oatmeal closer to him. He propped up his head on one hand and with the other, lifted the milk bottle and poured. Then he added sugar from the shaker and stirred the mixture briefly before he started spooning large bites into his mouth.

Her daddy walked past Kenny and reached out to touch his

shoulder.

"Well, the tournament starts next week, son."

Kenny perked up at the mention of basketball. Nell tried not to seem too interested in what her brother had to say. She listened closely, though, because she thought she might hear something that would be good for her story.

"Yep," Kenny said. "If we can just get past Belfry, we've got a good chance to go to state. Coach says he thinks we've got a real good chance."

"Yeah, and everybody else does, too. You keep playing hard like you been doing, and they won't be no stopping you, son. You all go to state, and they'll be scouts from all the big schools coming to watch you play next year." Like most of the families in the county, the Parkers bled blue, and Kenny's dream was to wear the deep, royal blue jersey of the Kentucky Wildcats. Nell thought maybe that dream was more Daddy's than Kenny's, but that didn't change the fact that her brother seemed to be counting on good things happening to him because of what he could do with a basketball.

The children finished their oatmeal and bundled up. Mama pushed them out the door with a hug for each. "I'll see you kids this evening," she called out as they hurried up the road.

Alma looked up at her sister and made a face. "Ha Ha, faker. You have to go to school just like Kenny and me. You ain't sick at all."

"You hush, Alma," Kenny said. "If Nell says she don't feel good then you don't say no different." Kenny liked to pull rank with his sisters. When they argued Kenny was often the referee. Sometimes he sided with one, sometimes with the other.

"Well, I don't think she looks sick," Alma whined. Kenny shot her a mean look and she didn't say another word until they got to Jessup's.

The bus was almost ten minutes late, and Nell was about to say to Kenny that maybe they should just go on home, that maybe school had been called off or something, but before she got the words out, the familiar flash of yellow turned the curve down from the store. Moments later Nell, Alma and Kenny were on board and sitting with their friends.

"I almost got to stay home today," Nell said, as she slid into the empty seat Sarah had saved for her. "Mama almost let me, then changed her mind, damn it." She whispered the last two words. "She'll come and get me if I tell Miss Elva I'm too sick to stay, though."

"You gonna tell her?" Sarah asked.

"Sure am. Right before lunch." Nell put her books on her lap with her lunch box on top, and settled back to think about what she would say to Miss Elva.

The bus was warm and mostly smelled like sausage biscuits and wet wool, the aromas mixing from still warm lunch bags and drying coats. Before leaving home Sarah had dabbed on a drop of Midnight in Paris perfume, and Nell twitched her nose at the too-sweet smell, which threatened to drown out all others.

Behind her, she heard Kenny talking to Josh Stumbo, a good-looking guard on the basketball team. Nell wasn't the only girl in school who thought Josh was handsome. She and Sarah sometimes pretended to swoon at the mention of his name, and it was an open question among their friends whether or not Josh might be a good kisser and which of them might kiss him first. Sometimes Nell thought maybe she was in love with him. She had filled several pages in her diary with Nell + Josh and, for good measure, added a few big hearts in red ink. She liked to daydream about Josh taking her to a dance sometime. But dancing was clearly the last thing on Josh's mind right now. The boys were talking basketball.

"We're gonna kick Belfry's butt," Kenny said.

"Hell, yes," Josh said. "You know it."

Nell listened to the boys talk but tried not to be obvious about it. She hoped maybe Josh would say something about her. Wouldn't that be something? Then, another conversation caught her ear. In the seat in front of her, Nell heard Alma and her friend Sally talking about what they had in their lunch boxes. Still almost three hours till lunch time, she thought, and they're already hungry.

"I've got two peanut butter and blackberry jam biscuits," Alma said. "You wanna swap me one of your sausage and egg ones?"

Nell didn't hear the rest of their conversation. A sudden bump in the road caused her to look out the window. The sky was blacker than it had been when they left home. Trees along the road swayed with the wind. The rain had started again, and fat little rivulets chased each other down the windshield, like children in an endless game of tag. The narrow blacktop road to school ran parallel to the Big Sandy River, and today the water looked swollen and muddy. Jagged limbs, plastic milk jugs, parts of a wooden steering wheel and bits of garbage spun and bobbed in the rushing water.

Mama might not come and get me after all, Nell thought. She won't want to come out if the rain gets too bad. Nell was about to say something about this to Sarah when she heard a loud bang and felt the bus lurch hard to the right. From the corner of her eye, Nell caught sight of the front end of a car that somehow must have hit the bus, knocking it off the road, causing it to angle down the hill toward the river.

Children screamed and held to one another. Josh yelled out, "Holy crap!" and somebody near the back of the bus laughed. And then the bus slid into the river.

Time stopped. Nell was enclosed in a giant yellow bubble where none of her senses worked. No voices, no smells, no taste, no touch.

Chaos followed the silent vacuum of the plunge. In front of her she saw Kenny grab for Alma's hand. But before he could reach her, Alma was carried away in the tumbling, screaming mass of children. Nell's eyes met Kenny's for an instant and then he was gone.

Then Nell noticed a curious thing. Although the river surrounded them, no water had come inside. In spite of the madness around her, she felt safe. It's like we're on a raft, she thought. Like Huck and Jim floating down the Mississippi. She smiled, sure that they were all going to be all right. She reached for her diary, which lay on top of her other books, just beneath her lunch box.

"I'll write about this,' she thought, just before the water rushed in, cold as death, and took them to another place.

The Old Order Changes

"Kevin might not be at school tomorrow," Robbie says as he steps off the school bus. He picks up a handful of gravel and throws it at a big black crow perched on a fence post beside the road. The bird flaps its broad wings and disappears into the glare of the mid-afternoon sun.

"Why's that?" Karen asks. She pushes her short brown bangs aside and wipes her forehead with the sleeve of her Patsy Cline tee shirt. Robbie hands her his book satchel and reaches for another handful of gravel.

Karen meets her six-year-old son at the bus stop every day and walks him home. Her first question to him usually is, "What'd you learn today?" And Robbie bubbles over with stories about Dot and Jim from his first-grade reader or maybe a fight on the playground. Today is different.

"Well," Robbie says, "Kevin's mommy's going to college, and his daddy don't like it." He kicks at a post and throws the gravel at a maple tree already starting to shed its leaves.

"They've been staying at his granny's, and his daddy says he's gonna come and get 'em. If he does Kevin won't be on the bus."

"You'll miss him if he's not, won't you?"

She ruffles his hair and pushes at an untamed cowlick at the back of his head. A chilly breeze moves through, raising a clatter among the dead cornstalks on the other side of the fence. Far above their heads, a dark cloud like a giant blanket, wraps itself around the sun.

"Come on," Karen says. "I'll race you to the front porch 'fore it rains."

All through supper, over two-year-old Timmy's chatter, Robert's banter with Robbie and the warm smells of boiled cabbage, soup beans and cornbread, Karen thinks about what Robbie had said.

Tammy had been Karen's best friend in high school, and they'd both dropped out their junior year to get married. The idea of ever going back would have been as foreign to either of them as their chances of becoming Miss America.

By the time she finishes getting Robbie and Timmy to bed, it's after eight o'clock. Like always, she sits down on the living room couch with Robert to drink another cup of coffee and swap stories about their day. She puts her head on his chest and feels the protective, solid comfort of him. The quiet is uninterrupted except for a rhythmic ticking of the Seth Thomas clock on the mantel and sudden gusts of wind soughing like restless ghosts around the corners of the double-wide trailer.

After a while he hugs her and starts to get up.

"Five o'clock comes awful early," he whispers. "Guess we better turn in."

"I'll be in soon as I put your work clothes in to wash," Karen answers.

She gets up and walks toward the door leading to the back porch. She gathers up the grimy clothes Robert had dropped when he came home from the mine and puts them into the washer. When the machine begins churning through its noisy cycles, she picks up the phone. Tammy answers on the second ring.

"What's this I hear about you being in college?" Karen asks.

"Robbie come in talking about it today."

"It's true." Tammy's voice has a ring to it that Karen hasn't heard in a long time.

"Somebody told me at church about how you can get your diploma by passing the GED test, and then they'll let you sign up for classes at the college. You just go down there and fill out some papers, and they help you get money from the government.

"It ain't hard at all, Karen. You oughta do it." She hesitates. "I sure hope you don't have to go through what I have, though."

"What do you mean?" Karen asks.

"Well, when I told William about it, he throwed a pure fit. He was drinking and mad, and flat told me I was gonna stay home like I was supposed to. When I said I was going anyway, he hit me."

Her voice drops to a whisper and Karen knows she's crying. "That's when I packed up the kids and come over here to Mama's. You know how little and crowded her house is, but there wasn't no place else for us to go."

"Did you take many of your things over there?" Karen asks.

"No, Kevin and me's just barely got a change of clothes, and I had to cut up some feed sacks to make diapers for Billy."

Tammy's voice is so low that Karen can barely hear. "I'm scared to go back to the house. William's so mean since he got laid off. He ain't a bit like he used to be."

"Has he got any leads on another job?" Karen asks.

"No, and sometimes I think he's just about give up."

There seems little more to say, and Karen soon hangs up and goes to bed. Silently, Robert slides his arm around her, and she inhales the heavy dark scent of coal dust and Lava soap. His body forms a spoon against her back, the way they always lie to go to sleep. Minutes later she feels the deep regular cadence of his breathing.

Karen lies still, eyes open in the darkness, the window beside their bed and the open door into the boys' room outlined in the moonlight. New thoughts and feelings trail through her mind like wispy clouds over the moon. She'll put off saying anything to Robert for now, she decides. Better explore the situation a little further first. See if she can really do it.

Sleep finally comes, bringing images of classrooms and schoolbooks. She sees herself and Tammy, girls again, in pretty flowered dresses.

On Tuesday, she takes Timmy to her mother's and drives the five miles to the college. She feels self-conscious in her one good dress and Sunday shoes and the tight curls she's arranged in her short brown hair. She asks for directions to the Financial Aid Office, where she finds a room with a dark green couch, four matching chairs, and a table stacked with official-looking forms.

In the adjoining room, a heavy-set blonde woman with glasses sits behind a desk, talking to someone across from her. Occasional snippets of their conversation, like "hurt in the mines" and "total disability," come through the open door.

More than once during the next few minutes, Karen comes close to walking out the door and trying to forget the whole thing. She's trembling, and her mouth feels like it's full of sand. When her turn comes the woman invites her in and reaches for one of the white forms.

The interview is brief and the news good.

Karen can get enough financial aid for books and gas and tuition. She'll have to pass the GED, but they give refresher courses, and if she passes she'll have the same qualifications as those of a high school graduate. The woman tells her about some of the degrees the college offers, and when she mentions the nursing program, Karen knows this is the one for her.

She can't wait to tell Robert.

But when he comes through the front door after work, her heart sinks. His shoulders sag, and he has that look she's grown up seeing on her dad's and uncles' faces.

A lay-off. She knows without Robert saying a word.

His fingers fiddle with the handle of his lunch bucket, and he looks down at the floor. It seems like a long time before he speaks.

"We knew this could happen, Karen. Seems like it always does, sooner or later."

Then the worry on his face seems to lighten a little.

"Thank goodness we've been putting a little bit back ever week." He sets his lunch bucket on the kitchen table and heads toward the back door.

"Maybe we can make it last till I can find something else." Karen follows him and grabs his hand.

"We'll make it last, Robert. And I can make some pillows and dolls out of them old worn-out patchwork quilts of Grandma's and sell them out at the flea market."

She talks faster, trying to keep the fear out of her voice.

"People love them old things, especially tourists. I've even had people around here ask to buy the ones I made for us."

She's afraid to tell him about what she's done today. Maybe this is the wrong time to bring it up. But to wait until later might make it look as though she doesn't trust him to understand. Oh, God, she thinks, please help me explain it right, and let him not take it the wrong way.

When she speaks her voice sounds strange even to her. "Robert," she says, "remember what I told you about when I was little, how I wanted to be a nurse and wear a white dress and white shoes and stockings and one of them little caps?" She tries to smile. "I thought that would be the greatest thing in the world."

His look is blank and uncomprehending.

Keep going, she tells herself. You've got to tell him all of it. She holds Robert's hand in both of hers. "Well, that was just a little baby dream." She smiles at the memory. "But today I heard about something that sounds wonderful.

"They've got a program at the college where you go to school for about three years, and if you pass all the courses, you get to be a nurse."

She pauses to catch her breath then plunges on. "They even help you get your GED and money to go to school on."

She's talking faster and faster, watching Robert's face.

"I just went down there today to see what they'd say, and they said they thought I could do it.

"And Robert," she whispers, "if I went, I'd see to it that you and the kids didn't suffer. I'd always put you all first, before school, and . . ."

A knot in her chest halts her breathing, and she can't say another word.

Robert sits and looks at her for a long time, as though he hasn't really seen her before. Like there's something different about her.

He speaks slowly and his voice sounds far away.

"Karen, ain't I always tried to provide you with the best living I could and done my best to make you happy? I won't say this college idea don't scare me. It does."

He smiles. "Why my daddy would've hit the ceiling if Mama'd ever named getting a job, much less going to college." He pauses and looks at her closely.

"But it seems to me like whatever my wife does that makes her happy, that's bound to make me and my kids happy, too."

Karen feels her breath easing out.

"So, if your mind's set on that nursing course, I'll do everything I can to help you. Besides," he grins, "I think you'd be real cute in that little white outfit."

And he'd tried to help, too. When she started to school, he'd played with Timmy and washed the supper dishes while she and Robbie sat at the kitchen table and studied.

But the days dragged on, and nobody was hiring, and their nest egg kept dwindling. The monthly financial aid check bought gas and helped with the groceries, but it wouldn't be enough when all their savings ran out. Gradually, a cold fear settled in, stifling the playful tone of their home.

The first night he came home drinking, her heart nearly stopped. He ran into the coffee table and almost fell. When she tried to reach out for him, he pushed her aside and headed for their bedroom. When she lay down, he remained on his side of the bed and made no move to hold her.

The next day he looked sheepish and hangdog. He didn't mention what had happened, just got up and dressed, and said he was going to check out a rumor about a new mine opening up over at Grundy.

Mornings grew more and more hectic and the nights even worse. Karen still went to the college every day, taking the classes she had to finish before she could apply for admission to the nursing program. Tammy had stopped going months ago after William had made her come back home.

As the year wore on, Robert's drinking increased. At night she'd listen for him to come home, holding her breath when she heard the mumbling or singing that meant he would be beyond her reach. He'd fall into bed to sleep it off, then get up the next morning and go again to look for work.

Until last night.

That's when she'd heard him stumble before he got to the front door. Filled with dread, she'd hurried outside. She managed to get his arm around her shoulders and help him up from the porch, and they fell together into the living room. Her books and papers were stacked on the coffee table, where she had intended to study for the final exam in Human Anatomy. Robert swept them off the table and across the room.

"Damn them books!" he yelled.

He tried to raise up and look at her, but his arm slipped, and he fell back on the floor.

"Who in hell do you think you are, Karen? You think you're gonna come in here, all high and mighty, and make me look like a fool? Bringing in your stupid little check ever month to buy food for my kids. Well, not no more, you ain't..."

His words trailed off, but now he was crying, and the tears seemed to make him angrier. She cringed when he raised his hand as if to hit her. She prayed that Robbie wouldn't wake up and wondered what in God's name she would do if Timmy started screaming.

Robert was stumbling around the room now, searching for something. She remembered the pistol they kept in the bottom drawer of the chest on the other side of the room.

"Oh, please, God," she whispered, "don't let him be thinking about that now."

But she saw that he was only looking for his jacket, which he'd dropped on the floor just inside the door. When he found it, he pulled out a wad of paper and threw it in her lap. Hands shaking, she smoothed it out until finally she could see what it was.

A notice from the mine bosses that the layoffs were permanent. The mine was shutting down.

Now she understood. In the back of his mind, he'd kept hoping that somehow the old job would come back. This notice had killed that hope.

The rest of the night was a blur. Through some miracle the

kids didn't wake up, but every now and then she could hear
Timmy whimpering in his sleep. Robert got quieter as the night
wore on, and sometime toward morning she slipped over and sat
down beside him on the couch. His head fell over on her shoulder,
and she put her arms around him and helped him to bed. She didn't
sleep, but lay waiting for the first light to appear at the window.
When it came, she got up to make breakfast.

She tries to keep her thoughts away from the night before,
and the final exam she's had no chance to study for. Just before
time to take Timmy to her mother's, Robert walks out of the
bedroom. A stubble of beard makes his face look dark and
haggard. The rims of his eyes are flaming red circles.
"I can't remember much about last night, Karen," he
whispers. He puts his hand out as if to touch her, then pulls it back.
"I know it was bad. All I can say is I'm sorry." He looks down at
the floor. "This damn job situation's got me so tore up I don't even
know what I'm doing anymore. One of the guys said he heard
there might be a mine opening up over at Martin, and me and
William's gonna go over there today to check it out, after we do a
little work for his dad."
Karen is numb from worry and lack of sleep, but she
reaches out and puts her arms around him.
"Everthing's gonna be all right, baby. We're gonna make
it."
She holds him and croons the words like she does
sometimes when she's rocking Timmy. After a few minutes she
kisses him and watches him walk out to his pickup.
She closes the door. Time to get ready for school.

The final exam of the last course she must pass before she
can apply for the nursing program. She sits in her usual seat near a
window. Other students take advantage of the remaining few
minutes to study, but Karen stares out at the gray tendrils of mist
rising over the mountains, muting the colors of redbud, dogwood,
and pine. Her hands are cold and sweaty, and she feels her

fingernails dig into her arms.

The instructor walks around the room, handing a copy of the test to each student. Tension spreads. Karen is alone with the piece of paper, the only thing between her and the dream that has kept her going through the past long months.

After what seems like no more than ten minutes, the hour is up, and the instructor is making an announcement: "If you want to know your grade, come by my office any time after two o'clock this afternoon."

Karen hears the words through a fog of weariness. She goes to the library to wait for the hours to pass. She tries thumbing through magazines and puts her head over on a table when she can't hold her eyes open any longer.

At two o'clock she's waiting outside Dr. Clark's office. The instructor looks up when she knocks. "Hello, Karen. "Come on in and let's see how you did."

Driving home afterward, Karen laughs, sings, and acts a pure fool. Relief takes the place of fatigue. A 'C' isn't the best grade in the world by a long shot, but it's enough to pass the course, and tomorrow she'll go to the Admissions Office and put in her application for the nursing program. The radio is tuned to a country music station, and she taps her fingers to Buck Owens and his Buckaroos' "Sam's Place" and hums along with George Jones on "Walk Through This World with Me."

When she comes to the trailer, she parks and heads for the front door.

Inside, the rooms are quiet without the frantic hubbub of her family. What a luxury to stretch out for a few minutes before time to go get Timmy. She drops her sneakers under the bed and lies down, the familiar pillow and mattress cradling her as she drifts off.

The telephone rings three or four times before she wakes up enough to know what it is. She opens her eyes and sits up. Her mother knows she will be back early and is probably calling to see if she's home.

But the voice on the phone is not that of her mother.

"Mrs. Jenkins, this is Capt. James Stevens. I'm with the State Police. I called to tell you there's been an accident. Your husband and another man in a pickup, and a coal truck down here on 80 ..."

She hears, yet doesn't hear, the rest of it. It's like she's in a room with no air and no sound, and every once in a while, someone opens up a door somewhere and she hears a string of words; then they close it again, leaving her with only panic and suffocation.

Little by little, she understands the whole story. Early that morning Robert and William had started over to his dad's to help put up a shed and had stopped at a liquor store on the way. They hadn't seen the loaded coal truck when they pulled back out onto the highway, and there was no way it could have missed them on the steep grade.

The days after the funeral turn into weeks, but Karen hardly notices. She does whatever is necessary to take care of the kids, but sometimes it seems as though she isn't even there. As though she touches things but doesn't really feel them. Sometimes anger pushes out everything else, and she throws whatever is in her hand.

Late at night, a string of questions like disembodied spirits flit across the bleak landscape of her mind. Was it my fault he started drinking? Did he think I didn't love him, or that my going to college made me better than him? What could I have done different?

Endless questions with no answers.

Sometimes she sees the daylight slide in under the window shade and knows that she hasn't slept at all. When it's time, she gets up and fixes breakfast for Robbie and helps him get ready for school.

On pretty days she walks up on the ridge behind the house and remembers times she's walked there with Robert. How they'd laughed and held hands and dreamed about their future. She sits down on soft, dry leaves, drawing herself up into a tight ball, and remains there, feeling nothing except numbing, mindless grief. Later, she returns to the house to face its emptiness without him.

Today, she makes Robbie's oatmeal and sets the bowl in front of him, then sits down and puts her head on the table. Suddenly, she is aware that he is speaking to her.

"Are you ever gonna go back to the college, Mommy?"

She raises her head and sees that he's looking at her closely, as though hoping for an answer right now.

"What, Robbie?"

"I was just wondering when you was going back to the college. I used to like it when we done our lessons together."

She looks at Robbie, really seeing him for the first time in weeks. His eyes, so much like Robert's, gaze at her as if trying to send her a message from somewhere far off.

She looks out at the mountains for a long moment, feeling the shelter and protection of their massive shapes. Then she draws a deep breath and turns back toward her son.

"Oh, yes, Robbie, I liked that too."

She senses a new vigor in her voice and body. Like the big old maple in the front yard must feel, she thinks, when its sap starts rising in the spring.

"Today, I'll take Timmy over to Grandma's and then go on down to the college and apply for the nursing program. I hope I get in." She opens the door and hands him his coat and books.

"But if I don't, I'm gonna see what else they've got, and you and me'll sit right there at that table and do our lessons together ever night."

Robbie smiles and waves. "I'll see you after school."

Karen stands still and watches him go down the path and out of sight, into the morning sunshine.

Better Than My Own Life

Mary hadn't been feeling well for the past three weeks, ever since Holly took off to be with Tom when he found them that apartment up in Chicago. It had just about killed her when Holly left and took Mary's two grandchildren with her. She had never cared as much for anybody as she did for those children, especially the little boy, Charlie.

She'd felt so bad this morning that she didn't think she could stand to stay inside, so she got in her little green Escort and took off. She could smell out a flea market or yard sale where nobody else could, and she was always on the lookout for the signs and tables set up in people's yards. Her station wagon was trained to pass anything except one of those places where she could stop and look for antiques.

She wasn't concentrating as much as she should have been. As usual, she was crying over Holly leaving and taking the kids and rummaging around in her purse for a Kleenex. Because of these distractions she almost missed a sign stuck up on a pole with a tree limb and tall grass covering part of it. She just barely did catch a glimpse of it, more because of the shape of the words "Flea Market" than anything else. She was so used to looking for the signs that she could recognize them a long ways off. She threw her foot on the brake just before she got to the turn-off into the little country road. She rolled down her window because the road was so pretty. She could hear the birds singing and the gravel crunching, and there were shadows from the oak and maple trees that hung over on each side. Mary had always loved fall better than any other season, and this October was one of the prettiest ones in a long time. Today, it helped her get her mind off her troubles.

Mary nearly had a fit when Holly ran off and married Tom at sixteen. It didn't help matters any that she was already pregnant with Tabby at the time. Of course, Mary didn't know anything about that for a while, but she couldn't have talked Holly out of staying with him anyway, she was so crazy about him. And he was about her, too. At eighteen, he was not much older than she was, but they really were in love. Mary carried on and cried, and warned Holly that he would leave her when he got tired of being married and couldn't pay the bills or provide for her. Holly wouldn't hear of it for a minute. When Mary found out about the baby, she kind of gave up on the idea of getting Holly to leave him, and when Tabby came, Mary was like a new person. She loved that baby better than anything. It was like she could play with her, and cuddle and spoil her in a way that she never could with Holly.

That was a funny thing about her and Holly. They were never close when Holly was little and growing up because they were so different. Holly was a quiet child. If she could find herself a book, she could entertain herself for hours, reading or daydreaming.

When she was little, she would play "house" or "school" with made-up playmates. Out on the back porch, it sounded like there were two or three other kids playing. Holly could make the voices all sound different. If anybody asked, Mary would just laugh and say, "Oh, that's just Holly out there by herself playing school. She's the teacher, and she makes up a different voice for each one of her students."

And Holly was always such a generous little thing. She would give her last penny to anybody that needed it. One time a man came to their door and said that he was out of work and needed some money for food, and Holly gave him the money Mary had in her sugar bowl that she had been saving up to buy them a turkey for Thanksgiving. There was a war when Mary came home and found out about it, but that was just a perfect example of how they were. They always fought about money. Every time something like that happened, Mary would warn Holly about the danger of the "poor house," and Holly would just pull back farther into herself. Mary never forgot how hard her own parents worked to keep the family fed, and she carried the scars of want. She still felt guilty if she didn't put back a good part of whatever money she got, just to be sure she'd have enough when she needed it.

It was only about a year after Tabby was born that Holly

had Charlie, and then Mary's life really was complete. If anything, she loved Charlie even more than Tabby. She and that little boy were always off doing something, playing games, going to the grocery, pulling weeds out of the garden. He tagged along after her wherever she went. You could see that little blond head with the cowlick sticking straight up, and Mary's gray hair pulled back in a bun, and they'd be hunched over a book, not knowing there was anybody else in the world.

Tom did leave when he and Holly had been married about three years, and Mary knew that everything she had warned Holly about had come true.

"You remember what I told you about that man. I said he'd leave when he got tired of being married and the bills got too hard to pay. Now what'll you do? It's not just you to worry about. Now you've got Tabby and Charlie."

Holly tried to explain that Tom had just left to look for work and as soon as he found it he'd be back, but Mary couldn't or wouldn't believe it. That's why it had come as such a shock three weeks ago when Holly came in and told her that Tom had found work in Chicago with his brother in a meat-packing plant and had rented an apartment for Holly and the kids up there. He'd even sent bus tickets for them, and she was leaving as soon as she could get all of their things together. Of course, when Mary heard that, she hit the ceiling. She didn't trust Tom to take care of Holly and the kids, and this was all it took to push her over the edge.

She pleaded, begged, and cried, and when that didn't work, she tried scaring Holly into staying — telling her all the awful things she'd heard about happenings in Chicago. She might as well have saved her breath because no amount of carrying-on was going to have any effect on Holly. She was as good as gone when those bus tickets came. All of that had happened just three weeks to the day before Mary spotted this flea market, and she had been so hurt ever since, some days it was even hard for her to get out of bed. The worst part was knowing that she had got so hard-hearted toward Tom, and toward Holly for leaving, that she couldn't ever reach out to them.

She'd gone about a mile and a half on that narrow little road when she came up on a sign hanging by a nail or two on a rickety old wooden gate: "Trader's Paradise: Our Trash, Your Treasure." She got her usual rush of excitement when she looked over and saw all those tables and booths set up. She felt better in spite of herself.

Mary had more than one reason for spending so much time out looking for all those things she collected. Of course, she liked them, but there was the money, too. She'd had her a little booth out on the interstate at Trader John's Antique Mall for about three years now. Social Security didn't go far, and every little bit extra helped. So, when she went out junking, she always hoped to find something good to put in her booth. She kept up with what was being collected through *Antique Week*, and she could tell within a dollar or two what things were worth and how much profit she could make.

She hadn't been there long — all she'd seen were some used clothes, some romance novels, and a few dishes and pots and pans, about what you'd expect to find at a flea market — when she spotted the treasure. Right up in front of her, in the next booth, sat the most beautiful little red pedal car she had ever seen in her life. In fact, it might have been the only one she'd ever seen outside a picture in *Antique Week*. Those things were so rare that they hardly ever turned up anywhere except at antique toy auctions, where collectors would pay hundreds of dollars for them. Especially one in as good a shape as this one. It looked so new that she thought it was a reproduction until she got right up on it and could see that it really was old. She peeped around to see if anyone else had spotted it before she walked up to it, but there was nobody else near.

"I see you're looking at the car."

She turned around and saw a man about her age or a little older, standing behind his table, neatening up his dishes and books.

"I just put that out a few minutes ago. Never had thought about selling it before. We got it for Jimmy, Christmas 1945." He hesitated, and his voice got softer. "We lost him the next summer in the polio epidemic, and it's been setting up in the attic ever since. Now my wife's gone too, and I just thought some other child might get some pleasure out of it. Funny thing — something just seemed to make me go up and get it this morning.

Mary nodded and was just getting ready to ask him how much he was asking for the car when something made her look up, and she almost fainted. She saw a woman and two little children that looked so much like Holly and Tabby and Charlie that it could have actually been them. Put Charlie's cowboy boots on the little boy, and he'd look just like him. Mary noticed that the woman laughed and bent over to talk to the children in the same way that Holly often did.

Mary just stood there, watching them come on up the line of tables. Just before they got to her, they stopped and looked at the toys on the next table over. Mary saw the little girl pick out a blonde pony-tailed Barbie, and her mother dig around in her purse for two quarters to pay for it.

When they were almost to the table where Mary was standing, the little boy spotted the pedal car. It wasn't too late to ask about the price and tell the man she'd take it. Since she'd already shown an interest in it, the dealer would be honor-bound to sell it to her if they could agree on a price. But all she could hear was that little boy's voice — so like Charlie's that she thought for a minute that it really was him.

"Mommy, Mommy, look at that car! Can I get it?" He was tugging at the woman's sleeve. "You said I could have one thing out here today, and that's what I want!" The woman looked doubtful, like she knew the price would be more than she could afford, but she stepped up to the table anyway and reached out to touch the little car.

"It sure is a pretty thing, Kevin. I know I said you could pick out something, but I don't know if we can get this or not." She turned to look at the man behind the table, and Mary looked at him, too. The man was smiling down at the little boy, and Mary had the strangest feeling that he was seeing Jimmy and that Christmas so many years ago.

"How much're you asking for the car?" He didn't answer

her for a minute, and when he finally did answer, she thought he might have been crying. She'd had enough experience with that in the last three weeks that she could tell, even if the tears were on the inside.

"Well, I guess it ought to be worth ten dollars - that's what I was planning to ask." He saw the look of disappointment on the woman's face - she didn't have that much — so he hurried on before she could answer. "But if you're interested, I guess I could let it go for five."

"Oh, it's sure worth ten dollars — probably even more. And I thank you for offering to cut the price, but I don't have five dollars with me, and I wouldn't ask you to take any less. Sometimes you just run out of money before you run out of month."

She smiled at the dealer and then looked down at Kevin. "I'm sorry, Kevin. We'll try to find something else you like before we go." For the life of her, Mary couldn't remember exactly what happened next. She saw the hurt look on the man's face, and she felt his pain just like it was her own. He had no idea how to let her have the car now, as much as he wanted to. It was up to Mary, and she found herself standing beside the young woman.

"Listen. I was standing right over there, and I heard you all talking about the car. You're not going to believe this, but today's my birthday, and just as a present to myself, I always try to find somebody to give a present to. I had just about given up today. I hadn't found anybody, and I was beginning to think my day was going to be spoiled. But this is perfect! Your son wants the car, and I need someone to give a present to."

She knew she must sound like a babbling maniac, but she also knew that she had to say it quick, before the woman could refuse. As odd as all this must have sounded to strangers, anyone who actually knew Mary would have been flabbergasted.

Before the woman could say a word, Mary grabbed her hand and stuck the five-dollar bill in it. Her last glimpse was of the young woman handing the money to the man. She turned around as fast as she could and practically ran past the row of tables toward the spot where she'd parked her car.

An hour later, in her kitchen, Mary could still feel the warmth of that woman's hand as she placed the money in it. She sat looking at her telephone a long time before she picked it up and began to dial.

It was only when her breath escaped in a rush that she realized she had not breathed since she began to dial Holly's number. Fear gripped her when she heard the first ring. Two, three more, and then she heard the sound of the receiver being lifted.

"Hello." She heard Holly's voice for the first time since that Friday morning three weeks ago when the three of them had boarded that Greyhound bus.

"Holly? Holly, just don't say a thing for a minute. I don't blame you if you don't want to talk to me, but please, listen. I want to tell you; I know I was wrong. About Tom, about you leaving with the kids to go be with him, about everything I said to you before you left. 'Course, you had to go with your husband and their daddy. I know it now, but I didn't until just today."

She was crying, and it was hard to talk.

"I love you, Holly, and them kids, better than my own life. And I just had to call you and tell you now, today ..."

All the held back grief and hurt washed over her, and she couldn't say another word.

"Mama? Oh, thank God. I thought maybe you never was gonna talk to us again. We all miss you so much, and Tabby and Charlie ask about you every day. I was afraid to call, knowing how you feel about Tom, but oh, Mama, we're so happy. He's got a real good job, and our apartment is a dream. There's even a little park with a playground for Tabby and Charlie to play in right across the street. The only bad thing was not being able to tell you about it, or have you come and see us."

A few moments later, Mary replaced the receiver and sat very still, happy in a way she'd never felt before. For just a minute her mind went back to the flea market and the story of a little boy with a brand-new pedal car on a Christmas morning long ago. And another little boy, right now, playing with the same beautiful toy.

And then Charlie's face came to her as plain as if he were right there in the room with her.

Mary smiled, thinking about the little check she'd get from Trader John's next month, and the Greyhound bus ticket she'd be buying for herself.

The Lesson

Joe could never get over how beautiful Anna was, with her white hair wind-blown around her face and her icicle-blue eyes piercing through him to ferret out any thought he might try to conceal. He went to visit her every Sunday, in spite of the painful arthritis in his hip. Today as he got off the bus, he tried to remember everything that had happened during the week. Some of the stuff he was afraid to mention because he knew she wouldn't like it, but he had to tell her. She always knew anyway, so it was better for him to just go on and let it all out.

Sometimes she told him things. Like last week she'd told him how Pete was sneaking around and stealing stuff when Joe was gone. Joe hadn't missed anything, but he didn't tell Anna that. When she'd told him what to do about it, he'd followed her instructions to the letter, and he was going to tell her all about it today.

Anna had always had more zip than Joe, and she was smarter, too. Sometimes he'd be at a loss as to how to handle something, and Anna would know just the thing. Like that time years ago, when they'd repainted their apartment out of their own pocket, but the landlord wouldn't let them count it on the rent.

Anna said, "Put some sugar in his gas tank. That'll teach the old skinflint."

And she was right. Sam had to junk the T-Bird.

Then there was the time that Anna figured out how to get even with Jack Potter for letting his leaves fall over the fence into their yard. Jack had a pond way down in the field on the other side of his house that he always stocked with catfish. And he wouldn't let Anna and Joe fish there, even though it was chock full of fish. Stingy old bastard. So, Anna told Joe to go to the store and buy some rat poison and put a little of it in the pond. She said a dose of that would make all them big old catfish go belly up, and that would show the son of a bitch a thing or two.

Joe did it, but he never knew if Jack learned a lesson or not. All he knew for sure was that there was a pond full of floating dead fish out there, and Jack never could get it going again.

And the leaves kept falling on their side of the yard.

Joe always took Anna flowers on his visits, whatever was in bloom in their yard, and sat near her so he could hear everything she said. If he didn't get close enough to suit her, she'd get all worked up.

"Scoot over here closer, Joe," she'd say. "Don't you know all these long-tongued babbling busybodies are just straining to hear everything we say?"

And he'd move closer and hang on her every word.

Anna had always been the boss, but Joe didn't mind. He seldom had to make a decision on his own. When Anna was still at home, it was a lot easier for him because she'd just tell him what to do, and he'd do it. But now it had been ten years since she left, and the visits got harder every week.

"Well, it's about time you got here," she snapped, before he could even sit down. "What in hell took you so long? I thought you wasn't coming."

"What made you think that?" Joe asked. "When have I ever missed a Sunday coming? I got a little later start today on account of the misery in my hip. Took me longer to walk to the bus stop is all." He hurried on, anxious to tell her all he had done last week in order to carry out her instructions. "I laid out behind the shed Friday like you told me to, and watched to see if Pete would come by and try to get in and steal something."

Anna's rapid, raspy breathing told Joe she was listening closely, and he hurried to finish before she could interrupt.

"He did come by about nine-thirty, but all he did was pick a few flowers out of our marigold bed. He walked on like he was gonna go over to that park bench he sets on and reads his paper every day, and just like you told me, I followed him and stole his wallet out of his coat where he'd laid it down on the bench." Joe giggled. "Pete never even knowed I was there. I guess he'd just cashed his Social Security check. It was all in there. I took the whole thing and dropped it in a trash can. I guess that'll teach him not to go stealing from other people."

"That's exactly right, Joe," Anna said. She sounded pleased, and he basked in the warmth of her approval. "People got to learn they can't do just anything and get by with it. They've got to be taught a lesson," she said. "If you let 'em get by with one thing, they're just gonna try something worse the next time."

He'd heard that from Anna all the forty-eight years of their marriage, and he knew she was right. Today, though, he didn't know what to do. Should he tell her about Dr. Perkins? He knew he needed his medicine. His nerves had got really bad. He couldn't sleep, and he had horrible dreams. Old Dr. Stevens, the one they'd gone to for years, would just write out his prescriptions without even making Joe come in for a visit. But he had retired and gone to Florida or somewhere, and now this new doctor was telling him he couldn't have the medicine. Said he'd been "over prescribed," whatever that meant. Said he'd have to learn to get along without it.

Well, wonder what Anna would say about this? She sure wouldn't like it. She didn't trust doctors, anyway. Just because they had them big degrees, they could say whether a person could have their medicine or not, just by writing it down, or refusing to, on a little white piece of paper. He bet she'd say this doctor had to be taught a lesson. Give 'em an inch, and they'll take a mile.

"What do you mean, he won't give you your medicine?" she said. "Did you explain about your spells, and how you get them awful headaches? And them bad dreams? Did you ask him nice?"

"I done all them things, Anna, and it didn't do no good. He just said I had an overdependence on it, and he was gonna take me off of it for a while and see if I didn't get to feeling better without it." Joe could feel tears on his cheeks, and he hoped Anna wouldn't notice.

"Well, we'll just see about that. If he thinks he can come in here and start messing with us, he's got another think coming. He's got to be taught a lesson. Has he still got his office there in the clinic where Dr. Stevens used to be?"

"Yeah, he's in the same spot."

"That office is the first one you come to when you go in, ain't it? So, you wouldn't see nobody but the girl at the desk and him back in his office."

Anna's voice got low and secretive, almost purring, Joe thought.

"Now you listen real close. Unlock that drawer where we hid that gun — the one we bought the time we heard them prowlers around the house. Find the bullets we bought for it and load it up. I think they're in that same drawer. Find out what time in the morning he goes to his office, and you get there a while before he does. Soon as you see him go in, you go in there and let him have it. One bullet ort to do it if you aim straight for his heart.

"He has got to be taught a lesson, Joe, one he won't never forget."

He knew that, as always, she was right. Evening shadows had begun to settle, and bird songs were quieter. Now that he had told Anna everything and had her instructions, Joe was anxious to begin carrying them out at home. "Okay, Anna, I'll be back next Sunday, same as usual, and tell you how it all worked out. I better get going if I want to catch that last bus home. I brought you some marigolds. They're blooming real pretty right now."

He got up from the stone he'd been sitting on near her grave, carried the drooping flowers over, and placed them on the ground in front of it.

The words "Anna Belle Colvin, 1913-1990," were chiseled in the black granite. The letters seemed to sparkle and dance in the light from the setting sun.

Favoring his left hip, Joe started the walk back to the bus stop. He had so many things to do between now and next Sunday. He settled back on the slick brown vinyl seat and began to formulate his plans.

Walking toward his house after the bus ride, he passed the park where people sat on benches, whiling away their time and catching up on neighborhood gossip. Joe never went there himself although he had played there as a boy. Now he seldom talked to anyone except Anna.

As soon as he got home, he planned to go and look in the drawer for the gun and shells, and get ready for his visit to the doctor. Tomorrow he'd go down to the clinic early to see what time the doctor came in. By Tuesday he should be ready to carry out the rest of their plan.

He was beginning to see that if he stayed organized, he could get everything done by Sunday. Anna wouldn't have any reason to be mad, and they would have a nice visit.

He had been home only a few minutes when he heard a knock on his door. It was an unusual sound. He hardly ever had company. Who'd be coming to see him? He wondered.

Pete stood on the front porch, just outside the screen door. His head was lowered, and he held his old billed cap bunched up in his hands. The thin, stooped little man always put Joe in mind of a scarecrow. Clothes hanging loose, flapping with the slightest breeze.

Pete never had been very big, even as a boy, but now he looked even more drawn and shrunken. He had once worked as a lineman on the railroad, and one day he'd slipped and got caught under a hand car. Came in a hair of getting killed. His gimpy leg and twisted back had knocked him out of going back to work, and with age his physical problems had worsened.

Joe just looked at him, his mind blank. He'd been concentrating so hard on the week ahead that it took him a minute to shift his mental gears.

Pete peered through the screen.

"Joe, I'm sorry to bother you, but I didn't know what else to do. You're the only one I know on the street anymore. Everybody else is either dead or moved away, and I couldn't just go up to a complete stranger."

Pete's face looked more tortured than usual, and his words seemed to stumble over each other.

"I'm in real trouble, Joe. Someway I lost my billfold over at the park, and it had all my money in it. You know I pay by the week for my room down over the garage, and they won't let me stay there no longer if I can't pay the rent for next week."

Tears ran down his cheeks.

"Joe, you know I wouldn't ask you, but I don't know what else to do. Could you let me borrow enough to pay for my room until I get my next check? We've knowed each other a long time, and you know I'll pay you back quick as I get it."

Joe thought for a second before he opened the screen. He knew Anna wouldn't be happy about this, but an idea was shaping up in his mind that might please her if he could just work it right. He opened the door wide. "Why come on in, Pete. I've got some hamburger for supper that I was just getting ready to cook."

He motioned Pete inside. "Why don't you come on in and eat some with me? I've got a spare bed out there in that back room. You're more'n welcome to stay here till you can get your room back." Pete followed him inside, looking confused by Joe's warm welcome. When they were boys they'd buddied around together everywhere, but Anna had put a stop to that as soon as she and Joe got married.

Joe led the way back to the kitchen. "I'm glad you come by, Pete. Set right down there at the table. You can watch the house for me while I go see Dr. Perkins tomorrow."

Joe divided the hamburger into patties. He took down a skillet from the cabinet, set it on the stove and turned on a burner. While the patties sizzled, he got out bread, a can of pork and beans, plates, forks, and two glasses for milk.

Pete looked like a condemned man who had been granted a reprieve. He hung his cap on a peg by the door and sat down in the chair.

"This is great, Joe. I never expected you to take me in like this and even give me my supper." His face twisted into a rare grin. "Remember how we used to go camping up at Blue Hole, and take pork and beans and crackers and Vienna sausage? This kinda reminds me of that."

"Yeah, we had some good times, Pete." Laughing, Joe opened the can of beans and emptied them into a bowl.

"Remember the time you reached your hand into that log in the river, thinking there was a turtle in there, and pulled out a water moccasin? Boy, Pete, you sure got rid of that critter in a hurry. Wonder it hadn't bit you." He poured Pete some milk and passed him the food.

Now, he thought, to put my plan into action. His voice became warm and sympathetic. "Say, Pete, how'd you happen to lose your billfold, anyway?"

"I can't figure it out, Joe. I was real careful to put it in my coat pocket. After a while the sun started getting pretty hot, so I took off my coat and laid it right by me on the bench. I swear I never moved but once, and that was just long enough to walk over to the trash can to throw my paper cup in. Couldn'ta been more than twenty seconds, you know where that trash can is, and when I come back my jacket was right where I left it, so I didn't think to check on my billfold. Never missed it till I got back to my room." Pete's voice cracked again, and Joe thought he might cry. "I don't know if somebody got it, or I dropped it, I just don't know. All I know is, it was gone, and I never saw nobody nowhere near me."

Neither of them spoke again until they had finished eating.

Joe cleared the table, washed the dishes, and put everything away. Anna couldn't stand clutter, and he knew she'd be mad if he didn't leave the kitchen spotless. Last week he'd spilled some milk on the floor. He thought sure he'd got it all up, but he must have missed some because suddenly she was there and fit to be tied.

"That sticky stuff'll ruin my linoleum. You get down and scrub every bit of it up."

"Anna, what are you doing here?" Joe's eyes had searched the small room, but there was no sight of her. His heart pounded, and his words came out in a hoarse whisper. "I didn't expect you to be here with me no more." In all the years she'd been gone, this was the first time she'd come to visit him at home. He had waited a long time that night, but there had been no further word from her.

After supper Joe and Pete talked a while longer, and then Pete said if Joe didn't care, he thought he'd go on to bed. Joe pointed out the small storage room next to the kitchen.

"Holler if you need anything, Pete. I'll be up for a little while, and then I'm gonna turn in, too."

He heard Anna's dry, rasping laugh before he heard her voice. "I see why you let that old bastard in. You wanted him to tell about the billfold."

"Anna? Is that you?" Joe whispered. He couldn't see her, but he knew she was there, just as she had been last week.

"That really tickled me, what he said," Anna giggled. "You sure must've been slick when you took it, Joe."

"Oh, I was." Joe could hardly contain his excitement. "The minute he got up to take that paper cup over to the trash can, I ran over to the bench and grabbed that billfold just as quick as a wink. I kept on hiding behind the tree till he left, and then I dropped it in the trash can, just like I told you." As soon as Joe was sure Anna had left, he went to bed. His sleep was deep and restful and there were no bad dreams.

The sky was overcast Monday morning, and a slight chill in the air reminded Joe that it would soon be November, and cold enough for the winter coat Anna had told him to get a few weeks back. He decided that maybe he'd better go on down to the Goodwill and look for one today. If Pete wasn't up by the time he was ready to go, he'd let him sleep.

The Goodwill store was a dark red brick building that had once been a Western Auto store. To Joe's delight, Anna's voice followed him up and down the long rack of men's coats. Her visits to him were becoming more frequent.

"My God!" she said. "They want ten dollars for these coats. What a gyp! People just give 'em this stuff. Well, you've got to have one. That black one over there looks like it might do."

The coat she had pointed out slipped smoothly down his shoulders.

"Yeah, I think that one fits," she said. "Get it, and let's get out of here."

He paid for the coat, put it on, and walked the three blocks to his house. Pete would surely be up by now, he thought, but when he walked inside, he saw that Pete had left.

"Kinda funny he didn't stick around to talk awhile or drink a cup of coffee." Joe felt a little disappointed that he'd missed him.

"The old s.o.b. probably made some and drunk it before he left. Thieving good for nothing," Anna said.

Joe walked to the small desk in the living room and opened the top drawer, rummaging around until he found a small brass key and then easily opened the next drawer down.

There, where he and Anna had placed them years ago, was the small, shiny .22 pistol and box of bullets. He picked up the gun, turning it this way and that to watch the light play on its gleaming gray barrel, then laid it beside the stack of unpaid bills on the desk.

He still had to walk up to the doctor's office to see when his office opened in the morning. He dreaded the walk, but fortunately it was short. No more than three blocks. The pain in his hip seemed to be getting worse. Even small distances were harder than they had been.

"We need to do that replacement soon, Joe," Dr. Perkins had told him on his most recent visit. "Right now, it's down to bone on bone."

The doctor had stood and put his hand on Joe's shoulder. "If we wait too long you might be permanently stuck in a wheelchair." Joe remembered the concern in the doctor's voice, and it touched him now to think about it. The truth was Joe kind of liked the guy. Except for his refusal to give him his nerve medicine, Dr. Perkins hadn't really been a bad sort.

Shaking his head to clear his thoughts, Joe approached the doctor's office. A sign on the door indicated that the office opened at 9:00 a.m.

Better get here around a quarter till, he thought. He noticed a bench, partially obscured by a lilac bush, and shadowed by an ornamental pear tree. That would be a good place to sit while he was waiting for Dr. Perkins to arrive.

Approaching his house on the way back, Joe wondered again why Pete had left so early, and if he would be back. It was sometimes lonely at this time of year. The neighborhood children were all in school and their parents at work. He walked up the steps to his porch and opened the front door.

Pete was sitting in the easy chair by the reading lamp in the living room. His face was a study of anger, confusion, and hurt, and his eyes seemed to float in a clear pool of tears.

"Why'd you do it, Joe?" Pete's voice was so quiet Joe could hardly make out his words.

"I thought we was friends again last night when you took me in, and me about crazy with no place to go."

He paused for a moment as though unable to continue. "And then after I went to bed, first I thought I was dreaming. I heard you laughing and telling somebody about how you stole my billfold and threw it in the trash can. Who in hell was you talking to, anyway, Joe?"

He didn't wait for an answer.

"And I still didn't believe it this morning. I thought sure I must've just dreamed it. But Joe, I got up and went over there, and I dug around down in that trash can, and there it was."

He held it up for Joe to see.

"Looka here, Joe. Here's my billfold just where you said it was, with all my money still in it. You didn't even take it 'cause you needed it. You just took it and throwed it in there for pure old meanness. "Joe, don't you know you can't treat people like that?"

Pete's face had gone gray with fury. His words pierced the air like icicle daggers.

"You've got to be taught a lesson."

Joe saw the glint of metal at the same instant he remembered leaving the gun on top of the desk. He heard the explosion, saw the flash, and felt the crushing impact of the bullet to his body. Then there was only a cold dark silence.

Anna was standing in a corner, just behind where Pete had stood. Her piercing blue eyes illuminated the gloom, and her hair, as black as it was on their wedding day, lay in curls like playful snakes around her shoulders. Her body was draped in the gauzy white garment Joe had chosen for her ten years ago.

She held her arms out to him. "So, he thinks he can get the

upper hand on us, does he?"

She moved toward Joe, smiling in the cunning way he'd always loved. A rustle of air seemed to carry her over the floor, the folds of her shroud billowing around her ankles, and releasing fragrant clouds of "My Sin," her favorite perfume.

"Well, we'll just see about that. Come on, Joe. Let's go figure out how to get even with this old bastard." She took his hand and led him down a dark hallway where red and yellow shadows danced on the walls.

Nothing No Stronger

A hard snow had come that night, leaving drifts in the fence row by the cornfield and a covering of three or four inches on the ground. The wind whistled softly around the corners of the gray, weather-beaten tenant house, finding its way inside through small cracks in the walls. There were four people in the house. Three of them — a man, woman and baby — shared a bed covered by thin Indian-patterned blankets, which the couple had ordered from Sears and Roebuck when they married almost a year ago. A seven-year-old girl slept fitfully on a cot in an adjoining room, near a pot-bellied stove whose fire had died out hours before. From time to time the girl whimpered in her sleep, as if troubled by dreams.

"Whose is it?" Pearl had gasped when she caught up with Viney. "Ernest's or George?" Her chest rattled from her struggle to catch her breath. She was a tall, ruddy woman, big-boned and strong. From the kitchen window she had spied Viney heading for the barn, clutching a bundle under her apron. Only one explanation for her sister's behavior came to Pearl's mind: She's trying to get rid of one. Still holding the wet dishrag she'd been using to wash the breakfast dishes, she grabbed Viney's arm and jerked her around to face her. "Well," she repeated. "For God's sake, whose is it?"

"George," Viney whispered. Dropping the bundle to the ground, she raised her hand to cover her mouth. A kitten-like moan escaped through the cover of her fingers, and another time Pearl might have reached out to comfort her. Her rail-thin body, clad in a faded blue cotton dress, appeared even smaller beside the bulk of her sister, four years older and forty pounds heavier.

"Thank God," Pearl said. "What on earth would we do if you brought in another one by Ernest?"

The women shivered in the early December morning. Wind

whistled through the bare branches of a walnut tree on the slope below. A column of gray smoke rose from the stone chimney atop the small clapboard farmhouse, carrying a faint odor of wood and with it, a reminder that it would soon be time to get dinner on the table.

Pearl's face gradually lightened. "Well, you'll have to get married this time," she said. "And you'll have to take Nancy with you. I know she belongs to Ernest, but you're her mother, and we can't hardly feed the four we've got."

"But Pearl," Viney whispered, "she don't hardly know I'm her mother. She calls me Aunt Viney and you, Mama. She's six already. How's she gonna stand leaving the only home she's ever knowed?"

"No way around it, Viney. You know you all can't stay here no longer." She kicked aside a piece of the limestone rock that littered the little farm. Viney and the children had spent countless hours clearing a few acres, but it would take much more work to make all of the land fit for the plow. Ernest had planted tobacco or vegetables on every available square inch of soil, and he cursed and complained when there was no space left.

His cousin George, a quiet man who seemed content to work like a pack mule from sunup to sundown and expect only food and a place to sleep in return, had left a job on the Buffin farm to come and help Ernest with the planting. The extra hand, however, had only made the challenge of rock clearing more evident.

"We'll have to tell 'em when they come home at dinnertime," Pearl said. "You and George can take the wagon and go get a license today."

Viney thought of the long road to Lancaster. Nearly ten miles. She knew that no amount of crying or wishing would change anything. She tried to imagine what it would be like to be married. The only married people she knew well were Pearl and Ernest, and she hated the thought of having a life like theirs. Amid the endless drudgery of maintaining the farm, the babies kept coming every ten or twelve months. She had heard of married love, but she was certain that she felt nothing of the kind for George, the man she would have to marry almost immediately.

"Listen, Pearl," Viney said, "You know I didn't plan on none of this."

"Hush," Pearl said. She thought of the looks Ernest had given Viney, and the touches and tickling she'd pretended not to notice when her sister first came to help. She'd been shocked and scared, all right, but Ernest was a brute of a man. She knew that nothing she could say or do would stop him from taking advantage of Viney if ever he got the chance. Besides, she'd asked herself, what about me and my kids? So, she'd held her tongue and hoped for the best.

"It ain't all your fault. Maybe not even most of it," Pearl said. She looked out over the rocks and hills. No green anywhere except for a small grove of cedars down near the creek. Long time till spring, she thought. She looked at the shivering girl, her baby sister, whose eyes put her in mind of a terrified rabbit.

"We'll just have to do the best we can. Maybe you and George can make a go of it." She put her hand on Viney's arm and nudged her toward the house. The sounds of a baby crying and older children yelling over something — a biscuit, maybe, or a toy — grew louder as they neared the back door.

"God knows," she whispered. "At least you'll have to try."

Viney's baby girl came that summer. When it was six months old, a lingering spell of croup had left its breathing ragged and hoarse. Its body felt hotter than it had when they had first gone to bed. Perhaps sensing its mother's wakefulness, the child whimpered a little and thrust its arms upward, demanding something she couldn't give. Despair overcame Viney as it always did when she had to attend to this baby whom she had neither asked for nor wanted.

Had she felt any pleasure that warm September day when she'd let George run his hand up her leg and touch her, let him keep on until it was too late to stop? Why didn't I learn after

Nancy come? She thought. Wish to God I had.

Memory of that other earlier time washed over her like a surging river, and though she fought it, no respite came. That filthy pig, Ernest, she thought. The sweaty smell of him. The terror when he grabbed her in the henhouse, pushing her down, forcing himself upon her. She'd hated her sister then for not killing him. Silly me, she thought. That was before I understood the way of things. Before I knowed they was nobody there to help.

Thinking the child might be hungry, she pushed the cover aside to offer her breast, hoping nursing might quiet it and allow her to sleep. Instead, it started to jerk and shake, its body contorting into a quivering, tense, unyielding form. Its lips were turning blue. She could see only a horrible whiteness where its eyes should have been, and she knew they had rolled back in its head.

Her body felt light, almost weightless. She was lying on a strange cot. A patchwork quilt had been pulled up around her arms and shoulders. Her feed-sack gown was tucked around her. It was damp and heavy, but warm. Her feet were numb at first, but a terrible ache set in as heat replaced the cold. Maybe to help it dry sooner, someone had straightened her hair out on the pillow in lines like those she'd seen somewhere, radiating out from a picture of a holy woman.

Voices like burbles rising from boiling water gradually became closer and clearer, and she realized it was George talking to another man, whose voice was faintly familiar. George held his black wool cap in his hands, and his high-top brogan shoes gapped open where they had not been tied. Snow had melted onto the floor under his chair, and Viney saw that he had pulled on his heavy corduroy jacket over the dingy white underwear he slept in.

She closed her eyes and let her mind wander back to the day she and Pearl had hurried out to meet George and Ernest, riding in the wagon, returning from the barn where they'd been stripping tobacco. Saw them look down in surprise as the two women approached them. Saw the anger on Ernest's face when he heard the news.

"Get married and leave here?" he'd sputtered. He stared at Pearl like she'd lost her mind. "What about the goddam rocks? What about George plowing and helping me with the tobacco and Viney taking care of the kids? What about everything else that's got to be done around here?" He would have gone on, louder and angrier with each breath, but there was something implacable in Pearl's face as she stared him down. This was one argument he could not win. Finally, he dropped his head like a beaten dog.

Viney could also see the fear in George's eyes as he looked at her. But there had been something else, too. Something like tenderness. And he had quietly agreed to Pearl and Viney's plan.

"I couldn't stop her, doctor. Once she got out the door, I couldn't catch her, neither." He glanced down at his gimpy left leg, broken in a fall from a run-away horse when he was eleven. The leg hadn't healed right and had left him with a bad limp. "She didn't even stop to put her shoes on. Just held the baby against her and started running."

"My God," said Dr. Anderson. "No wonder she was nearly frozen. It must be half a mile from here to your house."

Viney could see the two men from where she lay. They were sitting beside each other on a wooden bench a few feet from a silver-colored heating stove, not looking in her direction. She heard the popping and cracking of burning wood and saw a faint red glow on the stove's surface. White lace curtains hung on a window near her, and red and blue-flowered wallpaper filled the room with color.

A dresser on one side of the room held three pictures in wooden frames. One was of a pretty young woman with her hair arranged in an old-fashioned wavy bob. A faint smile on her lips suggested contentment. Two others held sepia-toned photographs of a young boy and girl. Like everything else in the room, the pictures had a well-cared-for look as though they had often been picked up, looked at and dusted.

As she gradually regained some memory of what had happened, images of past experiences with the doctor came to her mind. She would never forget the day Nancy was born when she had hardly known what was happening to her. How he had carefully explained each step to the barely grown girl she had been then. The feel of his gentle hands helping her through her agony that sweltering June day when this baby had arrived. Of an earlier time when one of Pearl's babies had been stillborn and Ernest was passed out drunk somewhere. How he'd talked so kindly to her sister and tried to ease her grieving. The time when little Samuel, Pearl's youngest, swallowed lye and almost died.

He adjusted his glasses and ran a hand through a thick shock of white hair. An elderly widower, he took care of the medical and, often, the emotional needs of the community. Now he was holding her baby and listening to its heart through a stethoscope.

"She's got pneumonia," he said. "When Viney ran in here with her, she was having a convulsion." He wrapped the baby in a thick blanket and handed her to George.

"No doubt but what Viney saved her life. She couldn't breathe. Good thing she got her here when she did."

He walked over and patted Viney's shoulder. "This just proves what I've seen over and over again. There's nothing no stronger than a mother's love."

Viney kept her eyes shut and pretended to sleep. She lay still a little longer, then raised up and looked around. George and the doctor were silent, their conversation finished. George was a man of few words, and the doctor had done what he could for the baby, leaving little else to be said.

Noticing that she was awake, Dr. Anderson carried the baby over and placed her on Viney's breast. "Well, little mother," he said, "you did a wonderful thing tonight. Hadn't been for you bringing her here when you did, this one wouldn't have made it."

He went to a cabinet across the room and withdrew a small blue glass jar. "Keep her chest greased with this Vicks Salve and see she don't get choked when you nurse her."

He reached for his coat, hanging on a peg by the door. "Wait a minute and I'll run you all down to your house." He glanced down at her bare feet. "You can't go outside again dressed like that." He picked up the quilt from the cot and held it out to her. "Here, wrap this around you." He looked over at George who was bending down to lace up his shoe. "Baby's name's Jenny, isn't it?"

George stood up straight to answer the question. "Yes," he said. "Jenny May Bradford. Named her for my mother."

There was a ring of pride in his voice, and Viney cringed. She jerked the quilt tighter around the two of them and the baby uttered a weak squall.

"Well, we better get on home, then," she said, walking toward the door.

She followed George outside to the doctor's car. Dr. Anderson loved his 1927 Tin Lizzie. The black car was almost six years old, but he kept it polished to a mirror-like shine and allowed no mud or grime to settle on its pristine surface.

"Here, George," the doctor said, handing him a curved iron tool. "Crank her till I get 'er started and we'll be on our way."

Nancy sat shivering on her cot, wrapped in the blanket she'd slept under. She hovered near the cold stove, hoping that proximity might give her some warmth. She didn't move, even when she heard a car stop in the yard.

The door opened and George and Aunt Viney came in, stomping snow off their feet. Viney walked over to Nancy and thrust Jenny toward her. "Here," she said. "Take her so I can cook some breakfast." Looking back over her shoulder, she added, "Better keep her wrapped up. Doctor says she's got pneumonia." With that, she turned and walked into the bedroom.

She returned minutes later wearing a gray cotton dress and heavy black shoes, laced and tied around her ankles. She had brushed her wavy black hair back behind her ears, accenting her fair skin, which had lately taken on a yellowish pallor. There were dark circles under her deep-set blue eyes. She held her hand to her throat and leaned for a moment on the edge of the kitchen table.

Then she straightened up and went about making a breakfast of biscuits, milk gravy and fried potatoes. When it was nearly ready, she called out to Nancy, "Put her down now and come in here and set the table."

Nancy had taken Jenny from her aunt Viney and carried her to a rocking chair in the tiny living room. "Come on, Jenny," she'd whispered. "Let's go ride the school bus." Now she carefully got up, laid the sleeping baby on the cot, and hurried into the kitchen.

The bond between Nancy and Jenny had begun the day Jenny was born. The heat of the day had prompted Nancy to take refuge in the leafy branches of a cherry tree out behind the smokehouse. Hidden there, she listened to the screams coming from the house. She thought Aunt Viney might be dying. What if she did? Nancy wondered. Would she go back home to Mama and Daddy and her brothers and sisters? She'd never understood why they left in the first place.

She thought back to the day when she had moved here with George and Aunt Viney. The children had cowered in a corner of Mama's kitchen, watching the puzzling activity in the bedroom. Clothes being thrown into paper sacks. Aunt Viney crying quietly, moving slowly, as though trying to hide in plain sight. Heavy silences broken with whispers, tears, or shouts. When Mama put my clothes in a sack, she remembered, that's when I knowed none of us was ever coming back. When it was time to go, Mama and Aunt Viney cried and hugged each other. Daddy and George stood back a ways, not saying much. All the kids cried, but little Samuel cried the hardest. Me and him played together the most. He couldn't talk too good where his throat was burned, but we could always understand each other.

Sometimes Nancy felt as though she had been pulled up by her roots and transplanted in bad soil. She hunkered down and made herself as small as possible among the branches of the cherry tree. She covered her ears with her hands and let her mind wander, both to drown out Aunt Viney's screams and to keep from mourning her own losses.

The afternoon dragged on while the sun cast ever-lengthening shadows. Eventually, it dropped behind the hills, bathing the world in a warm purple afterlight before the spread of darkness. When the screams stopped Nancy left her perch and approached the house. She sat on the wooden steps outside the door and waited.

At last, the doctor came to the kitchen and talked to George. "She'll have to rest a while and get her strength back," he said. "Just let her sleep till she wakes up." He picked up his black leather bag and headed out the door. Seeing Nancy, he smiled and patted her on the head. "You have a sister, young lady," he said before returning his attention to George.

"I think she'll be all right when she wakes up but come and get me if you need me."

Aunt Viney nursed the baby, then handed her to Nancy. "Here, take her," she whispered. "Change her when she needs it. Give her a bath if you want to. Don't bring her back here till she needs to nurse again. I'm going to sleep."

Aunt Viney's voice was so weak that Nancy had to bend over to hear. She took the baby but had no idea of what to do next. Aunt Viney had said something about giving her a bath, and that sounded like a good idea. She went into the kitchen where a kettle of warm water sat on the stove. A gray granite wash pan hung by a nail on the wall, and she brought it to the table and poured warm water into it. She dipped a finger in to be sure it was not too hot, then undressed the baby and lowered her into the pan. Jenny fussed a bit, but not too much. Nancy lathered her with Ivory soap and rinsed her in the lukewarm water. She was asleep again before Nancy had time to dress her.

"You and me is sisters," Nancy whispered. "We love each other now and always." Days turned into weeks and weeks into months as Nancy held tight to her prize.

If Aunt Viney loved either of them, she didn't let on.

George and Viney seldom had conversations, but when they did, Viney did most of the talking. She usually chose the mornings for her rants. Her voice grew loud and shrill as she recited a litany of worries. The complaints varied with the changing of seasons and the needs of the moment.

"How on top of God's green earth are we gonna get coats and shoes for these kids?" she'd say. "Nancy'll start back to school in three weeks, and now that Jenny's walking, she'll have to have shoes." Or, "We're about out of lard and flour." The dwindling twenty-five-pound flour sack and the almost empty fifty-pound tin lard bucket always sat in a corner of the kitchen. "Look how low they are. What're we gonna do if we run out before you go sell the tobacco?"

"You all come on in here and eat," she would finally call out, and Nancy and Jenny would make their way to the kitchen. George would be sitting beside the stove, ready to go to the barn or to the fields as soon as he had eaten his breakfast. He never uttered a word, so far as Nancy could hear, during Aunt Viney's tirades.

Viney managed to dodge George's amorous advances most of the time. He was not too demanding in the bedroom, so occasionally she gave in, always hoping that would do him for a good, long time. Afterward she would worry until her period came. About a month before Jenny's third birthday, Viney realized that she was pregnant again. Awful, awful, awful kept running through her head. All those miserable months ahead. And after that, God help me, another baby.

Then a strange thing happened. Panic gave way to calm, then peace. A baby was coming, it was true, but this time without shame. There would be no reason to cringe when people looked at her, knowing she'd been ruined before she got married. Not like with the girls.

As her body changed, Viney began to look forward to the baby's arrival. Why, she thought, it would be almost like this one cancelled out the others. Who knows? It might even make up for all the misery they had caused her.

She took for granted that Nancy and Jenny would continue looking out for themselves, coming to her only when they had to. There were not many times when they really needed her anymore.

It had been almost two years since she had weaned Jenny, but occasionally she remembered how awful the experience had been. She had paid little attention to the baby when she was at her breast. At times Jenny had seemed to gag at the taste of the milk as if she were accepting it only to keep from starving. Weaning her had brought welcome relief to both of them.

It was a cold day in December when Dr. Anderson came to their house again, and this time there were no leaves on the cherry tree behind the smokehouse. Icicles had replaced the heavy fruit of summer. The doctor told Nancy and Jenny to stay in their room until he said they could come out. Nancy loved to read stories from *Grimms' Fairy Tales* to Jenny as much as Jenny loved to hear them. They sat wrapped in their blankets for hours, reading the stories, while, only a few feet away, Aunt Viney struggled to give birth.

"It's funny, Jenny," Nancy said. "She's hardly screamed at all." She turned a page and started to read about an ugly old troll who lived under a bridge and was always looking for somebody to eat. She grabbed Jenny and tickled her tummy. "I'm going to eat you," she growled. Jenny giggled and tried to bite her nose. All at once, from the next room, came a thin high-pitched wail. "It's here," Nancy said. They put the book aside and strained to hear the low voices of the doctor and George.

"Let them sleep," the doctor said. "Tell the girls to be quiet so they don't wake them." He raised his voice a bit as he opened the door to leave. "I'll stop by tomorrow to be sure everything's fine." Then, almost as an afterthought, he said, "Congratulations, George. You got yourselves a boy this time."

"Much obliged, Doctor," George answered. "Viney's been looking forward to this one for a long time."

Viney was happy. Sometimes, on pretty, warm days she'd walk to the grocery store for a few small things, always carrying little Tom Jeff, eager to show him off. If someone asked after his name, as they sometimes did, she would proudly answer, "Yes, I named him Thomas Jefferson. Might as well give a little feller a name to live up to." She would hold the baby up until she could look directly into his eyes. "You're gonna make your mama proud, ain't you, Tom?"

When he blinked and squinted in the bright sunlight, Viney would laugh. "See?" she'd say. "He knows exactly what I'm saying." Then she would balance her groceries on one hip, the boy on the other, and practically dance out of the store and down the road.

Sometimes she'd croon a little tune to him, like "My Bonnie lies over the ocean / My Bonnie lies over the sea / My Bonnie lies over the ocean / O bring back my Bonnie to me." Then she'd cuddle and coo, and he'd open his mouth wide and coo back. Other times she'd recite a nursery rhyme, bouncing him on her leg to the cadence of the lines. "Tom, Tom, the piper's son, stole a pig and away he run," was a favorite, but she'd always add a cautionary word so he wouldn't get any wrong ideas. "Mama's baby is a good boy. He never would steal nothin', would you, Tom? Tom is such a good boy." Nancy and Jenny, now and again, wanted to play with the baby, but Viney wouldn't allow it. She saw that Nancy was pretty much raising Jenny, and that was fine. Let them be together, she thought. This one's mine.

November, again. Where did the time go? The cold had come early. Hog-killing almost always took place after Thanksgiving, but this year the temperature had dropped enough by the end of the first week of the month. George, with the help of some of the other farm hands, had butchered their hog, dressed it out and hung it in the smokehouse.

Viney bustled around the kitchen, getting ready to finish the remaining chores — rendering the lard, mixing the sausage, making souse meat — all the things that would assure her family of having these provisions for several months.

One of the most important jobs was soap making. Scrubbing clothes on a washboard every Monday required lots of good strong lye soap, and she needed to make enough to last. She had carried the big black iron kettle from the smokehouse to the backyard near the old walnut tree and started a wood fire under it, being careful to place it as far as possible from the house so that the fumes wouldn't choke anyone.

The five pounds of lard she'd put into the kettle slowly melted. She went out to stir it occasionally and then left it alone. She already had her lye solution in the kitchen ready to pour into the pot when it, too, had cooled enough. How many times had she and Pearl done this together before she had to leave? How many times had they seen their mother do it? Viney could almost make soap in her sleep.

Tom Jeff had started to toddle within the last month. He was so quick she had to keep a close eye on him. Sometimes she marveled at how he could climb a ladder or a chair within the few seconds it took her to turn around. She usually smiled at this. He's starting out young, she'd think. No telling what Mama's boy's going to do when he grows up. Maybe even live up to the name she'd given him. She allowed these delicious thoughts to carry her away to a place she could scarcely imagine. Her boy, an important man. Loving his mama and treating her better than she had ever been treated. Not like the girls. Viney was sure they would never amount to anything.

Smiling, she turned to look at the spot where Tom had been playing on the floor near the door. It took a few seconds for her to realize that he wasn't there. She had left the door cracked a bit in the process of moving back and forth between the kitchen and the hot kettle. If he wasn't in the kitchen, he must be outside. She almost didn't have time to feel the terror before she heard Nancy yell.

"Stop, Tom! Stop! That's hot! It'll burn you," screamed Nancy. Viney ran to the door. Jenny, a few feet behind her sister, stumbled over a rock, fell, jumped up again, ignored a bloody knee and echoed Nancy's cries. "Stop! Stop, Tom! Stop, stop, stop!"

Viney could neither breathe nor move. Then, as if rousing from a catatonic state, she lunged toward her baby just as he reached the kettle, knowing full well she would be too late. Images flashed past her, as fast as lightning: a crow's glittering black eyes staring at her from a nearby fence post, a cold wind raising chill bumps on her bare arms, the smell of hot lard and burning embers, the sight of her baby a second away from the unthinkable.

Then Nancy was there, like a leaf lifted by the wind, snatching the child's hand from the steaming cauldron. On the other side of her, Jenny grabbed his tummy. The three of them rolled backward onto the safety of a flat limestone rock.

Viney felt like she would vomit. Her stomach roiled. To keep from falling, she grabbed at a low-hanging limb of the walnut tree. For the rest of the day, she kept Tom Jeff within arm's reach. By full dark she was exhausted from the work and from thinking about what had almost happened. She was so tired that when the girls wanted to play with their brother, she allowed it.

All three children seemed happy.

He loves them girls and I guess they love him, too, she thought. Somehow this astonished her. Then, a stray thought came into her mind. They're mine, all of them. She felt a strong urge to cry, but she didn't. Not long after, she sent them off to bed. If she had known how, she might have told the girls she loved them.

And maybe it was true.

Acknowledgments

There is a pattern for our lives which we cannot discern, much less understand, until we reach an age that enables us to see it backward. Only then does the pattern become evident, and we perceive how small choices and decisions determine who we are and what we become. The writing of these stories, indeed, their very survival, has depended in large measure upon my interaction with certain people who have helped me to birth them.

One of these people is Connor Reeves, a young friend of mine whose understanding of the workings of computers surpasses my imagination. A few years ago, when my old MAC computer died, taking with it stories that seemed beyond reclamation, Connor, in an effort reminiscent of Christ raising Lazarus, was able to retrieve them. These stories are included in this collection, and my gratitude to Connor is inestimable.

Another dear friend, writing partner and former colleague, Dr. Marie Parsons, has always been there to help me overcome the crankiness and vicissitudes of my computer and get me on the track to structuring and compiling the collection of stories included in this volume. My gratitude to her for her encouragement, her technical assistance and her academic input as she read and reread my work knows no bounds.

The Reverend Dr. Sonya Jones, a.k.a. Swami Schrahananda, another dear friend and unending source of encouragement, has been a constant positive factor in my life and my writing efforts, offering her academic, technical and spiritual support in ways only she could provide. My gratitude to her is everlasting.

I am also grateful for the encouragement of the "usual suspects" in LaGrange, Springfield, and Bardstown, Kentucky. If not for their support and enduring interest in my progress I might never have successfully completed this project.

Many other people have influenced my life in so many different ways that recounting them would be impossible. Among them are beloved teachers, Wyatt Shely, Lillian McGuire and Rena Calhoun; my sister Wanda; my parents and other siblings; and legions of former students and colleagues who have remained friends over the years. All have sewn their pieces into the tapestry of my life.

To them, I say thank you.

www.ingramcontent.com/pod-product-compliance
Lightning Source LLC
Chambersburg PA
CBHW050458160726
48003CB00001B/69